Please note that *Eight Weeks in Paris* deals with issues related to homophobia, both external and self-internalized, including a forced coming-out.

# EIGHT WEEKS IN PARIS

### S.R. LANE

carina
press

carina
press®

ISBN-13: 978-1-335-62392-8

Eight Weeks in Paris

Carina Press
22 Adelaide St. West, 41st Floor
Toronto, Ontario M5H 4E3, Canada
www.CarinaPress.com

Printed in U.S.A.

Recycling programs
for this product may
not exist in your area.

# EIGHT WEEKS IN PARIS

# *Chapter One*

grapevine.us/2024/01/12/the-throne-live-action-cast
10:44 am

## BREAKING: Nicholas Madden cast in live-action adaptation of LGBTQ masterpiece *The Throne*

Nicholas Madden was cast this morning as "Frederick" in period piece *The Throne*, confirming rumors to that effect.

Cast alongside him are Sir Reginald Jarrett as "Hubert," Andrée Belfond as "Jehanne" (it's been so long since the French *gamine* has been on our screens!), and Jason Kirkhall as "Ambrose" (an odd choice, as Kirkhall is best known for his superhero franchises, but he can be versatile...if one overlooks his long nights out).

We expect some drama out of so capricious a cast—lest we forget Kirkhall's flighty liaisons with starlets and K-Pop singers, and Sir Reginald Jarrett's infinite on-demand supply of apricot tartlets. But even they are put to shame by Madden's legendary strops, his short-fuse temper, and his rank distaste for misbehaving costars. As the man critics have dubbed the Big Bad Wolf of Hollywood, Madden hits all the stops in the actor bingo, from "extraordinarily talented" to "a proper prick, actually."

Madden's fan base, trusting in their idol's penchant for dramatics, has set up an online clock ticking down to the first on-set breakdown (see it for yourself <u>here</u>).

Despite these apparent drawbacks, *The Throne*—with Priya Chaudhuri set to direct and the Henderson siblings producing—may well turn out a number of award-worthy performances. Chaudhuri, to whom official recognition is long overdue, is a hot bet for Best Director noms next year. *The Throne* might become her golden ticket into Hollywood history...if Kirkhall can keep it in his pants and Madden can keep it together.

Set in turn-of-the-century Paris, *The Throne* was for decades a lost novel. Rediscovered in the early nineties, it was heralded as a masterpiece of LGBTQ literature. The love story at its core is frequently cited by modern critics as a rare early portrayal of a non-tragic gay relationship—though its depiction of bohemian queerness during the Belle Époque is not without its flaws and prejudices.

With Madden cast as one of the two mains, only "Angelo," the novel's most complex and controversial figure, is left to cast.

While Madden will have his work cut out for him as dark, brooding Frederick, Angelo may prove a challenge for the most seasoned actor (as the disastrous stage adaptation from the early oughts has eloquently shown). Whoever bears the brunt of that role and shares the stage with Madden—a man unaccustomed to sharing the spotlight—will have to be an egoistic diva in his own right, or risk being utterly outperformed. With how many times *The Throne* has been in and out of production, those who claim the novel incompatible with the silver screen may well be proven right...

14:01

**UPDATE:** Cast! In a strange turn of events, *The Throne*'s Angelo will be played by Christian Lavalle, better known for his Calvin Klein and Armani campaigns and his 1.5M Instagram followers than for his acting history. Lavalle, 25, became a Dior mainstay at the tender age of sixteen and has been steadily acquiring modeling gigs ever since; but his experience as an actor is limited to a few appearances in French soaps, television gigs, and international ads.

Casting a newbie to act opposite Nicholas Madden is certainly an odd choice. Can he strike up the right kind of chemistry with the Big Bad Wolf, or will Madden have to carry the movie's huge emotional arc on his shoulders? Will *The Throne* crumple under its own weight?

At least he's French.

Filming is set to begin in June.

## June 2024. Paris.

Christian Lavalle was one of two things: a vapid boy-king without the skill and understanding to rival his good looks, or a *devastatingly* talented actor.

Nicholas very much doubted he was the latter.

The Parisian sun in June, warm and soft, spilled like liquid gold over the cobblestones of the Place Colette, the butter-soft columns of the Comédie-Française, and the polished red tables of the café terrace. It was a gorgeous day in Paris. On a late afternoon like this, all one wanted to do was relax in the sun, wear a cool suit of clothes and sip a cocktail.

Nicholas mostly felt hot and overdressed. The sparkling water he had ordered had done nothing to cool him down. It had scattered strange butterflies in his stomach.

He and Lavalle had arrived within minutes of each other to their non-official meet and greet. Lavalle had immediately been waylaid by a horde of fans, and did not seem inclined to put a stop to their fawning.

Nicholas was not a patient man.

But the lean young man who held court in the middle of the Place Colette, surrounded by the gaggle of his devotees, drew his gaze and attracted his attention, inescapably.

Because Christian Lavalle *demanded* attention. His beauty was compelling and undeniable. In a lily-white shirt and black jeans he looked infernally cool; the heat seemed to be beneath his notice. In his ad campaigns he had been merely exquisite; in motion he was...*distracting*. His hair, made golden by the sun, just touched the corners of his smiling eyes. He was laughing.

"Don't look so offended, Madden," said Madalena, slipping into the seat next to his. She stretched out her arm along the back of his chair and crossed her long legs. "The boy's done nothing to deserve your wrath except land the job. This is a very good look on him. Very *chic*."

"He's twenty-five years old," said Nicholas. "Hardly a boy."

"Then *you* are positively ancient."

Madalena grinned at him. In the Parisian sunshine, she, too, was more beautiful than usual. Her dyed hair was burnished to an auburn sheen; with her white skirt splayed over her crossed legs, her sweetheart neckline betraying a fair amount of brown-skinned cleavage, she looked like an actress right out of the nineteen forties. A shame she had never shown any penchant towards the vocation. She was content to be his PA, to haul him out of bed in the mornings and drink his expensive coffee. Nicholas dreaded the day when she grew tired of him and went off to ru(i)n someone else's life. He suspected her exorbitant pay had something to do with how long she'd stuck by him.

But she *was* beautiful, and he was—even an ocean away from home—famous, and people looked at them, attracted as moths to the flame of recognition and notoriety. The rare few who could tear themselves away from Christian Lavalle were already turning their smartphones on them, daring to take candids and tapping away. He could imagine the tweetstorm.

@somenosyfucker
y'all nicholas madden is in paris and hes not lookin happy about it

@noprivacy
someone dare me i'll totally ask for a selfie

@celebsenlive
c'est qui elle??? depuis quand il a une copine?

@unautreconnard
Nicholas Madden est à Paris? Il tournerait pas un film? 😲

Pictured: a scowling man, hands stuffed in his pockets, glaring at his prospective costar.

It didn't matter. He was in Paris for *The Throne*. The table read was scheduled in less than two days, provided Lavalle could shake off his fans for long enough to make it. Nicholas found the prospect sadly uninspiring. The thrill he'd felt when the script had finally, *finally* landed in his lap had now all but faded. *The Throne* was something real, a period piece with modern sensibilities, a project he could back without feeling that he was giving in to mediocrity. He was an ardent lover of the novel. He'd been waiting for that opportunity for... years. Years. He had made *damn* sure he'd be getting the role.

And then the Henderson siblings had chosen Christian fucking Lavalle, prima donna sublime, to play his Angelo. He was a *fashion model*, for god's sake, an Instagram *influencer* with a reputation for flightiness and barely any acting experience; and nepotism, or beauty, for all Nicholas knew, had landed him the role. It was sacrificing quality to sell tickets. No doubt production had meant to appeal to twin demographics: those who were young and online and celebrity-hungry, and those who were easily distracted by a pretty face. Nicholas had no patience for it.

Madalena tsked at him. "Keep making that face and it'll stick that way. Wind's a-blowing."

"We're supposed to have a—" Nicholas's voice lowered into scorn. "A *meet and greet*. Basic courtesy; the regular fare. I've been here half an hour. He lacks even the professionalism to know when to put away his fans."

Madalena shrugged a smooth shoulder, and produced a tablet from somewhere. "He posted a picture of the Comédie-Française on his Instagram account. Fans flock to him like bees to honey."

Nicholas closed his eyes briefly. "Of course he did."

She turned the tablet. Lavalle's Instagram account was a steady, pastel-colored stream of pictures of Paris, himself, himself and dogs, himself and fans, promo shoots for ad campaigns he was plugging, more dogs, and more Paris. *Amélie*, times ten thousand.

"A disaster," Nicholas said shortly. He doubted Lavalle had even noticed him. Smiling for the cameras must take up the entirety of his cranial activity.

Madalena hummed, scrolling through pictures of honey-gold buildings and bright sun. "Chaudhuri called."

"Pardon me?" Madalena's job was to field his calls and deflect the loonies from his path, not to hit voicemail on the fucking director of the fucking movie.

"Calm down," Madalena said, still not looking at him. "She wanted me to pass on a word, that's all."

Nicholas was only mildly appeased. "Anytime you feel willing to share, Madalena—"

"They've chosen a location for the café. There's a neat little underground bar near Bastille they can convert to Belle Époque aesthetics, whatever that means. She wants you to drop in tonight, get a feel for the place. Food looks good. Very classic. The menu boasts touches of, I quote, 'bistro avant-garde'—whatever *that* means."

Avant-garde food tended to be jelly-colored foam on foal-liver crostini: the sort of thing that was both inedible on the tongue and offensive to good taste. Not a single good medium-rare steak in sight. "Fine." Nicholas glanced away. The gardens of the Palais-Royal glimmered across a plaza of black-and-white marble columns. It was tempting to escape there for a few hours—to stretch out his legs on one of those green iron chairs between the trees, take in the sun, turn off his phone. *Rest.*

"She wants you to bring Lavalle along. Have a private chat. Get to know the guy."

Hell. Well, there went that fucking idea. Nicholas cast her a dark look. "Say that again."

She lifted her eyebrows at him. "Dinner with Chris Lavalle." She pointed, helpfully.

"Thank you, Madalena, I know where my damn costar is." So did the rest of the world, apparently. Regrettably.

"And here you are: glaring exquisitely at him, in full sight of every Parisian in the neighborhood, which is doing no good whatsoever for your optics—I say this out of love, not just because your job is also my job. You haven't exchanged a word with the man. Give him a chance," she coaxed, as gentle as with a lion. "Talk to him. He might turn out to be a kinder soul than you think."

Nicholas didn't need a kind soul. He needed a costar—an

equal, a partner, a man he could respect. "He's a diva. An influencer. He isn't an actor. His English is atrocious."

"His accent is lovely. And you barely speak French."

"I know enough." He could say *bonjour*, *merci*, and *sortez de mon chemin, bordel de merde*, which was usually enough for his purposes.

Madalena brushed sun dust off her skirt. "You keep looking at him."

"The entire blasted world is looking at him. He's making damn sure of it."

"The entire blasted world isn't about to play his lover. And you've been furiously eye-fucking him for half an hour. People are bound to notice." She wriggled her smartphone at him. "I noticed."

"You had better," Nicholas growled, "not be looking up pictures of your employer on that thing."

"I don't need to look you up. You're trending."

"For fuck's sake, Madalena!"

Laughing, she swiped to show him. And there he was—in his expensive sweater, in profile; his elbow was resting on the table next to his coffee cup, one hand covering his mouth. Half in shadow. He looked pensive. Absorbed. Odds were, any one of the morons pointing their expensive smartphones in his direction had caught *who* he was looking at, too. *Goddamn it.*

What the hell *was* wrong with him? Was he a green boy, untrained and inexperienced, so easily distracted by a pretty face and a lithe body that looked as though it had been made for—

He stopped that thought right the fuck there. And handed the phone back, grimacing. "I've been…preoccupied."

"He *is* gorgeous," said Madalena.

"His job description is to look handsome and wear shiny things. Of course he's beautiful."

But Nicholas thought it a weakness. Beauty of that kind

meant men like Chris Lavalle could coast by in the world, safe in the knowledge that they would always be loved. Beauty of that kind was too great for this life. Nicholas had worked with good-looking men and women in the past; but never before had it got so much…under his skin. It was an irritant. He disliked it.

"You put too much pressure on yourself, Nicholas," Madalena sighed. "Get a good look at him now; everybody does. He expects it, I suspect. You're gonna get closer to him than anyone else around here ever will," she added. And wasn't that the root of the problem, Nicholas thought, somberly. "Better get over it now, while you're still at arm's length. He might lose some of that attitude once he's in the water with you."

The script had several nude scenes. Nicholas had dismissed them as a regular day's work. Then he had learned whose mouth he would kiss, and who would touch him—so intimately. And things inside his head had gotten a hell of a lot messier.

Theoretically, sex scenes were about the least *sexy* scenes one could film. Nicholas had shot plenty of them in the past. Nudity did not trouble him; he'd kissed enough people on-screen to shrug off the intimacy of it. The technique—the skill—was in looking believably sensual while fighting off the intense foolishness of gooseflesh and wearing a skin-colored sleeve over one's cock. The best way to achieve this, he had found, was to hold himself at a distance from his costar, and manage, however awkwardly, to laugh with them: make the whole thing a day's trip down insanity lane.

He doubted he could laugh with Chris Lavalle.

He was a young Apollo, too lovely and too magnetic to be real. You couldn't laugh with someone like that: you could only worship them or scorn them.

As though summoned by the thought, Lavalle turned across

the Place Colette and met his gaze, despite the sunshine in his eyes, despite the distance between them. Nicholas's hand stilled around his coffee cup.

He had remarkable grey eyes. He was a cliché of a Frenchman, charming and remote.

"He's coming over," Madalena observed, chin upon her hand.

"No; is he?" Nicholas muttered.

Christian Lavalle, having at last shaken off his posse—who remained hovering, though thankfully distant—came to a stop beside their table. He gave them a smile: cordial, diplomatic. He met Nicholas's eyes for a moment, then moved on to Madalena with a polite confusion that soon melted into polite disinterest.

"Hello," he said, in a soft voice. "Shall we get on?"

His English was stilted, as with non-native speakers who learned it early on but never fully grasped the measure of the language. His voice was overly formal, and oddly accented, a little deferential.

"Get...on," Nicholas repeated.

Lavalle shrugged. "They have told me to meet Priya at *Le Renard d'Or.*"

*Priya*, Nicholas thought, with vague disbelief. Priya Chaudhuri. Their *director*. He glanced at Madalena, who helpfully said: "The Golden Fox. The bar I told you about."

"We are to have dinner." Lavalle widened his eyes a fraction, smiling. It was a fantastic smile. Nicholas had given the press many a fake, charming grin in the past; this was the best of them all combined. The simmering hatred of them, streamlined, brutally tailored down to an art.

He realized abruptly that Lavalle had no better an opinion of him than *he* had of Lavalle. Hands in his pockets, rocking slightly upon his heels, he looked entirely at ease.

This was his city. His ground.

"Dinner," Nicholas said softly.

Lavalle glanced down, then up again. His lashes were long and fair against his cheeks. "*Mais bien sûr.* I have made a booking for eight."

Nicholas had assumed Chaudhuri meant for them merely to look about the place. Eight was late for dinner—though not so late for Parisians, who enjoyed eating late into the night; give them a bottle of Beaujolais and a platter of charcuterie, and they would cheerfully wait out the sunrise over the Seine. Lavalle seemed intent on fitting himself to the stereotype as closely as possible. He now turned his lovely smile on Madalena, who—to her credit—neither blinked nor blushed against that frontal attack. "A table only for two, I'm afraid. Although... I am sure I could call...?"

"Oh, no." Her voice was amused. "You two will want to get to know each other." She extended a hand. "I'm Madalena Torres. The PA. Get him home before midnight, yeah?"

Lavalle ducked his head, his smile fading; a flush was just touching his cheekbones. What measure of *control* could the man have on his facial expressions? It was insanity.

"We should go then," said Nicholas shortly, standing. Somewhere to the left of them, someone was snapping pictures. It was grating; yet Lavalle seemed content to linger, presenting his best profile. He was used to it. His job was to look his best for photographs—candids and otherwise.

Nicholas hated amateur paparazzi with the same fervor he hated professional ones. He always visualized the headlines, the tweets, the bloody BuzzFeed captions. "Traffic'll be hell," he grunted, to speed things along. Madalena held his phone hostage on most occasions, or he'd have called his chauffeur.

Lavalle blinked at him. "Traffic? Nobody drives in Paris."

Nicholas looked at the endless flood of cars exiting the

arches of the Palais du Louvre, streaming towards the Opéra Garnier.

"Nobody from Paris drives in Paris," Lavalle amended. *"Ah, mais, mes Américains!"* He sounded amused. "We will take the bus. If we walk to the Seine we will find one going directly to Bastille, alongside the river. It will be much more pleasant. Being stuck in traffic is a…a pain in the ass. *Non?"*

Nicholas couldn't remember the last time he'd taken public transportation. His chauffeur would think he'd been kidnapped.

Nevertheless, with Madalena's generous blessing and her kiss burning upon his cheek—a little teaser for the cameras—they found themselves no later than a quarter hour later in one of Paris's green, foul-smelling buses. No seats; these had been optioned by what looked like half the little old lady population in the city. Instead they stood, and swayed.

Lavalle curled both hands around the metal railing, balancing himself with familiar ease, and stared out the window with distinct interest, as though there was something captivating about the view. In profile, he looked abstracted and sad. Did he sweat, or was he utterly unaffected by the heat? Nicholas was mildly impressed. If this was a character he was playing, Lavalle had gone full method.

What the fuck was Chaudhuri thinking? Casting a model who'd never acted in anything much bigger than a late-night soap was courting misery. For a movie that was already heating up next year's award season talk, of all things. Angelo ought to be played by a Frenchman—or at least someone who could speak the language well enough to bluff international audiences—but he was a baroque, interesting character, full of contradictions. He required *talent*. To have him played by a wannabe comedian with his sights on another Dior campaign was nothing short of an imposture.

Lavalle looked the part, at least. In a silken waistcoat, he would be the perfect Belle Époque debauchee. His proud manner, and the haughty curl of his mouth, would suit Angelo's cynical nature to a fault. And he was deeply, notably beautiful—the kind of beauty that was not easily overlooked, not even in Hollywood. His eyes, most remarkably, were grey and clear as still water. All-seeing. Nicholas thought of classical statues, marble-white and merciless and blind.

But Nicholas knew *The Throne* inside and out, and he would not be fooled by appearances.

Angelo was no indifferent torso of Apollo, listless and diffident. He was a man who had been betrayed often, who had loved and who had lost. He did not show emotion easily. He kept his cards close to his chest, an act Nicholas doubted that Lavalle—who did not so much wear his heart on his sleeve as display it prominently on every social media platform known to man—could achieve with any kind of subtlety.

"I don't get tired of it."

"What?" Nicholas, torn from his preoccupations, was brusque. Lavalle didn't seem offended.

He pointed at the view. The bus was coming up to the unmistakable arches of the Pont Neuf, and beyond it were the tall, dark spires and pale beige buildings of the Conciergerie, holding court above the brown, rushing river. The sun beat down hard, and the sky was a pale, Venetian blue. White slips of cloud were streaming away to the east, towards the hidden towers of Notre-Dame. It was only just the beginning of summer, the longest hours of sunlight in the year, and the days ran long and luminous.

"I've been here a thousand times," said Lavalle. His glance at Nicholas faltered just on the side of charming, as though sharing an intimate moment with a near-stranger was something he wasn't used to; as though he didn't invite intimacy with every picture, every selfie, every #nofilter #homesweethome #liveyourbestlife he posted a couple times an hour. "But I've never grown tired of the view."

Nicholas stared at him. Lavalle held his gaze for a moment, then glanced away. His hair fell softly into his eyes. He'd have to cut it, for the role.

He *had* to be a con. No one was this…this naturally unaffected, to the point that artlessness itself became an affectation. Nicholas could barely figure him out: every second he spent in Lavalle's company troubled him the more.

Lavalle was disconcerting. He kept reinventing himself. He was no longer the elegant, charismatic young man from the Place Colette, who had posed and smiled and allowed his congregation to take an endless stream of selfies. Nicholas had no idea who *this* man was, with that shy smile, those pale sleepy eyes. He only knew that his body was responding in kind—was roused as though from deep slumber into some new state of being, more febrile and more real.

The bus lurched to a stop at a red light—Place du Châtelet, a green plaque said—and with a startled noise Lavalle stumbled against him. He was a sudden, warm weight against Nicholas, who, having wisely braced himself against the railing, captured his elbow in his hand. Muscle and tendon and sheer vitality. Lavalle's eyes lifted to meet his.

They were almost the same height. Nicholas was a touch taller, and broader about the shoulders. He had the sudden urge to slip one arm firmly around Lavalle's waist. Lavalle's hand had landed on his chest, and as the bus resumed its course it remained there, his fingertips tangled in the wool of Nicholas's sweater.

"Pardon," he said. The *n* was softened in his accent, barely there.

"Sure," said Nicholas. His own voice, he realized, was hoarse.

# *Chapter Two*

**[CHRIS LAVALLE—DISCUSSION]**
**Weekly Thread—24/06/08-24/06/14**

REMINDERS: THE SHORT VERSION
- be good to each other.
- don't violate Chris's privacy! only approved pics are allowed!
- don't post speculation about where he lives. there's fannish and then there's just creepy.
- no body-shaming of any kind; mods reserve the right to delete without notice.
- content warnings for triggery material are appreciated.
- no real person fic in this thread! go to the [rpf thread] for that.

The full rules can be found here.
Questions to the mods go here.

[page 45 of 45]
[[< < 1 2 3... 45 > >>

**[mod] LavalleNation**
pics of our fave boy today 😄
instagram.com/p/pm8je55nf

instagram.com/p/pp95cbr9
instagram.com/p/2djr885d

**unautrejour**
ahhhhhhhhhhhhhh he's so pretty. it's so unfair. it takes me 30 min in the morning to look halfway put together and it's like he rolled out of bed looking like a greek god

**aimeesays**
ikr 😒

**marsalawine**
tbf for all we know it takes him an hour to look like that too??

**unautrejour**
lol i mean yeah obvs
but let me dream 😊

**mameme**
I love what he's done with the embroidered white shirt! so simple and so elegant!

**politenessisoverrated**
oh no he's wearing makeup oh no

**politenessisoverrated**
on closer inspection: that's eyeliner and highlighter at the VERY least
our boy is taking good care of himself

**WeStanChris111**
Where is He????

**jaicruaudiable**

That's the place colette in paris

I was there

**WeStanChris111**

Did you Speak to him?

**jaicruaudiable**

I did! He was v nice and personable but kind of...distracted?

idk

**Vero**

i was there too! I was so shy though ☹

but he was super sweet

**madnessisastateofmind**

...is Nicholas Madden just chilling there

**slamdunksammy**

that's not madden lmao

**aimeesays**

Wait. Is it?

**jaicruaudiable**

Is THAT who he is? Huh. Interesting

**WeStanChris111**

Wait Why????

**jaicruaudiable**

I mean I thought he was just a dude Chris was supposed to meet

They talked for a little bit and then I think they left together?

**[mod] LavalleNation**

W H A T

Nicholas Madden hated him.

Unquestionably. Unmistakably. He detested him. Half an hour in his acquaintance had made that clear.

Their shoulders brushed as they turned into the rue de la Roquette, and Madden pulled away stiffly at the unexpected touch. His body language was about as forgiving as that of a hyena forced to attend a charity function in a three-piece suit and a red nose.

It wasn't a fair comparison. Madden was vastly more handsome than a hyena.

But he would look about as ridiculous as one if he were to put on a red nose. His eyes—deep-set, and dark in the falling evening—were grave. He gave off the distinct impression that he had been unimpressed by *all* he had seen of Paris thus far.

Chris hadn't expected to make a particular friend of the man, knowing his reputation, but he would have appreciated simple, plain, basic courtesy.

Not this black hole of emotion.

They were met in the lobby of *Le Renard d'Or* by Priya Chaudhuri, an intimidating soul with Hollywood cred the length of Chris's arm and the keenest eyes he had ever seen. In a red leather jacket and tough knee-high boots, she looked ferocious, unstoppable. Surprisingly, Madden unbent enough to kiss her cheek. *Well*, Chris thought: they had worked together many times. Looking up her work, Chris had seen his name listed among her cast more often than not. Unlike other directors, Chaudhuri seemed willing to put up with Madden's caprice and thunder.

It was an advantage Madden had on him. Chris only had the advantage of charm, and a smile he had fought to perfect for the last half decade.

Chaudhuri seemed pleased to see him. Surprisingly, she looked pleased to see them—together. "Hello, Christian," she told him, and stretched out both heavily-ringed hands to him.

"Chris," he reminded her.

*"Chris,"* she repeated. Then she grinned. "My thanks for the recommendation. The Golden Fox! A gorgeous name. Eminently suitable for *The Throne*."

"It will do, then?"

"Modifications will have to be made. Period-appropriate furniture, for a start. Paintings. Art Nouveau… But it's just *underground* enough. I like it very much."

At his side, Madden had gone tense. He waited until Chaudhuri had waved them away to a booth against the far wall, before saying in a low, displeased voice: "This was your recommendation?"

Chris took a seat. He had a feeling being courteous with this man was an exercise in frustration. "I mentioned it to the producers."

"I suppose friends of yours own the place?"

He did know the owners, though he wasn't about to admit it. He watched as Madden sat opposite him and jerkily snapped up a menu, then said mildly: "I dine here often. It seemed like a pertinent choice."

Madden didn't look up at him. "What made you assume the producers didn't already have accommodations in place?"

As unbelievably provoking as his manner was, Madden's

voice was tremendous. Slow, low, dark. Chris found it—and the man himself—troubling. It made something inside him quiver, to hear him talk so; to be called to heel in this way. He brought himself to reply.

"Nothing. I heard they were still scouting for location. I made the call myself."

Madden laid the menu down slowly and leaned back in his seat. "A little high-handed."

"Perhaps so. But I came here often when I was reading the novel. The connection seemed inescapable."

That was a palpable hit: Madden blinked. Chris leaned his cheek on his fist, and smiled his most disarming smile.

"You *have* read the novel, then."

Madden made it sound the way he might say: *You* do *read, then*, and that would have stung if his behavior hadn't been disparaging from the moment Chris had introduced himself. Too bad. Chris could handle comments like these every day.

And, usually, he did. The internet was not a kind place.

Madden did not like him. Nor did he think Chris up to the task of playing Angelo.

Fine.

Chris left his menu untouched. He knew it well, and he had his favorites. He was on known territory. Madden was not. "Of course I have. Have you?"

Madden's mouth thinned. "I was fourteen when I first read it. The past two decades have given me many expectations of a film adaptation, as of any actors who might be cast."

*Quel connard*, Chris thought tiredly, accepting a complimentary cocktail from an eavesdropping waiter. Mojito with extra mint. The staff knew what he liked. Madden eyed his own gin and tonic with distaste.

So. Madden was every inch the asshole he was rumored to be; he was just subtle enough that he could get away with the most underhanded of insults. It seemed a shame that life had bestowed some of her best assets on a man so undeserving of them. He was a tall and handsome man, black hair and tan skin—one of those rare specimens who could pull off a short beard without looking like a lumberjack. His eyes were keen under heavy brows, and his mouth full and dark.

In his angora sweater and expensive trousers, he ought to look overly warm and uncomfortable. He did not. Instead he was cavalier and proud. And he had loathed Chris on sight.

It was a sad fact of Chris's life that he was vulnerable to a haughty, arrogant disposition. Madden suited the type perfectly. Something in those dark eyes seemed to see right down to his very soul, and to judge with stark contempt whatever sins they found there. It was in the set of his elbow on the tabletop, in the harsh decision on his face. He looked at Chris dead-on, without a hint of uncertainty, as though he could see nothing but the truth. And Chris was...touched, by this.

A second waiter detached himself from the bar and made his approach, doing his best to fit the part of the haughty French *garçon*. Madden gave him one glance, tapped his knuckles against the menu, and said to Chris: "Do you know the menu well enough to recommend—anything?"

"I know the menu," Chris replied tartly. "Not your tastes. I'll have the *sole meunière*," he told the waiter, in French, nearly biting his tongue at his own petulance. If he was trying to impress, he was failing. Spectacularly.

Looking distinctly scornful, Madden said: "*Steak au poivre*. And a green salad." The waiter nodded blandly, and then turned on his heel and raised an eloquent eyebrow at Chris.

Chris shook his head imperceptibly. He cultivated a working relationship with the staff of *Le Renard d'Or*: they supplied him with hard black coffees and oozy croque-monsieurs when he wandered in after a long, grueling week of shoots, and he tipped them all excessively well. They were gathered around the counter in an indolent group—gazing curiously at Madden, and whispering amongst themselves. Gossips, the lot of them.

"I see you have admirers," Madden said dryly.

Well, let him think that.

"I imagine," Chris said, "that you are used to being watched while dining out." And added cheerfully: "Eavesdroppers are *so* old-school."

Madden was on record for having excoriated a paparazzo with such vitriol the man had been hospitalized for a torn eardrum. So rumor went. More likely the pap had milked the situation for all it was worth, casting Madden in the part of a fiendish monster. And yet Chris could imagine him very well, castigating the miscreant with an acerbic tongue.

He suppressed a shiver. It must have been a sight to remember.

Well, never say never. It was possible this night would go down in infamy, too.

"Let them talk," said Madden, shortly. He cast a meaningful glance at Chris's phone, resting quietly on top of his napkin. "So long as this dinner does not end up online by other means, I can't be bothered to care."

Chris was briefly tempted to Instagram every course. It would be petty, and it would alienate his closest costar for the entirety of the filming, but it would be deeply satisfying to see Madden's scowl get a fraction darker every time he used a hashtag.

"You read *The Throne* when you were fourteen," he said instead. Throwing the gauntlet down. "What did you think of it then?"

"I thought it was a masterpiece."

"At fourteen! And now?"

"It is a *flawed* masterpiece."

Chris smiled. "I must admit I did not read it until two years ago. It is not in the French curriculum. Our understanding of American literature is limited to Hemingway and Steinbeck."

"Neither of which you hold in high esteem, I take it." Madden was maddeningly unmovable. He accepted the plate that was set before him with a single nod, and did not move to pick up his fork.

Perhaps he was used to being hand-fed by that pretty assistant of his. Chris declined the privilege of imitating her—though it would be a strange thing, to have Madden gone quite still under his touch, his lips half-parted, his eyelashes soft and dark.

"I am bored with the plight of straight men," he replied. His *sole meunière* came a moment later. The fish's flesh was beautifully seared; the golden sauce shimmered with butter and lemon, threaded through with fine herbs. It was a delicacy he didn't eat often. His time was limited when he was on a shoot.

"A bold statement," said Madden, "for one whose country produced the likes of Balzac and Flaubert."

"Ah! You *have* read them? French classes in high school, I suppose?"

"For my sins."

At last Madden unbent enough to take a bite. His eyes widened: only just, but enough to tell. He next speared a small, joyful pearl onion and ate it without a word. When he returned to the steak, the knife sliced in so smoothly it might have been butter. *Le Renard d'Or*'s specialty was in *bistro* dishes—Crêpes Suzette and Steak Diane, chicken rillettes, onion soup, flaky sweet-and-sour lemon tartlets, rich moussey *cafés au lait*. It was gratifying to see that Madden was human enough to appreciate simple pleasures.

If this was what he looked like when he was just sampling good food, then—

Chris stopped that thought right then and there.

"This is delicious," Madden admitted. He looked like a bemused panther.

"Hmm. I am glad you think so." Chris nursed his glass of iced water. Madden drank Bordeaux, red and full-bodied. Chris didn't feel the worse for his abstinence: the mojito had satisfied any craving he might have had for booze, and he preferred to be sober for this little tête-à-tête of theirs. He had no nose for wine, and was unable to discern much difference between vintages: some were red, some were white, some were a pleasant pinkish hue and paired well with smoked ham and raspberries. There was something, though, about watching the lazy swallow of Madden's throat, and his lips stained with wine...

Chris put that thought aside, too. "You say you had great expectations of the casting."

"I did. I do," said Madden.

"I imagine I fail to impress."

"You do."

Chris ate a small, finely-seared potato. "May I ask why?"

Madden leaned back in his seat. His hand covered his mouth: a gesture to which, in interviews, he defected while he searched for the right words.

In this particular case, the right word could only be a deliberate insult.

Finally, with a shrug, he said: "Angelo is a complex character."

"Ah," said Chris.

Somehow this odd, misshapen diplomacy was more disrespectful than an insult.

"Forgive me," said Madden, sounding distinctly unapologetic.

"No, I understand. It is a—how would you say?—a deliberate *failing* of our society to see models as little more than brainless, vapid airheads. I'm told we can't think our way out of a cardboard box." Chris took a sip of water. "I had not expected you to adhere to that line of thinking. Idiotic, of course."

Madden's anger—simmering and low like lamplight—looked beautiful on him. His brows pulled together, his full mouth thinning. "Idiotic?"

Chris looked up, eyes wide. "Would I have been cast, otherwise?"

"You look the part. I daresay that was enough."

"I'm sure Chaudhuri would be delighted to learn you think so little of her judgement."

It was a cheap shot, but Madden rose to it strategically. "You have very little acting history," he said slowly. "If you have any talents outside of looking exceedingly beautiful in low light, I have yet to spot one of them."

...well.

That was...unexpected. Insulting. Flattering. Chris felt heat rise to his cheeks—he had the sort of fair complexion that made blushing an inevitability—and saw Madden respond to *that*: the widening of his eyes, the slight parting of his lips. Then he looked away.

"What do you make of Angelo?" Chris asked, to parry the thrust.

Madden glanced back at him. "What?"

"Angelo. You say I am unfit to the task of playing him. Tell me why."

Madden finished his steak with a flourish of his fork, then picked up a piece of bread to soak up the sauce. He looked like he was doing some very quick thinking.

"He is callous," he said finally. "Cruel. Childish, in a sense. He thinks he is incapable of affection. He has high expectations of his lovers; he knows himself impossible to refuse. His meeting with Frederick is an exchange of power, exclusively—at the outset. Desire directed at him is habitual to him—but he doesn't know where to begin when it comes to his own." He met Chris's eyes, and suddenly the brutality of their conversation was gone—in its place was a thoughtful, profound fondness.

Madden *loved* Angelo, Chris realized. Loved *The Throne*, wholeheartedly. It was a howler of a book, twisting the knife in deep, and Madden was a howler of a man.

"He reminds me of an expressionist painting," Madden went on. "He doesn't think outside of absolutes, but he acts... exquisitely. It would be difficult for a seasoned actor to nail the part. An amateur with pretensions of grandeur couldn't begin to understand how to play him."

The words, spoken low and swift, slid through Chris like an arrow. He felt light-headed: the insult was unforgivable, and the challenge irrepressible.

"Give me your hand," he said.

Madden's eyes snapped to his. "What."

"As you say. Angelo and Frederick's first meeting is one of power." Chris held out his own hand, palm up. Open, vulnerable. "But Angelo desires him instantly, and he does not... control it...until he has proven to them both that he can harness that desire and force it into shape."

It was one of the first scenes in the script: a slow, intoxicating seduction. A play on desires. Angelo fascinated Frederick and then threw him aside.

Chris repeated: "Give me your hand."

Madden hesitated.

He lifted those somber, tender eyes to Chris's face, as though searching for the answer to an unworded question. But then he did unbend…he discarded the napkin he had been clutching, and with a jerking motion laid his own hand on top of Chris's.

"Thank you."

He touched Madden's warm, calloused palm with the tips of his fingers, then the back of his knuckles. Then laced their fingers briefly together.

*"Your hand is beautiful."*

These were Angelo's words, the words he was *going* to speak—in a life that was no less true, no less poignant, no less real, for being fictional. More so, perhaps.

Madden tilted his head to the side. Chris watched him take in a breath. Then he, too, became other than himself—suddenly he was Frederick, wary, wan, austere, the only sober man in a room of absinthe-drinkers and opium-lovers.

He said: "I—" and came to a stop. His hand jerked in Chris's grasp, as though he wanted it back, but couldn't bring himself to move away. Frederick was taken, seized, from the moment he saw Angelo. He didn't *want* to desire him. But desire was there, unbroken, unspoken.

His throat worked. *"I—thank you."*

*"A writer's hand."* Chris turned it, tracing the fragile pattern of palm-lines with the side of his thumb. *"A long life. A love line."*

Madden's fingertips curled very slightly around his own. *"Are you a fortune-teller?"* he asked, his mouth curling, displeased. Frederick was an ascetic. He didn't approve of charlatans.

*"Oh, no. Only I appreciate beautiful things."*

A laugh. *"Then you are not speaking of me."*

*"Don't you think so?"*

Chris had tried to understand Angelo then. This was such baseless, pointless cruelty. Soon Angelo would throw Frederick away, a casualty in the war he was playing against himself, scarcely regretted. But Madden's words put it into perspective: Madden's body was responsive, instinctive, reactive.

Was this how it would be, on camera? He could almost imagine it. Acting, like this, with his man.

Just like this.

Instead he meticulously fitted Madden's palm against his own. *"I think so."*

Madden's silence was deafening. Chris bent his head, and put his mouth against the back of Madden's fingers. Then turned his hand over and kissed the base of his thumb. The hollow of his palm. Carefully stroked up to Madden's sleeve cuff and touched his lips to the thin, soft skin of his wrist. There he repeated: *"I think so."*

Madden's hand curved. Trembling, it brushed Chris's cheek. Chris leaned into the touch.

When, going through the script, he had read these lines, he had thought Angelo's response wholly fabricated. A seduction conducted with painstaking discretion: going just far enough to be believable, yet not so far that he might endanger his own heart.

Now he realized Angelo had been captured the moment his lips had touched Frederick's palm. How could he not be, when Nicholas Madden was looking at him with a pained, shocked tenderness that felt—unearned, as though he had yet to know him? To deserve him?

Madden's thumb stroked his cheekbone. Madden's eyes were on his mouth. Chris held the line a moment longer, and then—he let it go.

# Chapter Three

**Chris Lavalle** @chrislavalle • 59m
while I appreciate the sentiment, I require no medical intervention following my business dinner with Nicholas Madden.

**Chris Lavalle** @chrislavalle • 58m
but the rumours are (for once!) true grapevine.us/2024/01/12/the-throne-live-act...

**Heart Eyes, Motherf\*cker** @bisonwhatbison • 56m
@chrislavalle OH GOD MY HEART STOPPED BEFORE I SAW THE LINK //SHAMEFACE

**Chris Lavalle** @chrislavalle • 55m
please send appropriate well-wishes and congratulatory chocolates thru the usual channels. #blessed

Priya Chaudhuri was a visionary.

She expected hard work and accepted nothing short of exceptional dedication. Her movies were vibrant, cinematic operas, never shying from vivid emotion; her actors went hungry and sleepless for their roles. She was devoted to her craft. She did not understand anyone who was not.

Nicholas had coveted the role of Frederick since the project had been pitched. He had made no mystery of it. He doubted there was a single actor in Hollywood who did not know they were going up against him if they auditioned, and he ensured that, once he had been in front of Chaudhuri and the Henderson siblings, the deal had been a cinch.

His fervent belief in the role was at once an asset and a handicap to the producers. He knew his character inside and out, and he was a reliable investment whose name would pull in fans. But his personal stake in the story meant he and Chaudhuri might very well be at each other's throats within a few days of filming.

Nicholas had a reputation. So had Chaudhuri. Between them they could make or break an actor.

None of this would have mattered—Nicholas was a difficult performer, but he respected Chaudhuri, and respect was hard to come by in the industry—if some hard-ass casting assistant with their eye on social media hadn't cast Christian Lavalle to act opposite him. Chris Lavalle, who had little to no acting experience, and was dangerously beautiful.

Nicholas had no idea what Chaudhuri thought of the choice. She played to high stakes: millions of dollars in film revenue, every year bang on the dot. He had no hope of reading her. With Lavalle she was polite to a fault.

The rest of the cast—all French and American, with the British exception of Sir Reginald Jarrett—were, thankfully, seasoned actors. Lavalle's main talent lay in keeping still under strobing lights and pouting.

And yet the memory of their dinner kept intruding on Nicholas's thoughts. The memory of Lavalle's lips touching his wrist, his warm breath, his fluttering eyelashes. Beauty itself was not enough to describe him. A deeper game had been at play; a game which Nicholas had only awoken from in the taxi back to his hotel, as though a dream had broken open.

Nicholas frowned, got a firmer grip on himself, and turned back to his heavily-annotated script. The effort he put into ignoring Lavalle was a distraction he couldn't afford.

The first table read had gone without a hitch.

The second table read, which was core-cast only, was fast becoming an unmitigated disaster.

Production had commandeered a large suite over the Grands Boulevards, lined in blond wood and parquet, tall windows and white ceilings. Below the windows were rows of spring-green trees and café terraces, packed with late lunchers enjoying a post-food espresso coma. The suite had been a tight squeeze yesterday, with the whole cast present—likewise some of the crew, the producing team, several smartphone-wearing PAs, and a responsible-looking security lineup. They had worked quickly and easily, and the overall mood had been hopeful, joyful. A smattering of applause had punctuated the end of the day. The crew had gone for cocktails afterwards.

Now, as only those who had been deemed essential remained—a tight table read was one of Chaudhuri's trademarks, meant to hone down the finer details, the intimacy of shared scenes, the nuances too quickly glossed over the day before—the cracks in the veneer were starting to show. Those cocktails were feeling entirely premature.

They were only sixteen around the table; even security had been banished beyond the double doors. Sixteen: Chaudhuri; Katherine Henderson, the better half of the Henderson siblings; Julian Chamberlain, who soon, Nicholas had no doubt, would be accepting multiple awards for Best Adapted Screenplay; Nicholas, and Lavalle next to him; the rest of the cast, looking hungover and skeptical.

Not a good look. Nicholas couldn't blame them.

The core of *The Throne* was a small, intimate set of familiars, the lives of whom the course of the novel charted, in an underground café in 1900s Paris. Artists, actresses, lost souls, immigrants, foreigners, and inverts, they were strangers caught in a storm: they were lost without one another, tossed wherever the wind blew, and mistrustful, bitter, solitary. They could not survive alone, and they resented it.

At their heart was Angelo, angelic as only Biblical angels were: cruel, sublime. And among them came Frederick, an intruder, another lost soul from beyond the ocean, who found in Angelo an object of abject fascination. They loved and they loathed one another, and in loneliness they found companionship. In the final pages of the novel, Frederick was set upon and beaten half to death, a flashing act of violence that threatened to ruin everything they had worked for. And Angelo became wholly human, at last.

When Frederick came back from the dead, *The Throne* found its final, singular, shining resolution: a way out of the darkness.

These were the performances around which the film's axis revolved: Nicholas's Frederick, the jaded newcomer slowly seduced into a set of bohemians, and Lavalle's Angelo, decadent and cynical, who lost himself in absinthe or opium, who cared precious little for his own life—or anyone else's.

If Nicholas did not portray Frederick's wary, weary fascination with his lover, the film would fail.

If Lavalle did not convey Angelo's bitterness and conflict, it would fail.

The rest of the cast could turn out stellar performances, and it wouldn't matter: if Nicholas and Lavalle had no chemistry, *The Throne* would crash and burn.

There had been a shift within him last night, and Frederick—Frederick as he had always thought of him—had changed. Nicholas's certainty of him, that constant, starlike surety, no longer fitted the perimeters of the story, now that he was made to share space with Lavalle's Angelo. He had had to face costars who changed the script before, but none of them had ever managed to change the way he constructed a role.

When it was his turn, Chris spoke with grave attention, neither quite reading his lines nor acting them through. That, too, worried Nicholas. He did not know what Chaudhuri and the Henderson siblings had seen in Chris during his audition, but surely it could not be only *this*: this thoughtfulness, this delicacy, which lacked something of Angelo's callousness.

Some actors played it up during read-throughs: hands moving, voices rising. Chris did not. But neither was his Angelo flat or dull—the subtlety of him danced just out of reach for Nicholas to grasp what he was doing with the character. If indeed he was doing anything at all, and wasn't just coming to the spotlight with a lot of goodwill and little skill.

Nicholas gritted his teeth at the thought.

As Andrée Belfond and Jason Kirkhall slowly worked their way through a scene that would have to be pared down for size, Nicholas found it increasingly difficult to follow each beat and each nuance—and, equally, increasingly so, to ignore the man sitting next to him. Lavalle, resting his chin upon his fist, was tracing with a fingertip the edge of the page they were reading. He'd cut his hair. Where the sunshine fell across his brow, an errant blond wisp was just touching his temple. He looked calm, focused, well rested.

The third time Jason Kirkhall fumbled a line, Chaudhuri released a rare, frustrated breath. Andrée looked briefly murderous, before she blinked the expression away.

Nicholas had little patience for Kirkhall's barely-old-enough-to-drink shenanigans. He found himself flipping ahead, skimming the lines he already knew—he and Lavalle were up next, a long, torturous, intimate scene that had their characters pare away at the barricades between them. Lavalle turned his head slightly, following the movement of his hand. Nicholas cleared his throat.

"Everyone take five," Chaudhuri said, when the scene was blissfully dropped. "Chris, to me."

Lavalle scrambled up, brushing Nicholas's shoulder, and somehow managing to make even awkwardness seem graceful. Nicholas exhaled through his nose, and went to one of the open windows to breathe.

The air was mild and bright. It was an early Parisian afternoon. Down below, cars were purring softly at a red light.

"The boy is out of his league."

Sir Reginald Jarrett, fatuous and British, asked for a light with a heavy wink.

"He'll be fine," Nicholas said shortly. "Chaudhuri is scaring the lights *into* him now."

Jarrett lifted his eyebrows, then turned to light his cigarette with a faint smile. "I meant poor Jason, to tell you the truth. But I suppose Lavalle is newish as well. Pretty, though." An appraising glance behind them. Nicholas declined to look. Lavalle had shown up wearing jeans that looked all but painted on. "Shame this is off to a bad start, really."

"Truer words," said Andrée, ambling over. She made a space for herself between Nicholas and the banister. As *The Throne*'s doomed poetess, she had had her hair lightened to white-gold, and her fine bone structure made her look almost eerie. Nicholas shifted to make room. Unlike Reggie's, her company was…tolerable; she was intelligent, and knew when to leave well enough alone. "At this stage," she added, "it's even odds the project will be sunk in a week."

"Come now," protested Jarrett. "Can't be that bad."

"You're too easily distracted by the pretty," said Andrée,

bumming a smoke. She glanced at Lavalle, who was listening to Chaudhuri and Chamberlain, looking intent. "And he *is* pretty. I've seen the—was it Armani? The campaign he did last year. Gorgeous. He knows how to...frame himself, which is half the job."

"He's used to cameras," said Nicholas.

"I thought you were dead against his casting."

"I was. I am. He—" Nicholas paused. "If either he or Kirkhall are dragging us down, it is on us to have the common sense to cut them loose before they get in too deep."

"*Merde* to that," said Andrée. "I am here to do my job, which is not nannying."

Jarrett chuckled. "My dear, whatever happened to patriotic solidarity?"

"*Merde,*" Andrée repeated, with feeling. She leaned her head back, exhaling a lungful of smoke. "Oh, listen. I don't know. This matters to me, too, you know. But I cannot be expected to baby my costars."

"If Lavalle doesn't come up to scratch," said Jarrett, switching gears, "it will be on *you*, Madden. You bear the brunt of your scenes together."

"I am aware."

Lavalle glanced back at them. He looked tired and sad. He looked as though he knew they were speaking of him, all three of them in the window. The cast had exploded starlike into small groups, drinking foul coffee from paper cups.

Of course he knew, Nicholas thought. Beauty like his, he was used to people speaking about him. He must recognize the look, the intent of it. He might as well not be in the same room, for all people cared. But when Lavalle's eyes met his, they softened. It was not quite a smile, but a—measure of connivance. Of understanding.

He remembered Lavalle's mouth touching his wrist.

"*Very* pretty," Sir Reginald sighed. "Were I but ten years younger!"

"Chaudhuri would take you to the cleaners, Reg," said Andrée.

The thought of Sir Reginald Jarrett—as ponderous in fashion sense as he was in conversation—engaging Lavalle in any manner of courtship and improbably succeeding was laughable, though Nicholas could not ignore the spark of irritated discomfort that went along with it. He looked out the window.

Andrée was right, though. Chaudhuri was famous for her intolerance of romantic liaisons among her cast and crew. Affairs were a distraction; love was, at best, a one-trick pony. The work was the work.

It was a pretty solitary life.

Spouses made distant contact. Significant others sent emails and gift baskets. For the most part, though, this was celibacy central. They had known it coming in; they would know it again. Working with Chaudhuri was a privilege, and those for whom the work did not come first were not granted entrance into the inner sanctum. Nicholas's own feelings did not come into it. He had sacrificed much to be here, in this moment, and would do it again, if he had to.

He *knew* he would have to.

"Alright, repeat," Chaudhuri said, as Lavalle stepped away.

The star system reorganized itself. Reggie patted Nicholas's shoulder; Andrée threw her cigarette butt out the window; Nicholas took his seat beside Lavalle again, their wrists brushing as they reached for the script together. He—his shampoo, perhaps—smelled faintly sweet: vanilla and bourbon.

"Skipping to scene 45," said Chaudhuri, and Lavalle pulled away.

Chamberlain, who had taken on the task of narrating, read in his soft voice: "*FADE IN: Int. ANGELO's room, late evening.*

*"This is the first time Frederick has been to visit him. The room is almost bare: a mattress, blankets, a writing-table, a washing basin, a small glass shelf. Books are strewn about the floor.*

*"ANGELO is lying on the bed, in his shirtsleeves. He is apparently, but not entirely, asleep."*

Nicholas stroked his thumb underneath his line. *"Are you still abed? The sun is getting low. People will wonder."*

*"If the sun is low there is no point in waking,"* Lavalle said.

In this read-through, action was not required. But emotion— expression—were. Chaudhuri's eyes on them were hard and keen.

*"Your friends ask after you. It's been two days since you've left your rooms."*

*"My friends,"* said Lavalle, with a touch of raspiness, *"know where I am."*

Chamberlain quietly put in: *"A small bottle is dangling from ANGELO's fingers."*

*"I see the green fairy has claimed you,"* said Nicholas, and it was not difficult to find Frederick's disapproval, his distaste and concern for Angelo, like an itch at the back of his throat. *"You have given much of yourself to her of late."*

*"Ah!"* Angelo should have laughed, pretty and wild; Lavalle's laugh was a tired chuckle. *"But what care have you, great Hadrian? I choose the green-eyed lover for myself, and you resent me."*

*"Resent you! You mistake me."*

*"Do I?"* Lavalle shifted slightly, though his eyes were averted. *"Isn't that why you've come to see me?"*

*"We are friends, I thought. That is why I came."*

*"Friends! Friends are not friends who care so little for each other. I loathe the very sight of you, my dear. And you care not at all."*

Nicholas took in a breath. When they filmed, he imagined he might kneel at Angelo's bedside. It was easy to see Lavalle's body there, languid and lost to the shallows of absinthe, in a loosened white shirt; his low, hooded eyes, his unresisting fingers as Frederick pried the phial from his grasp. His eyes had the right weariness to it, that Belle Époque *spleen*. But underneath it ran a vein of something brighter and angrier.

"*Loathe me, Angelo?*"

"*I have found no other word for it.*"

"*Is this what you must resort to, then? Absinthe and laudanum? Even I—devoid of experience as I am—can see you will lose yourself to them.*"

"*It is not experience you lack.*" And *those* words were not the mocking retort they should have been, but a genuine, hard-edged reproach. Lavalle was changing the script. He was making Angelo resentful, brittle, bitter. "*It is perception. Pleasure.*"

"*What pleasures can be found in hypnotics and absinthe are none I care to experience.*"

"*Yet you are here with me. Do you not wish for a taste? I have hashish, to mix the absinthe with, and sugar, and the little spoon.*"

"You'll want to get closer," Chaudhuri said. She sounded as though she spoke from a great distance. "Touch him, if he lets you."

Obediently Lavalle turned towards him; he made as though he would lift his hand to brush Nicholas's face, but, in the end, did not. But remained, silently, steadily, close enough to touch. "*Such fright! Won't you join me? Are you certain?*"

"*No. No... Angelo—*"

"*What harm is there in it?*"

"*I wish,*" Nicholas said, tasting the depth of Frederick's misery, the push and pull of his attraction and his repulsion, mixed together, indistinguishable, "*I wish that you would not hurt yourself so, Angelo.*"

"*Is wanting such a hurt?*" Lavalle's lips were parted, his eyes very bright. He looked feverish: nothing of Angelo's listlessness, but instead a pain so clear, so transparent, that Nicholas could not fathom how to grasp it—take it between his hands and let it run clear.

He said: *"This want?"* He was supposed to look at the bottle, then at Angelo's mouth. He watched Lavalle's mouth. *"This hurt?"*

*"I—"*

There was a pause. Chamberlain cleared his throat. *"A kiss."*

"You'll want to watch out for yourselves," said Chaudhuri ruthlessly. "We're not looking for *fast*. This is a slow, slow-*going* scene. Think of your body language: make it difficult, make it tentative. Angelo is mired in self-hatred; Frederick in self-doubt. You've spent six months wanting each other. Show it clearly."

*"Angelo,"* said Nicholas, in a voice so soft he thought only Lavalle, whose pale eyes were lifted to his, could hear it, *"Angelo. Angelo—"*

*"Ah,"* Lavalle said, and then leaned in. His hand was on Nicholas's cheek. His forehead brushed against his. *"And I thought I was alone."*

No words were spoken afterwards. There was no tenderness here; no laughter. Their bodies were victorious, though their minds knew better. In the morning they would part bitterly, and Frederick would walk to the Seine and watch the dark river.

*The Throne* was a slow descent into hell. The better ending, improbable and uncertain as it was, was nothing short of a miracle.

Chaudhuri was silent. So was everybody else. Nicholas was breathing fast. The sourness and the intimacy of their words made his blood beat hard. What was supposed to be a scene of opposites—Frederick's severity and Angelo's debauchery—a heartless seduction—had been turned inside out. Frederick had found himself making advances, and Angelo had held himself away.

"Interesting," Chaudhuri said at last.

Chamberlain was frowning. "It's not what I thought it could be. But—". He glanced at her. "I don't know. It isn't what viewers will expect, surely."

"It's interesting," she repeated firmly. "But I want to see more. I want the *two* of you—" she gestured between them, and with an indrawn breath Lavalle pulled away, putting some distance between them "—to practice this. Together. On record."

"It's a pivotal scene," added Chamberlain helpfully. "Perhaps the most significant in terms of Angelo's character early in the narrative."

*All the more reason not to run it through the gamut*, thought Nicholas, *of an amateur's interpretation*. But he, too, was shaken. Nothing, until now, had ever altered his perception of Angelo, whom he had loved for eighteen years. Lavalle had taken him, made him other, made him *different*, and Nicholas was drawn to his bitterness and wariness as he might not have been to anger or to rage.

At his side, Lavalle was quiet.

In another read-through, being sent back to practice a scene might have felt like chastisement. Any other director might have slapped down the law and sent Lavalle's personal approach to the role back to...well, to acting school, except Lavalle hadn't even attended that. But Chaudhuri looked calculating. She notoriously disliked wasting time on an endless stream of takes. She preferred having a vision of the scene as it unfolded, and expected her actors to provide a full-bodied character. If she approved of Lavalle's interpretation—

In the business, for Chaudhuri to demand several practice runs of any particular scene was a privilege. It showed trust. It meant power.

Nicholas wondered if Lavalle was aware of that.

"I have a hotel room," he heard himself say. "We can run through takes there."

Lavalle glanced at him so briefly he caught only a flash of startled grey.

"Perfect," said Chaudhuri—already the problem was secondhand to her. Her trust in them was staggering. "Then we move to 51. Sir Reginald, if you would."

They worked through the remainder of the script slowly, working out crinks as they went: small matters of vocabulary, of voice pitch, of connotation and subtext. Out of all of them, by Nicholas's estimation, only Andrée had a solid grasp on her character; a vein of tragedy ran through her lines, giving her a gravitas the rest of them could not match yet. Reggie was playing Sir Reginald, a sorry consequence of becoming a stage fixture people paid merely to show up. Jason Kirkhall had no business arriving hungover at a table read. And Nicholas was—rattled.

Lavalle did not look at him again until their final scene, which was the novel's single moment of hope—the world opening, the unexpected miracle: Frederick, thought dead for two months, returning to Angelo's rooms in the night, finding him there, finding his hand—their trembling, tentative embrace in the dark.

They had nothing to say. Relief and joy were too strong for words. But Lavalle touched his arm as Chamberlain read the final lines, a mere touch of his knuckles; and when Nicholas met his eyes he said: "Are you alright?"

"I stay at Le Meurice for the duration of the shoot," said Nicholas.

A faint smile touched Lavalle's mouth. "Of course you do."

"Tomorrow," Nicholas said.

"Tomorrow. I'll bring croissants. For breakfast."

# *Chapter Four*

www.60seconds.co/2022/06/12/interview-with-nicholas-madden

**60 Seconds:** Do you find it difficult to interact with other actors?

**NM:** I find it difficult to interact with bad actors.

**60 Seconds:** By whose judgement?

**NM:** My own.

**60 Seconds:** You don't get lonely?

**NM** (after a pause; briefly)**:** Never.

At eight a.m., the bakery at the corner of the rue des Saints Pères and the rue Perronet was a warm, golden haven of light. Chris, dragging off the cords of his earphones, pushed open the chiming door. The baker exclaimed to see him, threw her hands out at him, and presented a floury cheek to be kissed.

He laughed, admiring the day's offerings: the racks, as yet mostly untouched, were loaded with oven-hot sourdough, crisp traditional baguettes, milky brioche, multigrain loaves, and pastries of all kinds. *Pains au chocolat, chaussons aux pommes*, caramelized *mendiants*, buttery *sablés*, chocolate *éclairs* and

coffee *religieuses*, flaky apple tartlets—and the ubiquitous croissants, crescent-shaped, and still warm.

He bought four. Madame Dumont threw in five sugar-
studded *chouquettes*. He bit into one as he stepped back outside:
the soft choux pastry burst in his mouth, light as air, and so
sweetly melting on the tongue he wolfed down all five before
he even reached the Seine.

It was still early enough that the sky was a peculiar shade
of turquoise downriver, but to the east it was almost white,
the clouds parting at last. The last stars were fading out in the
distance. He meandered towards the Pont Royal. He preferred
the shaded bicycle lanes of the quays, though he had to dodge
the occasional jogger in bright fluorescent leggings, over the
busy fracas of the rue de Rivoli further in on the right bank;
but, by the time he reached the Louvre and plunged into the
Tuileries Gardens, the sleeping city had slowly awoken.

Cars, heavy double-buses, harried-looking metro commut-
ers, speeding bicycles, all were hustling along towards a thick
knot of traffic in the Place Concorde. The Tuileries were still
mostly deserted—though the emerging sun and the mildness
of June would soon bring out *flâneurs*, young families, and
students skipping the last days of school to suntan on the geo-
metric lawns and the low chairs. Then, stepping smartly up
towards the arcades, he came into sight of the shining doors
and marble floors of the Hôtel Le Meurice.

The doorman pushed open the glass pane for him supercil-
iously, eyeing with some disfavor Chris's worn pullover and
ripped jeans. Chris gave him a blandly pleasing smile, and
inquired at the desk for Nicholas Madden. The bag of croissants dangled from his hand; in his off-duty clothes, he could
be a university student.

More superciliousness, then, at the reception, though that
man was younger, and he glanced up at Chris, twice, not quite
placing him… Chris was polite, placid, and gave his name.

"Oh." A pause. The receptionist hesitated, then looked conspiratorial. "Is he expecting you? Sir."

A world of innuendo in that last word. Chris stifled a sigh. "Yes. Call him up, if you will."

He did. The call was short. When he hung up the receptionist's mouth had thinned at the corners. "Third floor, sir. The Napoleonic suite."

Madden would have a Napoleonic suite. "Thank you."

The young man apparently assumed he could allow himself to make confidences. "He didn't sound like he was in a good mood, sir."

"He never is," said Chris sadly. Secretly he hoped he had torn him from sleep. Take it as revenge for Madden's surliness during their dinner, for his disbelieving looks during the read-through. Take it as retribution for that intense focus, that powerful fixation, those somber eyes that made Chris feel as though he were too young and too inexperienced to get on Madden's superior level. He waited for the elevator, shivering at the memory of that dark regard.

Madden looked as collected as he ever did when he opened his door and stepped aside to let him in. He wore not the t-shirt and sweatpants one might expect of a man in the privacy of his own hotel room, but black pants and a white button-down, crisp and cool. And truly Chris had not expected him to wear pajamas. Nicholas Madden probably went to bed in a three-piece suit.

Or naked.

Chris couldn't stop picturing those long bare arms curled around thick pillows, and the dip of a muscled, naked back... he cleared his throat.

Madden looked briefly alarmed at being handed a paper bag of warm, buttery pastries, but handled them with grace. "I—thank you. I suppose." Stiffly. "Coffee?"

On the table between the bow windows was a breakfast

tray: porcelain cups, a bowlful of sugar, a plump pot of milk, a heavy plated jug of coffee. "Please."

Besides this, the room was sparse, tall-ceilinged, and very white, the furniture well-made and delicate. On the low table lay a tablet, a copy of the script, and one, fairly dog-eared, of *The Throne*. A set of large double doors opened into the bedroom, which was painted over in cream and cool tones. Through the windows the sky was lightening slowly to the deep blue of a true June morning. Nowhere did there seem to be any sign of Madden's living arrangements.

"It's charming," said Chris, dryly, thinking: *Very you.*

Madden shrugged a shoulder, seating himself by the window, and reached out to pour the coffee. He did so with alarming grace, as though he'd had training. The shirt thinned slightly over his shoulders; it was exquisitely tailored. But Madden, normally so mordant, seemed...tired. His eyes were dark. The rising sun caught shadows and angles in the bone structure of his face. "Sit. Sugar?"

"No—I take it black." A quick, interested glance at that. Madden added milk and sugar to his own, handed him his cup, and lifted with two knuckles the side of the paper bag.

"Croissants."

"I did say I would bring some."

"So you did." Madden extricated two. "Do you eat them plain?"

"When there's no jam." There *was* jam—little pots of orange marmalade and blackberry preserves—but Madden did not touch them: he ate neatly, with appreciation, licking his fingers, unspeaking until he was done. Chris, fascinated, left his own mostly untouched. It was not the French fashion to eat in silence. As Madden swallowed the last morsel, he glanced up at Chris—a gesture strangely reminiscent of the boy at reception, downstairs, who had stolen glimpses at him—but this was a long, careful look, made darker for the fall of his lashes. These were quite long, brushing his cheekbones when he blinked. Chris was touched by it, somehow. It gave his face a boyish look, there one moment and gone the next.

"What are you thinking?"

"Of you," said Madden.

"That's either flattery or an insult."

"Neither."

Chris cocked his head, somehow pleased, somehow flattered, though there was nothing in Nicholas's manner that hinted at deeper feelings. "What, then?"

"You puzzle me."

Chris laughed. "I'll take the compliment."

"Don't," said Madden, coolly. "I mean neither to stroke your ego nor to bolster your self-esteem. Merely—as an actor to another—" He paused. "Well. What would persuade a man of your social caliber..." He angled his head, glancing briefly at the tablet; then with a sour twist of the mouth: "A man with a media presence is bound by pressures and influences. Yours are among the worst. You're bringing into my industry all that is loathsome about yours: shamelessness, self-centeredness, a loose grasp on reality. What in the world are you thinking?"

The coffee was strong and black, very hot. Chris drank as calmly as he could. He knew what they would look like, as seen by an outsider. Madden was dark and neat, dressed to impress. And *he* was in jeans ripped at the knees, and in the worn oversized sweater he wore whenever he preferred not to draw attention.

He let out a breath, and lifted his eyes to Madden's. He did not know why Nicholas's words electrified him and pained him in equal measure. He was used to such comments, and agreed with the criticism to some extent. But Madden's piercing, bitter cynicism was hinting at something deeper; something within himself he had never wholly understood, and was only just beginning to feel his way around. It wasn't doubt, or even mistrust. It was sadness.

"You believe me unethical."

"I prefer irresponsible."

"I see. An interesting choice of words. *Your* industry, of course, is known for its equal pay, diversity, and fair opportunities." A dull unhappiness was beating against his ribs. He was normally so careful about not entering into comparison games; Nicholas aroused in him all manners of reactions, and this blunted grief was offset only by the joy of having found a real opponent. "But that isn't the problem, is it? I've been hoping above my station. Is that not what you think?"

"No." Madden had a miserable look about his eyes, as though he knew he had, somehow, stepped over an inner line, which he had set himself, and had not meant to overlap. "I don't—understand it. You."

"There," said Chris, quietly, "we agree." He sat for a moment, looking out the window: they were high enough to see into the Tuileries, where the summer fair would soon come, and fill the air with the smell of burning sugar. For now, however, the gardens were still mostly quiet, and through the double-pane glass no sound of the traffic below could be heard. "I don't understand it either."

"Then why take the job?"

Chris blinked at him, not sure he understood. "The audition was offered to me. Chaudhuri called, personally. Like a miracle. I did not question it. Would you have?"

Madden looked blank—as though a sudden gust of wind had blown away the emotion in his body—and then, almost rueful. "Lavalle—"

"Chris."

"I—"

"Yes, really."

"Alright." Madden's hand was on his wrist. Chris glanced up from it to his face, and did not find it altered in any way—only something about his eyes had grown mildly pained. "I did not know that."

"You thought," said Chris, scornfully, "that I had slept my way to the top. No? Or pulled strings, perhaps…no wonder," he added, "that you loathed me on sight."

Madden's fingers tightened, and Chris, turning his hand over, touched their palms together in a sad mockery of his play at seduction in *Le Renard d'Or*.

"I wanted it, though. The part. Wanted it awfully."

"So did I," said Madden, and Chris saw in him, suddenly, briefly, for the barest second, a man so powerfully affected with artistic longing that it overwhelmed everything else, even loneliness. A man whose words he could trust. "I know the feeling."

"Tell me about Angelo," said Madden, after a moment lost in the further consumption of coffee and croissant. They had returned to their natural places; contact, briefly achieved, had been broken. Chris broke off pieces of pastry between nervous fingers.

"You don't need me to tell you about him," he said—then added more dryly: "You have made it clear you know him better than I do."

Madden waved that aside. He had beautiful hands; long, bony, graceless, but expressive. Chris adored hands in a man. Madden was ticking all the boxes, one after the other. "I only know Angelo as far as my point of view goes—my understanding, which is Frederick's. We never see into Angelo's head. As I see it, you have the harder job of either of us."

Chris was silent. Then he said, "Tell me about Frederick."

"Frederick's the simpler one."

"I don't think so."

"He's the narrator, Lavalle."

"*Chris*. But he doesn't have insight into himself."

"Who does? Nicholas, then." Chris absorbed this. A world in which Nicholas Madden was on first-name basis with any- one other than his bathroom mirror seemed vaguely surreal. "Alright. Sure. There's a line in—chapter four, I think— about photography. Negative images. That's Frederick. He's a shadow. Unknown to himself."

"Until he meets Angelo."

"Yes."

"Then take Angelo as its opposite: not as a shadow but an actor—"

A brief, startling smile touched Madden's mouth: he had very straight, white teeth, and the smile threatened almost to transform his face, making it temporarily charming. "Now you're just playing."

"On words. But I mean it," said Chris, "I don't think An- gelo sees himself, ever. Or likes himself, much," he added. He was surprised to taste, on his tongue, a strange, astringent bitterness.

"He doesn't like Frederick much either."

"I disagree. He likes him very much—terrifyingly—and from the start."

"We," said Madden, his dark eyes darkening still, "have a very difficult task at hand, if we disagree so much on every particular."

"Then," said Chris, in sudden irritation, "trust me to do *my job*."

"Your job!" Madden laughed in his face. Whatever charm- ing truce they had found, that sweeter turn their conversa- tion had taken, rattled away like a screeching needle. Madden stood and loomed—he had a good figure for looming; tall, and impeccably dressed—his face twisted up in scorn. He had a stifled movement, as though crushing his anger under his heel, and spun towards the window, against which he leaned his back, arms crossed, and glared. "Alright, then. Impress me, Your Highness."

"*Va te faire foutre,*" Chris said, tiredly.

Madden's mouth twisted. "Insults and injury. You're not so smooth at all outside the smartphone screen."

"Do you imagine I'm a different person online and off?"

"I do. I know it. I know the kind of person you are."

"No one knows me," said Chris.

Madden stared at him, teeth clenched against what must be a scathing reply—something to flay him open with rage. But then he looked away. In profile, his face was sharp, jarring to look at. He was a handsome man, intimidating, too proud by half. Chris had met his type before; had fucked his type before. He was a special kind of heartbreak.

Half-mad, people said. The greatest narcissist on the red carpet; the Big Bad Wolf of Hollywood. Rude, overbearing, a diva, elitist, insufferable. But the man standing now at the window was more human than paparazzi candids and bad-tempered interviews would allow the public to know. In the golden June light that streamed in, fine as lace, through the windows, he looked tired and almost sad. Chris could see the line of his jaw underneath the black, groomed beard, and the soft faint lines of worry or laughter at the corners of his eyes; his posture, his body language, his arms crossed against his chest, were tense. He'd gotten up this morning and put on carefully dry-cleaned, pressed clothes, had left no trace of his living arrangements present in his own suite, but had thought to ring up room service for a breakfast tray. There was a strange, unhappy vulnerability in him.

Chris's hand twitched, as though he wished to reach out. To touch. To take for himself this odd, somber man, with his

cold opinions and his bleak manner, and to try and find inside him the little kernel of warmth that needed to blaze up,
outward and outward until it flared into a fire...

*"You know me,"* he said, quietly, taking Nicholas's words
for his own—but they were Angelo's in truth, Angelo's words
from the final chapters of *The Throne*, at the end of the world,
when everything went to hell, and the battle was lost. *"I think
you're the last man in the world who knows me."*

Nicholas's throat worked as he swallowed. *"I thought I did."*

He came, as Frederick might, to kneel at Chris's feet. It
should have looked absurd, suggestive. But with every appearance of chastity he leaned his weight against Chris's thighs,
and bent his dark head, resting his arms on his lap.

The words were all wrong. The gesture was all wrong. In
*The Throne*, this was a moment of separation: the point of lost
hope, of resentment, of isolation and misunderstanding. Frederick was going home. He was leaving.

But instead the words felt like recognition. It felt like being
touched on the elbow by a stranger, and, turning, finding a
friend.

Chris touched his hair. It was very thick, sun-warm, and,
when Chris stroked his fingers through it, Nicholas's breath
came out of him in a shuddering sigh. Which was wrong, too.
Frederick was supposed to be callous and cold, too hurt by
Angelo's selfishness to forgive him his faults, too entrenched
in his own self-loathing to dare love him.

Angelo had swallowed the shame of himself like a star, and
set himself to a life of cynicism and perdition. Frederick—
ascetic, corrupt, Puritan Frederick—adored him and loathed
him, and was lost.

Nicholas was a master at it. He portrayed internal and moral
conflict with reserve and power. He had, during yesterday's table
read, shown Frederick's repugnance and self-flagellation with

nothing more than a touch, a glance, a twist of the mouth…now it appeared that the battle *was* lost. He was prostrate, abandoned.

Tenderness was not in the script. Nicholas, who infamously detested improvisation, had gone off-base, off-earth, off-nature.

*"You will drive me mad."*

*"I wish that I could. Then you would stay with me…madmen in our own madhouse."* Chris kissed his hair. He couldn't have stopped himself if he'd tried. *"Stay. Stay. Stay here."*

*"I can't."* But Nicholas's hands tightened around his knees, an absurd, reassuring caress.

*"You don't care to."* Angelo's jealousy was easier to find. Chris had shared that terrified anger for too long to mistake it. *"You goddamn hypocrite. Cold, cold hypocrite—what do you care for? Your own small, cheap, shameful pleasures—and I, the worst of them all."*

*"Angelo. Angelo. Look at me—"*

Chris wouldn't; he couldn't; couldn't look at him, or Angelo would come up in him, in his mouth, and he would say something absurd and real, horrifying.

Nicholas pulled away. His hair was in his eyes, falling over his brow. He reached for Chris, who turned away, but it was a caress—his hand stroked past his ear to the nape of his neck, and tangled in his hair. The script said, *A kiss.* There was no reason why they *should* kiss now, in this sham of a rehearsal session. But Chris thought…well, he thought. He was wrong. Nicholas brushed his thumb against his mouth instead, so gently that Chris only had time to take a breath and pulled him down to rest against his shoulder. Chris's heart gave a pained beat.

His lips pressed against Chris's ear. *"Goodbye, Angelo."*

## *Chapter Five*

**@chrislavalle** makeup fun! Gold tints and bronze accents in today's session with @a_mell before the shoot for rights4all, donation link in bio!

It was a lot of fun to strip for a good cause. Though i've been in the industry long enough to feel comfortable with my own body, working with the amazing @trampling on different poses and angles helped me understand when and why i've experienced body shyness in the past, and what I can do to combat it in the future. nudity can be fun and empowering, but it can and must only be on your own terms and boundaries.

rights4all empowers charities and schools across europe with means to help lgbt+ youth, especially homeless and trans teens, with education and habitation costs. this photoshoot features fifty renowned lgbt+ campaigners from across the european union, posing nude or semi-nude as a pledge to combat the stigma attributed to queer bodies. we want to highlight diversity and beauty across the gender spectrum and from every age and demographic...

*Hello, Chris.*

Nicholas stood. He went straight to the breakfast tray and poured himself a cup of coffee, still miraculously semi-warm;

to this he added two sugars and enough milk to turn it light as a nut, and drank it down. Chris was moving slowly, a little awkwardly, just out the corner of his eye. It was a grim sort of victory, to have forced him out of his charming ways at last.

The moment had broken down into absurdity. He'd been absorbed by his own performance, by Chris's reaction, by his responsiveness. Acting opposite Chris was dangerously close to not acting at all.

Damn the man. When Nicholas had let him in, he had been…oddly fascinated…by Lavalle's worn, oversized sweater, which hugged his shoulders and his arms, but fell softly in his lap when he sat. The effect was devastating. In expensive clothing Lavalle had been merely stunning; ripped jeans and mussed hair made him look unexpectedly young and tender, and Nicholas had had to force down the sudden desire to pick him off the floor and carry him directly into the bedroom. If he'd kissed him, he would have tasted the jam and sweetness of the croissant, the sour black tang of coffee.

*Unacceptable.*

He had been intolerably rude, a situation that was becoming alarmingly common when they were in the same room. Nicholas disliked that in himself. He needed a tighter rein on his temper.

But Chris had held the line and carried it through. Yes, it had been Angelo he'd ached to kiss, Angelo with his self-loathing, Angelo with his cynical bitterness. Only at the last moment, with his hands on Chris's thighs and their lips inches apart, had he remembered himself.

"Forgive me," he said. The words tasted strange. He didn't say them often enough.

Chris glanced at him, reaching for his own cup. His hair was worse now—rumpled and soft in the semi-light. "What for?"

"That was unprofessional of me. And you," he added, in fairness.

"Yes," said Chris, frankly. A smile tugged at the corner of his mouth, teasing a dimple. "I won't tell if you won't tell. But we have found something now, no?"

That was one way of putting it. He sounded as though he'd not done anything more consequential than trying on a new outfit. But Nicholas had never been so shaken in his certainty of a character—not one of his proudest costars had ever succeeded in forcing him where he'd not intended to go. And Chris had done it without knowing it, with nothing more than the touch of his fingers, and a kiss in his hair. Chris, with his sweet manner and his lovely, lonely eyes.

Frederick, rigid and demanding and cold, had gone to his knees in front of Angelo. Nicholas himself couldn't fathom kneeling to anyone. But he had done it—done it gratefully. That kiss had felt like the favor of a prince.

He said: "Perhaps."

"You disapprove."

"I don't know that I do," Nicholas said slowly. "But you might run afoul of Chaudhuri if you keep reinventing yourself."

"You forget," said Chris, "that I only invent Angelo as far as you're willing to bend to me."

The phrase awakened incredible desires in him; the smile which accompanied it was unreadable. It might as easily be purely innocent as...not. But Nicholas was aware of *him* now, in a human, animal way: he was powerfully aware of Chris's tall, lean body, the lingering presence of his touch, his long fair eyelashes, eyes lowered. He smelled warm and good. A young David in ripped jeans in the sunlight.

Something buzzed between them, and, startled, their eyes caught; and then Chris seemed to become aware of what he had said, and opened his mouth, flushed slightly, and looked away. He found his phone. Grimaced.

"Work?"

"No. No. It's nothing, I…" Chris looked a little foolish, a little irritated. "I should call them back."

"Do. We're done for today," said Nicholas.

Their separation was awkward, hard-edged. Disliking the French fashion of kissing cheeks in parting, Nicholas held out his hand. Chris's hand was strong, his grip firm. At the door he seemed on the brink of saying something more.

"I'll see you in two days," said Nicholas, to prevent it.

"Ah." Chris smiled, shrugged. "Yes."

Nicholas watched him until he stepped into the elevator, leaning against the doorjamb, then returned into his suite alone. As he crossed the room, he became aware that his windows opened onto the arcades; that, if he only stood there long enough, he might see Chris cross the street towards the gardens. He did not plan on standing there unmoving. But he found himself gathering the coffee cups, returning the plates to the tray. He still felt the strange displacement that had begun when Chris's fingers had strayed into his hair—as though he had stepped into an alternate timeline.

It took a couple of minutes. Chris stepped out from under the arcades, hands in his pockets. His hair caught the sun and shone bright as a new penny. Nicholas watched, waiting for the moment when he would look back.

*Look back.*

He did not.

Because these things had an old, superstitious tradition in them, filming began at midnight.

Midnight in June was still warm, and the place Dauphine was a contrast of deep sweet shadow and pooling streetlights.

Shops and cafés were darkened and shut up. The film crew looked incongruous, with their beetle-like cameras and expensive microphones, and their voices were hushed and quietened, as though they felt the passing of time in this place as a measurable thing, a palpable thing, that they could mold and shape to their own desires. Perhaps they could.

Nicholas was waiting. At his side, in mannish pants and a cinched shirtwaist, Andrée lit an anachronistic cigarette. The tip of it burned cherry-bright, flaring up.

"Well," she said.

Nicholas said: "Well?"

"Here's a pretty mess. We really and truly are in for it now."

This echoed Nicholas's sentiments: it was a moment of grace before the cameras started rolling. He could feel Frederick settle inside of him, a possession. "Indeed."

She swept her gaze around the set, nodding briefly at a few privileged persons. Chaudhuri stood across the length of the square, some way away, and discussed sight lines with her cameramen. Andrée drew on her cigarette thoughtfully. "I thought this was below her. You never know… Everyone bows to power from on high, even the great and the mighty."

"What?" said Nicholas absently. Already he was looking for a golden head among the crowd.

She peered at him. "You haven't heard? It's all anyone is talking about."

"Have we lost our funding?" Nicholas inquired dryly.

"No-o." She shrugged, and dragged on her smoke, grimacing.

An odd choking clenched Nicholas's chest. "This is about Lavalle?"

"Rumors, Madden. Only rumors."

"What then?"

She grew more distant, and less affected. "There's some say

that…persons above were involved in his choice. French, influential persons. His uncle is a former secretary of culture."

"Ah."

He was not surprised; he could not be. An unknown quantity with very little acting experience could not work his way onto an A-rate cast without greasing some hands. The clenching sensation returned, strangling his heart. It ought to have confirmed all his worst suspicions about Chris's lack of acting ability.

But he had seen Chris's Angelo; he had heard him, had *felt* him, had held him. And, now that the man had come out of the limelight to rest beside him in the dark, he did not want to believe he could be a sham, anymore.

"Is this certain?" he asked. It alarmed him also that Chaudhuri should have given in to outside pressure. She was not the sort to give in to nepotism of any sort. What fate this spelled for *The Throne*, he did not know.

Another very French shrug. "Our government is keen on Hollywood revenue," she said, damning her country with faint praise and with a flick of her burning cigarette. "Somehow I wanted something else for the kid, though. Don't suppose it'll be good for his career if he can't turn out a good performance."

Nicholas closed his eyes. Then he opened them again. Andrée patted him on the shoulder and pushed off. Nicholas remained where he was, the still center in an ever-moving world. Around him the set spun. Cameras and ever-bright spotlights. Actors moving about, melting voices. The slow trenchant movement of blurred light.

Then a minor commotion brought confusion to the crew—people in the way of his line of sight shifted and danced—and he saw Chris.

He stopped short. Absurdly, it had been evident to him that he would know the moment Chris made his way on set—he would feel it, would know it in his body, like a ripple in still water. Instead, nothing. Chris had arrived unnoticed. Chris probably had been there for quite some time, and he was alone now, leaning against a bench, his golden head lowered as he read.

He was reading the script. He was going through his lines. His chin was propped against his fist, his elbow on his knee.

He was nothing but scrupulous in his work. Unlike Jason Kirkhall, unlike Reg, he was alert and attentive, plainly wishing to please—even, Nicholas thought with a stab of pain, to please *him*: to give in to his caprices. In return Nicholas was detestable, Chaudhuri impatient, and the cast suspicious. Chris endured the suspicion and contempt of cast and crew with smiling composure; and if he privately damned them all to hell, he took care to do so out of earshot.

Nicholas was no stranger to nepotism in Hollywood. It was baked in, essentially, into the business; he might not, himself, have landed some key roles, if it hadn't been for a well-placed word with the right people. No—it wasn't blatant favoritism that stuck in his throat, nor even the loss of what another, more experienced actor might have brought to the character. It was the hypocrisy he couldn't get past, the thought that Chris must be a different person underneath his beautiful smiles. He despised a lack of sincerity. He could not abide being lied to.

*Had* Chris lied to him? Had he smiled, and smiled, and wheedled pretty words, and spoken nothing but falsehoods right to Nicholas's face? Had that been the case in Nicholas's own hotel room, when Nicholas had knelt at his feet?

They hadn't come across each other often over fitting week. Those few days before the start of filming were always a frantic, heady rush, when costume fittings, location scoping, and logistical details had to be figured out last minute.

Only once had they met, outside costuming. Startled, Chris

had tripped on the doorstep of the trailer, catching himself on Nicholas's arm with a light grip. He had been dressed in a white shirt and dark trousers, a beautifully embroidered waist-coat opened to reveal part of his throat and his collarbone. His golden hair was slicked back, his mouth bitten-red.

That was all. Two days ago.

Nicholas hadn't been able to stop thinking about it since.

When a makeup artist came up to Nicholas, wielding brush and powder, looking away was a relief.

This was only a short scene, a chance meeting between their characters. Filming, as they usually did, out of order, they would repair afterwards to a pair of ancient maid's rooms, set into the brickwork of a building that probably *did* date from 1900, for a longer and more intimate shoot. Production had planned the timing closely, for they intended to last no longer than the summer in Paris, a mere eight weeks of shooting; despite this, it wasn't till past half past one that Chaudhuri called for action. The cast and crew waited, their impatience and nervousness rising.

"Nerves?" he asked, when another sea-change in the crew brought him close to Chris. Chris glanced up at him, chin on his fist, and smiled.

"Not at all. Isn't that funny? I'm used to cameras."

"This is another sort of camera," said Nicholas dryly.

But Chris shrugged and said, "Well, and so? I know I photograph well."

"There's more to acting than good looks."

"So everyone keeps reminding me," Chris said, ruefully. And then, at Nicholas's sharper look: "Not in so many words, they don't."

"You're an unknown quantity."

"There's that too."

"If," said Nicholas, "you prove them wrong tonight, I'll buy you a coffee."

Chris's smile reappeared. He touched Nicholas's shoulder. Nicholas shivered, and had to resist the urge to cover his fingers with his own. "I will hold you to that."

It was possible that his timidity and reserve weren't just for show. The first four takes came out flawlessly; Chaudhuri requested they try again from a couple of different angles, but *The Throne* was off to a rocking start. A subdued thrill was running through the crew, like a shared fever.

Crew knew immediately when they held on to a winner. Crew recognized talent.

They recognized it now. Andrée, waiting on the sidelines for her cue, had her mouth set in a curious frown. Chaudhuri's face was grave. Across the set, actors and DAs and camera crew were all looking at Chris.

Nicholas was looking too: the trouble was looking *away*. Chris was enthralling.

His Angelo was by turns infuriating and lovely, selfish to the point of loss and charming to the point of disbelief—his hands nervous, his body active and mobile, his face changing emotion in a flash. Nicholas kept breaking off, catching onto a different thread of action, meeting Chris's motion with his own. Like a dance.

He wasn't used to being led. But this was not quite like being *led*.

It was moving in one direction, and finding the movement echoed in another body. It was like having two bodies…

When Chaudhuri called for a break, they stayed together. Acting was a peculiar drug: it amplified feeling. Frederick loved and loathed Angelo, and Nicholas felt a fraction of that emotion resonant in his own body, whenever he looked at Chris.

Chris himself looked tired, determined, hesitant.

"I wish," he said softly, when the PA who'd brought them bottled water had assured them of her assistance, congratulated them, beamed, and taken herself off, "that I knew what *this* look of hers means."

He nodded towards Chaudhuri, who was unreadable. He pressed the cool bottle to his burning cheek.

"Chaudhuri's fine. Ignore it." Nicholas had seen many a seasoned actor reduced to crippling indecision by Chaudhuri's thousand-mile stare.

But Chris, after a moment of trepidation, gave in to a smile. "She does let us have a frightening amount of self-determination."

"She trusts us," said Nicholas, "to do our job."

Chris raised his eyebrows. "I've earned that distinction, have I?"

"You are spectacular tonight," said Nicholas, "and I'll owe you that coffee." And then he knew he'd surprised him: Chris's face went entirely blank, lips parted, eyes widening.

"I—"

"Dare you to keep it up," added Nicholas, more lightly. Chris's eyes went softer, and he bumped his shoulder with his own, companionably enough.

"I did not imagine you like this, Nicholas." He pronounced his name the French way—the *s* softened so far as to be almost inaudible—and Nicholas found that he liked the sound of it; liked the way his mouth shaped his name, the low amusement in Chris's eyes. With a smile, Chris brought his water bottle to his mouth. His throat worked as he swallowed. He brushed Nicholas's lapel with the backs of his knuckles, as though to sweep away dust—and then left his fingers lingering there.

"How did you imagine me?" Nicholas's voice was a little

rough. They stood in the circle of the cameras' cyclopean eyes, a little apart from the rest of the crew. The light of a streetlamp fell directly over them. Nicholas could see every one of Chris's golden eyelashes, kissing his cheeks.

Chris shrugged a sloping shrug, and said: "You have a *terrible* reputation." He sounded so earnest that Nicholas laughed.

"All well deserved, I assure you."

"You *were* abhorrent to me," said Chris, cheerfully, "when you thought I had slept my way into the cast."

"I," said Nicholas, and then frowned, and swallowed back his instinctive retort. He admitted: "I don't know what I think of you now."

"I suppose that's fair enough."

"It isn't." He sighed. "It's professional mistrust. It's one thing to assume emotion in a take like this—" it was a panoramic scene, and Chaudhuri had so far held off on the closer shots; those would come, later, when in the privacy of Angelo's garret clothing came off and skin touched skin "—and another to keep it up in a closer shot."

"Ah." Chris seemed to think this through. "Intimacy breeds contempt."

"Something like that." The truth was that Nicholas had never been partnered in a sex scene with anyone but a woman. It was not his first gay role—no man went to Hollywood without playing some bit part kissing another man; it was a professional rite of passage—but certainly his most explicit. With women, playing up an attraction he did not feel was easy enough. With Chris, though…

"Then I have the better of you." Chris's voice was amused. Nicholas glanced at him, and he looked away. "I'm used to the intimacy—and the contempt. Photoshoots, you know…" He let that statement float into space, waving his hand in a vague

fashion, as though the concept of tasteless nudity in advertis-
ing was better left unsaid.

He had modeled Calvin Klein underwear. He had worn
Levi's jeans tight enough to showcase his rather delectable ass.
He must have weathered the worst of it all: the horrors of the
fashion industry, the small cruelties, the dastardly pitfalls, the
pettiness and the malice.

Again Nicholas had to resist the urge to touch his hand.
Chris's face was sad, and all he could do was admire that bravery. He cleared his throat.

"Posing's hardly enough. There's more to a sex scene than
looking artfully beautiful."

"Then I *must* be out of my depth. What, then?"

Nicholas said slowly: "Power, I suppose. Kindness."

"A strange association."

"It's an equilibrium."

"Not that different from actual sex, then," Chris said. His
eyes were low-lidded and meaningful. *There is a wicked streak
in him*, Nicholas thought. *Be careful.*

So late at night, with his hair slicked back and his clothes
artfully mussed, Chris looked the type to eat men's hearts for
breakfast. Perhaps he did. Nicholas had no idea what he did
outside of Instagram filters and costume fittings. Perhaps he
went out at night, perhaps he picked up in bars in *le marais*;
perhaps a man almost as beautiful as he was was waiting for
him in his bed.

*Which is none of my fucking business.* Wondering if his costar
had a *boyfriend*, for fuck's sake. It was as unprofessional as it got.

But the idea of it was inescapable. Worse still was the
thought that only a few hours' time separated them from a
bed of their own. *A bed of our own.* The possessive pronoun
changed everything.

It was one thing to see Chris in these proper, tight-fitting clothes. Another thing entirely was being the one who got to pull them away from his body, to undress him like a present, to run his hands over Chris's skin—

It was a gambit on Chaudhuri's part. She had elected to throw her actors into the intimate center of the film's emotional story line: a sex scene in Angelo's bed. They would have to wait, nude and embarrassed, for the filming to kick-start into motion. It was a risk not many directors would have taken.

But Chaudhuri didn't care about appearances or embarrassment, and bulldozed over awkwardness with frank dislike. There was a twisted logic in it. Angelo and Frederick were strangers too—they would discover each other, uneasy and hesitant. As actors, Nicholas and Chris were only the shadows through which their characters got to exist. But those were *their* bodies, and *their* mouths, and *their* naked skin. It was Chris he would be touching.

The thought was so startling and so erotic that Nicholas reached out to cover Chris's hand just as he moved away. His fingers brushed his arm, feeling the curved bones of his wrist, his palm opening under his own. Chris twisted his wrist, and then it was almost as though they were holding hands; as though they were bracing themselves against the incoming storm. As though they had nothing left but each other.

The contact was short-lived. Chris's hand fell away.

Nicholas did not meet his eyes when they returned to their cues. He felt as though he was looking at himself from the outside.

# *Chapter Six*

**The Throne Cast & Crew** @thethronecast • 15m
Filming starts at midnight on the dot for #TheThroneFilm!
Follow us, @TheThronePR & @SHenderson for news, can-
did pics, exclusives, cast & crew interviews, and more...

**The Throne Cast & Crew** @thethronecast • 13m
#firstlook: Priya Chaudhuri at the helm!
[pic]

**The Throne Cast & Crew** @thethronecast • 11m
#firstlook: @AndyBelfond in last outfitting checks a few
minutes before filming starts!
[pic]

**The Throne Cast & Crew** @thethronecast • 8m
Isn't the Paris night beautiful though? crew selfie #say-
cheese
[pic]

**The Throne Cast & Crew** @thethronecast • 3m
#firstlook: Nicholas Madden, looking broody, feat.
@chrislavalle, looking lovely
[pic]

★ ★ ★

The garret had been an old servant's room—a *chambre de bonne*—high in a building circa 1899, somewhere close by the Pont du Carrousel.

It was, in fact, not far from Chris's own studio in the rue des Saints-Pères. At dawn, looking outside the spare, ancient windows, you could catch a glimpse of the river, fogged-over and white. Once the crew had set up, the necessary last checks had been made, and the light fixtures had been adjusted a final time, the place was tiny. White sheets were thrown over the bed, easels and canvases strewn about, books of poetry half-opened and forgotten.

They didn't have much time to play with. It would be a matter of one, two takes, maybe three: the light might rush up upon them, and Chaudhuri's schedule could stand no delay. The crew felt anxious about this. If anything happened to mess with the shoot, they would have to start over the next morning, and this could derail the rest of their calendar.

But in Chris's chest a steady, fizzing excitement was rising, as step by step Angelo came further and further into the light. He found it easy to change into him—to wear his clothes, to shed his own skin. Angelo, he felt, had burrowed inside of him, and it would be the very devil of a thing trying to pull him out. He wondered whether Nicholas, too, carried around the ghosts of his own roles, or if he would find that notion distasteful and absurd.

It didn't help that Nicholas stood a few meters away from him, patiently letting a makeup artist smooth fixing gel through his hair and touch up his face with a dab, dab, dab of concealer. Chris, who had gone through that rigmarole first, stood on the edge of the circle of cameras, and tried not to look at him too much. *Tried* was the operative word.

It was ridiculous. It was *ridiculous* to be so attracted to a man who, by all accounts, held nothing but contempt for him. But Nicholas had only to look at him for a moment—to smile that stolen, fleeting smile he shared with so few of his colleagues—and Chris felt like a high school boy with a crush.

He'd posed in lascivious positions for fashion campaigns, had sprawled languidly over the semi-nude bodies of his colleagues; he knew how his body must look when it needed to fit an erotic checkbox. He knew, too, that his hair—his mouth—his hands—were all pretty spectacular. He knew it abstractedly, without self-possession or pride; or, well. Perhaps a little pride. But the *spectacle* of eroticism was unconnected to intimacy, or gentleness, or affection.

A hand touched his elbow. "Hullo! Are you alright?"

Reginald Jarrett. A few days ago, Chris had been impressed by the privilege that was meeting him: Jarrett had played his way up and down Hollywood for the past forty years, and lived by his roles with pomp and sensitivity. Closer up, though, his knowing smiles were irritating at best and unsettling at worst. He was too quick, too familiar with the *my boys* and the *old pets*.

"Yes, of course. I did not know you were filming tonight." Chris furrowed his brows in mock chagrin, and smiled his airhead diva's smile. Jarrett chuckled.

"Oh, no. No. Priya wouldn't ask that of me. But my insomnia is a fickle mistress—and so I thought I'd pop in. See how the young 'uns are carrying on…"

For god's sake. He was a cliché rolled into another cliché. "I wonder," said Chris, pleasantly, "that you decided to come—it is *so* early. And this is a very *private* scene. No need for outside intervention."

"Mm-mm. One-*on*-one, I should say—eh?"

Chris glumly contemplated the oncoming likelihood that

he would soon have to take his clothes off with Reginald Jarrett for an audience.

"Nerves?" asked Jarrett, oddly awkward. Chris might have found this charming on another occasion; now he was startled and embarrassed. And yet—after all—Jarrett's naive, chummy nature meant he probably trampled boundaries every day without knowing it. Quite likely he would be horrified if he was put off too rudely. Chris said, keeping his tone light:

"Not quite."

"You are used to it of course."

Chris swallowed that. "Yes."

Jarrett hummed, smiling a small, sagacious smile. He glanced towards Chaudhuri, who was in deep talks with her main cameramen. "She has not put the fear of her wrath into you yet, I take it?"

"Not yet," Chris laughed, and was preparing to politely excuse himself when a cool voice said behind them:

"I would thank you not to scare off my partner, Reg."

"Scare him! Your partner! My dear boy, our Christian has nerves of steel."

"Is that so," said Nicholas, settling down against Chris's side, his shoulder just touching his. "Oh, get on with you, you frightening old cove. You've no business being awake at this hour."

Chris hid a smile. He could have sworn Nicholas's fingers brushed his, between their bodies.

"My insomnia," Jarrett protested, but he gave way, and patted Chris's hand in a vague sort of manner before pushing off. The crowd had thinned by now. Chaudhuri, despite her penchant for hands-on materialism—or perhaps because of it—had shooed off all but her essential crew, trusted producing assistants, and cameramen. Even security had been pushed firmly out, and the makeup department were just finishing up. The set looked like that of a small, intimate independent movie, instead of an expensive production.

"Reginald is a character," Chris said. He tried to force his focus away from Nicholas. Mistake. He looked at the bed they would soon be lying in, and felt his cheeks heat.

"Reginald is an old bully," said Nicholas, bluntly. "He never notices other people's discomfort. Never mind that he is a fatuous man, who should damn well know better than to—anyway. You shouldn't let him push you around."

"Is that what I was doing?"

"Were you?"

"I don't...think so. But then—it is true I am...a little uneasy."

Nicholas cast a contemptuous glance at the unmade bed, the clothes left on the floor, the half-finished easels: the small room, the confined space, where Angelo might have lived.

"You should be," he said. "You're playing a hellish ghost of a character."

Chris gave him a startled glance, knowing Nicholas's thoughts so close to his own, and then found it very difficult to look away again. Nicholas's beard had been trimmed for the part, and his hair, like Chris's, was slicked back, though more severely, as befitted Frederick's puritanical notions of manner and dress. Angelo's character was debauchery and dissolution, Frederick's starched austerity. The contrast was poetically fitting.

Chris suspected that Chaudhuri wanted to force a confrontation by throwing them headlong into a sex scene: she wanted a clashing of forces, until, exhausted by the fight, the two of them fell, half-desiring, half-incredulous, into one another's arms. Frederick and Angelo's bed was a battleground.

He had a flashing vision of what it might be to lie in this man's arms—for a true purpose of tenderness, not this sham version of it—and had to suppress a shiver.

But thinking about sweet and intimate things wouldn't do. Chris's pride wouldn't stand it, when the story was over and Nicholas walked away.

"Look at me," said Nicholas, abruptly. "While we're shooting. Look at me."

He caught Chris's hand. Chris stared down at it.

"You want direction," said Nicholas.

"And you," Chris said, "are appointing yourself as—my polar star?"

"If it gets the job done."

"Is the *job* all that matters to you?"

"Yes," said Nicholas, frankly, and Chris frowned at him, stung. "The work is the work."

"That is Priya's philosophy."

"And mine."

"It's inhuman."

"You think so?" Nicholas glanced at him, then away, and then back again. "Would you sacrifice the integrity of an important photoshoot for the sake of one photographer's whims?"

"That's—" Chris paused. Reflected. "I suppose not. Very well: integrity for integrity's sake. But the photographer holds power; *there* is the difference."

"Not in your case. If you threaten to bail, that's the whole campaign falling apart. Where will they find another actor as beautiful as you? If *you* fall apart, where is our Angelo?"

Chris's mouth opened; his amazement must have shown, for Nicholas looked down, flushing darkly.

Before he turned away, he said: "Make yourself ready, whatever you do."

It was a scene of silences. It relied on the performers' chemistry and charisma. This, Chris reflected, was the final test, the last threshold into the inner sanctum: if he pulled it off tonight, he was an actor made. Fail, he would become another beautiful washout within the next three years.

Nicholas's eyes were unsympathetic, but he, at least, did not look as skeptical as Jarrett—and Chaudhuri, in her unguarded moments—had been. Chris was thankful for that unflinching conviction: it seemed that, having put his trust in him, Nicholas would remain by his side until proven wrong. His polar star, Chris had called him, half in jest and half in truth, and it now appeared that Nicholas shone brightly for him and him alone. Chris grinned at him.

Then all at once the cameras were rolling. They were very close together. In Chris rose a vital impression that he could not fail now. He obeyed the instinct, and kissed Nicholas at once.

An intake of breath. Chris pressed Nicholas gently against the door, his hands stroking over his shoulders and down over his chest, his mouth gentle on Nicholas's. Nicholas made a soft, unexpected sound, and opened up to the kiss. The set was wholly silent. The kiss deepened. Lips parted lips. Then another, more tender and more real. They clutched at each other, pulling close; Nicholas's hand was warm against the side of his face. Chris felt him angle them slightly sideways— back into the shot, he realized, so that Chaudhuri would have her close-up—and shivered. It was still so hot. Nicholas was a tremendous actor.

*"Angelo,"* Nicholas murmured, and, shuddering, leaned into him, leaned his head against his. His face against Chris's neck. His arms came around him, and then they were hugging, a fierce, ragged embrace that felt truer than words.

Chris pulled away first, shakily. He took Nicholas's hand. He led them into the makeshift bedroom.

There he kissed him again, taking control of the embrace without much grace or effort. It had never been so easy to shape his body around another man's. Nicholas seemed to anticipate his thoughts, coming to him with a stifled gasp, burying his hands in his hair. Why had he thought the man inflexible? Nicholas was willing and sweet. He moved them slightly, so that the cameras trained on them could capture every moment and every angle. It was a gentle, tired kiss. When they parted again he leaned his forehead against Chris's.

*"Are you afraid?"*

*"No."* Wonder and surprise. *"No, damn you."*

Chris entwined their fingers. *"Then come."*

Then the bed. A continuous shot—from the side and from above—as they navigated the logistics of it.

This was more awkward. Chaudhuri called for a cut twice, rearranged them on the blankets, offered suggestions. Chris waited, his left arm slung around Nicholas's shoulder, his back against the mattress, pressed down, feeling the weight and the warmth of Nicholas's body pushed up against his. Skin to skin.

With the awkwardness there came, suddenly, a sensation of pure excitement, as though the thrill of the moment had lightened and lightened. It was in the touch of Nicholas's fingers around his bare shoulder; the push of his thigh against Chris's hip; the brush of his breath against Chris's cheek. Should he turn his head *just* so, he would be able to catch his mouth again, he would feel the caress of Nicholas's lashes against his cheek—

Nicholas let out a shuddering breath, as though in response, but before Chris could speak Chaudhuri called for action all over again.

They tried it over once more, but the awkwardness still lingered, and this time the break was longer. They had to stay there, and tried to fit without squashing each other in strange places. The scene felt implausible. Chris watched the sky slowly lighten to a pale lilac outside the narrow window.

Then Nicholas shifted, pushing his knee in deeper, and Chris bit back a groan.

No. This was real.

"Sorry," murmured Nicholas.

"At this point," said Chris, with a sigh, "we might as well get comfortable." He stretched out his arm, wincing, before settling his wrist gently back on top of Nicholas's shoulder.

Nicholas held for a longer moment, then sighed and relaxed as well—his firm hold on his arms gave way slowly, until he was lying half on top of Chris.

"That's good," said Chaudhuri, from a distance. "Hold it."

When he turned his head, Nicholas's mouth brushed Chris's cheek. "She'll keep us here until dawn."

*I wouldn't mind*, thought Chris, so abruptly that he forgot to answer for all of ten seconds, before, swallowing, he said: "It'll be sunup soon enough. The light—"

"God forbid we have to return tomorrow." Nicholas's eyes had drifted shut, but he was scowling still. He was so, so warm.

*I wouldn't mind*, thought Chris—again—and had to jerk away from his wandering thoughts, finding purchase on the emptier side of the bed.

As though on reflex, Nicholas's hand skimmed over his side, just brushing the loose linen of his shirt. He was—he was *soothing* him, as one would soothe a frightened kitten. Chris fought down a giggle. His amusement was heightened by a fizzy sensation, like champagne bubbling up inside his lungs.

"Alright?"

"Yes." Chris opened his eyes. Nicholas was watching him. "Yes."

Nicholas nodded, but something in his face had gone odd. Searching. "Chris—"

"Alright, boys, start over," said Chaudhuri. "To the top. Back into gear."

The scene became harsher, more brusque. Chris tore a line into Nicholas's sleeve and stripped his shirt off of him. He felt Angelo's fear on his lips and pulled him into a scathing kiss, and Nicholas responded in kind: he backed Chris into the wall, gripping his hips so hard Chris would have bruises come morning. Nicholas kissed like a man drowning. Chris held on to him fiercely.

*"Are you afraid?"* He made it an insult.

*"No."* Nicholas was looking at his mouth, eyes dark and hot. As though out of patience he kissed him again. Then tore himself away. *"No. Damn you."*

Chris's lip curled. *"Then,"* he said, *"come,"* and he shoved him towards the bed.

When it was done, when it was all over, when Chaudhuri called for her final cut, he dressed himself quickly, shoved his legs into his jeans, shrugged on a crew t-shirt, and fled.

He stepped out onto the balcony of the neighbor bedroom, likewise commandeered for Chaudhuri's purposes, in which props and tools had been stacked up.

The sun was rising.

"Fuck," Chris said, with great feeling. He dug into his pocket for his phone, found instead a crumpled pack of cigarettes, and lit one with relief.

The sweet smoke curled down his throat into his lungs, and he found that he could breathe again. He needed four shots of espresso, ten hours of sleep, or a long hard fuck, preferably all of the above in sequential order.

Sex scenes were an awkward business, and Chris was no stranger to enforced intimacy or casual nudity.

He had been attracted to his coworkers before, and each time had been a disaster in the making. His attraction to Nicholas was tied up in the man's infuriating manner: his odd sweetness, his scorn, his exasperating kindness.

Chris did not know why, having discerned that Nicholas could not like him, he had not simply ceased to want him. His body wasn't responding right.

He found his phone. It was a heavy, reassuring weight in his palm, anchoring him in the moment. He held it tightly, brushing his thumb over the smooth screen, and then he turned it on.

He had notifications plenty. He cleared them all without looking at them, and called up his voicemail. One call was from his agent, which he ignored, feeling the dim guilt of it churn in his stomach for the few seconds it took for the next message to play. Listening, he finished his cigarette. Then he hit call.

Antoine answered after the second ring.

"*Mon chou,*" he said, in his strange lilting voice, "why do you call so early? You could have woken me."

"Were you asleep?"

"I was not."

"Well, then."

"Alright—" Antoine sounded amused. Antoine always sounded amused. "Then why are you calling me at the break of dawn?"

"Just done for the day. Will get to sleep soon." The sky in the east was now decidedly blue. Clouds were streaming above the rooftops of Paris, purple-white against the rising light.

Antoine hummed, agreeably, and then said: "They're making it quite hard for you, no?"

"No. Well. Some of them."

"Madden? I heard about his tantrum on the set of *One for the Gold*. Has he broken a camera yet?"

"No, he's—" Chris faltered, at a loss. Nicholas Madden existed so wholly, so distinctly in the world, that describing him seemed a thankless task. "Sweet."

A pause. "I see." Antoine knew, better perhaps than most people in Chris's life, how dangerous it was to fall for a co-worker. "Chris…"

"I know." Chris stubbed out his cigarette, then ground it under his foot. "Bad idea. I'm holding off."

"You should. Nicholas Madden, of all people," said Antoine, sounding exasperated and fond.

"Where are you?" Chris asked, shortly. "Still Bombay?"

Antoine accepted the change of subject without another word. "Oh. No. Did I not tell you? No, I'm back in Paris. Back here for—oh—a few months; at least."

"You wouldn't be opposed to getting a drink?" Chris asked, wincing at the plaintive note in his voice. But he wanted a friend! Someone who knew him and loved him, and who was game enough for getting a bit—more than a bit, to be honest—drunk. Antoine's presence in Paris in itself was rare.

The day they'd met, Antoine had been back from two back-to-back trips to Rio de Janeiro and the Rockies, and had arrived on set hungover, still wearing sunglasses and crumpled designer jeans, swaggering, exhausted, drinking black coffee by the gallon. Chris had liked him instantly. Over the years, they had become truly and meaningfully close.

"Mmm. Maybe Tuesday. Tomorrow, I mean. Real tomorrow, not today tomorrow. Yes?"

"Yes. I've the morning booked shooting, but free from noon. *La Planète*?"

"Alright. You'll tell me all the sordid details there," said Antoine, affectionately. "I have to go, my dear—this man in my bed appears to be waking."

"Oh!" Chris was still laughing as he was summarily hung up on.

## Chapter Seven

**Spotted!** *The Throne*–rising star and fashion icon Chris Lavalle seen embracing mysterious man...

In a twist we should have seen coming, pretty-boy extraordinaire Chris Lavalle has a boyfriend? Maybe? He was caught kissing and hugging another man in the Tuileries Gardens, in Paris, yesterday afternoon. We are bound by journalistic integrity to allow that this could be a close friend—reminder that the French kiss everyone hello: one kiss on each cheek is customary in Paris—but our body language expert has detected an unusual tenderness in the two young men's encounter. The positioning of their hands and the unusually lengthy embrace might even be hinting at a deeper, more intimate relationship... (See more pictures on p.6.)

Lavalle, known for his massive Instagram following and for his surprise casting onto one of the most talked-about movie sets of the year, is playing Nicholas Madden's lover in *The Throne*. That unlikely pair were spotted during an intimate one-to-one dinner before filming officially began. What the appearance of our mystery man in the Tuileries might mean for Lavalle and Madden's work relationship (or non-work relationship?) is still up in the air. More to come soon, we hope...

★ ★ ★

Nicholas woke on Friday with a headache to rival the devil.

He had slept for four hours, if that. It was six a.m.

He *hadn't* been drinking, and it struck him as grossly unfair that his head should feel every bit like the worst of hangovers. His blood was pounding in his ears, hot and angry, and his mouth was parched and dry and sour. Groaning, he rolled onto his back, and thence onto the floor in a half-controlled slump.

Coffee, he thought, blearily. Coffee would make this better. That, or an axe to the head.

By the time he had ordered breakfast, dragged himself into the shower, recomposed himself into a semblance of self-possession, and pulled on some clean pressed clothes, he felt marginally more human. To the credit of Le Meurice's staff's prompt service, an embossed silver breakfast set was waiting, coffee still steaming, butter glistening, on the low table of his drawing room when he stepped outside of his bedroom suite. The weather outside was bright, clear. Another brilliant summer morning. Chaudhuri would be pleased: it made for good filming weather. The sun over the Seine was extraordinary. They were scheduled to shoot two scenes at dawn the next day.

Two soft, flaky croissants had been placed neatly upon a plate. Nicholas, fastening his shirt buttons, thought of Chris, standing in the window—Chris in those sinful ripped jeans, his hair messy and curling around his ears. Chris's kiss in *his* hair. What might Chris look like when he was just emerging from sleep? Nicholas almost turned back to the bedroom, half expecting to see him in the doorway, yawning, hair a mess, without a stitch on—

"For *fuck's* sake," he said, exasperated, and sat.

But his own voice rang loud in his ears. He felt shatteringly alone.

Madalena, he found, had texted him. Thought you should

see this, it said, followed by a winking emoji and a URL. He opened it on his tablet, sipping his first, perfect, sweet cup of coffee.

*REVEALED: BOYFRIEND OF FRENCH INSTA-GRAM STAR CHRIS LAVALLE!!!!* said the headline plastered over his newsfeed, because of course it fucking well did.

Below it was a picture of Chris, his hands wrapped around the waist of a tall, dark, handsome man. He was laughing. They were both laughing.

Well.

Well? Well, so what? Was it truly shocking that Chris was dating? If, Nicholas thought, swiping through the article, he *was* dating at all. Chris must have friends of his own—modeling acquaintances, or something of the like. This man of his was certainly hot enough to *be* a model. The two of them made quite the picture: Chris's hair bright in the sun, the unknown friend's brown forearms under his rolled-up sleeves. Theirs were the easy smiles of those who stand on more than familiar terms. Nicholas didn't think he'd seen Chris smile so freely in the month since they had met.

On set, Chris was a mostly silent figure, unfailingly polite, scrupulously professional. He had never once posted set pictures on social media. He was kind and distant.

The crew didn't dislike him, but they were puzzled by him. He didn't belong. The news of his family's nepotism had surprised nobody. In many respects Chris was a creature of another world, at once too genuine and too fake to fit Hollywood's strict stereotypes.

It troubled Nicholas that he had no idea exactly how genuine—or how fake—he was capable of being. Was the melancholy young man who'd sat in this room the assumed persona, or was he the Instagram star who coolly memorialized his privacy for the eyes of a million strangers? Was he the actor Nicholas had met on set? Who was the man who had so sweetly kissed him in that cramped servant's room? Who had watched him out of Angelo's cold, cold eyes? Who had lain with him half-naked on Angelo's and Frederick's bed, for an hour, squirming against the chill?

Nicholas swiped left. The article had a full dozen pictures of the encounter. It detailed its finer points with glee. The meeting, the customary kisses on each cheek, the easy physicality between the two men, and the moment—cinematic suspense at its finest—when the stranger removed his sunglasses. He had the most unnerving green eyes.

The smile on Chris's lips was nothing like Nicholas had ever seen before. He looked young. Carefree.

With a soft sound of exasperation, he tabbed over into his email, and applied himself to reading one of the scripts his agent had sent out for his consideration.

His phone pinged with notifications some time later, an unwelcome reminder that he was scheduled for an interview with *Paris-Match* on the Champs-Elysées in less than an hour and a half. He had no great desire to go. But Madalena showed up, at eleven, wearing a designer Parisienne off-white blouse and enormous sunglasses. She shoved two Starbucks cups into his hands, and maneuvered him deftly away from his gloomy melancholy.

"You look like hell," she said, in the car. "Rough night?"

"Can't remember."

She nudged his coffee with her own monstrous Frankenstein-like caramel confection. "Drink up, then. Look pert for the cameras."

Nicholas sipped, obediently, and was surprised to find she had shelled out for a vanilla macchiato. She was already looking at her phone—pulling up his schedule, by the looks of it—and did not appear to want to be thanked. Madalena was one of the few people on earth aware of his coffee preferences; most people just assumed he took it black. But the taste of vanilla was sweet and mild on his tongue.

They were idling at a red light just beyond Concorde when Madalena made a soft, choked-off sound.

"Problem?"

"Mm-hmm."

"Madalena."

"Nothing dramatic," she sighed. But then she glanced at him and said, in dramatic undertones: "Damien Jones is scheduled for the interview."

"Ah." Damien Jones was a dickhead of the first water.

"Don't let him rile you up."

"I promise not to throw any furniture," he said, dryly, mostly to see her smile. She didn't.

"He threatened to sue. Last time."

"Last time he intimated I had instigated a sexual relationship with my female costar. My *underage* female costar."

"He wants a scoop," said Madalena. "Don't give it to him. Do *not* antagonize him, Madden. He'll sink his teeth into anything."

This was true. Jones was one of many in the paparazzi crowd who wanted tabs on Nicholas's sexuality, and scented out scoops and candids as sharks would take to blood in the water. They flatly disbelieved the possibility that he might be straight, which complicated the defense, as Nicholas refused to bend so far as to appear romantically linked to a woman. His agent had long ago abandoned that part of the fight, and had stopped hooking Nicholas up with premiere dates entirely. It was an endless, relentless push-and-pull between his own reality and everybody else's.

Still, Jones's presence in Paris spelled trouble. If he had taken the pains to fly over, he either knew something Nicholas

didn't—in which case Nicholas didn't pay Madalena enough—
or he hoped Nicholas would betray some extraordinary sentiment when confronted with a direct question. From there it
was no great leap to Chris. Chris was the unknown factor in
the equation. Chris was the trump card in Jones's sleeve: the
convenient, beautiful, unashamedly gay costar.

If Nicholas did not manage him with the most skillful of
touches, Jones would *know*. Jones had been sniffing around him
for years. Jones knew damn well he had something to hide.

"Christ," he muttered.

"Stick to the script," said Madalena.

"He won't stay anywhere close to the script."

"I have faith in your powers of improvisation and devastating snark."

Nicholas was silent for a moment. Noontime traffic in Paris
was dreadfully slow. They drove up the Champs-Elysées towards the Arc de Triomphe at a frog's crawl. The great buildings lining the avenue were biscuit-colored and formidable
in the sun.

"Have I made a mistake?" he asked, finally.

Madalena raised her eyebrows, then removed her shades,
blinking at him. "I never thought I'd hear you say that, you
know. Ever."

"Em—"

"My god, you *are* in too deep." She grinned at him. "You
haven't called me Em since college."

"Be serious."

"I'm always serious." But she gave the question some
thought. "I don't think you—blew it, to put things bluntly.
But it sure is rocky terrain."

"I *have* taken gay parts before."

"Sure. Has any one of them mattered so much as this does?"

*Did you ever have to play opposite Chris?*—Madelena was pointedly polite enough to leave it unsaid.

With a sigh, Nicholas knocked his head back against his seat. "I don't know."

"You've been open about your attachment to this story," Madalena added, amiably. "People are bound to draw conclusions. I thought—well. I thought you would take the opportunity to—"

"To come out."

"In so many words. Yes."

Truth was, he *had* intended this. A part of him, at least, had looked on the part of Frederick as a chance to be as honest as he couldn't be permitted to be off-screen. The world—the prying, voyeuristic world—would understand, even if he never did put words to it. It was so unlike him, to leave it to chance and guesswork, instead of being forthright in all things, and true, that he felt abruptly disgusted with himself.

Madalena, perhaps sensing his discomfort, grasped his shoulder briefly. "If you do ever decide to…"

"I know." There was despair inside Nicholas, as though Paris and all its beauty was only highlighting the misery he was beginning to become aware he was feeling. He had sacrificed too much to stop now. He had given up too much of his own past, of his own life—of what he loved, and what he hated. Sacrifice had made him what he was now. There was no coming back from it.

"So long as it doesn't bankrupt us both."

"No chance of that," said Nicholas, dryly.

Damien Jones was an asshole, and yet Nicholas felt a disgusted sort of kinship with him.

He was a little man, in spirit though not in stature (in truth, he towered three inches above Nicholas, who was no small man himself), and would cheerfully commit bloody murder if it got him the scoop he wanted. These days, though he had in the past written a rare few thoughtful pieces, he limited himself to sex scandals and their ilk—kinky business, hushed-up affairs, closet cases. He had outed many a B-lister when he had nothing better to do, leaking pictures of club outings and back-alley blowjobs without a missed heartbeat.

But Nicholas was a celebrity and a notoriously private man. A choice target, but a chancier one.

He had in the past ambushed Nicholas on set, ratted out his room number from unsuspecting hotel grooms, hunted him down on red carpets; he asked private, inconvenient, probing, shamelessly insolent questions in public spaces, clamoring for honesty when he, himself, had none to offer. He had for two years rather infamously penned a pseudo-anonymous call-out column, from which no one in Hollywood remained unscathed. He had accused Nicholas of every professional sin under the sun, and a few personal ones to round it all up. The horrid business about his *One for the Gold* costar had only been the latest of them.

More worryingly, he remained well enough on the acceptable side of the law to write lucratively for the high-end rags in the business. Absent Nicholas's categorical refusal to deal with the man, though, his agent could do little to fend him off; the best he had been able to do was limit one-on-one interviews in scope and in number.

"Why not refuse, then?" Madalena had asked.

Nicholas had shrugged, and said, "I will not give him the satisfaction."

"You're proud, Madden."

"For my sins."

But now—now, Nicholas thought, as Jones obsequiously made the opening serve, inviting him to sit and offering him coffee—he was badly tempted to take a vow of silence. Something about Jones's oily smile was disquieting.

"I hope we aren't disturbing your schedule," Jones said, after the necessary pictures had been taken.

"We aren't filming today," said Nicholas. His coffee was black and strong and bitter. He sipped it without a grimace.

"Oh? None of you? But the weather is so nice. True Parisian weather."

"Some of us may be. Andrée will be on set this afternoon, I believe."

"I see. Is it begging too much to ask how the filming is going on?"

He was too calm. He was hoping for something. Nicholas set his cup down on its saucer with a soft click. "I wouldn't dream of divulging sensitive information."

"My sources—" Jones clicked his tongue. "My *sources* have it the set can get quite—hot."

Nicholas frowned, irritated. Jones shouldn't have any sources on set. "I can't imagine why."

"No? Mr. Madden, I hope you don't think we've forgotten *One for the Gold*—the public certainly hasn't."

"I should hope not," said Nicholas, mildly. "I won a Golden Globe for that role." *And you accused me of sleeping with a seventeen-year-old.*

"Ah. Of course." Jones laughed. He had a nice, honest laugh. It made people trust him, to their detriment. Nicholas would not make that mistake. "Selective memory, eh? Can't recommend that enough."

"That must come in useful."

Jones blinked, then grinned. "You have no idea."

He proceeded to ask the customary questions—what was it like working with Chaudhuri again? Did he find the confines of a pre-existing canon restraining or liberating? Did the cast get along, or was there friction in the mix?—small, mundane stuff, which Nicholas could answer in his sleep. He praised Chaudhuri, weighed in favor of reading the novel prior to watching the movie ("a full cinema-going experience," he said, "allows for a deeper understanding of the source material when you come out of the theater," to which Jones replied, "oh, really? imagine that"), and allowed himself a few choice, good-humored sound bites about Jason Kirkhall's partying habits. He kept himself shy of mentioning Chris.

"I must admit," Jones said at the end of the half hour, fiddling with his tablet, "it was expected of you to see working with Jason Kirkhall as a hardship. A young man like him…"

Nicholas smiled. "Jason is a very professional young man, his libations notwithstanding."

"First-rate actor," Jones agreed. "But *he* has been in the business since he was—oh, eight? How long ago was that?"

Nicholas flicked away some invisible dust with his fingers, his irritation brewing hotter. Jones's subtlety was not in his questions: it was easy to recognize he was leading up to the core of the matter, and it was not Jason Kirkhall he was most interested in. "I have no idea. I'll make sure to look at a calendar when I get home."

"I imagine he and Chris Lavalle must get along very well."

"I couldn't say," said Nicholas, blandly.

"Two young men, close in age… Though, of course, their realm of experience differs widely." Jones swiped at his tablet's touchscreen, seemingly distracted. "Was it a surprise?"

"The casting? Of course. For everyone, I believe, including Chris."

Jones's coy look would have been irritating in a younger man; on a man of forty-odd years, it was laughably insulting. "Anything to say about that?"

Nicholas crossed one ankle over the other. "No."

"Mr. Madden, surely you understand our readership is looking *forward* to this unusual partnership."

"I'm sure they are."

"Do you find him an able costar?"

"He's perfectly capable. Honestly—" Nicholas said, deliberately: "I think he'll surprise you."

"Mmm. Can you give any credence to the rumor—unsubstantiated, of course, as *yet*—that his casting was due not to any particular talent of his own—though I'm sure he is a very *nice* young man—but instead to upstream influence in his favor?"

Sweet as milk. The goddamn fucker.

"I have heard no such rumor," Nicholas lied, smooth as his black coffee. His calm demeanor was hard-won, and he needed to hang on to it. Jones would *adore* getting him riled up. "I do, however, find it rather insulting that those aspersions should be cast on Priya Chaudhuri's integrity."

"Of course."

"He has made the part his own," Nicholas said quietly. "I could not imagine another Angelo now."

"That's—" Jones blinked, thrown. "Praise indeed."

"If you will call the truth praise. Yes."

"What do you have to say about Lavalle's tendencies towards sexual exhibitionism?"

And there was the whiplash. Nicholas opened his mouth, then closed it.

Something distressingly close to triumph flickered in Jones's smile. Without a word he held out the tablet. A flick of his thumb, and there Chris was—Chris posing, half in shadow, limned in gold, tastefully nude. An aptly placed thigh only just maintained his modesty; he sprawled, on his back, one hand over his brow, his hair mussed. He was smiling at the camera, eyes shadowed. He looked young and painfully vulnerable.

Beautiful.

Nicholas swiped down. This was a series. This was—*huh*—a

charity photoshoot. He'd never heard of rights4all. *LGBTQ+ youth and homeless teens...*

"Well," he said, distantly.

"Any way to draw attention to yourself, eh?"

Nicholas kept his voice bland. "You could say that." He handed the tablet back, much though he wanted to keep swiping through the photoshoot. Something about Chris's vulnerability fascinated him. Exposure was no weakness for Chris: it was a form of pride, of self-expression, of naked honesty. There was power in that. There was bravery. He felt a taut desire to experience it for himself.

"I'm surprised," said Jones. He laid the tablet down on the sofa but did not turn it off: his fingers lingered on Chris's picture. "Not afraid of bad publicity, are you? Bit of a change since 2022."

"Is it."

"I'm almost certain you once lambasted Mason Purnell for mooning reporters during the filming of *Halo*."

"You should know," said Nicholas, smiling.

"Can't remember?"

"I do remember. I was there, as were you. The relevancy of that anecdote to the present situation escapes me, however."

Jones switched tactics in a flash. "What makes Chris Lavalle more deserving of your indulgence?"

*The fact that he's raising funds for a charity, you moron.*

"Is he? A young man starved for attention acts out online and reveals more than he should. News indeed." Nicholas stood up, reaching for his jacket. The Big Bad Wolf of Hollywood would never abase himself to show vulnerability the way Chris did so simply. He must always be trenchant and forceful and a right prick, rather than allow himself to be thought weak. "We're done. I can't imagine anything more of value could be said now."

## Chapter Eight

Priya Chaudhuri, though an intensely private person in every respect, was kind enough to welcome EW.com in her Parisian hotel suite on a beautiful June afternoon. Chaudhuri, who is in Paris to film her latest movie, The Throne, is a busy woman. After the universal success of Made in Kindness, for which she earned a Golden Globe, a Directors' Guild of America Award, and two Oscar noms, she has launched herself straight into this adaptation of the well-known early-twentieth-century novel, casting in quick succession several giants of the industry (Andrée Belfond, Reginald Jarrett, and Nicholas Madden were given key roles) alongside a few resounding surprises (party boy Jason Kirkhall as a golden child of turn-of-the-century French bourgeoisie, and Hollywood unknown Chris Lavalle, of Instagram fame, as Madden's immediate costar). This stellar yet intriguing cast, working under Chaudhuri's skillful direction, is already the center of much media attention and awards season interest.

Chaudhuri does not let this acclaim go to her head. After three straight years of outstanding filmmaking, during which she directed and co-produced beauties such as Made in Kindness, Last Stop, and The Dress, she is used to the attention any new project of hers inevitably garners. As she let EW.com into her inner sanctum, she was calm, self-possessed, and willing to offer inside information...to a point.

**EW**
*Any chance of an exclusive scoop about* The Throne?

**Priya Chaudhuri**
*[laughter]*

**EW**
*I had to ask!*

**Chaudhuri**
*I plead the fifth.*

**EW**
*Fair enough. You surprised many when you cast...your cast. Not all actors, either, to begin with.*

**Chaudhuri**
*Mm-hmm. I think more people have asked me about Chris Lavalle in a short amount of time than about any other actor I've cast in years.*

**EW**
*It is a very surprising choice. Nobody expected it. What made you decide to cast him?*

**Chaudhuri**
*He was a shoo-in after his audition. He made a very definitive impression upon us [Chaudhuri and the Henderson siblings, producing]. We realized that he would be a very different Angelo—not at all the character that we'd envisaged while working on the script—but a fascinating new take on the role.*

**EW**
*This must have come as a surprise to the rest of the cast. Nicholas Madden was vocal in his support for this project—*

*he plays immediately opposite Lavalle—what was his reaction to the casting?*

**Chaudhuri**

*[laughter] Nicholas was perfectly reasonable.*

**EW**

*After his behavior on the set of* One for the Gold...

**Chaudhuri**

*What most people don't remember about* One for the Gold *is that filming was an absolute mess. Henry [Paulson, director of* One for the Gold*] has since said that he regretted the way he went about it. The producing team and the cast were unable to foster a meaningful relationship, and tempers ran high. Nicholas Madden was not singly at fault.*

**EW**

*Still, he has a reputation as a diva.*

**Chaudhuri**

*Be that as it may, he has never been anything less than ruthlessly professional on my set.*

**EW**

*He approved of Lavalle, then?*

**Chaudhuri**

*He had reservations, like many others. Nonetheless, he and Chris have been able to bring out a great deal in one another. Chris's inexperience finds an anchor in Nicholas's wealth of knowledge—but Chris brings a fresh understanding of the source material to their partnership.*

**EW**
The Throne *is a love story...*

**Chaudhuri**
*It is. It stands to reason that the main actors should be influencing each other and supplementing each other's interpretation of the text.*

**EW**
*It's also a queer, historical love story. A bold choice?*

**Chaudhuri**
*We didn't think so. It's been a long time since* Brokeback Mountain. *It's no longer a risk to portray queer bodies on the big screen. Complex portrayals of LGBT relationships are—if not quite the norm—at least much more often represented in mainstream filmmaking. There is still much progress to be made in terms of representation—especially non-white, non-cissexual representation—but we are taking steps in the right direction.*

**EW**
*You are one of the flagships of modern filmmaking; your record speaks for itself. This is your first foray into period pieces. Why France in the 1900s?*

**Chaudhuri**
*Well, the fashion, for one. [laughter] But sentiment and emotion were entirely foreign then to our modern sensibilities. Self-repression was the norm; self-expression was performed in nuanced, intricate, exclusive ways. Behavior was a code—language, family ties, social relationships, class ascension—all of these were factors into social relationships. We think that we have forgotten them, and yet...* The Throne *is a beautiful portrayal of a bohemian subset of society that has since*

*disintegrated and recreated itself over and over during the following decades. Underground Berlin in the 1920s, sexual liberation and the counterculture of the '60s—it's all there in potentia.*

**EW**

*Let's talk about place-setting. You decided to film on-location...*

June streamed towards summer. Soon, in August, Paris would be mostly empty of Parisians, left to the tourists' tender mercies, and the streets deserted and hot. Until then, though, the weather was beautiful, the days long, and the sun over the tall towers of Notre Dame golden and soft. Already, at eight in the morning, the first lounging sun-lovers were settling in on the quays around the Pont-Neuf and the Ile de la Cité, nibbling on croissants, sipping milky coffee, and looking curiously at the closed-off enclave of *The Throne*'s set. They were young, mostly students in their twenties, sharing an early breakfast by the river before classes started, farther up Saint-Michel, in the Sorbonne and the Pantheon.

Chris, work done for the day, feeling tired and tender, leaned against one of the cream-colored balconies of the Pont-Neuf, and wished for his bed. Failing that, he wished for better coffee.

He was finding his sea legs. The terror of the first days of shooting—the dread of failure, the hope of success—was ebbing away, leaving in its place a sense of lingering accomplishment. He had not been thrown out on his ass for being miserably terrible at his job. He held his own. That was a relief.

Angelo helped. Beautiful, egoistic, unhappy Angelo. He was so angry—so alone—so terribly sweet, in his own selfish way. It was a joy to be him; to feel what he felt, to love what he loved.

It helped also that Nicholas—though temperamental and brash in all other aspects of his life—had stood true to his promise: Chris only had to look at him while they were shooting to find direction and judgement. A look, a touch, was enough for them to work smoothly together. Nicholas was steadfast and certain, and while Chris duly enjoyed being an everyday witness to that chiseled body and that strong jawline, Nicholas's trust in him was even sexier.

"Here."

Blinking, he looked away from the sun on the water. Nicholas had apparently found a coffee shop. "Thank you." The paper cup was hot between his fingers.

"I owed you one," Nicholas said, sitting down. He stretched an arm out over the stone, looking up at Chris. "Black, right?"

"Yes." Chris glanced at him over the rim of his coffee. "You?"

A smile flitted over Nicholas's lips. "Vanilla cream, when I can get it. One sugar."

"Cream!" Chris shuddered. "Americans! You balk at drinking whole milk, yet you put cream in your coffee. Blasphemous."

Nicholas laughed—a soft, low laugh, that meant nothing, gave away nothing, but was pleasant to hear, nonetheless. "Good work today."

"Mmm. You, too."

"You're getting good at this."

Chris smothered a smile, feeling his cheeks heat. "Faint praise."

Nicholas hummed, smiling, and bumped his shoulder against Chris's hip. They drank in companionable silence; it was, Chris had found, simple to be silent alongside Nicholas. These moments of quiet never stretched out into the uneasy awkwardness of strangers, even though they *were* strangers. It was an odd thing to think about a man he had been naked with twice in a week.

It was Friday again. They had the weekend off. Chris wondered whether he could dare ask Nicholas to join him for a stroll one afternoon. They could make themselves look incognito: put Nicholas in faded jeans, instead of his immaculate pressed trousers and shirt—or glasses, the better to conceal his spectacular eyes. And then go to Montmartre, have some crepes on the grass below the Sacré-Coeur; or else to the Musée d'Orsay. Nicholas seemed a man capable of appreciating art. Renoir, Cézanne, Degas: the men who had painted Angelo and Frederick's Belle Époque.

Chris tried to imagine it. Nicholas, his hair gelled back, in casual clothing, with his hands in his pockets, standing below the works of Van Gogh and Monet. Rolling his eyes at the stream of smartphone-wielding tourists. Taking his time. All that formidable energy, that physical presence, channeled into a different stream of being...

He was about to ask when Nicholas said, "What is that man doing?"

"What?"

"We have a pap on the premises."

"I don't mind," said Chris, before he saw Antoine. "Oh." He sighed. "No. He's—that's a friend of mine."

Nicholas looked back at him silently. Antoine—in slim cream jeans and a close-fitted Henley—put down the camera and waved.

In a minute, the two worlds had collided: Nicholas silent, forbidding, closed-off, already, to this invasion of privacy—Antoine, as charming as usual, smiling, kissing Chris's cheek.

"Hello, you."

"*Salut.*" Chris drew him away slightly. "What are you..."

"I heard you were filming here—you're trending; did you

know?—and thought I'd come see you." Antoine gave him an assessing glance-over. "This fits you. Though I would've opted for a blue waistcoat instead of the grey."

"I'm surprised you're even awake."

Antoine's lips quirked up. "You're assuming I slept. Are you finished?"

"For the day, yes. Are you going somewhere?"

"No. Will you have breakfast with me?"

"If you like," said Chris, laughing. Antoine was like a summer storm—he charged in, changed everything, turned the world upside down. It was a bewildering task to be his friend. It was very like him to swagger in on the set of *The Throne* like he owned the whole thing.

Antoine's fine eyebrows hiked up. He nodded subtly towards Nicholas. "You won't introduce me?"

"I can introduce myself," said Nicholas. It startled Chris—they had been speaking French—but Nicholas evidently knew more of it than he let on. Blinking, a little touched, a little flustered by Nicholas's ongoing attention, he stepped aside.

Antoine held out a well-manicured hand. Nicholas hesitated only for a moment before he shook; Antoine kept his hand lingering in his own for a second too long, and then pulled away, a smile tugging at his mouth. "Nicholas Madden," he said, savoring the name.

"You have the better of me."

"Antoine Charpentier," said Chris. "A friend. A photographer."

Nicholas took in a brief, sharp breath. Chris wouldn't have noticed it, if he hadn't stood so close to him. "Not a celebrity photographer, I hope."

"My god, no." Antoine had slipped into his usual, informal English—fluid, scrupulously correct, but intensely French in intonation. "I photograph only beautiful things."

Chris had the rare pleasure of seeing Nicholas look thrown. He handled it creditably well. "I understand the reticence."

"Will *you* join us? Breakfast," said Antoine. "Somewhere in the Île Saint-Louis, I think. Has Chris not shown you our usual haunts?"

"Not yet."

"I was going to," said Chris, dryly, "before you butted in." Antoine laughed. "My mistake!"

Nicholas was looking at Chris, though. "Were you?"

"I was," Chris said, with a bashful smile. Nicholas smiled back at him, as though genuinely charmed, and then they were standing there, grinning at each other like fools.

"Mm-hmm," said Antoine.

"I can't," said Nicholas—not quite regretfully, though he angled his body towards Chris's, brushing their arms together. "I need some rest. It's been a long night. Breakfast sounds— exhausting. If I'm honest."

"Fair enough." Antoine didn't look in the least put out. "Come out with us tonight, then. Yes?"

"I—" Nicholas looked bewildered. "Where?"

"Oh," Antoine said, shrugging, and Chris was struck with the suspicion that this had been his goal all along, talks of breakfast on the Seine notwithstanding, "anywhere. A bar. There is a place that sells by-the-hour margaritas behind the Hotel de Ville."

"I'm sorry," said Chris. "*Were* we going out tonight?"

"Were we not?"

"I imagine we were," Chris said, elaborately thoughtful. "How strange that I forgot."

"*Good* boy."

"I'll—" Nicholas was frowning. "I'll think about it."

"I hope you will," said Antoine silkily. A delicate silence

fell; then, stretching himself, he added: "I really do think we should go. The best seats will be taken by the brunch crowd."

"Go on ahead, then, and get us a table," said Chris, in French. "I'll have to wrap up things here. Le Meunier? In twenty minutes?"

Antoine brushed his arm, smiled at Nicholas, and stepped aside, pulling his phone out of his pocket. Nicholas, dark-eyed, watched him go.

"So."

"So," Chris said.

"That's your—?"

"My—? Oh. No." Chris sighed. "Antoine doesn't do serious, and I don't do casual. We wouldn't fit." He was intensely aware that Nicholas's gaze was on him, dark and meaningful. "We've known each other for years. Better to be friends and commiserate over the state of our love lives together. Antoine is rarely in Paris. He's—not always so—"

"I didn't mind," Nicholas said.

"He's a good friend," Chris said, glancing at him. "He wouldn't publish anything without your consent."

"I'll take your word for it," said Nicholas, but he was smiling at the ground, and in his face was a tentative sort of eagerness. Chris wanted very badly to take his hand in his—to hold it in the private space between their chests just long enough that their heartbeats could merge. For a moment they stood in silence, watching the traffic pick up on the other side of the river.

Then Nicholas said, slowly: "This bar…"

"You don't have to come, Nicholas."

"I think I want to," said Nicholas, wryly. "I only have—some misgivings. Is it a gay bar?"

Straightforward. He was rarely ever anything less. "No. It's fairly diverse, though. No one would look twice at two men or two women together there."

"I see."

"Will you come?"

"I want to," Nicholas repeated.

Antoine, damn him, engineered a strategic takeover of Chris's wardrobe. By the time Chris was walking up the stairs of the metro, as dusk fell around him, he was wearing a pair of tight black jeans and a cashmere pullover he normally reserved for more extravagant occasions. He felt self-conscious, which did not happen often—it took a certain kind of shamelessness to display his body to the world as often as he did—but this evening felt off-kilter, as though the earth had been knocked an inch or two off its axis.

Right. Fine: he was man enough to admit to an attraction, at least. Nicholas Madden was hot. Take it as a fact.

Chris had always had a weakness for an arrogant, overbearing type of man. It had led to many heartbreaks in his past. But Nicholas, though prickly and grim, had proven to be sweeter than anyone thought. In the long creeds gossip magazines published to detail his many tantrums on set, you never saw *and then he brought coffee to his exhausted costar after a night of filming* tacked on at the end.

You never knew that he could thread his fingers through his costar's hair to soothe him, while they played lovers, lying in the same bed and trying to fight off awkwardness.

Instead, Nicholas seemed…lonely. Chris didn't know that he had any friend in the world apart from his PA. He never talked about his family, and if he had had a partner in the past, no one had ever been able to find out.

Chris was reasonably certain Nicholas was single. He was reasonably certain that Nicholas was not straight. He was even reasonably certain Nicholas felt at least a fraction of the attraction Chris felt for him.

Nicholas also wasn't *out*, and had betrayed no sign that he ever intended to be. His cautious question about the bar's leanings had made that quite clear. He would play a gay part, that much was accepted within Hollywoodian double standards—but there was a gigantic leap to be taken from that to being seen in public with a male partner. Nicholas would not (could not, perhaps) take it.

He was entitled not to. Chris had once felt a thread of impatience when his friends refused to own up to their own sexuality—until he had realized that what came to him as simply, and truly, as his liking for black coffee, was the result of much self-deliberation on the part of many others. His sexuality, which had never failed to be anything less than utterly clear to him, was not so easily found in another body. He had made his peace with that.

*I'll respect his reserve*, he thought, kicking his heels on the Place du Châtelet. *If he decides to do something about it—we'll see. But I won't push...*

Despite this, he could not help but feel a pang of disappointment when a car came to a gentle stop at a red light, and Nicholas's PA stepped out ahead of her employer.

Her silk blouse and dark blazer gave her the look of a businesswoman on the town. She looked like a million dollars. By contrast, Nicholas was—trying to blend in, in a way: he had put on dark jeans and a black button-down, which would have looked dressed up on anyone else, but on Nicholas Madden seemed almost casual. Giving them a wave, Chris had a brief image of Nicholas as he must be at home—truly at home, not in a swank Parisian hotel room with nothing to wear but businesslike suits—in sweatpants, in a close-fitted t-shirt that would, perhaps, delineate his pecs and his abdominal muscles. Sweatpants hanging a little low, just enough to glimpse at the ridges of hip bones, the rise of a well-defined ass. The thought of it made his heart race just a bit faster.

"Hi," he said, when they reached him. "Madalena—is that right? Are you acting bodyguard tonight?"

"Chaperone," she said, grinning, and kissed his cheek without a shred of self-consciousness.

He knew better than to expect that sort of greeting from Nicholas, who did—to his credit—appear to move in for some kind of bro hug before he remembered where and who he was. Chris grinned at him.

"You look good."

Nicholas's eyebrows rose. "High praise, coming from you."

"Hardly," Chris laughed. "Those jeans must have cost half as much as my entire wardrobe."

Nicholas looked down at himself, and then, inexplicably, blushed. Madalena, noticing this, hustled them right along before Chris had time to parse out what he felt about it.

They fell into place naturally: Madalena on Google Maps, Nicholas half a step behind her. Chris found it easier to match his pace to his; Madalena's high heels looked downright lethal. "I must tell you," he said, in a low voice. "It's Friday. Antoine's crowd will be there tonight, so soon after he's come home."

Nicholas glanced at him. He'd burrowed his hands in his pockets. "Is that a problem?"

"Not as such. They've all—we've all—had our hands burned at the fire of celebrity: our own, or other people's. They're not fond of any invasion of privacy, especially their own."

"And they're your friends. We are protected by proxy."

"I don't think you'll have to worry about anyone taking candids," said Chris. "Or recognizing you. Most people will be drunk, or dancing, or both."

"But?"

"But, well. I know you want to be careful. I brought you these."

Nicholas received his gift with a bemused look, turning it between his hands. "You—glasses. You bought them?"

"They were cheap," said Chris.

"I—" Nicholas hesitated, then forged on. "Thank you." He put them on, and grinned, suddenly. "You know it's an awful cliché?"

"Let me keep my dreams," said Chris. His voice softened in spite of himself. "You look like Clark Kent."

# *Chapter Nine*

@lavallenation • 11m
Latest pics from the set early this morning
[pic]

@lavallenation • 10m
Don't forget: don't tag Chris in the pictures you take of
the set! He may pose for them, but he doesn't necessarily want to see the fandom's dark depths, lol

@lavallenation • 10m
Our boi looks damn fine in period clothing
[pic]

@lavallenation • 9m
He's talking to esteemed director Priya Chaudhuri omg
[pic]

@lavallenation • 3m
Wow, okay, madden fandom woke up this morning &
chose violence. Don't let them rile you up!! If they can't
get past their fave playing a gay role, smh

@lavallenation • 2m
listen @ all newbies you can stan for madden all you like
but leave your homophobia at the door

@lavallenation • 1m
Madden fandom: HDU BESMIRCH OUR FAVE
Madden and Chris: lol
[pic]

Chris was wearing eyeliner.

*I might as well be a teenager with a crush.* Nicholas's hands were balled up in his pockets. Of all the damned things to find utterly fascinating.

Chris did, however, have gorgeous eyes. And—with *those* jeans on—a pretty near perfect ass. It was a wonder he'd managed to pull them on. His hair didn't bear thinking about, let alone looking at.

It had been a long time since Nicholas had felt such a rush of exhilarated lust at the sight of anyone, let alone a coworker. Chris had turned the rules upside down.

Their fingers brushed as they walked down the street. It was coming on dusk; the light was a pale dusty gold, touching their steps as Chris pointed ahead.

The bar was a narrow dive tucked in between doorways, in a cobbled side street, where tourists and residents came to sit in the restaurant terraces and on the steps of porches, smoking, drinking white wine out of clear plastic glasses. Chris led the way, touching his fingers to Nicholas's forearm as they stepped inside.

Inside was warm and dark. Under their feet a heartbeat drum thrummed, and it took Nicholas a moment to realize it was the sound of muffled music. Chris pointed at the stairs to the basement. They pushed in. He shouldn't have been worried about anonymity, he realized: it was late enough that the bar was crowded, every table taken, feet overlapping. Here was a girl in a red leather jacket, her drink sloshing out of her cup as she hiccupped with laughter; here, a guy in a plaid shirt gesturing for the bartender; there, a group of university-age students, shouting cheerfully at each other, carrying on a conversation in the thrumming dark. Chris wound his way through, unhesitating.

They reached the bar. Chris greeted a woman with colorful tattooed vines twining up her arms with easy familiarity, ordered three drinks in rapid-fire succession, and turned back to them with a smile.

"Beer?" he prompted, holding one out.

"Sure."

"There's Antoine."

Here *was* Antoine, holding court in a corner, who, upon catching sight of them, lifted a hand in welcome. He extricated himself from his circle of admirers with a wave and a kiss, and came up to wrap Chris up in a hug.

"Hello, I don't know you," he said, to Madalena, and then, with an arch look in Nicholas's direction: "I *do* know you."

"My thanks," said Nicholas. "For inviting us."

Antoine's smile grew a fraction. "My pleasure. What's your name?" To Madalena, again.

Introductions ensued, whereupon Antoine appeared to adopt them as his new best friends, and insisted on presenting them to his posse. "First names only," he added, with a flitting grin.

There were six of them, and Nicholas remembered none of their names before the half hour was through. They, like Chris and like Antoine, were tall, elegant, and beautiful—models, he assumed, before one woman was introduced to him as the new hope for French journalism, and another, a sharp-eyed, haughty-looking young man, as the best attorney on this side of the Seine. Here were, apparently, the top of the crop—the *crème de la crème*—and they were drinking shitty beer in a Parisian dive. Madalena would fit right in.

Nicholas was keenly reminded, as the conversation swirled, of his own lack of sociable feeling. Once in a while was well enough—you could hardly survive in Hollywood without attending parties and soirées by the handful—but keep him for a few long hours in a room full of people and he felt ravaged, exhausted.

It accounted for some of his short temper (though not, admittedly, all of it). He wasn't a social creature. Performing to a camera was an easy task, considering the alternative: he disliked performing *himself* to strangers. So much of his time was spent playing an act, he had very much lost track of who Nicholas Madden was when he wasn't the Big Bad Wolf of Hollywood.

Chris tonight was strangely quiet. He followed Antoine's meandering conversation with a faint smile, eyes half-closed, one hand curled loosely around his beer. They were seated together, opposite Madalena, crowded on a velvet-backed bench against the wall, in a darkened corner. In the light of the burning lamps, Chris's face seemed older, and his eyes were dark and sad.

Nicholas brushed his knuckles against his hand as he lowered his pint. "Alright?"

"Alright," Chris murmured, quietly. He was silent for a moment, then added: "I don't—I don't find this easy."

"Evenings out," Nicholas surmised.

"People," Chris admitted. He caught Nicholas's look, and smiled, briefly. "It's easier when I'm on a job. Work is work. This, though—" He lifted a shoulder. "It's...different. Harder."

"I know the feeling," Nicholas said slowly.

Chris turned enough to look at him more fully, and watched him for a few seconds, unspeaking, before he said, "Yes. I'm starting to understand that."

Nicholas looked at him. Their hands were very close together on the tabletop; it would be the work of an instant merely to touch him. Chris's eyes were on his, thoughtful. All-seeing.

"Let's dance," said Antoine, and that focus was lost.

They were swept away. Down they went, into the dim,

thick, incense-smelling basement: down a flight of rocky stairs and into the club itself, where music thrummed heavy and sensual in the dark. They were separated, and Nicholas hesitated on the edge of the dance floor; then Madalena caught his wrist and drew him in, and the music took them.

He'd not gone out dancing in years. It wasn't a thing he *did*. It wasn't even in the realm of possibility. Had Nicholas been told a week ago—hell, twenty-four hours ago—that he would find himself dancing in the seedy underbelly of a Parisian nightclub, he would not have believed a word. But the music was close and deep, the kind of music that sank into your bones—the kind of music you couldn't not dance to, on some deep-seated level— and Madalena was laughing and drawing him into it.

Nicholas was no longer twenty years old. His idea of a good time was a glassful of something rich and amber and an evening away from his phone. He'd all but forgotten how to dance. But now he was twenty again: and dancing was easy.

It was like riding an elephant. You never really forgot.

Madalena was swept away, after a time. She was replaced by faceless strangers. None of them recognized him; none of them cared, and the anonymity was soothing. Men danced with men and women with women. There was a safety in that, a familiarity, an acknowledgement. How long had it been since he'd last stopped pretending to be straight? How long had it been since he'd let himself watch a man's back, the muscles of his shoulders, the slimness of his waist, for anything longer than a passing, shameful glance?

The crowd heaved and changed. The music switched beats, and dropped into something heavy and dark, a lifeblood-thrum that made the dancing harder. And then, as though Nicholas had summoned him, Chris was there—a hand on his arm, the hint of a smile in the flashing strobing dark lights—then pressed flush against him, smelling like alcohol and long nights out.

God, but Chris could *move*. No longer the softer, silent young man he had been in the bar above: he was a vision, a supernatural apparition in the strangest of places. A stranger. His hair was darkened with sweat, curling against his neck; his eyes were wide and bright, his mouth red with biting or kissing. He curled one arm comfortably around Nicholas's neck as the crowd pushed them close, and brought his mouth close to his ear and said:

"I never pegged you for a man who could dance like that."

"Like what?" Nicholas shouted back. His hands found their way to Chris's hips. Chris made a soft, purring sound, and pressed up closer, leaning his forehead against Nicholas's temple. They were of the same height, just about. They were pressed together in all the right places. Thigh to thigh. Hip to hip. Chris was solid angles and warm body, knowing hands, a winning smile.

"Like you want to fuck," Chris said.

*I want to fuck you*, thought Nicholas. Chris blinked at him. Then he grinned, a sudden brightness, illuminating his eyes in the changing lights of the club, and slipped both his arms around Nicholas's neck. He shook his head.

"Dance with me," he said, against his cheek.

Once or twice another dancer attempted to cut in: a hand on Nicholas's shoulder, a lithe body pressing against Chris's back. Each was dispensed with firmly and kindly. Chris's chest was pressed to his own, his fingers lost in his hair. He was humming to the song's beat. Though the room was too resonant to hear, Nicholas felt the soft thrum of it against his own skin.

Only once did they break off, to drink again: shots, this time, of tequila, and something sweeter, something like lime and pop, and Chris swallowed them back like water, shaking himself afterwards, and grinning. He remained close to Nicholas, side to side, his head tucked comfortably against his. At some point in the proceedings his hand slipped into Nicholas's. Nicholas saw no reason to take it away.

When they made their way to the dance floor again, it had got late enough that the music was leaning towards the slow and sensual end of the scale. Here Chris was in his element. Taken out of his usual persona, he was charming and a little tipsy, a little handsy, full of joy. "Come here," he said—shouted, really, above the music—and tugged on Nicholas's hand, bringing him into the middle of the dance floor, where they were lost in a sea of anonymity.

They might have met each other in the club, found each other dancing. They might have met here on any night out on the town, strangers in the dimming lights, body to body, touch to touch, mouth to mouth. Nicholas might not have hesitated then to take him by the hand and lead him towards a quieter, darker corner, where they could have enjoyed a nameless and mutually satisfying tryst, back pressed to a bathroom stall, hands wandering underneath clothes, finding smooth skin, taut muscle, willing promise. It felt like mischance that they had already been naked together. They had bypassed a million steps and jumped straight through to intimacy.

Chris knew, as well, that something between them had shifted. When he brought Nicholas closer to him again, he did so with intent. His hands slipped around his neck to cup the back of his head.

They were barely dancing—they were more intent on touching subtly than on moving. This was dancing as Nicholas remembered from being young and foolish in love, the first boy he'd ever wanted when he'd barely been more than a boy himself. Only...only he was thirty-two, and Chris was a grown man, who wanted him. There could be no doubt about it. Judging by the look in his eyes, the smile on his lips, he knew it, too.

By mutual agreement though not by design, they gravitated

towards the darker corners of the club. Here was quiet, and the
assurance of total privacy, amid perfect strangers. Chris was
breathing softly, his nose brushing Nicholas's cheek.

He was trembling, a fine tremor. Nicholas laid his hand
against the small of his back, pulling him up close, and said:
"You're shaking."

"Am I?" A wisp of laughter. Chris touched his nose to
Nicholas's jaw; his mouth was just open. "I don't—I don't
know why."

"Chris," said Nicholas, turning his head, to find his mouth.
His fear had abandoned him, somewhere between the bar and
the basement. Chris was warm against him, and gentle.

"Ah. Yes." Chris's lips curved. Then he kissed back, his lips
parting to meet Nicholas's.

Even odder, that he should already know how Chris kissed.
His mouth was familiar. But—no—no: Chris was not, after
all, Angelo.

Angelo, by turns teasing and violent, kissed without meaning or kindness, without giving away an inch. Chris had more
purpose. He was softer. But underneath the softness was steel.

He pulled away from Nicholas, their mouths just parting, and
then he *touched* Nicholas's mouth—with the backs of his fingers, of all the inane things. Nicholas said his name, and barely
heard himself over the roar of the music. Chris leaned in again,
and, gently, kissed him, again; so, so gently, as though he imagined Nicholas might break apart in his arms. Nicholas's breathing came harder. He opened his mouth to the first, tentative,
almost shy brush of Chris's tongue, and then gave in, entirely,
when Chris wrapped his hands around the back of his head and
kissed him with more intent. Good Lord. He kissed as though
he meant something by it.

They stumbled away against a wall, and, catching themselves, found that they had fallen into a narrow, carpeted al-
cove, shallow, in which they were all but invisible. Their

mouths parted only so long as they could take a breath, before Nicholas trapped him in and pressed close…and gathered
him up against him, fitting both of his hands around Chris's
slim waist. Chris made a soft, dangerous sound of encouragement, in the back of his throat—almost a growl, possessive
and sure—and threaded his fingers through Nicholas's hair,
slowly, cradling his face, his neck, the back of his head.

They were chest to chest; Nicholas could hear the hard
thrumming of his heart. Pressed together like this, he could
feel the hard muscle of Chris's arms, the flat plane of his belly,
and even—when Chris, in a moment of madness, hooked a
thigh around his hip—the hardness in his groin, impossible
to mistake. *Is that a gun in your pocket—?* The thought bubbled
up into laughter, and Chris smiled against his mouth, giving
his lower lip a teasing nip.

"Bad idea," Nicholas murmured.

"Mmmmm," said Chris, his thumb pressing hard against
Nicholas's cheekbone, his breath hot against Nicholas's neck.
"I don't care. Kiss me again."

Nicholas obeyed, his lips barely touching his. Chris almost purred in response. He was magnificent. He showed
want without shame, without prudery. His hips were working against Nicholas's. He twitched when Nicholas's hand
dropped from his waist to his ass, and then *moaned*, opening
his mouth again to Nicholas's tongue.

They were rocking against each other now, slowly. The
pressure against Nicholas's aching cock was immense and unbearable. He wanted Chris right there, against a dirty wall in
the basement of some nameless bar, while behind them music
pulsed and strangers might be watching, might be—no, they
were hidden from sight here, concealed by the darkness—but
anyone might come: anyone might be in search of them now.
What a spectacle that would be. Nicholas Madden and Chris

Lavalle, caught frotting against each other like a couple of horny teenagers in an underground bar.

Then they *were* caught, and the worst became true.

"Oh. Nicholas—"

Madalena's voice penetrated through the haze in Nicholas's skull like a burning star. Against him, Chris went very still.

"Nicholas. I'm sorry."

Nicholas pulled himself away. Madalena was *there*, two steps away, her eyes ablaze with worry.

"Paps. They must have followed us."

Damn, damn, *damn*. Nicholas tore himself out of Chris's unresisting arms, and Chris remained pressed against the wall, breathing hard. Nicholas didn't look away from him. He looked painfully vulnerable, and absolutely devastated— his hair a mess from Nicholas's fingers, his mouth red with kissing; his eyes were wild, worry and regret warring with arousal in his face; fuck, *fuck*, Nicholas wanted him, wanted him so badly he could choke on it.

"Nicholas, we need to *go*."

"Go," Chris choked out. "Go. I'll—find Antoine. Give them something to look at instead."

Nicholas felt powerless to stop him. "Be careful."

"Always am," said Chris, with a sudden, sad smile, and he slipped away, brushing against Nicholas's chest as he went. He did not look back. Nicholas felt the loss of him as though a bird had lived in his chest for years, and had just taken flight, never to return.

Then he looked at Madalena, and the regret transformed into grim determination.

"Come on; this way," she said, pulling on his arm, and to-gether they slipped through the back door and into the soft summer night, as the thrumming sounds of the club fell away behind them.

# *Chapter Ten*

closeup.com
08:08 am

## Caught! Chris Lavalle of *The Throne* Drinking & Flirting During Bar Outing

**Spotted:** *A boyfriend on the horizon?* Chris Lavalle and mystery man seen embracing outside a bar in gay Paree Lavalle, latest Chaudhuri protégé and new hope of gay love story *The Throne*, was seen drinking heavily in underground French bar...

The next few days passed as in a dream.

Chris's agent sent him a sternly-worded email about boundaries and career-making decisions, and Jason Kirkhall, who until now had regarded Chris with little more than indifference, appeared to have a change of heart, and invited him out for a night out. "Boys' night," he said awkwardly, standing in Chris's trailer with his hands shoved in the pockets of his Armani jeans. "Dancing, shots—"

"I don't think it's a good idea," Chris said gently.

Jason's face fell. "No?"

"My agent," said Chris, with a shrug and his best *what can you do?* face, "recommends I lie low for a little while. No bars, no alcohol..."

"Awww. Bummer, man."

He looked so downcast on Chris's behalf that Chris couldn't help but smile.

They had only a few scenes together, and most of these were ensembles; he had had very little opportunity to speak to Jason, and had not taken it. They were about the same age. Jason was not disagreeable to look at—tall, broad-shouldered, very blond—and though his conversation skills were limited to his own likes and dislikes, he was a pleasant guy to talk to. He had been in the industry since he was a child, and seemed to take his own Hollywood cred for granted, although he had, until now, mostly starred in action flicks and the occasional indie. His reputation as a lady-killer preceded him, and (to Nicholas's intense disgust) he enjoyed partying a little *too* much.

Then again, perhaps any kind of partying was distasteful to Nicholas. Their night out together had been…exceptional. But it was, and must remain, an *exception.* Chris knew that Priya Chaudhuri disapproved of affairs and trysts between her stars: she wanted them focused, with their mind on the job. She would not be well pleased if she learned that Chris went around making out with Nicholas Madden in dark corners.

He couldn't afford to displease her. As a model, he was aging out of the industry. *The Throne* was his ticket out to a different kind of work. The sort of work that demanded intelligence and serious engineering, if he wanted to make it.

But, god, what a kiss…

None of Chris's former boyfriends had been lacking in that department, and yet Nicholas had flown above and past them all. He was a powerful, demanding kisser, the sort who pushed and pulled and took whatever he wanted, and wanted nothing short of absolute dedication to the moment. Nicholas *was* absolute: he pushed things to their limits.

When he played Frederick, he did so with gravitas and

interest and a sadness so peculiar to the character that Chris could no longer imagine him any other way. When he spoke, he spoke with emphasis, every word weighed and measured against its meaning. When he kissed, he did so with abandon, throwing himself into pleasure.

Chris had tried, and mostly failed, not to imagine what he might be like in bed. All that coiled power, all that repressed desire, given physical form…

"Lavalle?"

Chris resurfaced. "Sorry. Oh, Chris, please."

Jason broke into a grin, and said in passable and surprising French, "Sure. Don't mind my horrible accent."

"It can't be worse than mine," said Chris, laughing, and Jason took this as an invitation and perched on the side of the dressing-table, stuffing his hands in his jeans pockets.

"You been in the business long? I mean, not—well, you know."

"Modeling? Yes, a little while. Almost eight years, now."

Jason whistled. "Long time in the industry."

"I suppose. I wanted a career change, though."

"And you sure got one," said Jason cheerfully. "Pulled plenty of strings to get there, I bet."

"I—" Chris was startled. "I wouldn't say so. I auditioned for Chaudhuri…"

"Ah, we all know how it starts," said Jason, with easy dismissiveness. "Don't worry about it: everyone went through that rig one time or other. It's no biggie. That's how Madden made his start, too. You know, my agent wanted me to audition for Frederick? But *that* was a lost cause. Madden wanted the role so bad he'd have killed anyone else in the running."

"Is he that bad?" Chris asked, curious, and leaving aside the subject of strings that needed pulling for the time being. "On set, I mean."

"Oh, he's alright. Barely ever talks to *me*, anyway. Of course there's all sorts of rumors, but what can you do? Guess he threw a lamp at a director once, that was a thing."

"I...see. I have been tempted to throw things at photographers before," said Chris, making a note of asking Nicholas—if he could bring himself to face Nicholas ever again—about the lamp incident. There was probably a good story in it.

"Haven't we all?" asked Jason, very much entertained. "Deserved it, if you ask me."

Chris's second visitor that week was Andrée Belfond, who cornered him on set after a particularly grueling day of shooting. The weather had turned for the worse, and everyone was irascible and wet and beginning to doubt *The Throne*'s chances of success. Nicholas was particularly somber, coming and leaving without rest or pause, and barely looking at Chris in the intervals between scenes. Chris wasn't quite sure whether he was thankful for it or not. Their kiss was always intruding in his thoughts. Sometimes he wanted more. Sometimes he thought it should never, never happen again.

But Andrée, sitting down beside him one evening between takes, and lighting a cigarette, disarmed him with sincere concern. "You alright?"

"Alright?" Chris repeated, taken by surprise. "I—yes?"

"You don't look it," said Andrée, calmly shielding her smoke away. "What's gone on between you and Madden? You can barely stand to look at each other."

Chris was silenced.

"Like that, is it?"

"No," said Chris quickly.

"It's alright," said Andrée. "Keep it from Chaudhuri, that's all."

"That's not—what I mean. I mean, there's nothing. I don't think he likes me much. I'm sorry, why do you care?"

Andrée laughed. She had a lovely laugh, vivid and bright; her face, haloed by her white-blond hair, seemed to lose ten years when she smiled. She leaned her elbow against the armrest of her chair and said, "Merely curious. If it's not like that, then, why? Madden was your knight in shining armor for a couple of weeks there."

"Was he," said Chris, doubtfully.

"Oh, entirely. Of course at first he was dead set against your casting. But something about you must've caught his attention. He's been defending you against the press lately." She must've seen some emotion pass over his face, because her eyebrows hiked up. "Didn't you know?"

"No?"

"Damn," she murmured, digging out her phone. "Hang on. There's this guy—this journalist—who loves to rile Madden up. Here."

Chris read the interview with some disbelief. He'd never heard of Damien Jones. He'd not been aware that Nicholas was even giving interviews.

*I think he'll surprise you.* The words were so honest, so purely Nicholas, that something stuck in Chris's throat. He skimmed the rest of the article, biting his lip, and handed back the phone without a word.

"Illuminating," said Andrée, with an amused snort. "Jones is an asshole, though. Madden hates him. Always pushing for the sordid little stories, the things nobody says…"

"Oh?" said Chris, faintly.

He looked across the length of the set at Nicholas, who was in deep conversation with Chaudhuri. The set was bright with spotlights, the cameras ready for action; everything else was in shadow, and all he could see of Nicholas were his shoulders, his hands, his profile lit up at an angle. "I…suppose someone like me is a source of gossip for reporters like him."

"Fresh blood," Andrée agreed, drawing on her cigarette. "Always good intel. Plus, you're clickbait. People like your face."

"I can't imagine why," said Chris blandly, and Andrée went up in a shout of laughter.

Nicholas glanced back in their direction with a thunderous look.

"Oh, look at him," said Andrée, thoughtful. "Very *tall, dark, and brooding*, isn't he? Good casting. So were you," she added, suddenly, surprising Chris. She looked at him, measuring, from the tips of his hair to the tips of his shoes. "I didn't think so at first. Thought you were out of your depth, to be quite honest. But you're not. Oh, you're lost, sure—first-timers always are—but when it comes to the camera, nothing in between, nothing but your face and your voice and your hands—you know what you're doing. I don't think any of us expected that. Except Chaudhuri," she added. "But god knows what Chaudhuri's thinking."

"There was a compliment in there, I think," said Chris. "Thanks, I suppose."

"Don't thank me," said Andrée bluntly. "I know movies like these: I have a few of them under my belt, too. They take your guts and they tie them up into knots. They hollow you out, and whatever gets poured back in, you have to be damn sure you can handle it…don't you feel it? The feeling that Angelo's got you by the throat? Hang on to that feeling. If you can control it, you'll get out wholly yourself. If not, he'll always be there."

She left on that prophetic note, crushing her cigarette butt under her heel. Chris was abandoned to his own thoughts. He watched Nicholas, who was now allowing a makeup artist to touch up his face and hair. He was wearing one of Frederick's dark suits, so well-cut and so well-made that he looked all but poured into it. *Tall, dark, and brooding.*

Then Nicholas looked back at him, and Chris caught his breath.

After a moment Nicholas waved away the makeup person, and made his way over. Chris's smile was irrepressible. He couldn't hold back a frisson of excitement.

"I see Andrée is making friends."

"It's kind of a shock, you know," said Chris, thankful to find that his voice was even. He could even smile. Nicholas barely smiled back; but he leaned against the seat Andrée had abandoned, as though he meant to stay awhile. "She's a very famous actress. Imagine having Marilyn Monroe walk up to you…but then, I guess, so are you."

"A famous actress?"

"Well. You would look…adequate in a dress," Chris said, biting his lip in his amusement: secretly he thought Nicholas would look goddamn fantastic in a bit of red silk. Whoever dressed him for official events should have more *fun* with that brilliant body.

"I pull off dresses pretty well, thanks."

He sounded so much like the stuck-up prick Chris had first met in the *Renard d'Or* that Chris could only laugh. "I've worn a few in my time. My work requires some dressing-up. Ripped-up tights. Lingerie…"

"Yes, I know."

It was a moment before Chris caught up with his meaning. "You—"

"I've seen a few pictures." Was he *blushing*? It was adorable. Chris caught his eye. Cleared his throat.

"Right." He was silent for a moment, and Nicholas, evidently unwilling to push, looked away. "It was kind of Andrée to try and cheer me up. She and Jason have been very—sweet to me this week."

"Jason," Nicholas repeated, without inflexion.

"Mmm. He wanted me to go clubbing with him."

Nicholas looked momentarily outraged. It lasted a second, if that, but Chris saw it nonetheless, and carried on quickly: "My agent wants me to steer clear of clubs and—and bars. For a little while."

"Probably a good idea."

"Yes."

More awkward silence. Was this how it was going to be? Nothing but careful words and meaningful, double-edged looks?

Chris couldn't bear it. He brushed his hand against Nicholas's arm. "You know I wouldn't. Say anything. Don't you?"

Nicholas looked up at him, uneasiness in his gaze; but after a moment he nodded, and covered Chris's hand with his own, for a bare second of affection. "Yes, I know." Then he added, "Thank you."

"There's nothing to thank me for," said Chris, a trifle sadly. "It's basic human courtesy."

"Most human beings aren't so kind."

There was something bleak in his eyes. The lines at the corners of his mouth were tight. *Damien Jones*, Chris thought. And others of his ilk, poking and prodding at Nicholas until he broke, and in breaking gave them the ammunition they needed to call him unhinged. How had he ever believed Nicholas was the tyrannical diva the trashy press insisted he was? He had a temper; he was arrogant; he was also clumsy in social interactions, gentle in strange moments, and unfailingly loyal. Chris had known celebrities who treated people like shit. They didn't act the way Nicholas acted with Madalena, or Chaudhuri, or even Sir Reginald, who, though not unkind, was certainly exasperating. Nicholas handled him with amused temperance.

"What did Andrée say?" asked Nicholas, after a longer but easier silence. He wasn't looking at Chris; his eyes were on Chaudhuri, across the set, where she and the production manager were looking over the location fixings.

"She—oh, she warned me to be careful."

Nicholas cut him a glance. "About?"

"Angelo. Seems he's the kind of role that never lets you go."

"That's not untrue."

"Is that why you tried to put me off entirely? That *wasn't* what your opening gambit was all about; don't deny it now."

"It was—but only in part," Nicholas admitted. "I acted in good faith. I didn't think you were right for Angelo: too young, too inexperienced, not enough understanding of what the work entailed…"

"Yes, Andrée said something like that too."

"But I knew, too, that Angelo was the sort of character who would gut you if you played him wrong. I stand by what I said: Frederick is the easier part to play. And yet you—" He paused, visibly frustrated. "I don't know how to phrase it. You play him at the right distance. You're not a method actor."

"I'm not an anything actor," Chris said, laughing.

"No; but you are. You're different."

"Is *that* a compliment?"

"I don't know yet," Nicholas said softly. "I just know that when you play, I don't want to look at anyone else."

Chris lifted his eyes to his, a little breathless with the desire to charm, to tease. "That's…take care, Nicholas. That's a little close to intimacy."

He was aware, quite suddenly, of Nicholas's warm, animal body next to his: the breadth of his shoulders, the hands he had stuffed in his pockets, the stubble on his jaw.

Physical intimacy was a strange thing between them. They had seen each other naked, and lain in the same bed, and yet they did not share the easy affection of lovers. They had kissed for the camera, and kissed for themselves, and each experience had held its own share of delights. Chris had kissed many people for work and for leisure, and yet each kiss with Nicholas seemed a treasure trove of unexplored wants. He was acutely conscious of his own body, of his own breath, of his own desire to reach out and place his hand flat against Nicholas's chest. He wanted to touch; he wanted to thread his fingers in Nicholas's hair again, and hold him close, until Nicholas's pride finally gave way and his arms finally came around him.

It was a very strange thing to be longing for a hug. It was not in the least romantic.

*And yet here we are*, he thought, and felt blood rush up to his cheeks. Nicholas blinked, and then glared at the floor as though it had done him personal offense.

"We're bad at this," he muttered.

"Very," Chris agreed breathlessly.

"Look—" Nicholas sighed, then ran a hand through his hair, no doubt mussing up the work his hairdresser had put into it. "I don't know—if you know this, but your friend—Antoine—he texted me this afternoon. I guess Madalena gave him my number."

"Oh?"

"He wanted me to know you'd be doing a shoot for him in a couple of days."

"I am," said Chris, bemused. It wasn't a big thing—Antoine liked to do private shoots every now and then, with friends. Chris liked those intimate shoots among people he trusted, when having a body was just something beautiful; something really, profoundly good.

Having a body and living in it: it hurt, sometimes. Antoine had a way of framing the light so that it hurt a little less.

"He asked if I'd come too," Nicholas said.

That was...unexpected. "To shoot?"

Nicholas shrugged. "If I wanted, yes."

Chris was intrigued, and more than a little curious. He wondered what Antoine was about. "*Do* you want to?"

"Let's say I'm intrigued. Would you mind?"

"I wouldn't," said Chris, automatically, and then thought twice about it, and rephrased: "If you don't think it crosses a—a boundary, that you don't want crossed—I'd understand."

"You know," Nicholas said, "I think you actually would. You're probably the only person in the world who *would* understand. I like that about you."

And then, as though he hadn't just decimated him in five words, he added over his shoulder: "I'll think about it."

# *Chapter Eleven*

## [DISCUSSION]
## Weekly Thread—24/06/29-24/07/05

[page 76 of 77]
<< < 1 2 3... 75 76 77 ]] >>

**aimeesays**
[pic]
[pic]
[pic]
😕

**madnessisastateofmind**
Man, I don't know how to feel about any of this.

**aimeesays**
It just feels very out of character for him?? When has Chris ever been a party animal, idgi

**madnessisastateofmind**
Yeah like
Okay, he's in the industry, drinking and going out are part of the job I'm sure.
But I kinda feel like the papers are milking this & making it into

a Thing when maybe Chris just went out with some friends and wanted to have fun

**slamdunksammy**
lol i agree, Chris was just having a drink and the paps made him out to be a Heavy Drinker™
smh @ everyone who's taking this srsly

**aimeesays**
Also the sex thing??????? wtf

**politenessisoverrated**
the sex thing is some prime bullshit. Chris has always been super private about his love life, we don't even know if the bloke in the pic is his boyfriend, idk whose ass they're pulling that one out of but it's certified drivel tbh
AND ALSO
remember the guy he was dating a few years ago, Mark or whatever? Chris wasn't half as influential then as he is now, especially with the movie coming up, but the hot goss sites were all over how cute they were and how goals their relationship was…and then when they broke up they were falling over themselves trying to find some kind of radical flaw in Chris when it was just an amicable separation. imagine what they would do to him if it had been a bad-break-up! no fucking wonder he's so private about it.

**jaicruaudiable**
I mean…he's French. People loooooooooove to think French people are super promiscuous, hon hon hon and all that. ☹

**aimeesays**
Thanks!! I hate it!!!

★ ★ ★

"This," said Madalena as they got out of the car, "is a *spectacularly* bad idea."

"You're exaggerating."

"Barely. Have you asked Slater about this?"

Jim Slater, Nicholas's agent, would doubtless be deeply annoyed with him for accepting Antoine's invitation. Nicholas was not slated to appear in unplanned photoshoots without prior agreement—and a fair amount of money changing hands.

"No. I don't intend to. I'm only here to watch, Em. Whatever else happens…happens."

She was silent, taking his arm as they walked up to the warehouse. It was an old building, a deconstructed depot turned into avant-garde art studios; the façade had been graffitied in bright pops of color, and, when they ducked inside, they found a landscape of open spaces, tall windows, radiant sunshine, and exposed beams, twining upward and upward, dizzily. "Like a cathedral," Madalena murmured.

It was an accurate description. Their footsteps echoed against the white-parquet flooring. Across the open span, where a small group of people was in a cluster, a tall, dark man looked round at the sound, and came quickly to greet them.

"Madden! I'm glad you've come. Madalena too! What luck!"

"Antoine," said Nicholas, shaking his hand.

Antoine laughed at his formality, gave Madalena a quick one-armed hug, and tucked his hand possessively in Nicholas's elbow. "Come on. I want you to see this."

*This* turned out to be Chris, sprawled in a Louis XIV–style armchair, his eyes closed gently as a makeup artist worked on his face. Shimmery highlighter brought his cheekbones into stark contrast, and his golden hair was slicked back from his temples, not a strand out of place. He was wearing a white t-shirt and black jeans. His simplicity was breathtaking.

"I'm...surprised," Nicholas admitted. "I imagined you went for wilder things."

"Oh, I do," said Antoine, cheerfully. "But Chris deserves a classic look. He's very feminine like this, is he not? I like showing off that aspect of him."

He was. He also looked—to Nicholas's surprise—intensely masculine. Not in between, but both, at the same time. It awakened strange desires inside Nicholas's chest: this duality. Chris was so wholly alive, so intensely real, that Nicholas's early assessment of him seemed now a distant dream—a shallow set of beliefs that had dissipated at the approach of daylight. Everything prior to his meeting with Chris seemed shrouded in shadow.

Chris opened his eyes to the sound of their voices. He met Nicholas's gaze, and for a moment Nicholas saw delighted disbelief in his face. Chris hadn't thought that he would truly show up. He sat very still, allowing the makeup artist to fuss over him one last time, but didn't look away from Nicholas for a single moment. Then, when she had finished, he stood quickly and came over to them. Then came awkwardness: it felt too strange to be shaking hands, as though they were strangers. A nod was impersonal and absurd. Chris hesitated, then moved in for a rapid, breathtaking hug.

"You came."

"I said I might."

"Yes, but—" Chris broke off with a smile. "Are you here to watch, or to participate?"

"I don't know yet," Nicholas admitted. "If this is a private party—"

"It's not," said Antoine, amused, and Nicholas broke eye contact with Chris. "I'd be happy to fit you in. The two of you make a stunning contrast. You don't have to decide now, though; there's plenty of time. Chris..."

"Yes, of course. I'm ready."

They moved into position. Chris was a little self-conscious, an odd reticence passing over his face. But soon this was swept away, and as Antoine had his team move up the lights and the décor, Chris arranged his limbs into position, allowed his head to loll against his shoulder, and watched the camera with half-lidded eyes.

"That's good," Antoine said to him. "Hold it for a sec."

Chris's lips curled into a smile.

They all moved with the precision of a team well used to a professional photoshoot. As the light changed, clouds moved over the sun, and time went idly by, Chris went through a succession of poses, each as self-possessed and calculated as the next. Nicholas, standing to the side with his hands in his pockets, wondered that he had ever thought him a vapid, in-sipid diva, without talent or vision. This was self-control in a nutshell. Chris's poise, his smile, the look in his eyes, the way he took in the sun—he moved like a dancer, shifting position with fluid attention to detail.

Antoine barely had to direct him. Shielding his eyes from the sun, Chris was bashful and a little shy, his face just turned away in the shadow of his arm. Hands in his pockets, staring straight at the camera, he was defiant and cocksure, his mouth cocked up in a brash smile. Crouching, elbows upon his knees. His fingers in his hair. The light through his eyelashes, cas-cading shadows. His back, turned away sulkily, and the white shirt so fine Nicholas could see the lines of his bones through it—his hair, a little mussed now, soft curls brushing the back of his neck—and then a look over his shoulder, casual and teasing and so intimate it took one's breath away.

"That's lovely," Antoine was saying. "Look back at me. Now arch your back. Now smile. There."

They took a pause one hour in. Chris took a bottle of water

from one of Antoine's assistants and tipped back his head as he drank, his eyes falling shut.

"Thirsty work," said Nicholas.

"Yes, isn't it? I like it, though. Antoine's pushy. He's always asking for more."

"Isn't that an issue?" Nicholas thought back to the number of photographers he'd worked with, most of whom had directed him this way and that without a second's thought for his own comfort. He was used to wearing hot, too-fitted suits and to sweating underneath spotlights for hours on end.

Chris seemed to thrive under the pressure. He was more visibly tired than he had been at the start of the shoot, but a live energy was running through him, lighting up his eyes. He brushed the back of his hand across his mouth, thinking about it.

"Not when it's Antoine. I trust him," said Chris, with astonishing simplicity.

Nicholas couldn't remember the last time he'd trusted someone with his own body. It was rare that he allowed himself that vulnerability; in these last few years, sex had been non-essential, and prior to that he had been too concerned with thoughts of discretion and caution to open himself up to somebody else very often. Madalena was his truest friend, but even she, who could take on the world, could not handle him when he was at his angriest and his most lonely. "That kind of friendship is a rare thing."

"It is." Chris smiled at him. "Sure you won't try it?"

Nicholas glanced at Madalena, who was peering over Antoine's shoulder as he showed her photos on his laptop. "Without a contract?"

"These pictures likely won't end up anywhere but in Antoine's portfolio. He respects people's privacy—yours and mine," Chris said, brushing his hand against Nicholas's arm. "As do I. As *will* I."

It was the first time they had touched since the kiss. Nicholas's breath caught, and Chris, with a swift little jerk, brought his hand back to his chest. Their eyes met.

Chris was the first to look away, and that moment—the slow lowering of his eyelashes as he glanced to the side—kicked up a great fracas inside Nicholas's chest. He was caught, brutally, on the very edge of a cliff so high up he could not discern what the ground far below looked like. But then he caught the hint of a blush on Chris's cheekbones, in the angled light that fell across his brow, and he found himself wanting to reach out again, to take him by the shoulders, to say—

Well, and why not? Nicholas was tired of having a body that belonged to everybody but himself. His agent, Madalena, directors, casting crews, production managers…they carted him to and fro, in front of cameras and crowds and audiences, until *Nicholas Madden* became a rich commodity, a Hollywood persona, a self out of the self. He appeared in magazines, did photoshoots for *Vanity Fair* and *Vogue* and *Premiere*; he posed on the red carpet in Hermès suits; he smiled at interviewers' bad jokes, replied scathingly to criticism, and nourished a reputation as the Big Bad Wolf of Hollywood. None of that meant anything at all. None of it mattered a damn.

What mattered was this: Chris's fingers brushing his hand, and Chris's grey eyes meeting his, without fear and without pride, only steady acceptance. It was the look of an honest man.

There were so few of them in the world.

"Antoine," said Nicholas.

Both Antoine and Madalena looked over their shoulder. Madalena's eyebrows hiked up.

"Think you could draft me a contract?"

"Sure," said Antoine, slowly. "If you're certain."

"I am."

★ ★ ★

It took an hour for makeup and costuming. The light had changed fast—it was near on six o'clock—and now streamed, golden-warm, through the tall bow windows, casting immense shadows out of nothing. Chris had his highlighter and eyeliner touched up, while Nicholas submitted to the desires of the makeup artist.

"Nothing exaggerated," said Antoine, critically. "We want a natural look, not something overdone. You *could* pull off some lipstick; but we'll refrain this time."

Chris, laughing quietly at this little speech, returned wearing cream jeans and a fitted sweater, hair lightly pulled back from his face.

"For contrast," Antoine explained. "No, keep the trousers. Hang on, we'll find you something. Here—"

*Here* turned out to be a very nice dress shirt, white as snow, which fitted Nicholas perfectly. "You were so sure I would say yes?"

"I hoped you would," said Antoine, without a hint of a blush.

"Don't mind him," said Chris in an undertone. He gave Nicholas a slow, appraising once-over, which Nicholas *felt* to the tips of his toes; then a sudden smile came to his lips. "You look *good*."

"Thanks." Nicholas's heart was beating a wild tempo.

"Can you waltz?" Antoine cut in abruptly. Startled, Nicholas broke away from Chris.

"I—what?"

"He can," said Chris.

"I...can," agreed Nicholas, bewildered.

Chris's smile was blinding. "*Wild Thing*, four years ago. I remember."

"You saw that?"

"In the theater."

Nicholas laughed. "Well, I *could*, as a matter of fact; whether or not I'll remember how is another matter."

"I'll lead," said Chris, with a bright, wicked look.

Their first few attempts were awkward. They stood too close together, then too far. Chris clasped his waist a shade too tightly, making Nicholas hiss; Nicholas tramped on his foot, and Chris erupted in nervous laughter. They were stepping in the wrong direction at the wrong time. There was no music at all. Chris was frowning. Nicholas wanted to smooth the lines from his brow.

Chest to chest, hand in hand, they tried a spin—missed—Chris stumbled over his own feet, and they veered to a stop.

"Right, yeah," said Antoine, "no. This isn't working. What's got into you?"

"Sorry," Chris said, breathlessly, and moving away. His hand pushed back against Nicholas's chest, and then...stayed there.

"I'm out of practice," said Nicholas.

"No, that's not it." Antoine's gaze on them was impersonal. Critical. Not unlike Chaudhuri's. "Both of you know the steps. You even know how to move together, and that's the main thing."

"No music," said Madalena, brandishing her phone.

"Certainly not. They don't need music. They need to get *over* themselves. Start over," said Antoine, turning his back on them. "From the window."

The next try flowed better. The following one was even graceful. Chris's hand, clasped in Nicholas's, was warm and dry; his body was a solid line against Nicholas's side, and, once he got the grasp of leading, their movements became smoother, calmer. Twist, spin, turn, look. Chris's eyes met his, full of undisguised mirth. After the first, the second, the third go, they had got the hang of it, and then they could do poses, and make every move sharp—then smooth—then sharp. They turned, turned again—switch—leg—look. Nicholas's head was spinning; he wanted to laugh, incongruously, as he had not laughed in years: Chris's amusement was undeniable, irrepressible, and all he wanted to do was to follow him wherever he led. It wasn't dancing so much as a succession of poses: Chris's hand in his hand, Chris's forehead against his, Chris's fingers curled at his waist, his thumb pressing against Nicholas's side, through the dress shirt. It felt extraordinary.

Antoine called for a pause, and Chris broke into a laugh, leaning his head against Nicholas's shoulder. Nicholas felt the vibrations of his laughter against his skin, his breath trembling against his jaw, and shivered too, one hand running up the small of Chris's back. They stood together in the sunlight, head to head, Chris's fingers brushing his side, stroking up and down.

Antoine cleared his throat and broke them apart.

"Better," he said, appraisingly. Resting his chin on his fist, he peered at his computer, switching through pictures. "Now try for something more provocative."

"What, wasn't that enough?"

"Two men dancing? Not nearly enough. Madden—" Antoine shrugged. "You know how to brood, and that's half of the work done. But, ah, Chris! You are more professional, normally! Stop giggling, *merde*."

"Forgive me," Chris said, mastering himself. "A moment of madness."

"I bet," said Antoine, darkly. "Back to your places, gentlemen."

This time they found their rhythm almost immediately. Chris had got used to leading; Nicholas only had to follow. It was a change from his usual—he was so accustomed to being the one in charge that the haze of it went up to his head. Chris moved smoothly, the bare touch of his fingers on Nicholas's enough to say *this way, like this, trust me, come with me...*

Nicholas was light-headed, as though the light itself was dazzling champagne, bubbling inside his throat. Chris was *moving* him. He did so subtly, with great care, with no intent to offend. Nicholas looked at his mouth, a little furrowed, and thought of kissing him.

He said, to avoid that outcome: "You're good at this."

"You sound surprised."

"I suppose I am," Nicholas admitted. "You constantly surprise me."

Chris looked up at him, a luminously amused glance, piercing him through. Then he shrugged the minutest of shrugs, gently pressed Nicholas to turn in time, went with him through the length of the movement, and said: "I could return the compliment. You are not what I expected—you know—at all."

"I do know," said Nicholas dryly. "I must have seemed a very monster."

"A very attractive one," said Chris, laughing.

"Stop fucking talking," Antoine called out to them, and they sobered, and covered in good time the length of the warehouse, dancing in and out of the fading, brilliant sunlight.

And then again, and again, again, until Antoine, his voice sharp and mellow by turns, declared himself satisfied. Chris's hand relaxed in Nicholas's hand. Chris's body relaxed against Nicholas's body.

"That was—" He was smiling. Then he stepped lightly away, stroking his fingers down Nicholas's chest. "Interesting."

Unexpectedly, Nicholas found he could only agree. "I don't...do photoshoots. Very often. Much less the improvised kind."

"Do you regret it?"

Nicholas let go of his hand. The last of the light touched Chris's temple, teasing his blond curls to gold, tangling in his eyelashes. "No. No, I don't."

They went out for dinner. Nicholas, gravely attentive to detail, wore the pair of glasses Chris had bought him, which delighted Chris: he tucked his hand with sudden affection around Nicholas's elbow, and said: "You see? I was right."

"About?"

"Everything." The joy in his face was contagious. Good god, he was lovely. He was so intensely charming, so catching in the light, that Nicholas felt it in his body: a sharp pain, an arrow in the heart.

"I'm glad—" He stopped, thought again, rephrased. "I'm glad you got the role, Chris."

Chris paused, in the street, shoving his hands in his pockets. He looked at Nicholas for a long moment, suddenly quite serious. Then he held out his hand.

Nicholas grasped it.

They went in to dinner.

# Chapter Twelve

**INT—Angelo's ROOMS—Morning**

FREDERICK is leaving. He has convinced himself that this will be the last time. He sits on the edge of the bed, watching ANGELO sleep.

ANGELO wakes. He doesn't say anything, but leans up for a long, slow kiss.

The bad weather held on. It rained often, and they were obliged to shoot indoors; outside scenes were few and far between, and most were so dark and so deeply depressing that Chris found himself returning to Nicholas's trailer oftener than was strictly advisable.

They worked through their lines. Nicholas was a patient teacher, for all his pretenses at exasperation, and worked with him swiftly, helping to fill in the gaps Chris was uncomfortably aware remained in his approach to acting. In another life, he would have made a good theater director. He knew how to make Chris move, act, and speak; he knew how to translate the artfulness of modeling into the artlessness of acting.

They moved between poses, debated Angelo's thought processes, debated Frederick's, rehearsed lines with as little prejudice as Nicholas was prepared to bring to the table. There was still a stiffness about him, a hard knot in the center of him, a yawning emptiness he only very rarely allowed himself to show. He had driven away people with his temper as a younger and less experienced man, and it was assumed that he was still as brash, still as dangerous, at the age of thirty-two, as he had been at the age of twenty-three. He loathed the press and mistrusted all manner of social media. No wonder. They preyed upon him like a pack of vultures.

"Too cliché," said Nicholas, when Chris shared the sentiment. His voice was a little hoarse; he had been caught in the rain that morning, and was cursing the storm.

"You are a harsh critic."

"Call them rats, if you like. Or hyenas." He was lying on the couch in his trailer, his forgotten script left half-open on his stomach. His eyes were closed. "They accused me of sleeping with every single one of my costars. Including the underage ones."

"Every one?"

"Well. Every female one. Only one male costar."

"What happened?" Chris asked, carefully. He had seated himself at the far end of the couch, legs gathered to his chest; now he put down the script, leaning his cheek against his knee.

Nicholas's hand clenched into a fist. "The rumor was swiftly quenched."

Chris's lips parted. He was reminded once more that a few years lay between them; the entertainment industry had changed, or had pretended to change, during the decade that separated their respective entry into the realm of Hollywood. Nicholas had endured that rough environment on his own, and had survived it with only bad temper as a character flaw. It spoke to his steadfastness and resolution. "That's terrifying."

"Call it Hollywood."

"Do you not find it—" Chris hesitated, wondering how to put the matter with some delicacy.

"Troubling?"

"Oppressive. Stifling. Yes."

Nicholas's eyes slitted open. "I do. But it…it becomes something one is used to. After a while, it no longer hurts. Or it does—but so far away—that it barely seems to matter, when I have been given so many chances to act…"

"Act your heart out."

"Mm."

"Is it worth it?" Chris wondered. *Would I find it worth it? Is acting that meaningful—to me?*

No. It wasn't. But he hadn't the passion for acting that Nicholas nourished. It was a live fire in Nicholas, an old echo of the ancient Greek tragedies—acting that took you by the throat and didn't let you go. Acting you lived by and died for. And if it meant alienating those around him, if it meant he walked a lonely road, trapped in the nighttime of his own mind; well: who was to know of it? Who would ever care?

Chris's chest ached.

Nicholas's socked foot knocked against his knee. "Don't make me into a martyr. I'm a very privileged man."

"I know." Chris wrapped his hand around Nicholas's ankle, feeling the hard press of bone under the skin. "Still, Nicholas, I wish that—"

"Don't," said Nicholas roughly. "Don't wish. Let's not think about it."

Chris was silent. After a moment he said: "You don't fear that people—the press—will think the same thing now?"

"That we're sleeping together, you mean."

"That—well. That filming *The Throne* means outing yourself."

Nicholas looked at him. He had the darkest, most soulful

eyes Chris had ever seen in a man. Even lying down on the couch, his head pillowed against a cushion, he was brooding. Chris had never known anyone who could brood in their socks.

"That's. Part of it, yes."

"Playing Frederick." Closeted, self-hating Frederick, who wanted Angelo so badly it gnawed at his soul.

"He...resonated with me."

Chris curled his fingers around his ankle. As protective gestures went, it was remarkably futile; but Nicholas smiled at him, a brief upturn of his lips, before letting his head fall back against the cushion. There was such trust in the gesture—the baring of the throat—that Chris felt choked with affection. He did not know when his careful examination of Nicholas had turned into outright emotion; he did not know when it had begun; he knew only that a man who let him see him at his most vulnerable was one he ought to protect, and one he ought to trust.

Chris had been a model since he was a teenager. The industry, a pitiless bucket of crabs, had shaped him. It had taught him never to trust anyone easily. He made friends, certainly, and sometimes charmed the pants off some peculiarly interesting person; but trust was harder to come by, and apart from his family—safely at home in the Dordogne—and a few rare close friends, he found that he was better off journeying on alone. Like Angelo, in his way, though Angelo was cruel and playful by turns, and Chris did not enjoy bitterness as he did. Angelo drank the last dregs of a society that repulsed him in his absinthe glass, and slept the sleep of opium-death.

Chris went through the motions of his life with an absent smile upon his lips, looking pretty for the cameras, and choosing, though he never gave anyone much joy, never to give much hurt.

There was a soft knock on the door as he paged through his script. Nicholas grunted, half-asleep, and with a sigh Chris got up and went to open the door.

He had expected Madalena. Sir Reginald stood clumsily on the trailer steps instead, his hand lifted once more to knock.

"Oh! Dear boy, what are *you* doing here?" he asked, peering into the trailer.

"Rehearsing lines," said Chris, by rote, moving back as it became obvious Sir Reginald meant very much to come in. The air was wet. It was about to rain again.

"I...see," said Jarrett, with a perceptive look at Nicholas, who had lifted himself up on one elbow.

"Reggie. What the hell do you want?"

"Be civil," Jarrett chided. "I wanted to say—" He cast a quick glance at Chris. "Well! Was I interrupting something?" he asked, with a canny look.

"Yes," said Nicholas. "My nap."

"It takes a brave man to stay in alone with Madden, you know," Sir Reginald confided in Chris. "Lion's den, and all that."

"I enjoy Nicholas's company," said Chris, blandly. Nicholas gave him a look of outright amusement, and sat up, setting his elbows on his knees. Chris, possessed with mischievousness, added, "He is a very patient teacher."

"Patient!" Jarrett seemed at a loss. "I must say, you seem to have tamed him. He is positively pleasant tonight."

"Don't try my patience," Nicholas advised. "Whatever you came to say you may say to Chris."

"Hiding nothing from each other, are you? Hm. Well. Can't say it would be the first time for costars to—well! Doesn't matter. I meant to say, they are canceling tonight's filming. Rain, you know."

Nicholas frowned. "Could Madalena not come herself?"

"That lovely girl? No, I told her not to bother; I would tell you myself. I had a few little matters to bring up—about journalists, and the proper way to speak to them, my boy, but—ah, well, it can wait. We'll have a private chat, Madden, just you and me. I wouldn't *dream* of troubling the two of you now, when things are so...sensitive."

Chris opened his eyes at Nicholas over his shoulder and saw him stifle a smile. Sir Reginald saw it, too. He was plainly curious; he could not say anything; he bowed out of the trailer with many apologies for having interrupted Nicholas's *nap*. Chris shut the door behind him and leaned hard against it.

"Oh la la," said Nicholas, dryly.

"Rumors of our mysterious but steamy affair may soon be doing the rounds among the crew," said Chris, a little rueful.

"I hope not," said Nicholas, standing, and reaching for his shoes, "Chaudhuri would have the skin off our backs for it... mine, anyway; *you* would charm your way out of the path of her wrath."

Right. Chris had not forgotten that Chaudhuri and the Henderson siblings would descend angrily upon them if they heard the barest rumor of an affair. But he had allowed it to slip his mind, to be only a distant consideration—it was so easy to lean into the desire he felt for Nicholas, to let every move, every breath be filled with simple affection. He picked up his jacket, putting it on slowly. Nicholas reached around him for his sunglasses.

"Here."

"Thanks." Nicholas didn't move away. His hand landed on Chris's jaw, and tilted it up. He hesitated, for a long, long second, and then leaned in, brushing his lips to Chris's. One kiss. Then two. Nothing more.

When he pulled away his eyes were closed. He opened them. Chris could not read his expression.

"Was that for me or for Angelo?"

Nicholas's thumb brushed his cheekbone. "Both of you."

They were due to kiss again not twenty-four hours later.

It was a hard scene to shoot. They were at it for hours. By the time an hour and a half had gone by, the frustration was getting to all of them. Chaudhuri, unhappy with their performance, pushed them and pushed them again, until Nicholas was snapping at Madalena and the makeup guy and the producing assistants, and Chris felt overheated and unhappy. A headache was starting to pound at his temples. When a costuming assistant came to put his waistcoat to rights he sat obediently, and let her manhandle him.

Kissing was a joy. Kissing was one of the sweetest pleasures in life. To fail at it so obviously, so publicly, was an exercise in frustration. To have fifty people looking on as he and Nicholas tried and failed to find the right tone was far, far worse.

Nicholas's body felt like a stranger's now. Chris could trace every line of it with his hands, and it wasn't *doing the job*.

Across the set, Nicholas sank into a chair, his head in his hands.

"Someone should check on him," the costuming assistant said. "You guys are friends, right?"

"That," said Chris, tiredly, "doesn't mean I like being barked at. He's in a dark mood."

"I get that," she chuckled. "There you are—all done."

"Thank you." He gave her a weary grin and reached for his bottle of water. Chaudhuri was talking to Nicholas in a fierce, angry whisper. Chris watched them through the crowd of PAs and cameramen and sound designers. Nicholas, folded up in his chair, his brow dark, looked like thunder and lightning. Chaudhuri probably wasn't willing to risk the storm. She gave his shoulder a squeeze, and called for order.

"Last take. Get ready. Chris!"

He got to his feet.

The previous takes had been careful, painful, and slow affairs. But whatever Chaudhuri had said to Nicholas had changed him. He glowered at Chris as though wounded.

He reached him in two strides the moment Chaudhuri called action. His hands caught Chris, cradled his head and his shoulder; pushed him against a desk so hard it knocked the breath out of him. Nicholas's mouth came down on his. The kiss became at once brutal, and hot, and *wonderful*. Chris's hands rose to sink into Nicholas's hair. His mouth opened to Nicholas's tongue.

He was aware that the cameras were swarming around them, beetle-like and watching. But Nicholas was kissing him, bracing both of his hands around him, pressing him down, his body a hard, solid line against his own. Chris moaned, more incoherently than not, and locked a leg around his hip. Nicholas's lips brushed his jaw, his cheekbone, the corner of his mouth. He nosed at his throat, kissed his Adam's apple, went lower, opening his shirt, finding skin. And the cameras no longer existed. The set was no longer real. There was only Nicholas's body pushed up against his own, only his hot mouth parting over collarbone, his tongue stroking against Chris's skin.

"*Angelo.*"

The name was jarring. Chris caught his breath. He ran his hands into Nicholas's hair, pulling him up to his mouth. He found Angelo's words.

"*Don't stop.*"

Nicholas flinched away, and the pain was drawn so starkly on his face that Chris almost believed in it. His fingers touched Chris's cheekbone, his jaw, his lips. Then he closed his eyes. *You will make me mad.*

Chris's grip tightened in his hair.

*"When I am with you,"* Nicholas said, resting his forehead against his shoulder, *"When I am with you I no longer know myself."*

*"Is there someone to know?"* Chris asked viciously. *"I do not know you. Nobody knows you. Come to bed, Frederick——there's an end there, at least, if nowhere else."*

*"Is that all that you want?"*

*"Yes,"* Chris lied, his lips numb.

At last Nicholas moved away. *"Forgive me. I hardly know what I'm doing."*

*"That is blindingly clear."* Angelo's thin-edged cruelty was easy to find. But he, too, was weary: weary of fighting and fucking and then fighting again. They were nearing the end of the story, when Angelo and Frederick's carefully self-contained myths were starting to crumble.

He and Nicholas had rehearsed this scene ten, twenty, thirty times. Sometimes they'd kissed.

More often they had not.

It hurt, now.

*"What do you want, Angelo?"*

*"Nothing. Nothing. I want nothing from you."*

Nicholas fell silent; then, with a long and shuddering sigh, he surrendered, and bent down again to kiss him. A silent kiss, this time, a quieter kiss, full of hurt and longing.

Chris felt it down to his bones. He shivered in Nicholas's arms, and, when the time came to move aside, to pull himself away, he found that he missed the warmth of him, and the immense physicality of his body. He missed the softness of Nicholas's slicked-back hair under his fingers, the rough linen of his shirt.

"Good," said Chaudhuri, later. She had sought Chris out

and found him in his trailer, wiping foundation from his face. "You did good tonight, Lavalle."

"Chris," he reminded her.

He was rewarded with one of her crooked smiles. "Not everyone stands up to Madden half so well."

Chris looked at her in the mirror, then away again. "Sir Reginald agrees with you." He was tired of the rhetoric. Did no one see Nicholas as he was? It seemed absurd. Nicholas was a brave man, a *proud* man; and yet it was impossible that Chaudhuri, as clairvoyant and perceptive a woman as she was, could not see beyond his temper. Nicholas's explosive anger at the world concealed the deepest, sweetest solitude.

"That's not what I mean," said Chaudhuri, not unkindly. "He is an extraordinary actor. Living up to his mark is not something everybody can do."

"I had the feeling he led me for a fool in that scene," Chris admitted ruefully.

"I had the opposite impression." Chaudhuri seated herself on the corner of the makeup table. "The two of you are perfect contrasts. I like that you move against him."

"Is that why you cast me?" He caught her surprised look. "You knew that Nicholas was Frederick. He knew and you knew. There was never anybody else in the running. Why choose me to play opposite him? I was barely an actor before this."

"Call it a trial by fire," Chaudhuri said lightly. "There are many reasons why I chose you, Chris. But—yes—I *was* thinking of you as opposites when you were cast. Nicholas shows pain so well. He ought to play Shakespeare—Macbeth, maybe, or Coriolanus."

"Or Angelo."

"Or Angelo," she agreed, with a grin. "We needed someone who could bring out the sweeter part of him."

"And that's me."

"It's part of you."

"I don't know whether to be insulted or flattered."

"Be neither. Be both." She reached out to squeeze his shoulder. "Be an actor."

Chris nodded, but absently so. He was conscious of Angelo, standing over his shoulder, with all his repressed urges and all his impossible desires; the line between the person and the shadow seemed thinner than usual. Angelo's emotional journey was moving so swiftly that all Chris could do was grit his teeth and hope he didn't come out the other side with a broken heart.

The trailer door opened. Nicholas came in, looking down at his phone, and nearly collided with Chaudhuri. "Oh. Sorry." He looked inquiringly at her. Silhouetted in the dark doorway, hands braced on either side, he towered above her. There were dark circles under his eyes.

Chaudhuri glanced between him and Chris, her impeccably penciled eyebrows rising. "Madden. Good: I wanted to talk to you."

"Oh," he repeated, pocketing his phone. "About?"

"There'll be a livestream of tomorrow night's filming." Her voice was disapproving but resigned. "Instagram stories, small interviews, for an online release. A lot of promotional nonsense, but the Hendersons insisted. I recommend you be more than willing to present the best of yourself. Be charming. Be gallant."

"I believe I can do that," said Nicholas, with a wry twist in his voice.

"You had better," she said bluntly. "No spoilers. Nothing negative. They'll ask about the two of you: be sure to act as friends. Fans will jump on any rumor of a fight and make a mountain out of a molehill. Don't give them the ammunition."

"Of course," Chris said, blankly.

Neither he nor Nicholas started to breathe again until she had bidden them both good-night and stepped outside. The door slammed behind her. He caught Nicholas's eye. Nicholas lifted a shoulder and dropped it again, amusement and rage warring in his eyes.

"Our roles are written for us, it seems."

"Scripted," Chris agreed, with a touch of rasping irony. Nicholas hesitated, then came to sit in the chair next to his, resting his elbows on his knees.

"Listen—"

"It's alright."

"I mean: about tonight."

Chris hesitated, and looked away. Blood beat at his throat, like a bird caged. "What about tonight?"

"It got...intense. Some scenes change when you play them—become harder. Stranger. And we get harder and stranger with them. Are you okay with that?"

Chris looked at him. Nicholas's eyes were intent on his, his mouth set in a hard, dark line. He hesitated. "Neither of us are method actors."

"No."

"And this is something else."

"It is something else," Nicholas agreed softly. He ran his hand over his eyes. "Ah. What a fucking mess."

# Chapter Thirteen

*…Tonight we are interviewing the cast of* The Throne, *Priya Chaudhuri's latest period piece, to find out the secrets of this reputedly secretive shooting. We are in Paris, France, it's nine p.m., things seem to be getting busy around here…the weather has been unreliable lately, let's hope nothing comes in the way of the filming tonight…here's producing assistant Mel Al-Amin, who will show us around the set, backstage, and even (if we're lucky!) the dressing rooms… Hi, Mel, what are we doing tonight?…*

The whispers started around nine thirty. Soon the entire cast and crew were looking alive and alert: the journalists had arrived. Mel Al-Amin, towering above them in Louboutin stilettos, led them around the set, keeping up a bland, polite, steady commentary, and diplomatically steering them away from the cameras. Nicholas kept an eye on them. They were a small team, young, starry-eyed, more than a little impressed by the fracas of a professional nighttime shoot. When Andrée, arriving unaware on set, was collared by Mel to give a sound bite and pose for photos, the cast sighed in collective relief.

"Better her than us," they murmured.

"They wouldn't care about us. They want the star factor."

"Imagine Madden submitting to that—?"

"Madden would as soon cough up his own lungs."

"Wouldn't want to risk his temper, if I were them. Why'd

they have to come tonight, anyway? Look, my makeup's all smudged."

"Nah, nah, you're fine. How's my hair?"

The extras murmured. Jason, as hapless as a newborn puppy, bounded over to Andrée and the camera crew. They were doing a tour. Andrée was smoking negligently, looking elegant and bored; Jason charmed the pants off each one of the newcomers for a solid half hour. But the camera guy was getting bold, and the interviewer had started to ask awkward, probing questions. Mel, mellifluous, diplomatic Mel, looked a little harassed.

"No, I'm afraid Priya Chaudhuri is not available for comment. We are waiting for her now… No, Sir Reginald Jarrett is not shooting tonight. We do not know… Yes, Nicholas Madden is here now; I'm *sure* he will be delighted to speak with you."

They descended on Nicholas. *Hyenas.*

The questions were slow, low-tier, and only just barely researched. He gave mechanical answers. He was proud of working with Chaudhuri again. He liked France well enough. Yes, there had been a dreadful amount of rain. No, he hadn't gone to the Louvre yet. All of his costars were excellent.

"All of them?" the interviewer, a relatively well-known journalist called Mira Everley, squeaked.

"Every one," said Nicholas.

"Even—I mean—even Chris? Lavalle? He is so—*new*," Mira Everly hedged. "Rumor says you did not approve of his casting?"

Nicholas felt himself bristle in instinctive protectiveness. "I fully trust in Priya Chaudhuri's power of decision."

"Surely there is *more* you can tell us about that. What is he *like*?"

"He likes his coffee black."

The camera guy glowered at him. Mira just looked blank.

"Chris's a good dude," Jason volunteered, cheerfully.

"Yes, but isn't it awkward? Playing lovers, I mean. I mean— with someone you don't even *like*?" Mira floundered under his stare.

Nicholas kept his voice noncommittal. "I'm sure it must be."

"I'm sure," said Chris, amused, behind him.

The interviewer squeaked again. Chris held out his hand to her so charmingly she could do nothing but shake it, then gave Nicholas an unimpressed once-over. "Have you been telling horrors about me?"

"Yes. I've divulged your coffee-drinking habits to the gutter press. May the vultures descend."

"Hyenas."

"Whatever."

Chris leaned in to say, in a mock-whisper, in Mira's mic: "The abominations he drinks cannot be called coffee. Vanilla syrup. Whipped cream. I've seen his Starbucks fidelity card."

Nicholas found that a smile was pulling at the corner of his mouth. "My reputation, Chris."

Mira got her breath back. "You—uh—um. Is it—" She gave Nicholas a failing glance, then braved onwards: "Is it very hard to work together?"

"Not at all," said Chris. "Nicholas is wonderful to work with."

"I concur," said Nicholas.

"Hush; she is speaking to me. No: truly, I would not be standing before you if it were not for him. When I have despaired, when I have thought I was not up to the task before me, he was there. Ever helpful. Never a word out of turn—"

Nicholas moaned pitifully. "I'll never recover."

Chris grinned at him. Then his smile dimmed. "I could not wish for a better costar."

"Nor I," Nicholas admitted.

"Um," said Jason.

Mira looked like she barely knew where to put her head. "That's—certainly—uh—*intriguing.*" She lunged on another tack. "Is that something you draw from? Christian Lavalle, you have only made a few appearances in TV shows before—you have never been cast in a high-budget movie—is that right?"

Chris's smile went a little rigid. "Perfectly right."

"You were not daunted by the task?"

"I was. I still am. It's absolutely daunting. But I have found real purpose in the work." That was as bland a reply as it could get—like oatmeal in lukewarm milk. Chris delivered it with a smile so sweet Mira barely noticed.

"Nicholas Madden—you have worked with Priya Chaudhuri before—is she a very harsh taskmaster?"

"Careful!" Jason laughed.

"She is," said Nicholas. "A fantastic one, too."

"Your hopes for this movie are high?"

"Astronomical."

"Why *The Throne*?"

Nicholas stilled, feeling a little caught. Mira's bubbliness had reminded him that the rest of the world did not see his involvement in *The Throne* as clearly as he or Chris did. The truth of his emotional investment, which he had kept so dearly close to his chest through years of self-repression and restraint, was starting to crack open, and light was beginning to shine through. It was illuminating entire landscapes, flooding over the world.

Then he mastered himself. "That's a very complicated question. It is a stunning story, of course. Working with the Hendersons and with Priya Chaudhuri is an honor few would dare to refuse."

"Of course," she echoed, a little doubtfully. Her gaze went to Chris again. "You were not afraid of some—presumptions— which might be made, regarding your choice of role?"

"No," said Nicholas, bluntly. Chris was looking at him, his grey eyes calm and steady. "I wasn't."

And then added: "I am not."

"I need a cigarette," said Chris, once they had made good their escape. *"Mon dieu."*

"Mm," said Nicholas.

"Are they all like this?"

"Worse."

He shivered in mock-fright. "Come with me? There's a quiet spot upstairs."

It was a balcony, overlapping the square below, the terraces and cobblestones. It had rained that afternoon, and the air was humid, the heat of July penetrating the evening; the street-lights were dancing with the shadows of the trees, casting long skeletal silhouettes across the wet pavement. In the distance, a church bell was ringing eleven. A strange sound: it was as though centuries of time were ringing the hour, cloaked in golden stone and stained glass.

"Want one?"

"No, thanks."

He watched Chris light his cigarette: the careful curve of his fingers around the match-flame. His face was, for an instant, illuminated as Nicholas imagined the old saints' heads must be, in the ancient Norman church windows; then, eyes half-closed, he shook the flame away, and the light died. Then the tip of his smoke flared red, and Chris took a long drag, exhaling in a sigh. Smoke bloomed between them, sweet-smelling and bright.

Nicholas leaned hard against the railing. He became aware, with sudden and brutal honesty, that Chris had carved a place inside his rib cage, where his affection for him lay. Real affection, barbed and bare. Emotion of a sort he hadn't felt in a very long time. A little more than a month, and Chris had opened up new paths in his chest. The dark woods were parting.

He asked, "How long have you smoked?"

"Since I was...oh, a teenager." Chris leaned his head back, holding the cigarette with some distaste. "It's a bad habit."

"But hot."

Chris smiled, eyes closing. "You would say so. I don't give in to the habit often. Sometimes, though..."

"You did well tonight."

"Yes? I hope I did. I barely knew what to say to her."

"You handled it as well as you could be expected to. Chaudhuri herself would not have known what to say."

Chris laughed, ducking his head. "Thank you very much."

"It's a good thing. You're used to attention online. But this is a different game—hyenas, vultures, and so on. The gutter press will try to fit you in a category, any category, as long as you don't conform to expectation... You'll be a whore or a martyr or a reprobate, and you'll have to smile and bear it."

"Is that what you do?"

"No, I'm just a bad-tempered asshole." Nicholas gave him a wry grin. "Angelo is only the first role. Who you present as on the red carpet is another."

"I hadn't wholly realized that when I auditioned," Chris admitted, his eyes distant. "I thought I knew exactly what I was getting into. But every day has a new revelation—people are already calling *The Throne* Oscar-bait. We have a fan base. I didn't expect the...promotion side of things...to be so exhausting, and so demanding."

Nicholas's hands felt achingly empty. Taking Chris in his arms now, when unknown cameras were swarming the set, would be a brilliantly bad idea. "For better or worse, your name is tied in to *The Throne*'s success. Chaudhuri put her trust in you. What you choose to do with it is up to you."

"Have I *your* trust?" Chris asked brutally.

Nicholas glanced at him, then reached out to take the cigarette from his fingers. He brought it to his lips. The smoke sank into his lungs, lovely and ashy and foul. "Does it matter?"

Chris was staring at his lips. "It does. To me."

Nicholas took another slow drag, swallowing the smoke, then handed the cigarette back. Their fingers brushed as Chris took it. "Do you trust *me?*"

"Not to make my coffee. No; but I do," said Chris, with a very French shrug. "It's the strangest thing that's ever happened to me. I didn't expect to find a friend in you."

*Is that what we are? Is that* all *that we are?* Friendship was the last thing Nicholas needed. Compassion came with strings attached; recompense and gratitude made relationships into exchanges of power. He didn't want Chris to pity him. He had always wanted an equal.

The thought went unsaid; but Chris must have seen it in his face. He reached out to cover Nicholas's hand with his own.

"Nicholas—"

"Don't."

Chris's grip tightened. "Shall we play pretend, and claim nothing is wrong?"

"Nothing is wrong. Let it go, Chris." Nicholas pulled away, and shoved his hands in his pockets, staring somberly down at the square below them. The streetlights flickered, shivering. After a moment Chris leaned against the railing next to him; he sighed, but said nothing, and only smoked another cigarette. The bright, sweet smoke rose in the air between them.

The phone rang at fuck o'clock the next morning.

Nicholas, whom the streaming sunlight had for once not woken early enough that forming coherent sounds without caffeine intake was a challenge, grunted. The ringing did not stop.

"*God*. Fuck. What."

He found the phone buried underneath a mass of cushions. "What?"

"You sound like shit," said Slater, unsympathetically. Nicholas winced. He rolled over and pulled a pillow over his head. "What the fuck is this?"

"What the fuck is what," demanded Nicholas, eyes closed.

"This publicity stunt you did last night. Why was I not informed? Why the hell did I not sign off on this?"

"Stunt—oh. That."

"That," said his agent, dry as the Sahara desert. "You and Christian fucking Lavalle, hamming it up for the cameras. Do you know how many views you've garnered in the past six hours?"

"I have a feeling you're about to tell me."

"Half a million, Madden. Half a million people watched you flirt with the French pretty boy. And boy *oh* boy *do* they have something to say about it."

A chill stole through Nicholas's lungs. "What do you mean?"

"I mean I've had three requests for an official comment on your sexuality, and it's barely midnight on *this* side of the pond. People are asking if *The Throne* is an opportunity for you to make your way out of the closet. Now—stop me if I'm wrong—but I remember you insisting that coming out was not anywhere near the fucking horizon. I *vaguely* recall that Priya Chaudhuri does not look kindly on her cast doing the horizontal loop-de-loop behind her back. I *emphatically* remember telling you that consummately reinventing yourself was, is, and will for the foreseeable future be an idiotic career decision. Did I misremember any of that?"

Nicholas sighed. "No."

"Wait until you're forty-five, I said. Call it a midlife crisis and get yourself a boyfriend half your age, I said. Wait until they call you daddy on Twitter."

"For god's sake, Jim—" But he was wincing. Slater wasn't wrong; he was just an even worse asshole than Nicholas was.

"He's got to be good in the sack if you've decided to ruin your best shot at ever playing for Costa or Melchior again. For your sake, I hope he is."

"I'm not fucking Christian Lavalle," Nicholas said, finally, having exhausted all other avenues of thought. *I'm not fucking him* was his last line of defense. It was the only thing he *could* say without perjuring himself.

"Then why the hell are you mooning over him all over the news?"

"It can't be half that bad. We're a small, intimate cast. *The Throne* isn't under any kind of spotlight."

"Tell that to BuzzFeed," Slater snapped. "And the Academy Awards next February."

Nicholas's phone pinged. He put Slater on speakerphone and glanced at his notifications. Fifteen WhatsApp messages from Madalena. Eighteen emails.

*Well, shit.*

Nothing from Chris. But one email was from Chaudhuri's PA, which was an ill omen. Nicholas groaned, and dread settled in his chest, heavy as lead.

"There you are, then," said Slater, with uncompromising smugness. "Am I going to have to come to France, or can you shut up the boy toy before he blabs?"

"He won't talk." *Fuck.* "Don't call him that," said Nicholas, tiredly. He disliked the roles Slater was putting them into—as though the fault alone resided in Chris; as though their feelings for each other did not resonate through him every time he thought of him.

Slater let a pregnant pause settle uncomfortably between them. "You're *sure* you're not fucking him."

"Positive," Nicholas snapped, somehow finding a measure of gravity. "Chris is as possessive of his intimacy as I am. Perhaps more so. Banging the Big Bad Wolf is not going to help his career take off."

"Really," said Slater, doubtfully. "Looks pretty plausible to me. Bag an A-list actor and you're in tabloid fame forever."

"He doesn't care for the tabloids," Nicholas said shortly. "Nor do I," he added, sitting up and throwing off the blankets. "Look, you don't need to come. It'll blow over as soon as the filming is over."

"And if it doesn't? Should I have a backup plan ready for you? I can call around, see if any starlets need a boost up to—"

"I'm not going to fake date some poor girl just to keep people from trash-talking me. They've done it before; they'll do it again. They'll have a different target next month."

Slater sighed, a great elephantine sound. "You gotta understand, Madden. Mike Costa wants you in his next production this fall. There's plenty of offers waiting for you now—you'll have your pick of 'em once you come back to the States. *And* you're long due a golden statuette next winter, if I'm any judge. Would be a shame to throw that away for a pretty piece of ass."

Nicholas gritted his teeth, but Slater's words hit home. *The Throne* was not the end game of his career; he had to think in absolutes, had to think long-term. Mike Costa was one of the most acclaimed directors in Hollywood. "I'll talk to Chaudhuri."

"Be sure you do. Keep me posted."

Slater hung up. Nicholas flicked through his messages—increasingly worried ones from Madalena, an astonishing number of unknown callers, and the dreaded email from Chaudhuri's PA, which noncommittally desired his presence with her production manager and the Henderson sibs at noon. He was still shirtless, in his socks, and glaring down at his smartphone when Madalena's hasty knock came on the door.

"Wow, well. You look like shit," she said, when he opened it.

"So people keep saying." Nicholas shrugged on his shirt. "What's the hellscape like?"

"Have you seen the BuzzFeed article?"

"I haven't. Slater rang me up."

She groaned.

"Chaudhuri wants a word, too. All the king's men and all the king's horses. Hell, Em." He scrubbed a hand over his face, all too aware that he was exhausted, shell-shocked, and in dire need of coffee. "I don't know what to do about this. I don't know that there's anything to do at all."

Madalena didn't answer. He looked at her. She was biting her lip, and frowning. "What?"

"I don't see you like this often."

"Under-caffeinated and grouchy?"

"Scared."

Nicholas stopped in his fruitless search for his shoes, then dropped down heavily on a low armchair. "I'm blowing this out of proportion."

"Maybe just a tad. This isn't the first time you've been rumored to sleep with a cast member. What makes this different?"

Eyes closed, Nicholas made an eloquent gesture. "Chris." To his own ears, his voice was uncomfortably warm, and for a second, behind his eyelids, he could almost imagine Chris there, in the room with him, rising from the couch to perch on the arm of his chair. Close enough to touch.

"Oh," Madalena said, and there was unbearable understanding in her voice now. "Have you talked to him?"

"Not yet."

"Coordinate your statements, then." She perched on the back of the couch and prodded his foot with her boot. "You're good at acerbic put-downs. Brass it out, act the way you do—be proud and imperious and cavalier with people's softer emotions—the world will forget about you by next week."

"Until some dickhead with a camera and an obsession catches me standing too close to Chris. Or anyone else," he added, wryly.

Madalena paused. Her eyes were sad. "That's the hazard of the job."

"I know."

"There are worse things than the world discovering you're human," she said softly. "Look, if you do want to come out—"

"I don't. I thought that—I don't know what I thought. *The Throne* was an opportunity, perhaps. Slater was dead against it; *is* dead against it; but I wondered… Oh, fucking hell. I'm tired."

"You really don't look so good," said Madalena, with a trace of concern. "Have you been sleeping?"

"Like the dead. My throat is hoarse, that's all."

"I'll buy you some cough syrup."

"I'm fine, Madalena."

"You don't *sound* fine."

Nicholas hedged, feeling like a coward. It was easier to deflect. "I'm perfectly capable of buying my own medicine."

"I'm your PA," she pointed out, reasonably. "Talk to Chaudhuri. Get a few days off. The weather has been horrible lately; everyone on set is coming down with a cold."

"I'll take your word for it."

"Come on." She hauled him to his feet. "I'll make us some coffee."

# *Chapter Fourteen*

**miraeverly**
♥ ♥ ♥ at these candids from last night's #thethrone-
livestream! Click thru for impromptu interviews with @
andreebelfond, @jasonkirkhall, @chrislavalle, and even
the elusive Nicholas Madden himself! Sir Reginald was
not available for commentary, but Belfond, Kirkhall, and
Lavalle guided us around the set of Le Renard d'Or.
Dream team!! 😁
Link in bio!
#thethrone #thethronelivestream #spoilers #spoileralert
#candids #ilovemyjob #sweetandsalty #lerenarddor
#parisnight #dreamteam #lavallenation #visionaries
#moviestars #cinema #art
15 hours ago
1,298 likes

**lavallenation** 👍 👍 👍

**parisgurl999** jason pLS

**babydonthurtme** Is that?? A smile??? On Nicholas
Madden's face????

**navigatemutual** this cast is gold

**mindhooves** I can't wait for this movie to come out!!
Why is january so far away ☹

"I'm sure you understand."

"I do," said Chris. "I'm not sure what I can do about it."

Katherine Henderson gave him a slightly forced smile. "Priya understands that neither one of you intended for any subtext to be inferred from your actions. We know where the mistake stemmed from, of course. Nicholas is so private a person that his friendship with—well, anyone at all—must be surprising to many. It's true, nonetheless, that we did not expect his relationship with *you* to develop so well."

"He's a good man," Chris said, carefully. There was plenty else he could have said about Nicholas—*he's the bravest person I know*, and *I want to be with him all the time*; he knew, though, that their producer would scent out the truth of his words like a shark scenting blood.

"He's certainly an excellent actor. Priya wishes for you both to keep your eye on your work, at least for the time being. Don't talk to journalists unless they've been personally approved by my team. Candids…" She made a *what can you do* gesture.

"I wasn't planning to talk to journalists."

"Then I don't think I need to keep you any longer," she said briskly. Her smile became more genuine as she walked him to the door. "Don't let them intimidate you. It's a rite of passage, really—the longer you stay in the business, the easier it'll be to ignore. Of course," she added, with delicacy, "you are used to the spotlight…don't worry. It will die down soon."

Chris walked out of her office, thoughtful and troubled. He had not expected the interview to have such an impact;

he doubted anyone had, much less Mira Everly, who, having discovered internet fame, was milking her fifteen minutes of glory for all that they were worth. His own Instagram account was blowing up with comments and DMs. Fans were going back through his stories and posts, looking for content about Nicholas, repeatedly messaging him with demands for contact.

Turning off the comments would, he knew, only have the worst intended effect. Posting nothing would heighten the rumors; posting about something unrelated would see him accused of burying the lede; addressing the gossip would only fan the flames. There was simply no way to win.

He made his way to the set. Jason, cheerfully shirtless, was getting fitted for an outfit. He caught Chris's eye, and waved him over with enthusiasm.

"Baby's first scandal," he said, beaming. "Proud of you, man."

"I could have done without it," Chris said dryly.

"Aw, it'll die out in a few days. Look at me—they're always on my case for dating so-and-so. Who knows how many people I'm supposed to have slept with. Hundreds, prolly."

"But you *are* dating people," said Chris gently.

"Well, yes. But that's the thing: that's *my* life. I love people. I love dating girls. They're soft, and they're lovely, and—" A sudden flush darkened his ears. "And I like it when they take control," he added. Chris smothered a smile. Jason, shrugging, grinned bashfully and added: "So I don't mind it when everyone is on my case for dating a beautiful woman, right, because hey! I should be so lucky."

"That's a nice philosophy in life."

"Always appreciate your partners," Jason agreed. "Not just the romantic ones, either. Look sharp—here he comes."

Chris looked around. Nicholas was walking on set, impeccably dressed in slacks and a white shirt, engaged in profound conversation with Chaudhuri. Well, and there went the option that he might speak to him before the authorities got to him. Fleeting sadness passed over Chris. He'd hoped that whatever was happening between Nicholas and him could stay, for the time being, private.

Falling for him felt like taking flight: a jump, heart in his mouth, and then, suddenly, the wind…

*Falling for him.* He frowned to himself. He'd not put it into words until now. But that was what it was: foolish, wonderful infatuation. He loved watching Nicholas move; he loved listening to him speak. He loved his long, graceless hands. A word of approval from him was worth a thousand compliments in someone else's voice. Chris wanted Nicholas's eyes on him when they were shooting: it was a staggering thing to put so much trust in one man, and yet his trust had come easily, painlessly, almost unnoticeably. Even now.

Nicholas and Chaudhuri had stopped on the edge of the set. Nicholas lifted his head and met Chris's eyes over her shoulder.

He looked haunted.

*Ah.* Well, that settled that. No doubt their friendship—such as it had been—would no longer be convenient for him to continue. Chris took in a breath, then turned away.

"Rough, buddy," murmured Jason.

Chris smiled at him, and made his way to the makeup trailer.

Nicholas found him there, an hour later. He popped his head in, took one look at Valérie, and said: "I can come back."

"No, I'm nearly done," she said kindly. "Come on in. Do you need a touch-up?"

Nicholas lingered in the doorway, hands dug deep in his pockets. "No. I wanted a word with Chris."

"Well, wait until I'm finished with the powder and I'll leave you to it," said Valérie, with prompt discretion. She made good on her word, finishing up and gathering her materials in record time, and brushed past Nicholas with an encouraging smile. Nicholas looked after her, then seemed to...sag.

"Hell." He leaned his head against the door.

Chris watched him silently. Nicholas scrubbed a hand through his hair and said: "Have you talked to Chaudhuri?"

"Katherine. She assured me that they knew nothing... untoward...was going on." Uncomfortable, Chris shrugged.

"That's one way of putting it." Nicholas gave him a wry grin. "Are you alright?"

The question took him by surprise. "I've lived through worse." He meant it, though he could not remember a time when his feelings had been so intemperate. Nicholas was clearly feeling the pressure of the expectations that were put upon them, and Chris was uneasily aware that this pressure was worse for a man who was not out of the closet. He knew he had to cherish their present relationship: it could all fall apart so easily. "Are you, Nicholas? You stand to lose more than I do if—well. You know."

"Chaudhuri puts her utmost trust in both of us," Nicholas said, by rote. He shook his head.

Now that Chris could take a better look at him, the haunted look was not an impression. His face was drawn, the lights of the makeup trailer casting his features into interesting angles and shadows—stark black lines, the bold stroke of his mouth, his straight jaw, the dip of his throat under his collar. His eyes very sunken under dark brows. And his voice was roughened, like old bark rasping against the throat.

Chris reached up to feel his forehead with the back of his hand. Nicholas blinked, very quickly, but submitted to his touch. His skin was clammy.

"Are you coming down with something?"

Nicholas groaned. "*Et tu?* Madalena is convinced I've contracted the plague."

"Madalena cares for you."

Nicholas's eyes fell shut, and he leaned slightly into Chris's touch. "Yes, well."

"If nothing else, you should take some ibuprofen—stave off the flu."

"I don't get sick," Nicholas said, long-sufferingly. "I haven't been sick in years."

"Then it would be a very sorry way to start, wouldn't it?"

Nicholas huffed out a laugh. His eyes were still closed, his lashes a dark sweep against his cheeks. When he opened them, the depths in those eyes were enough to make Chris's mouth dry. He didn't say a word. Just that deep, honest look, as though he was watching the gears in Chris's head work.

"You have a very strange idea of keeping it professional," Chris murmured.

"You make me strange."

"Mr. Madden?"

Nicholas jerked away. Chris's hand hovered in the air for a moment before he slowly put it down. A young woman with a PA's headset and a red afro was standing irresolutely behind them. They were silhouetted in the trailer's door, the bright light coming from within, gilding their bodies in pale gold. And they had stood intimately, heads close together, Chris's hand cupping Nicholas's face—

*This isn't helping our case.*

"What is it," said Nicholas roughly.

"Ms. Chaudhuri wants you and—and Mr. Lavalle on set in five minutes."

"Fine."

She lingered awkwardly.

"Is there a problem?" Chris asked, as Nicholas tensed beside him. He could not deal with Nicholas's temper now. Nor, by the look of her, did *she* want to.

Her chin tilted up. "*The Throne* matters to all of us, Mr. Madden. *All* of us. We don't like malicious gossip any more than you do. So don't worry about—about the crew talking behind your back. We won't. Even though you're a real beast sometimes," she added, with a defiant look.

Incomprehension flickered across Nicholas's face. He was shocked into silence and stillness for a long moment—long enough for the girl to start fidgeting again—then said slowly: "I...will keep that in mind."

Then added: "Thank you."

She nodded, clutching her clipboard against her chest, and fled.

Chris's laughter was irrepressible. "What loyalty you inspire."

"Chaudhuri chooses her people well." But Nicholas, ducking his head, was smiling.

Nicholas's voice became more and more hoarse as the month progressed, and the weather, as predicted, turned gradually for the worse. When August came, it came with dark skies and heavy rain, and Paris took on a blueish tinge, as though the cascading water had stained its buildings and its streets. It grew cold, and thunderous, as utterly un-summerlike as June had been a true month of spring.

Chaudhuri, much like the rain, never let up. Her schedule was demanding; her expectations were higher than they had ever been; she did not care any more for the bad weather than she did for such minor hardships as a broken camera, which had to have parts shipped in from the States, or the leg-breaking slipperiness of some of their on-set locations. Her actors braved the cold and the sleet for her; her crew, teeth chattering, stood in the deluge with parkas and hoodies, clustered around thermoses of scalding hot coffee.

Around them the Parisians went about their daily business with only a few looks of interest, streaming in and out of metro stations, their heels and umbrellas clattering against the wet pavement.

Then the rain became a torrent, and they were forced to switch exclusively to indoors scenes. Nicholas came to work early and left late. He read, over and over, the script he knew by heart. He worked with Chris on every scene, hammering out the minutest detail, so that every take could bring in more emotion, more concern, more despair. He abided no weaknesses and no mistakes, and seemed, in his quiet, relentless determination, willing to carry *The Throne* on and through to completion if he had to do it alone.

And yet he was tired. The lines of his face stood at a sharp contrast; his eyes seemed all but carved in. Chris did not think that he slept very much. He was wholly focused on the task at hand. Nothing mattered so much as the work.

It was a sentiment shared by cast and crew alike. There was a brightness in their eyes, a fever in their words. Every scene was jarring, heartbreaking, backbreaking: every scene a star slowly imploding, folding in on itself, going nova. Angelo and Frederick loved and hated and fucked and fought their way through hell, and the whiplash between passion and bitterness and horror put everyone on edge.

Chris adored it. The times when he acted with Nicholas were precious, glittering moments, and those when he was separated from him were blunt, dull, and obscure. They worked together on their characters' voices, and Nicholas was brilliant and considerate. They *worked*.

"Come on," he said, taking Nicholas's arm at the end of a punishing workday. "Let's get some noodles in you."

"We should rehearse," Nicholas said stiffly, before breaking into a hacking cough. *"God."*

"We'll rehearse," Chris said. "Come on. Some hot broth will do you good."

"Hot broth," Nicholas muttered disbelievingly. But when they arrived in the small, crowded ramen shop in the rue Saint-Anne he perked up somewhat. "This place is snug."

"Yes; don't you think?" Chris pulled out his chair. Nicholas glared at him, but sat, with a soft groan. He didn't speak at all until the noodles came, and then, streaming chili oil in the broth, said:

"Alright. You've made your point."

"If you mean to scare every PA on set with that scowl of yours," Chris said, not looking up, "I won't stop you."

"I don't." Nicholas swallowed, wincing. "I don't mean to."

"I'm starting to get that." Chris sipped his soup. "Now tell me."

"What?"

"You're a clever man. A brave man," he added, when Nicholas gave him a look. "You're an actor, Nicholas. I love watching you act. But playing Frederick is terrifying you. Why do you do it, then?"

Nicholas was silent. His chopsticks drummed a nervous beat against the table. He stopped abruptly, put them down, and said: "Call it a measure of protection."

"Against?"

"I don't know. The world, I suppose."

"Hollywood, distorting reality?"

"Cinema is...complicated. Acting is simple; acting is foolishly simple. Hollywood, with its celebrity status, its A-list and its B-list and its C-list, its defenders and its haters, its conspiracy theories, its nepotism, its award shows and dirty votes and fashion *faux-pas*—that is a lot to take on. All the time. Without respite."

"Is that what you want?" Chris asked. "Respite from the tumult of the world?"

Nicholas shrugged, coughing into his sleeve. "Isn't that—I guess everyone wants that. A place to rest. A coming-home."

"The eye of the storm," Chris murmured.

"Mm. This is good," Nicholas said, poking at his bowl. "Yes. I don't know. *The Throne* has meant so much to me over the years that not being part of it was unimaginable. I wanted it to be a real thing. A true thing. There's not a lot of truth out there."

*And you insist on truth*, Chris thought, watching him eat. *You expect everyone to show you who they are; and when they refuse to it hurts you. You're tired of liars, and pretenders, and fools—and you fear that you are a liar, a pretender, and a fool.*

*I can see you. I didn't for the longest time, but I do now.*

"And then," said Nicholas, not looking up, "Chaudhuri cast you."

"And I was fake."

"I thought so. My god, I was so damn certain you were. Instead—" Nicholas's eyes would not meet his. He was unexpectedly shy. The flu, Chris surmised. "You were true with me. There was an honesty about you."

"Faint praise," Chris laughed. "I don't feel real most of the time, Nicholas." There had been moments in his career, in his youth, when he had believed that the persona he was putting on the screen or on the stage were the real him; he now knew better. His character was endlessly divided. Who was he, outside of the Twitter hashtags and the modeling contracts? Who was Chris Lavalle when he was alone, facing his own loneliness and severity?

His relationship with his parents was a dead end. He had

few close friends. He had a million followers on Instagram, and they expected him to be smiling, to be charming, to sell them a perfect Parisian fantasy.

"Then you *are* a good actor. But I don't think that's all it was. You wanted to seduce me, that night, in the Golden Fox. Not me," he added, impatiently, when Chris opened his mouth in outrage. "You wanted Angelo to seduce Frederick—and he did. He did. You got me good."

"I," said Chris, distinctly, "am not Angelo."

"And I'm not Frederick. But they might as well be ghosts, hanging over us."

That was troubling. Angelo's flightiness and selfishness sometimes seemed all too real. Frighteningly so. Chris looked down.

"Once," said Nicholas, "you asked me if I thought Frederick belonged to me. And I do, in some measure. I have grown to like and dislike him so much that embodying him—his narcissism, his self-hatred—becomes second nature. But I don't hate myself, Chris, any more than you are going mad with absinthe and opium..."

"You're dedicated to your work."

"It's the only thing that matters. Don't you see? It's the only thing that makes sense."

Chris set his spoon down, swallowing. Nicholas was so certain, so beautifully earnest. He could see the value in this form of thinking: acting had become for him the chance to express ugly sentiments he was normally scared of confronting.

"And what about you?" he said softly. "I don't disagree, you understand. Anyone who sees you act can tell how much the part matters to you. It's stunning work. When you move, when you speak—there's nothing else. There's *no one* else."

"You see me," said Nicholas, with sudden, soft wonder. "That's it."

This was so close to Chris's own thoughts that he couldn't help laughing. "My god, Nicholas. Am I hallucinating this conversation? Are you?"

"It would help if we were part of a video game simulation, wouldn't it? Then there would be parameters to follow, and code to build on. Instead there's nothing but human behavior, and we're beasts, all of us, and we have to piece it all together star by star..." He sneezed.

"You're sick," said Chris. "I'm going to take you home. *And* call Chaudhuri," he added. "You can't shoot if you're hacking up your own lungs."

Nicholas looked mulish and stubborn, but he stood by while Chris paid, and then waited patiently on the curb for a taxi as a fine rain began to drizzle once more. "I'm fine," he insisted, coughing.

"You sound like you've swallowed a tornado, Nicholas."

"Acting," said Nicholas, not very coherently. "I like the way you say my name."

Chris stared at him. Then, with great tenderness, he slipped his arm through Nicholas's, and pressed it against his chest. "Come on, actor mine. Get in the cab."

Nicholas stayed close to him as the car navigated the darkened streets. After a while he leaned his head against Chris's head and closed his eyes. In the sweeping, golden streetlights, his face was tense and pale. There were dark circles under his eyes. *Tired*, Chris realized. *Exhausted*. He wasn't sleeping. And he had caught a cold. He was coughing weakly, and his hand was hot against Chris's thigh. After a while Chris caught it up in his own and held it tight.

"Hey," he said, to the driver. "I changed my mind. Take us to the rue des Saints-Pères."

## Chapter Fifteen

*"…it looks like we're in for a good stormy summer here. The skies will be dark for the next four days over the north of France, with heavy rainfalls and thunderstorms coming in from the east to cover the entirety of the Ile-de-France, Normandy, and Picardy regions. Temperatures are falling, and they're falling fast… Paris is sending out a flood alert for the 1st, 4th, 5th, and 6th arrondissements; take care out there, folks, and stay warm…"*

Nicholas woke to the soft, muted voices of the weather forecast. For a long moment he could not understand where he was.

He was lying in a bed that was not his bed, in a room that was not his room. It was late, and it was dark. Rain was falling against the window, a steady patter. From time to time a car passed down in the street below, its engine roaring in the near-silence, and white lights swept through the blinds, arcing over the ceiling and the walls. Then it fell away, and the room was in shadow again; only the blueish tinge of a laptop screen shone, gilding the edges of a window seat, a bookshelf, a desk.

The muffled voice of a presenter spoke gently through the quiet. Nicholas could not follow what they were saying. He was so tired. And the bed was warm. A fat duvet covered him.

He closed his eyes. He slept a while longer, and then woke again, abruptly, to a feeling of oppression and closeness. He tried to push himself up on one elbow, and that alone took all the fight out of him. He fell back against the pillows, breathing a little harder, and tried to think.

He remembered. The taxi ride, his head against Chris's shoulder, and then running, ducking out of the rain, pushing through a heavy door into a well-lit foyer. The stairs, narrow and close. Chris's hand in his hand. What had come after he could only very vaguely recall: Chris had told him to sleep, had said he would—call Madalena. Yes. Had found him clothes. Nicholas, feeling sluggish and slow, had put on the pants and t-shirt he had been given, and had crawled into bed without a second thought. He had been asleep before Chris had come back into the room.

Chris. He was sitting in the window seat: the laptop was balanced on his knees. Asleep? Perhaps. No; his eyes were open. He was watching the screen.

"*...lightning strikes...*"

"Hey," said Nicholas. His voice came out rough and very, very hoarse.

Chris glanced up at him. "Hey." Gently, he lowered the laptop screen and set it aside. He was wearing a soft-looking sweater and a pair of black jeans; his face was tired and his smile was wan. There were dark circles under his eyes, made starker by the light of the laptop, and, from time to time, a bright stroke of lightning illuminated all of his soft edges and angles.

"What time—?"

"Around three a.m."

"I'm putting you out of your bed," Nicholas said, without much conviction. The thought of getting out from underneath the warm, fluffy duvet was unbearable.

Chris tucked his hair back behind his ear, looking, quite suddenly in the dark, a little shy. Nicholas found the gesture unbearably endearing. "I don't mind. You should sleep."

"Work—"

"Is not happening tomorrow. The rain. Sleep."

Nicholas nodded weakly. He was slipping under again.

Then it was afternoon. The light had changed, though it was still raining, harder now, and the sky was like dark slate. He felt like hell warmed over.

Chris was gone. The laptop had been put away neatly on the desk, and a blanket was folded up in the window seat.

Nicholas tried to sit up, failed miserably, and had to fight down nausea. He settled back against the pillows, closing his eyes and battling the urge to be very, very sick. His head was pounding hard enough to break bricks. The light through his eyelashes was painfully bright.

The door opened. He heard Madalena take in a breath, before she came into the room and closed the door with a soft *snick*.

"You awake?"

"Hmmmm," said Nicholas, too tired to form words.

She came in and sat on the bed, folding up her long legs underneath her. "You look terrible."

"Thanks." His voice was gravelly, like old rust. "Where's...?"

"Chris? I got him to lie down for a couple hours. He stayed awake all night, poor fool. Are you up to drinking something? I've medicine for you to take. And we should get some liquids down your throat."

Nicholas opened his eyes a fraction to look at her. "Chaudhuri—"

"Has canceled the next four days of shooting. Apparently the whole crew is coming down with something—even Jason came in this morning with a sore throat. Our bright, beautiful summer! Anyway, there's a storm forecast. We wouldn't be able to shoot in the Palais-Royal Gardens if we wanted to."

Nicholas closed his eyes with a groan. "What a mess," he croaked.

Madalena's cool hand came to rest on his forehead. "You're very hot."

"I know."

"Cheeky. Here."

She helped him drink a tall, cool glass of water, and he levered himself up enough to swallow a couple of tablets. It was enough to exhaust him all over again; he sank back down, shivering hard. Madalena gathered the blankets about him, gentle as with a kitten.

"I haven't felt this terrible in…years." Nicholas kept his eyes shut: the light itself was painful.

"You've been running yourself ragged." Madalena's voice was quiet. "You don't take care of yourself, Nicholas. I don't like to think what could have happened if Chris hadn't brought you home. What would you have done: come to set and fainted in front of the whole crew? Where is your responsibility to *The Throne*?"

That seemed wildly unfair. "My responsibility is in showing up."

"Showing up doesn't help a soul if you collapse." She sighed, and her hand fell on his, lacing their fingers together tightly. "I worried. When Chris called me, I thought you'd been taken into the ER."

Nicholas squeezed her hand with as much strength as he could muster, which wasn't much. "Shouldn't. I'll be—" he sneezed, so violently it must have taken years out of his life "—alright."

"Obviously," she said dryly. "Get some more sleep. The doctor said you'd be out for twenty-four hours, and it's not been ten since he saw you."

"Doc—?" Nicholas said drowsily.

"Came this morning. You swore at him."

"Did I," Nicholas murmured, but already the long tendrils

of sleep were trailing into his bloodstream, and the bedcovers were becoming very, very heavy indeed.

He woke with a clearer head, though his throat burned, and he had a pounding migraine. He had no idea how long had passed—it could have been a year as easily as a second—but Madalena was gone, and the light had all but faded. A lamp was turned on in the window corner; the rest of the room was darkening into slow, tender, blue shadows. Chris was sitting where he had sat the night before, cross-legged underneath the lamp. The light cast the gentle slopes of his features in bright contrast, his grey eyes clearer and paler than they had ever been. There were still dark circles under his eyes, but he was wearing reading glasses.

Nicholas made a caveman-like grunt, and Chris looked up, smiling quickly. "Hallo. You're awake."

"Perceptive," Nicholas said huskily.

"*And* rude. I'll chalk that up to your feeling better." He had been reading; he put the book away now, and crossed the room. He was wearing a loose sweater, the long sleeves falling over his wrists, and a pair of grey, baggy sweatpants. It was, in fact, the most underdressed Nicholas had ever seen him. Even his hair looked a mess. A fuzzy, soft-looking mess.

His brain-to-mouth filter must be broken rather badly, because he said: "You look—good."

Chris's eyebrows hiked up. "I'm afraid I can't say the same. You look horrible."

Nicholas winced. "Mince your words, won't you."

"Sorry." He didn't sound sorry at all. "Sick and sweaty isn't a good look on anybody. Can you sit up?"

He could, though with some difficulty. Chris helped him to the bathroom, where Nicholas took a much-needed piss, and then looked with some dread at the shower. The need to be clean weighed heavily against the effort it would take to get there. Still, though, it would have to be worth it; he couldn't abide the feeling of the t-shirt stuck to his back and armpits.

In the end, the shower was not the dragon he had feared: the worst of it was getting out of the cubicle, when his head swam into white and he had to sit heavily down on the toilet seat. Chris had tactfully left new clothes on the rack, warm from the dryer, and very soft. Sweatpants. A black t-shirt, which was a little snug on Nicholas, but felt amazing against his sensitive skin.

"You hungry?" Chris asked, when Nicholas emerged, wet-haired and weak-limbed but happy, from the bathroom.

Nicholas's stomach quivered. "Let's not tempt fate. I've managed not to vomit yet."

Chris gave him a look. "I can think of something," he said, and brought him warm milk, something Nicholas hadn't had anybody do for him since he was eighteen. Warm milk and honey, and crumbling shortbread, buttery-sweet and perfect. They ate together in complacent silence, as the rain doubled down on the windows and the sky darkened to the purplish brown of a bruise. Nicholas watched Chris, who was absorbed in thought, his cheek resting against his fist.

When Chris caught him staring, he gave him a quick, wistful smile. "I have to admit," he murmured, "when I thought about you in my bed, this wasn't quite the scenario I imagined it would be."

Nicholas's laugh was a rasp. "Lusted for me, did you?"

"Badly," said Chris, very seriously. "Every night."

Nicholas's mouth quirked in a rueful smile. A confession was on the tip of his tongue. *Yeah. Me too.* He reached out and touched Chris's hair. It was exactly as soft as it looked.

Softer.

"What *are* you doing." Chris stayed still, though, letting him touch. When Nicholas cupped his cheek he smiled, and leaned into it, covering Nicholas's hand with his own. He glanced up at Nicholas through his eyelashes.

"You're lovely." Nicholas brushed his thumb against his cheekbone. "Have I told you that?"

"Not in so many words."

"I should have told you many times." Nicholas was conscious, suddenly, of a sadness, rising and rising within him. "I'll miss you when you're gone."

Chris, looking stricken, ducked his head to kiss his palm. "Where am I going?"

"Anywhere. You'll be a star after this. You'll take Hollywood by storm."

"What makes you think I want to?" Chris said quietly.

"Don't you? I thought you must."

"You and everyone else." Chris sighed. He took Nicholas's hand between his own, rubbing his fingers against his palm. It tickled. "And sometimes I do too. I hardly know what I want, Nicholas. *The Throne* feels like an opportunity. What comes after...comes after."

"An opportunity," Nicholas echoed.

"Yes, perhaps. A chance to be real. *More* real, I mean, than I am when I post pictures of myself online, or act in the small-bit soaps you think so materialistic, so vain. I *feel* myself becoming vain and materialistic. There's no writing in it, no real chance to act. When I had a chance to audition for *The Throne*, I thought I had that one shot. Strange, isn't it? I feel brilliant when I am next to you. I don't feel unreal. It's not something I'm used to—like I own my own body for once."

Nicholas squeezed his hand. "Come here."

Chris bit his lip, but let himself be tugged over against Nicholas's side. "You'll make me sick."

"Don't care."

He laughed. "Isn't that my line?"

"Shhh." Nicholas petted his hair, threading his fingers

through the fine curls. With a sigh, Chris tucked his face against his neck, and closed his eyes. Nicholas felt the brush of eyelashes against his skin. "How much did you sleep last night?"

"Not very much," Chris admitted. His breath was cool against Nicholas's heated skin. "I thought someone ought to keep an eye on you. Madalena was worried. She would have come in at two in the morning, if I'd let her."

"She's protective."

"As are you." Chris's fingertips rubbed against the collar of his t-shirt, where it met his skin. "You've been carrying the weight of *The Throne* on your shoulders for weeks. Took a fever to take you down."

"Stop speaking nonsense."

"Alright. Then…" Chris pushed himself up and captured Nicholas's mouth with his own.

Nicholas made a very soft sound, and kissed him back, opening his mouth, tracing his teasing teeth with the tip of his tongue. Chris cupped his jaw and stroked the line of his brow down to his ear. "Hang on," he murmured, and moved over to straddle him, resting his weight carefully atop him: his knees on either side of Nicholas's hips, his hand braced against the pillow. He kissed him again, lightly. One kiss, then two, lips barely parting. He tasted of honey and butter and milk.

"Whatever happened to not getting sick?" Nicholas asked against his mouth.

"I had a cold in April." Chris nipped at his lip, then kissed it. "I'll risk it."

Nicholas laced his fingers in his hair, took a good grip, and pulled him down.

Chris curled up again on the window seat that night, when they managed to separate long enough that sleeping became an option. Nicholas yawned in the middle of a kiss, and Chris leaned back, laughing, and booped him on the nose.

No one had booped Nicholas's nose since his little cousin's kitten. He'd been ten at the time.

"No, really," Chris said, removing himself demurely to the window seat with a blanket and a book. "You have fever sweats. I'd rather be uncomfortable than clammy hot."

That was fair enough. Nicholas didn't like it any more for it, though.

"You look distressed."

"Hardly."

"Proud, too." Chris turned on the little lamp and sat in its halo, running a hand through the hair Nicholas had thoroughly messed up. It floofed like spun gold. "It's a good look on you."

"Everything is a good look on me."

Chris hid a smile. It showed, though. There was something brilliant in his face, in the circle of light around it, that took Nicholas's breath away.

Then again, it might be the light-headedness. Nicholas lay down, bringing the duvet up and over his shoulder, and propped himself up on one elbow, looking at Chris. "Tell me something."

"What?"

"Why did you start modeling?"

Chris traced a finger down the spine of his book, looking thoughtful. "I was approached by an agent. I was…oh, sixteen. And I liked fashion—I liked the stylishness of it. I loved it for a while. The posing. Framing my body in different ways. Then Dior booked me as a main, and…" He made a slightly helpless hand gesture. "That was that."

He leaned his head back, looking at Nicholas through half-lidded eyes. "It took me a long time—years—to recognize that the industry is…rotten, where it matters. I still love fashion. But I loathe its lack of body diversity and its racism. Most models I know, especially women, suffer from eating disorders. Most models of color can't get a break in the industry. There's no space for LGBT representation, either, except when it's hot to have two girls embracing on a magazine spread. That's why I—after a while, I switched from mainstream fashion to more niche spots. I'd gained enough clout that I could make choices. I worked with photographers who wanted different body types, different skin colors. Trans people. Disabled people. Photographers who show beauty in everyone…" He took a breath, and gave Nicholas a wry smile. "I can get passionate about this."

Nicholas thought about it, with a little flush of shame. He was conscious that he had, early on, imagined Chris as shallow, petty, and trivial; someone who was not capable of such thoughtful commentary on his own career. Nicholas had been the shallow one in truth. A dull sense of admiration and culpability pounded through him. "I'm guilty of stereotyping, I know. You called me out on it the day we met."

"Yes, well. I'm used to it. When I moved into acting, most of the commenters thought the same way."

"Still. You shouldn't have to deal with that." He added: "I'm sorry."

Chris's eyes softened. "You don't have to apologize."

"I believe I do."

They were silent for a moment. Chris was touched, he could tell; but the thread of the conversation was lost.

"I wish you were with me," Nicholas murmured, a little helplessly.

"I am with you."

"In bed, Chris."

Chris's smile essayed a return. "I wish that too. Maybe later." He glanced out the window, and the light fell on his hair, his eyelashes, his cheek. His profile, limned in gold. "I love storms. Everything is heightened during a storm."

"Larger than life."

"What a strange saying." Chris's lips curved. "Does fame make you larger than life? Is that what happened to you?"

"No. I was always like this."

"I wish I'd known you then. Before."

Nicholas rolled over onto his back. "You might know me now," he said, meaningfully.

Chris laughed. "What happened to taking it slow? Or—well, not taking it at all?"

Nicholas had no reply to this. It was true that, until the very second he'd collapsed in Chris's bed, he'd not intended to take their...their shared emotions...anywhere closer to what he could very tentatively term a relationship than they had been before. But Chris was so *soft*, so lovely, so lonely, and the bed was so large and so very, very warm. It was a shame to be alone in it, when kissing him was sweeter than honey. The weight of his body against Nicholas's —the brush of his hands against Nicholas's chest—the touch of his fingers in his hair—his mouth opening under Nicholas's mouth—it had all felt like a mere expansion of who they were. They had been set on a path, and they had found each other in the journey.

Chaudhuri never had to know. Whatever happened, he was certain of this. Neither Chris nor he were so inexperienced that they would make the mistake of hurting their respective careers with a short-lived *affaire*. But they had this moment. This night, with the lamp burning and the sound of the rain. These short few days until filming started again.

"What are you reading?" he asked, instead of answering.

Chris's expression flickered. *"Rebecca."*

"Ah. Appropriate, of course, to the occasion."

Lightning struck, illuminating Chris's face.

There was something bleak in Chris's eyes. He looked away. "Go to sleep, Nicholas."

# *Chapter Sixteen*

## [RPF Thread]—#50

REMINDERS! READ THIS BEFORE YOU POST
- NO VIOLATING ANYONE'S PRIVACY.
- we mean it. no doxxing. don't look up actors' homes. don't FOLLOW them home. DON'T LEAVE GIFT BASKETS ON THEIR DOORSTEPS.
- seriously, just don't. you will be banned.
- remember that fiction =/= reality. tinhat and theorize all to your heart's content, but a) at the end of the day, you don't know these people, and b) you are not allowed to interfere in their lives.
- don't body-shame. anyone. ever.
- content warnings for triggery material are appreciated.
- weekly discussion posts roundup [here].
- be civil and courteous to each other, mods will delete if appropriate.

The full rules can be found here.
Questions to the mods go here.

**immortaldeath**
So…about that *The Throne* vid…
Madden/Lavalle, y/y?

**aimeesays**
So much yes. I've kept it to myself in the LavalleNation thread,
but I've been calling it for WEEKS.

**immortaldeath**
I've been following Madden for literal years and I've never,
ever seen him act like this with a costar. I mean. He was smiling? Like, genuinely happy-style smiling??

**mme999**
it's kinda sad that this is so rare ☹

**immortaldeath**
Tbh it adds to his mystique. 😀

**peacefulnewt**
imo no. lots of costars act like that.

**sika11**
Madden doesn't, though.

**peacefulnewt**
not convinced. come at me when you don't stan an asshole

**babydata**
lol don't even bother peacefulnewt HATES madden

**peacefulnewt**
so? lmao you sound so triggered that someone doesn't like
ur fave

**sika11**
I was just trying to have a conversation............

**aimeesays**
Fwiw sika11 I agree. Madden is notoriously standoffish with his costars, but with Chris he lights up. It's like the good time-line version of him.
I can't wait to see this movie, y'all! They look so good together in real life, what are they going to be like onscreen?

**unautrejour**
same same SAME. Have you seen what Chris has been posting on insta?
video of him and Madden in his(?) trailer
pic of Madden in the makeup chair
Madden on set before shooting

**immortaldeath**
Oh my god

**babydata**
Welp, I shipped it before but now I'm ready to tinhat. Who approved this??

**smolder**
oshit i see it lmao

**unautrejour**
Ahhhhhhhh *chef's kiss*

Chris woke at six with a light heart and a crick in the neck.

He slipped out of the bedroom without waking Nicholas, who had burrowed underneath the duvet and now slept on, uncaring of the world. An odd change from the Nicholas of two days ago, who had raged and fumed against the universe; an odd change from the Nicholas of two months ago, who had resented Chris's very existence.

Chris had a shower, long and cool, and then very thoroughly went about his hair care routine. He needed the distraction. The familiarity of each step and each pause gave him a certainty, a steadiness of thought he'd sorely lacked the last few days. Madness, to bring Nicholas home. He should have taken him back to his hotel and entrusted him to Madalena's care. Madness to have Nicholas in his bed, to hear his low, sensual voice speaking to him quietly in the dark, to see the shape of his body just barely touched with light. Chris had slept lightly and badly, and wanted nothing more than to crawl into bed with him.

Padding into the kitchen, barefoot and shivering, he put on the kettle and cranked up the heating. He was dogmatic about his coffee. He bought the beans fresh and ground them coarsely. Then the French press, carefully maintained and much beloved.

Then toast. He couldn't swallow eggs or bacon at this unholy hour of the morning.

The coffee was hot and smooth, with a smoky sweetness in the aftertaste. The sky outside was just as dark, burning with the lights of the city below. Chris lived on the last floor of a nineteenth-century building in the rue des Saints-Pères, just below the attics; the apartment was small, with high, slanted windows in exposed wood, and corresponding doors.

He was pouring a second cup when the bedroom door opened. Nicholas came in yawning, and went to him directly, slipping both of his arms around Chris's waist, as though, for all intents and purposes, he belonged there: pressed up against his back, the long, firm line of his body radiating warmth, his face tucked against Chris's neck. His breath was soft against Chris's hair.

"Good morning."

Nicholas's voice was sleep-roughened, though it had lost the coarseness of a sore throat. His hand slipped underneath Chris's shirt, splaying over his lower abdomen, where Chris was ticklish and absurdly sensitive. Chris closed his eyes, pressed back against him, testing the strength in Nicholas's thighs, the solidity of his shoulders.

"Hi."

Nicholas groaned, his lips open against Chris's neck. "Nnngh." He peered over his shoulder. "That coffee?"

"Fresh and hot."

"*God.* You're a wonder."

"I'd get you a mug," said Chris, "if you let go."

"I don't particularly want to."

"No coffee, then," he laughed. "But only ask, and I'll do it." He turned around in Nicholas's arms, and found him bleary-eyed but awake, and rather grumpy about it. His eyes were dark and tired, his hair a royal tangle; his mouth was set in a sulky, overly proud line. The black t-shirt was doing wonders on him. It was a shade too small, and the stretch across his chest and around his arms was very, *very* nice. Chris reached out to trace the muscle of his bicep.

Nicholas flexed.

Chris was still laughing as Nicholas kissed him.

"Coffee," Nicholas murmured, between kisses. "Huh." He pulled away long enough to cup Chris's jaw in the palm of one hand, and then leaned in, licking across his lower lip and into his mouth. It was a very light, very curious kiss, utterly unlike Frederick and Angelo's passionate embraces: no desperate plea for affection this, but affection itself, gentle and probing.

Nicholas's nose brushed against his. Their lips were only just parting, and in the spaces between there were worlds of meaning, unsaid but tangible, as though they understood at a word, at a touch, how emotion should be shown. Emotion given and accepted.

Then Nicholas kissed the corner of his mouth, then the line of his jaw. He nuzzled against his neck, pulling down the collar of his loose shirt, pressing his lips against every inch of skin he bared. The t-shirt slipped over one shoulder, and Chris shivered as Nicholas's mouth brushed his collarbone. He slid his fingers in Nicholas's hair. Tugged, experimentally.

A shudder went through Nicholas, and he pressed him harder against the counter, so that Chris caught the tail end of his meaning and hoisted himself up, separating them for a bare, longing moment before Nicholas spread his knees and crowded against him. Nicholas's hands on either side of his face cradled his skull; Nicholas's mouth met his mouth, opened underneath his, gave thanks.

The sky was markedly darker when they parted. As they caught their breath, with Chris's forehead pressed against Nicholas's shoulder, and his hands stroking absently up and down his bare arms, a shout of thunder roared through the house, and lightning forked, so close, so close together they could not have said which came first. Nicholas started.

They looked at the window.

Another thunderstrike—overhead, this time, almost. Chris laughed; the sound was torn out of him, unexpected and marvelous; and he caught Nicholas's smile, his falsely dejected shake of the head.

"End of the world."

"End of the world," Nicholas agreed. He touched his fingertips to the soft corners of Chris's eyes, to the soft corners of his mouth. "I don't mind."

"Neither do I—except," Chris said, "that it will hamper with the filming…"

"Filming will stand for a few days."

"Can you bear it?"

"So long," said Nicholas, with a world of understatement in his voice, "as I can stay here."

"You might want to call Madalena," Chris said, without making much of an effort to move away at all. "Make sure she doesn't risk fire and thunder."

"Mm." Nicholas brought him close for another, breathtaking kiss. Then he complied, pushing away with some regret. Chris cleared his throat and cleared off the counter.

He gave Nicholas his privacy while he talked on the phone, and reheated the coffee, which would have to do. He added a truly distressing amount of whole milk and sugar to one mug, and then came and handed it to Nicholas, who accepted it with a thankful nod, and lifted the mug to his mouth.

Those biceps. Chris bit back the want of it.

"...no need, Em." Nicholas sipped his coffee, and his eyes shut in pure pleasure. His next look at Chris was full of mischief. "Chris takes proper care of me. Lots of fluids. And bedrest."

Chris opened his mouth in protest, then closed it. Nicholas's mouth quirked up.

He was an *asshole*. Chris adored him.

"If you go out in a thunderstorm, I will fire you," Nicholas continued, distinctly. "It might as well be the apocalypse... No, I don't need—well, what I need I have here." A pause. "None of your business. Go back to bed, Em."

Chris nursed his coffee. The ceramic sides of his mug were warm against his palms. He found something inexpressibly touching about Nicholas now: in sweatpants, hair a mess, stubble on his jaw. He felt possessive, and jealous of anyone who had ever seen him like this, jealous even of himself, of the moment, the second, when he had had Nicholas in his arms.

"What on earth are you thinking about? You're smiling."

"Is that spot in my bed still open?" Chris said, before he could talk himself out of it.

Nicholas gave him a smile so startled, so brilliant, that he seemed another, much younger man altogether. Chris barely had time to put his mug aside on the counter before Nicholas reached out for him again. He let his hands settle on Nicholas's waist, unhesitatingly proprietary. Nicholas seemed pleased about it, though. Not threatened, but taken in.

"Come on, lover," Nicholas said against his ear. "Come on. It's been too long."

They ran into logistical problems. Unlike Frederick and Angelo, they were not so transported with joy and rage that it blinded them to the engineering of a successful love scene.

There were clothes to get rid of, and the occasional awkwardness of a sock refusing to come off, of Nicholas struggling with his too-small t-shirt, until Chris, laughing, helped him pull it over his head, and threw it away. And then the Problem of Kissing—they were getting distracted. Much too tempting to lose themselves in the easy pleasure of mouth moving against mouth, of slick tongues and roving hands. No wild throes of passion these: just standing in the middle of the bedroom, half-dressed and kissing, unhurried, with their arms around each other. Chris's arousal was a purring cat, laid out in the sun. No need to hurry. Nowhere to be.

"Oh, hello," murmured Nicholas, as Chris's palm brushed against the bulge in his sweatpants. The fabric was so faded, he felt the heat of him through it, the long, hard line of him. "Mm."

Chris explored, delighted, as Nicholas's hips stuttered at his touch. It was an easy task to pull down the sweatpants over the ridges of his hip bones, over the swell of his ass, and to let it drop—

Nicholas wasn't wearing any underwear.

"Oh," said Chris, not very coherently.

Nicholas's fingers tilted up his chin. "Eyes up."

He seemed wholly at ease. His eyes caught Chris's, tender and full of laughter. The harsh, disapproving man Chris had met in the Place Colette seemed light-years away.

"Now you."

"You'll be the death of me," Chris said, laughing, but he obediently removed his shirt, and stepped out of his own sweatpants. Nicholas hummed, tracking down the length of his body, moving backwards to get a better look at him; and for a moment they admired each other.

Naked, feet planted a foot apart, thighs strong, his thumb rubbing absently against Chris's hip, Nicholas was a gorgeous animal, with a repressed, lazy strength he showed without boasting. A great deal of pride, though, and a knowing look.

"You're not half bad, Lavalle."

"Thanks," Chris said dryly. "You're alright."

He touched Nicholas's chest, stroking up to his shoulder, curving his hand around the curve of his arm. Kissed him there, where the collarbone met the shoulder, and felt a hard shudder go through Nicholas. Chris's lips brushed his skin again, and Nicholas sighed, and bent his head, and nuzzled against his throat. Both of his arms came around Chris's neck; his fingers found their way in Chris's hair.

"This is a very peculiar love scene," he remarked, voice muffled.

"No script."

"No. We'll have to improvise."

"Get on the bed," Chris said.

Nicholas's eyebrows rose, but he obeyed. He obeyed with such readiness that he pulled Chris down with him; they fell backwards on the mussed-up duvet, legs tangling in their eagerness. And that was fantastic, too, the full sensation of naked skin against naked skin—Chris had taken it for granted for years, it seemed, had never quite understood how really, really *good* that sort of intimacy could become. It was nothing more, in the grand scheme of things, than what he had done with a dozen other men.

And yet—

Chris straddled him. Their hips jolted against each other;

yes, Nicholas was hard, his cock full and heavy against Chris's thigh. Chris reached down and curled his hand around him. He gave him a long, slow pump, and Nicholas's head went back, his fingers knotting in the pillow.

It was his turn to be incoherent. "Oh."

"Good?" Chris kissed his half-open mouth.

"Fuck. Go slow."

Chris went slow. He went so slow that Nicholas swore at him. He was braced half on top of him, one knee pushed in between Nicholas's thighs. He traced the line of his eyebrow, and watched as Nicholas's eyelashes trembled. Nicholas was an intemperate lover, a demanding lover, never satisfied; he worked against Chris, caught the rhythm and made it his own, sought his mouth. Time became elastic. There was nothing other than the slick glide of skin on skin, and Nicholas's low groans of hard-earned pleasure; nothing other than his own arousal, neglected but not forgotten; nothing other than the urgent want to watch Nicholas come.

He wanted to hold him when it happened. He wanted to see what he looked like, that proud, arrogant man, when he was finally all caught up in joy.

Nicholas came with a shout. He pressed his head back against the pillow; his muscles were taut, and his thighs were trembling. Chris worked him through it, riding out the hard movement of his hips. He didn't stop stroking him. Nicholas's hair was very black against the white pillowcase. Nicholas's body was rigid, as impossibly beautiful as the statue of David: each line, each smooth curve, as well-worked and as well-made as the finest marble.

He came down from it slowly, shaking. His mouth was open. Chris kissed his cheek and eased off a little. When he let go Nicholas took in a shuddering breath, and curled in on himself, stroking one hand down his chest, as though in search of the same pleasure.

"Chris." His voice was all torn up. "Fuck."

"One moment." Chris rolled away, reaching over the side of the bed for a tissue. Nicholas grabbed his wrist and weakly pulled him back. "I do have to clean up."

"Don't care."

Chris's voice shook with laughter. "Give me a second."

Nicholas made a displeased sound, but let go. He pushed himself up on his elbows, still breathing hard. His hair was matted to his neck where he'd pushed his head into the pillow.

Chris dropped the dirty tissue on the bedside table—something he would no doubt regret later, but for now couldn't bring himself to amend—and came back to lean heavily against him, smiling as Nicholas's arm curled immediately around his neck. He pressed a kiss against his shoulder. "Liked it?"

"*Liked* it," Nicholas repeated scornfully. "You don't have to ask."

"I suppose not." Sweaty and pleased to hell and back was a good look on Nicholas: he looked like he'd lost years of sorrow. His fingers were lost in Chris's hair, drawing pleasing trails down his scalp. Chris pressed his lips to his cheekbone, and hummed, smiling, when Nicholas's mouth found his. He was a marvelous kisser—deep and soft and inexpressibly powerful—and his hand on Chris's chest was warm.

"What—" Nicholas asked, between one kiss and the next "—do you want?"

"Me?"

Nicholas hooked an ankle over his. "Do you plan on remaining unsatisfied?"

*Oh.* "Oh."

Nicholas's knee pushed a little against Chris's groin, pressure and pleasure all at once. "My hand, or my mouth?"

# Chapter Seventeen

**The Throne** @thethronecast • 9m
Due to unforeseen weather conditions in Paris, filming this week has been suspended. We'll post updates as the situation continues. Stay warm, folks...

"God. Um." Chris had lost all power to speak, it seemed. "Whatever you prefer."

Nicholas had to smile. There was precious little light in the small bedroom, and now that he'd caught back his breath from the *spectacular* orgasm Chris had somehow given him, he found there was a great deal to admire by it. Chris's body was long and lean, elegant. His cock, half-hard against his thigh, was much the same. Nicholas pushed him gently on his back.

"Are you—oh."

"Oh," Nicholas repeated, settling between his legs. He smoothed his hands down Chris's thighs, parted them easily, hooked them over his knees. Chris was leaning back against the pillows, wide-eyed and amazed. He looked utterly glorious.

Nicholas kissed his knee. Chris's leg jerked.

"Are you—oh, *merde*. Okay, this is happening." Chris's accent came out more fully when he was aroused, a fact that Nicholas shouldn't find charming, but did anyway. "Are you sure?"

"Dead certain." He'd never been more so.

He wrapped his fingers around Chris's cock, gently lifting it from his belly, and brushed his thumb against the slit. Chris's breath came out of him in one long rush.

It was a bit awkward to bend over like this. He moved back enough to lie on his stomach, and lifted one of Chris's legs over his shoulder: much, *much* better.

He pressed his lips against the soft, soft skin of his sack, and Chris made a faint, punch-drunk sound in the back of his throat.

Nicholas licked a long, dirty stripe upward, and took him in his mouth. It was a very, very long time since he'd done anything like this—years: way back to when he was twenty-two and much of an arrogant idiot—but body memory kicked in, and he adapted fast. The taste went from strange to familiar in a half second, and then it was a hot, silky-smooth hardness, swelling against his tongue and pushing in. Nicholas swallowed around him, sank down a little deeper. Chris's hips jerked.

"Oh, god. Nicholas—"

"Mmmm." The groan was muffled. He pulled away enough that he could lave his tongue around the head of Chris's cock, then took him down again, bracing his hands on Chris's thighs.

"You're doing so well," Chris whispered, and something in Nicholas's bloodstream sang at the praise. "I—oh, oh, oh, do that again—"

Still polite, even now. He touched Nicholas's head, his fingers haplessly threading through his hair, but never quite pushing, never pressing in deeper. Stunned appreciation fell from his lips, fine as champagne.

Nicholas found that he liked it best when he had his dick buried down his throat, *just* on this side of uncomfortable, and could feel every tremor of Chris's thighs under his hands.

He had forgotten how much he loved this—his lips stretched around something large and heavy and hard and silky, the convulsing swallowing of his throat around it, the almost-pain that stretched into unbearable pleasure. His own cock was well spent, yet he could have gone again; he *wanted* to go again. Chris's breathing was coming faster and faster. His words had faded into soft, whining sounds, almost sobs, half French and half English, all pleading.

"Nicholas, Nicholas, I'm—oh! Don't—I'm going to—"

Nicholas pulled away reluctantly. He opened his mouth against Chris's hip bone, against the soft, soft skin between his groin and his thigh, tracing the long lines of muscle with his tongue, and took him the rest of the way there with his hand, jerking him off fast and sweet. Chris trembled. He came almost in slow-motion. His hips stuttered one last time and a harsh gasp was torn out of him; his thigh tightened over Nicholas's shoulder and pressed him close as slickness spilled over Nicholas's hand.

Nicholas kept going until Chris was whining softly, all the way past pleasure into delighted pain. He panted up at the ceiling, caught, for the first time since Nicholas had met him, in pure, absolute selfishness. It was a good look on him.

It was a *fantastic* look on him. As was pleasure, and the flush on his cheeks. He looked like a man well fucked.

Nicholas levered himself up, ignoring the momentary feeling of loss as he reached for the box of tissues. He cleaned him off carefully. Eyes half-lidded, legs spread, Chris let himself be manhandled.

And that was unexpectedly hot, too—the awareness of trust. It felt tangible between them. It didn't hurt that Chris looked fucking gorgeous like this.

"Come back," Chris murmured, and Nicholas—helpless against him—went.

★ ★ ★

Nicholas's stomach growled as he kissed a trail down Chris's chest.

"The romance lives," Chris noted cheerfully. "There's left-over pizza in the fridge."

Nothing sounded so appealing as cold junk food straight from the fridge. "Perfect." Nicholas pushed himself off of Chris and off of the bed. It was freezing out of the duvet, and he scooped up the sweatpants he'd abandoned as he went to the door.

When he came back, balancing a plate and two glasses in one hand and a bottle of water in the other, Chris had managed to emerge from under the duvet. He had not, however, managed to entangle his legs. His hair was a wild riot of golden curls.

Nicholas leaned against the doorjamb and looked grave.

"You should probably put on some clothes," he murmured.

"Am I distracting you?"

"I'm sorely tempted to jump you again," Nicholas said solemnly, bending to put down his offerings on the bedside table. He didn't miss Chris's appreciative look at his ass. "Pizza?"

"Please—I'm starving."

"Four-cheese," Nicholas remarked, sitting cross-legged next to him. "Good taste."

"I have *excellent* taste, as befits you, in my bed. Pass me that sweatshirt."

Nicholas handed it over. It had a Sorbonne logo stamped in maroon letters across the chest, and fell a little too large on Chris's lean frame, but at least it covered all potential... assets. Shame. On the other hand, there was something to be said in favor of the sudden appearance of modesty. It meant Nicholas could look at him without wanting to screw him into the mattress.

They ate cross-legged on the bed, too hungry to bother with manners, finesse, or restraint. The water was straight from the fridge, and cold enough to make Nicholas's teeth ache. His body ached, too, in infinitely more pleasant ways. He felt calm. Detached. Happy. The sensation spread out from his rib cage, a glowing little sun. It was like greeting an old friend.

"You look good like this," Chris said, prodding him with his toes.

"Debauched and dissolute?"

"Well, half-naked, to start with. Have I succeeded in a debauchery?"

"I should think you have," Nicholas said dryly. "As I am, presently, in your bed."

"*On* my bed. And not, presently, kissing me, which fails us both on the debauchery front."

"I find the taste of pizza thoroughly unromantic."

"Mm. Nicholas Madden, concerned about the softer emotions. Revolutionary."

Nicholas captured his ankle and dragged him closer. "I'll show you revolutionary. Come here."

The last of the pizza was left untouched and forgotten. By the time they emerged from the bed for the second time and lugged themselves into the shower, it was nearly four. Chris cranked up the heat as far as it could go and pulled Nicholas with him into the cubicle, stroking his hands down his hips and ass, soaping him up. It was absurd, Nicholas thought. He'd never taken a shower for any other purpose than the most pragmatic, and Chris made the whole expedition feel like a romantic overture.

Perhaps it was. He sank his fingers into Chris's dampened hair and cupped his neck between his palms, kissing him very thoroughly, until Chris made a mellow sound of sheer appreciation—"Mm, oh"—and opened his mouth. They were caught in a rhythm, rocking hips and wandering hands, until they were all but slow-dancing under the water, holding on to each other.

"We ought to call Chaudhuri," Nicholas said, when the last suds of shampoo were washed away and the water was turned off. Chris, reaching for a fluffy white towel, gave him a solemn look.

"Should I be concerned that you're thinking of our director while naked with me?"

"I'm trying to think of something *other* than you, naked, in my arms."

Chris threw the towel at his head and went out into the bedroom, promising to find something to put on. It was a nice sight.

Nicholas dried himself off. He barely recognized the man in the mirror, with his wild hair and his look of near euphoria. He couldn't stop smiling, and couldn't be bothered to care.

The phone call was blissfully short. Chaudhuri seemed preoccupied; she congratulated him on *staying with Chris to rehearse* without a trace of irony or distrust. Then Madalena: *she* made it two sentences before pausing, and abruptly saying: "Did you fuck him?"

"*Em.*"

"God. You did. Well—" Her voice was troubled. "Congratulations?"

Nicholas sighed and sagged against the bedroom door. Chris was crouching in front of his dresser, pulling out clean clothes. He cocked his head in Nicholas's direction, lifted his eyes to his. Nicholas shrugged, inelegantly. "I trust you can remain discreet about it."

"Please," Madalena said, scornfully. "You'll betray yourself before I betray you. Not that you should," she added, as an afterthought. "Chaudhuri would be furious."

"I know. Thanks," Nicholas said, to Chris, accepting the clothes. His fingers brushed Chris's, and he let himself linger. His thumb. His palm. The inside of his wrist, soft as anything. Chris leaned against him, the warmth of his skin like a little sun. Nicholas's hand wrapped around his waist.

"I'll leave you to it, shall I?"

"*Thank* you, Madalena."

The rain was not abating. It was late enough in the day that the sky was pitch-black, and the outline of the rooftops only barely visible in the deluge. In the small bedroom, though, the lamplight was golden-warm, gilding the edges of Chris's body. Nicholas watched him pull on the Sorbonne sweatshirt and a pair of old jeans, and was touched, for a moment, with the insanity of the situation. He hadn't been with another man in nigh on four years. It hadn't seemed…important. Jim Slater was right: it made economic sense not to come out until he was well into his forties and no longer leading man material. Once he had an Oscar or two under his belt—he was well aware of his own talent, and saw no point in watering down his chances—odds were he would be bankable regardless of his sexuality.

In the last decade, Hollywood's treatment of queer people had apparently changed in what felt like drastic and new ways. It put up a front of acceptance. But the hypocrisy rankled behind the scenes, still. Chaudhuri was one of those rare exceptions who would create stories for queer characters in ways that were not cliché, tragic, or martyrizing. The industry still teemed with discrimination, ingrained prejudices, and deceptive hiring practices.

And Nicholas had seen fit to obey those directives and bow to that hypocrisy.

Chris had come into the equation and changed every parameter. Nicholas could not, it was true, imagine what a serious relationship with him would look like. They lived half the world apart, and Chris was seven years younger than he was. *His* career was just taking off, while Nicholas was a known quantity. It was an absurd notion to imagine that they would keep this intimacy, this closeness, if they had to deal with paparazzi and privacy violations on a regular basis.

It was terrifying that he was tempted to try anyway.

He looked away. The bedroom *was* small, and cramped, and the bed took up most of the space; Chris had evidently favored comfort over capacity. The bookshelves were well stocked, though, mostly with French mysteries and historical fiction— not that surprising, considering. Some loose pictures were fanned out, not quite on display, but not quite hidden away.

"Your parents?" Nicholas asked, curious.

They were a middle-aged couple, caught in the middle of a lush dinner party, hand in hand, glancing with comically similar expressions of cheerful awkwardness at the camera. The woman had Chris's golden hair, and something about her mouth was very like him, too—a tendency to smile, perhaps. Her husband was taller, and in his square jaw and frowning brow was an obstinacy that marred the fondness of his expression.

"Yes," Chris said shortly.

Nicholas glanced at him. Chris put his hands on his hips. "You don't get on well?"

"No. They're very religious."

"Hence your name."

"And my distaste for it," Chris said, shrugging. He had been brought up within strict parameters. His parents had expected him to be moderate in his behavior, moderate in his appearance, moderate in his political opinions. They had not expected him to splash out his life online, nor to publicly advocate for positions they despised. "They weren't enthused about having a gay son, much less an agnostic one." He shrugged, stiffly and unhappily. "They live in the country; I don't think they're often on social media. My work doesn't affect them in any way, and still they disapprove of it. I warned them that I had got the part of Angelo, and..."

"And?"

"They didn't care. They'd never heard of Chaudhuri."

"Or me, I should imagine."

"Well." A rueful smile played on Chris's lips. "I didn't tell them about you."

"Take care, Chris. My pride has suffered many blows since I met you; I don't know that it can bear another." But the hurt look in Chris's eyes did not fade. Nicholas put down the photographs and slipped one arm around his waist. "You alright?"

"The storm." Chris leaned his forehead against his shoulder. "Electricity in the air. Bit of a headache."

"Right." Or, far more likely, he didn't care to talk about his neglecting, exhausting parents. Which was fair enough, but a familiar curl of anger coiled in Nicholas's stomach nonetheless. It was just as well the Lavalles lived away from Paris. He would *dearly* have liked to give them a good piece of his mind.

"Do we risk thunder and lightning? I want to go to the bakery down the street."

"For croissants, huh," Nicholas murmured.

Chris's smile became a shade more genuine. "I was thinking bread. Sandwiches. For tonight—oh, hell, it *is* night."

"Then I'll go down with you."

It was still raining, and the streetlights were steady golden glows in the darkened street, reflecting on the wet pavement and car windshields. No one around. Paris was sleeping under an enormous casket of lead. In the distance a pharmacy sign was blinking on and off, and the faint roar of a bike cutting a corner was deadened by the rain.

Chris, the hood of his sweatshirt tucked down over his blond curls, did not look at him as he caught Nicholas's hand in his. He stuffed them both in his coat pocket, out of the cold. A deep font of fondness rose in Nicholas then, and he had to swallow it down, force it away, lest he give in to the inevitable and kiss Chris where he stood. Perhaps against a doorway. Or against a car.

The bakery *was* open, its windows all fogged up in the cold and wet, but bright, and warm inside, smelling of hot bread and caramelized sugar. A young woman sat behind the till; she did not look as though she knew them, and only a little sullenly moved away from the space heater to answer Chris's entreaties. A loaf of spelt bread and a cracking baguette were set down on the counter, soon joined by two fat sandwiches and a fruit salad.

"Anything else?" the girl said listlessly.

"No, thank you. You're very brave to be open tonight," Chris said, in French, with a sudden, bright, winning smile. She blinked under the onslaught, and the tips of her ears pinked.

Typical, Nicholas thought, distantly amused, of Chris, to be charming the heads off everybody he met. *Including me.*

Yes, he *was* charmed. He had taken for himself the privilege of knowing what Chris looked like in bed, when his hair was in his eyes and his heart was in his throat. He knew, too, how Chris kissed, how he moved when he had sex, how deep and sweet his voice went when he pleaded for more. None of it would have mattered a damn if it wasn't for the way he looked at Nicholas: really looked, without prejudice, without pride, without exception, but only in his eyes a strange disbelief, a deep, troubling affection. Whatever it was, the emotion between them was close to a radio wave, an unending loop, that snagged and bounced back—and became stronger and stronger the longer they stayed on one station. It was unnerving. It was (god forbid) incredibly exciting.

Nicholas was thoughtful as they returned to the cold street, bags in hand. Chris looked at him, his pale eyes luminous in the semi-light, and didn't push.

Nicholas went about a hundred yards before giving in to the impulse to kiss him.

"Oh," said Chris, "oh, *alright* then," as he was pushed back in a darkened doorway. He was already smiling when Nicholas's mouth met his own. His cold fingers snuck under Nicholas's borrowed jacket, splaying over his abdomen. Nicholas cupped his jaw, cradled his skull against his palm, and kissed him beyond sanity, beyond hope, beyond uncertainty and pain. Nothing. Nothing but this.

It was four a.m. when the text came, lighting the bedroom in a ghostly blue.

Chris made a disapproving moan against Nicholas's neck and burrowed a little further down under the duvet. Nicholas, only half-awake, groped for a disappointing long time for his phone—it had fallen off under the bed, and he was groggy and sore and more than a little pissed off by the time he unlocked it.

Madalena. Exclamation points.

"What," Nicholas enunciated, "the fuck."

Chris peered up at him sleepily. "Wha'ssit?"

Nicholas clicked on the link, hoping for clarity to return.

He did not wholly understand what he was seeing for a solid twenty seconds. Then he scrolled down, and he found the picture.

Chris's hand skimmed against his side, a silent act of sleepy reassurance. "What is it," he mumbled again.

*Fuck.*

# *Chapter Eighteen*

celebslive.com/2024/08/18/latest/8f985/return=?

## CAUGHT! NICHOLAS MADDEN AND CHRISTIAN LAVALLE IN ILLICIT EMBRACE IN PARIS

Madden and Lavalle's unlikely friendship has raised a few eyebrows, after an intimate interview of *The Throne*'s cast showed the two stars in suspiciously close quarters. No comment was made on their behalf, and *The Throne*'s production team has remained tight-lipped about any potential love story.

An out and proud gay man, Lavalle has been for the past few years a fierce advocate of LGBT+ rights in fashion and on social media. His apparent friendship with Nicholas Madden, best known for his temper tantrums on various film sets over the years, has been one of the most surprising outcomes of *The Throne*'s casting, and has led to some vivid online speculation. Madden, who is rarely ever linked to anyone romantically, has had explosive relationships with newcoming costars and was set to dislike Lavalle, the unknown factor, from the outset.

Shockingly, the two men have since grown uncannily close. They are rarely to be seen away from one another, confirmed unofficial sources.

One source close to Chris Lavalle has indicated that they

spend most of their time together, and often meet "in secluded quarters" to "read lines."

After what is being called the <u>August Storm</u> hit Paris four days ago, filming for *The Throne* was stalled, and Madden and Lavalle conveniently disappeared.

Last night, on a now defunct Instagram account, a picture of <u>the two actors caught in a passionate embrace</u> was posted by an as-yet unknown user. The account was taken down (Madden's lawyers, no doubt acting posthaste) but the picture was swiftly circulated on social media.

Whether Chris Lavalle (prior to this a nonentity in the acting world) has achieved his *coup* casting via Madden's bed is at present firmly denied by Madden's agency and by *The Throne*'s production team. It remains to be seen what Priya Chaudhuri will have to say about her stars' willful decision to flout her "no filming romance" rules...

"I admit to being surprised," Chaudhuri said, her voice cooler than a Norwegian spring. "I believe I made it extremely clear that no distractions would be tolerated among the cast and the crew. You might, if you truly thought it necessary—" her voice dropped a couple more degrees "—have conducted this *affair* discreetly. God knows it wouldn't be the first time an actor of mine has gone against my express wishes. Although, to be quite frank, I had thought Jason the better candidate for going off-script. I had not expected it to be *you*, Christian."

At her side, Katherine Henderson cleared her throat. Her eyes on Chris were troubled, but sympathetic, a fact he should have found more reassuring than he did.

Chaudhuri ignored her. The pale sunlight of the after-storm washed over the tall walls of the suite over the Grands Boulevards into blinding white. It was devastating, that sunlight. The last of the rain had stopped, and the world was glittering.

"I have been under the impression that the rumors running about, concerning the two of you, were at worst slanderous and at best misleading. It is a blow to understand that they were, in fact, quite accurate. Am I wrong?" Chaudhuri asked, when Chris made a sound.

"No," he said, reluctantly. "And yes. Nothing had happened between Nicholas and I when the rumors started."

Chaudhuri closed her eyes very briefly. "And yet you thought to engage in an ill-thought fuck. No matter the bad publicity for *The Throne*, or for yourself."

"I don't think it's quite that bad," said Henderson in an undertone. She had a tablet with her, and was scrolling with obvious misgiving through a collection of photos. Chris cringed. He'd seen them, of course—there was no mistaking who the two men were, nor the embrace they had been caught in. The pictures were damning. "It *may* be spun in the right direction."

*Spun.* A story. A fling. Chris curled his fingers against his palms, willing himself to remain calm. Dread beat at his temples, and a bitter taste was in his mouth. He had not seen Nicholas in hours. Already he was missing him; fear and worry and grief were all mingled together, and he could not think of anything to say that would not make matters worse.

"The right direction," repeated Chaudhuri, weighing the word, "would have been to avoid this mess altogether. Madden! Of all people!" She shook her head. "I had not thought him so susceptible to a lovely face."

Chris stiffened. "Nicholas was against this from the start," he said, feeling as though each word was being torn from his guts. They spelled out what he did not want to face: Nicholas was facing down hell, and Chris could not go there with him. He was losing him, little by little. Last night, while they were asleep, while their pictures on social media were blowing up, he had already lost him in some great, tragic way. "He would not want to endanger his career for a—a fling."

"Tell that to the tabloids," Chaudhuri said. She was not cruel about it. Her furious disappointment was worse than even ruthlessness might have been. "Whatever happens next, *The Throne* will be the object of sordid speculation for months to come. Did you not *think*, when you were lazing about in Madden's arms, how disastrous an affair with a fellow actor, one with considerably more experience than you have, might be for your future prospects? Do you want to go down in history as the model who fucked his way into a high-end production? That is what they will say. That you slept with Madden to get the role."

"Chronologically impossible," said Katherine Henderson with a wince, "but, sadly, the tabloids care little for logic. They will make you out to be—"

"A slut?" Chris said bluntly.

"Let's say, an opportunist." It wasn't pity, the look on her face. It was an awareness that her profit revenue stream was getting curtailed at the source.

"How diplomatic." Chris knew perfectly well what the gutter press would say about him. The rumors of his incongruous casting had run long; the tabloids would be looking for fresh bait.

Nicholas, an established actor of certain renown, would see his career suffer and his prospects curtailed. Chris, an unknown quality, an outsider, would be cast into the ugliest of roles: the gold digger who'd sold himself out for a part in a Hollywood film. It would be disgusting at best, dehumanizing at worst.

"I want to say," he ventured, striving for solidity, "that it was in no part intentional—for either one of us—to become entangled in a...an affair. We were caught by surprise."

"You're adults," Chaudhuri said. "At some point it must have occurred to you that you would likely be seen."

It hadn't. They'd been caught in the rain from half a street away. The paparazzo had had an excellent camera, judging by the quality on those stolen photographs.

Damn it, he wanted Nicholas there. He wanted to hold on to his hand while Nicholas endured this shit. Chris had always ended relationships with a smile, a handshake, and no strong feelings of regret. Now it felt like having the heart torn out of him.

"Damien Jones has released an op-ed on the two of you," Chaudhuri went on, accepting the tablet. "He claims, I quote, that *Nicholas Madden has denied having any involvement whatsoever with Christian Lavalle—a denial that came with such fearsome ferocity one must be hard-pressed to believe him.* Charming. Friend of Madden's, is he?"

"I wouldn't know."

"No." Chaudhuri's dark eyes pierced his. "You wouldn't know."

She leaned back in her chair, looking, quite suddenly, enormously weary. She pinched the bridge of her nose, then removed her glasses and massaged her brow with her thumb and forefinger.

Katherine Henderson took over. "Politically, this is a PR nightmare. The two of you are consenting adults, it's true— but *The Throne* is no safe bet. Frankly, it needs revenue to justify its budget. As is, it stands on its reputation and on that alone. To have its two mains scandalously exploited on tabloid slick-pages goes against every promotional rule in the book. There is no critical acclaim for profit-grubbing manipulation; and profit-grubbing manipulation is what it will *look* like. Things might stand differently if you and Nicholas were of an equal footing. But you are not. He is, as far as celebrity goes, on a higher standing. Being so forcibly outed will damage his career, perhaps irrevocably. And you are the one who damaged him."

"I...see," said Chris, numbly.

"We in this room know that it isn't true," Henderson said, with a forced kindness that was worse than Chaudhuri's exhausted aggravation. "Nicholas is a grown man, and makes his own choices. But even he cannot control his bad publicity. He has, historically, been dreadful at it."

"*We*'ll proceed to damage control," Chaudhuri said. "I'd rather you and Nicholas no longer spoke outside of your scenes together. No late-night rendezvous in each other's trailers, no *reading lines*, no social media posts. Dead air. Don't give anyone any room to breathe. *The Throne*'s official stance will be strictly no comment."

Chris watched the dust motes dance in the thin, watery sunlight. Already the sky outside was lightening to a very pale blue. The world was returning to its natural state. But he felt changed, irrevocably. "Nicholas..."

"Nicholas will agree, or we'll have him against the wall for breach of contract."

Chris swallowed, feeling empty-hearted. They would, he had no doubt. The work was the work was the work. Nothing else mattered, not even—perhaps outstandingly so—the softer emotions and sexual embarrassments of *The Throne*'s cast. In production's eyes, they were being weak and unprofessional. But the weight of Chaudhuri's disillusionment was the harder to bear.

He looked out the window for a long, unhappy moment, then said: "I understand."

"Good." Her eyes were on him, keen as anything. "It would be *extraordinarily* foolish to let this incident define you. You are at the very beginning of your career. To hurt your chances so rakishly is...ill-advised."

"I can't go back in the closet," he said. If a trace of bitterness showed in his voice, he could hardly be blamed for it.

"No. You cannot," she said evenly. "Nicholas no longer has a choice. You and he will have to live with that."

"You alright?" Andrée asked, balancing her beer on her knee. Unlike the rest of the cast, who had given both him and Nicholas a wide berth, she had come into his trailer after tonight's shooting and cracked open a cold one.

Chris wiped the last of the foundation away and reached for the cleanser. "Have you taken up the role of confessor?"

"Nothing so Catholic." She gave him a wry grin. "Madden looks thunderous."

"He has every reason to be angry."

"Nonetheless. Are *you* alright?"

"No," Chris replied, after some reflection. "I don't believe I am."

"Won't talk to you, will he?"

"Oh, no." Nicholas had not given him a single look tonight. They were not shooting scenes together; their characters had been kept pointedly apart. Apart from a few glimpses of him across the set, Chris had not seen much of him at all.

He couldn't blame him. Being outed against his will, by, of all people, Damien *fucking* Jones, must be the ultimate affront Nicholas could stomach. One thing to have rumors running about, salacious and entirely fake details connecting him to his gay costar. Another to be caught making out passionately with said gay costar.

"Does it strike you as ironic—*non*?" Andrée said thoughtfully. "*The Throne* is a love story. We have been constructing it piece by piece; every word, every kiss, every inch of passion has been calibrated to render the most powerful impact. But if the story gets away from us, and takes shape in reality, *then*…it's time for damage control."

"I can face the facts," Chris said, wiping his eyes. The makeup remover stung, bringing up sudden, sharp tears. "It makes political sense for Nicholas to avoid the very sight of me."

"How melodramatic."

"We're in the business for it." He sounded bitter, and he knew it. It was getting harder and harder to maintain that focus, that selflessness. He wanted *out*.

She tipped her beer at him. "*Touché*. Still. You're being made into a convenient scapegoat. Oh, yes, I can see it," she added, seeing his grimace. "Production doesn't think about protecting you, so long as they need to protect the film. I respect their work ethic and despise their personal sympathies."

Chris gave a sour laugh. "That sounds harsh."

"I promise you, it will not prevent me from working with Chaudhuri again."

The door banged then, and in came Jason, still in his Belle Époque rags, but clutching a sleek, anachronistic smartphone. "Chris! Hey, man, I—oh, hello."

Chris watched, with some awe, as Jason went from frat boy extraordinaire to shy schoolboy in a second flat. Andrée, looking amused, made room for him on the makeup table.

"Hello, Jason. Good work tonight."

"Nrk," said Jason, coherently.

"Join the party, do. There's beer in the mini-fridge."

Thus armed, Jason seemed more capable of properly adulting. He gulped half of it down in one swallow, and said to Chris: "It's fucking bullshit, man."

"What is?" Chris asked, momentarily diverted from the pain that was slowly and surely squeezing out his rib cage.

"Business with Madden. The two of you not filming together tonight." Jason shrugged a haughty, rich-boy shrug. "Looney tunes. Like that'll make the pictures disappear. I should know," he added, as an afterthought.

"Yes; that's a regular Friday for you. How *do* you handle it when your personal affairs get aired in the tabloids?" Andrée asked, with the look of someone scientifically interested.

"Crash at a mate's for a couple weeks. Pay the assholes off. Get into a fight, that always helps."

"Bad publicity is good publicity. I like that."

"I can't imagine that would work for me," Chris said gently. "Nicholas has every right to stay away. His career is…vulnerable. I have to respect that."

"And what about you?" Andrée asked, her habitual bluntness cutting in. "You have as much of a right to establish your career as Madden has to preserve his own. Are you going to be the bad guy for the rest of the shoot? The promotion tour? The awards shows?"

Chris dragged a hand through his hair, loosening the pomaded curls. "I hardly know."

"If your agent was anything worth a damn, they would be demanding the pictures be taken down and the manageable speculation reduced to zero. You deserve protection, Chris."

Chris had been alone for so long—with only Antoine's comforting but erratic presence to act as a buffer against the world; with only his agent to field the jobs and audition calls that were thrown his way—that the notion of protection made little sense to him. He *had* felt well defended for the last few days, when the raging world had been condensed to his own cozy bedroom and Nicholas's arms. Nothing could touch them there.

Except something *had* touched them, by way of some dickhead's expensive camera, and now everything had gone to shit.

Fuck Damien Jones and his op-ed, and fuck production too. They wanted nothing more than for *The Throne* to succeed: he knew it and he respected it. But in their vision there was no space to breathe even a fraction of a breath out of turn.

"Hallo." Andrée reached out to cup his cheek. "That's anger, isn't it? First time I've seen you at it. It looks good on you."

"I mean, dude, you *get* to be angry," said Jason, helpfully. "Tabloids are trash."

"Hold on to it," said Andrée. "Nourish it. That anger will sustain you through the worst of it all."

The worst of it was Nicholas, looking drained and ashen, glaring at him under the too-bright spotlights.

They could not avoid a scene together forever, and Chaudhuri seemed intent on powering on without a word put aside for the awkwardness of the situation. Not forty-eight hours after the photos had broken out, Chris and Nicholas found themselves on either side of a large table, about to shoot the confrontation scene between Angelo and Frederick. Smart move, in a sense: to draw on the tense relations between them to feed the angriest, hardest scene in the script. Chaudhuri was a director first.

A smart move, but it would be heartbreaking to film. Chris hoped wistfully it would be one of Chaudhuri's famed one-take wonders, and they could all go home with some aspirin.

Or go out for a drink. A foamy piña colada with a neon-green paper umbrella sounded incredibly appealing right now.

Nicholas looked grave and ancient and horribly sad.

Chaudhuri spoke to him in hushed, angry whispers. She nodded over at Chris, and Nicholas closed his eyes.

"I know," he murmured, his voice just audible through the falling quiet. He sounded rough.

Chris set his teeth. He met Nicholas's gaze and held it. As badly as he wanted to cross the set and touch—god, merely to brush his hand!—they were separated by the rift of their own, personal tragedies, and touch alone would be little more than a momentary sop.

After a moment, Nicholas looked away.

*That* was the worst of it. No anger or shyness in Nicholas's eyes: but disillusionment. An overall aura of *I fucked up.*

*I did this*, Chris thought, dismally, and then, *No. I didn't. It happened to us.*

That knowledge didn't help one bit.

Chaudhuri gave Nicholas one last, hard stare, and then left. Then it was the two of them alone—with four cameras trained on their faces, and cranes overhead, and glaring spotlights casting long shadows out of the microphones. And a room full of people staring at them. Nevertheless, in this moment, in this small world, they were alone. It was a terrible loneliness, to be the center of attention, and so utterly isolated.

Chaudhuri called for action, and professionalism returned. They made it through the scene once, then twice, without much ado; Nicholas worked mechanically, and Chris took up his trail and played up to his strengths, scarcely remembering his lines. It wasn't bad. It just wasn't *good.*

"Cut," Chaudhuri snapped, after the third exhausting take was wrapped up. Angelo's cruel words stuck in Chris's throat, bitter-tasting. "Get your *bloody* heads into gear, both of you. I'm not wasting more camera time on this than I have to. You better get off your asses and *into* the mood."

"What else have we been doing? What have we done but obeyed your orders?" Nicholas snapped, a harsh tremor in his voice, and the crew executed a collective flinch.

The Madden Effect: when he looks for something to throw, cut and run far out of arm's range. But Nicholas remained seated, his hands clenched into fists. His face was carefully, meticulously blank.

"I haven't seen much proof of obedience," Chaudhuri said. She waved off her production assistant and left the camera. "Nor of competence from either of you. You may play the drama queen, Madden, as much as you like or think you deserve to—*when* we are done with the shoot. Once you're off my hands, you may do as you please. Until then, you're a goddamn professional with a goddamn job to do."

"She's right," Chris said quietly. Nicholas's eyes snapped to his. "We should wrap this up."

Nicholas looked briefly murderous. Then he swallowed, and looked down. "Alright." His voice was strangled. "As you like."

Chaudhuri made an approving sound and returned to her seat. Nicholas, eyes averted, was pale.

Again. Then again. The same lines, the same argument, the same self-hatred. It was Frederick's worst moment, when the very sight of Angelo was unbearable to him. Nicholas played him perfectly. While Angelo's words came to his mouth and Angelo's callousness rose up in Chris, Nicholas *was* Frederick, down to the core. His disgust, his rancor, his severity. Chris couldn't imagine another man in the role. He was, for a stunning few seconds, grateful that they had waited until now to shoot this scene.

It wouldn't have been half as good had Nicholas not loved Angelo.

The scene ended with Angelo pressed up against the table, white-faced and shaken, at last, out of his pride. The cameras pushed in for a close-up. Nicholas, with one hand on Chris's chest, was breathing hard and uneven.

He was looking at Chris's mouth.

Chris parted his lips, wishing irreverently that Nicholas would give up the ghost and kiss him. He wasn't meant to. Frederick was leaving Angelo; this was his goodbyes, his *adieux*, not a moment of tenderness or understanding. But Nicholas looked—

Well. He looked as he had looked when he was braced over Chris in bed, his hand wrapped around the both of them, with sweat in his eyes and Chris's name on his lips. Pleasure and pain warred in his shadowed expression.

His thumb brushed Chris's cheek.

*I'm sorry. I am so sorry.*

Nicholas took in a breath. His eyes were very black.

"Cut. That's the one," said Chaudhuri, pleased, and Nicholas pulled away so fast Chris was caught leaning against him and nearly fell over. He recovered badly. Nicholas's hand shot out and caught his elbow. The shock of it drenched Chris all over; he snapped his head up, and their eyes caught.

"Careful," Nicholas said, shortly.

"I—thanks," Chris said. He found his footing, and Nicholas dropped his arm, one hand still outstretched. When Chris looked down at it, he jerked it back to his side.

"It's nothing."

Nicholas hesitated, and seemed on the verge of saying something more; but Chaudhuri called impatiently for Andrée to make her entrance, and the moment was lost—Nicholas pulled away once and for all, and walked off-set without another word.

# *Chapter Nineteen*

**Chris Lavalle Fans** @lavallenation • 16m
With respect to the #TheThrone drama…gentle reminder that Chris is a very private person, who doesn't deserve to be harassed right now…as far as we can tell his relationship with Nicholas Madden was a) consensual and b) confidential. We were never meant to know about it 1/x

**Chris Lavalle Fans** @lavallenation • 15m
and we should be more concerned about how information gets circulated on twitter and adjacent platforms than trying to cast blame. Madden didn't deserve to be outed either. We, the fans, aren't entitled to every side of celebrities' lives. Even though sometimes we think we know them 2/x

**Chris Lavalle Fans** @lavallenation • 14m
we need to remember that they're people in their own right. Would WE want to have our privacy and intimate affairs revealed to the whole world? Would WE want people speculating on our sex/love lives? Would WE be as gracious about it as Chris has been? I mean, he's had to go offline because of 3/x

**Chris Lavalle Fans** @lavallenation • 13m
people asking him to comment and prying into his intimate details, trying to figure out where he lives, etc.
Remember that until a few months ago Chris's relationship with fame was limited! He wasn't the one outed,
but that doesn't mean he's okay with what's happened!
Respect his privacy, people. It's not hard. 4/x

**Chris Lavalle Fans** @lavallenation • 11m
(Can I just say I'm not impressed with #TheThrone's response to this affair as well? Like, damn, is it so hard
to send out a statement of support for your two main
stars? Smdh.) 5/x

**Chris Lavalle Fans** @lavallenation • 10m
TL;DR: don't be assholes. Chris is already bearing the
brunt of the blame for "turning" a famous actor gay.
Don't play into that narrative.

Nicholas returned to Le Meurice in a black rage. He wasn't
certain who it was directed at—production, or Chaudhuri, or
Chris, or Jim Slater, or himself. Anger had a way of burning
through his reserves and defenses, a slashing, scathing horror
that sank into his bloodstream and went straight to the heart.
He wanted to drink himself into dark oblivion and forget he
had ever come to Paris.

Madalena, knowing better than to knock the hornet's nest,
refused to engage. She tapped on her phone during the cab
ride, one well-heeled ankle propped over the other. Nicholas rested his chin on his fist, stared out the window at the
stagnant traffic and the infernally *chic* Parisians, and fumed.

"Damn them all," was all he found to say, once they had
let themselves into his suite. He tugged harshly at his collar,

loosening his tie. Jim Slater had insisted he be starched and formal in appearance for the foreseeable future. "What a *grand* mess this all is."

"Mm," said Madalena, still tapping. Nicholas gave her a black look. "There's no need to glare at me. You could have stayed and talked to Chris."

"Certainly not." That, too, was verboten, as per Slater's orders. And Nicholas's guilt and terror were too great to power him through a conversation with Chris. They had been apart for less than two days, and already Chris had grown...distant. Solitary. In Angelo's makeup, he played the part of the libertine with a startling abandon. It was, by turns, infuriating and arousing, and Nicholas could not stay alone with him, or else he would...break something, perhaps, or—worse yet— push him against a wall and let their mutual attraction wear out its course. He remembered Chris's burning kisses. He remembered the dizzying, spiraling feeling of Chris pressing his lips to his shoulders, his collarbone, his pectorals. He remembered Chris's body in his arms, his delighted laugh, his wandering, teasing hands.

Chris was young. No doubt the two days he had spent with Nicholas were, to his eyes, nothing more than a wonderful distraction with a regrettable ending. A quick exchange of pleasure. He certainly felt bad for Nicholas now: the pity in his eyes was unbearable. But whatever had powered his desire for Nicholas was gone. It showed in his eyes, in his faint smile, even in the way he stood: turned away, daring not to look at Nicholas, he kept himself distant, and Nicholas could not blame him.

Best to cut all ties now. If Nicholas remained in Paris much longer, he would have his heart smashed to smithereens.

Madalena put down her phone at last, and gave him one hard, long, mascara-black look. "Jim Slater wants you to call."

Of course he did. When it rained, it poured. "Fine."

Her voice softened. "You need to make a statement, Nicholas, whatever it is. The longer you stay silent, the worse the speculation will get."

"I am well aware."

He had not so much as looked at his phone since the incident. Damien Jones had boasted of his discovery to the point of vulgarity. Nicholas did not put it past him to have set paparazzo on his tail, looking for the moment to pounce; though, more likely, whoever had taken the pictures had sold them to the highest bidder. The story had been picked up by celebrity news, made the rounds on Twitter, and become an international scoop. Jim Slater had, in the past two days, sent more cease-and-desist requests to various media outlets than a straight actor would need in a long lifetime.

It was the worst-case scenario imaginable. The Shakespearean storm. To be outed for any reason would have been enough for a strategically public meltdown; to be outed on Chaudhuri's set was a horrible bet, never, he was sure, to be repeated; to be outed on the set of *The Throne* was dreadful publicity; and yet, even then, they might have turned the tide.

If the photos had captured him in an anonymous man's arms outside some nameless nightclub, the downfall might have been manageable: blame it on a drunken night out, blame it on stupidity, blame it on whoever and whatever was at hand. But he had been in Chris's bed, and he could not deny it. The truth was invulnerable. You could not kill it.

It could have remained a private matter. If he and Chris had stayed in from the storm—if they had played out their mutual attraction and exhausted it and walked away satisfied…no doubt, Nicholas thought—had to think, had to *believe*—they would have had some melancholic conversation about boundaries and discretion once filming was over, and parted ways with some relief. On-set flings happened, blazed fiercely for a few weeks, then fizzled out. It was the way of the world. Why should it be different for them? Why should they be *lucky*?

They'd thought they were safe.

*You were never safe.* The words echoed through Nicholas's mind in his own mocking voice, lilting with exhaustion. *You should have known better. You should have been smarter. You shouldn't have fucked your young, lovely, neophyte costar, for fuck's sake.*

For years he had thought himself above suspicion and beyond reproach. He had prided himself on his restraint. *And when it counted you couldn't keep it in your pants.*

He eyed Madalena's phone, and she immediately pulled it out of arm's range. "Nope. *Non.* You're not looking at this trash."

"Em—"

"Slater's orders. You pay him a fortune to keep you in the good books."

"I think the good books are closed for us now," Nicholas said flatly.

"To keep you out of the *bad* books, then." She tucked her phone in her skirt pocket. "Much as I dislike the guy—and I do, for all he's done and said to you over the years—he's very good at his job. If he says to keep mum and stay offline, I say listen to him." She paused, staring intently at him. "It would look better for you if you and Chris agreed on what to say to the press."

Nicholas dragged a hand through his hair. He felt long, long beyond tired. Exhaustion dragged at him. "That's not an option."

"Because he won't, or because you won't?"

"Both. Neither. We're not on speaking terms." His voice took on a distressing accent of longing. "He won't so much as look at me."

"His reputation will take as much of a hit as yours," Madalena said, in a quiet, polite, otherworldly voice. "He'll be the actor who fucked his way into *The Throne.* Forever." She caught his look of disgust. "Anyone who has met you will know you didn't compromise your ethos for a proper screwing. But most people, Nicholas, do not know you; and they'll have *opinions*."

"I know. Fuck, I know."

"Production isn't on his side. They want out of the scandal as fast as possible, and if they can kill it by casting him aside, they will. He's already out of the promotion tour—"

"What?" Nicholas looked sharply at her. "How did you come by that?"

"I know these things," Madalena said, with a touch of her old, airy manner. "The crew knows, more or less. Word came down from the Hendersons this morning. They boost his salary, discreetly, and he vanishes until the premiere. Prior commitments."

Nicholas's heart felt wrung-out and sorry. "I assume he said yes."

"Would you blame him? If I were him, I'd clear right out of the public eye. Stay indoors and never move from my bed again."

"No." Nicholas sank back down on the chair, closing his eyes. "No, I don't blame him."

Madalena's phone trilled. She extricated it from her skirt and peered down at it. "Slater. Should I tell him to call back?"

"No," Nicholas said again, and reached out his hand. "I'll take it."

The phone call was blissfully short. Slater had gone straight through astringent disappointment into businesslike bargaining. "You won't have to make a statement. It can be a one-off."

"So long as it doesn't happen again," Nicholas inferred.

"Yes," Slater said, bluntly. "You can't afford it, Madden. Costa has already called off the audition. So sorry, the role has been filled, never meant to raise expectations, yadda yadda. There'll be others like him—nothing on the surface, of course, they won't risk coming off the worse in the tabloids themselves, but down below that'll be the cause. Seems a shame to bet your whole career on a one-night stand, but what the hell do I know. Have you talked to him?"

Nicholas grunted. "No."

"Good. Keep it that way. Don't be seen together. There's, what, a week left of filming? Then back to the States, pronto. No dilly-dallying in Paris, you hear? You forget about pretty boy and you come and do *Deep North*. Alberta Fleischer is solidly Democrat, thank fuck."

*Deep North* was Fleischer's ice-cold Alaskan thriller. Nicholas had been looking forward to working with her; she was one of Chaudhuri's temper, though without the dire personal expectations. Now, though, that prospect seemed dull and lackluster.

Slater kept talking, and Nicholas closed his eyes, swallowing dryly. His thoughts kept returning to Chris—Chris in his studio, on that first morning at the end of the world, making coffee. The lines of his back underneath that soft t-shirt. The soft-looking curls at the back of his neck. Nicholas had stood in the doorway and had been struck by a sense of tenderness and protectiveness.

Then he had come in and slipped his arms around Chris's waist. He could still feel the weight of him, his body resting heavy against his chest. He could hear the smile in his voice.

"That should keep you out of harm's way until promotion for *The Throne* starts—and by then Jason Kirkhall will have mooned his adoring public, or some starlet will have had her mugshot hacked, or some similar bullshit, and you won't be the one in the hot seat. *If* you can keep a brake on that dastardly temper of yours." He broke off. "Nicholas…"

"What?"

"Allison Giannopoulos needs a date to the Make-A-Wish Foundation Gala."

A migraine was threading a fine iron wire from one of Nicholas's temples through to the other. "I don't know who that is."

"Oh, who cares? Figure skater. Came in second in the World Championships." He sounded as though he was reading off a list. "Twenty-one years old. Dark brunette—"

"No."

"You gotta think politically."

*So people keep telling me.* "I said no, Jim. As I recall, I said no three weeks ago. I'm not dating a girl barely out of her teens to butter my side of the bread."

"I may promise you it would butter hers too."

"I'm not an escort."

"And neither is she," Slater said, sounding hurt. "A purely platonic, mutually beneficial relationship. Date for a couple months, then move on; she gets a leg up, and you get the benefit of the doubt."

Nicholas set his teeth. "Cynical."

"Yeah. That's me: cynical. Up until lately, it was you, too. You were ready to commit murder for *The Throne.* Woe betide anyone who got in your way. This affair has made you soft."

"Perhaps it has," Nicholas said, unable to give a shit.

"No to Giannopoulos?"

"No. Hard no, Jim. I'll call you later."

He dropped the phone on the low table, breathing out a long, harrowing sigh. Madalena perched on the armrest of his chair, and wrapped an arm around his shoulders. "Nicholas." She pressed a brief kiss in his hair. It was foolish, superficial comfort, and Nicholas shouldn't have felt warmth creeping up his cheekbones at the unfamiliar display of tenderness. He took her hand, roughly, and pressed it in his own.

The final days of August burned to the touch—a final flaring of light before autumn and darkness came. *The Throne* wrapped up its last scenes quietly, without much online fuss, and, thankfully, with no more promotional stints. The crew was subdued, and the cast rarely spoke but to the purpose. There was hard work to be done, and in hard work they found a selfish devotion that bordered on the religious.

It ended, as it had begun, near the Palais-Royal Gardens, a breath away from the Place Colette and the Comédie-Française. Most of the cast had shown up. The final scene was a long and convoluted one between Chris and Reggie, set in the prologue of the film; the distortion of time, combined with the heady, collective thought of *soon we'll be done*, gave the set a golden, hazy edge, a blurring of the sun. Once this was over, everyone would be aimless and a little sad, and most would go out for a drink tonight, to while away their last hours in Paris. For Chaudhuri and the Hendersons, of course, this was only the beginning of the hellish stage known as post-production. Some of the cast would remain in the city a few more days; Nicholas was set to fly out the next morning.

Chris was sitting in the shade, talking to Reggie. He was more dressed up than he normally would be; Angelo's customary white shirt and cinched waistcoat had been replaced by a somber morning coat, a cane, and a top hat, which he drummed abstractedly against his thigh. He was made up to look even younger than his twenty-five years. He was Angelo before he became Angelo, eighteen and fresh from Provence, a shy newcomer to Paris, who must rely on Jarrett's steadying presence. A fine ray of sunlight touched his face, casting the lines of his brow-bone and jaw into sharp relief. Hunched forward, his elbows on his knees, he stared at Reg intently, mostly listening, sometimes speaking a word or two.

Reggie was being Reggie—flirtatious, bombastic, over the top, and Chris was smiling at him, a little tiredly. Nicholas kept looking over at them.

"That's an unlikely couple," Andrée said.

Nicholas gave her a glance. *She* had wrapped up her final scene the day before, and so had abandoned her character's mannish trousers and box-suit jacket in favor of a pair of jeans and a maroon bodice. Designer, by the look of them. Strange, and vaguely surreal—as though they had jumped forward in time; her white-blond hair seemed, suddenly, an affectation.

"Reg likes Chris," Nicholas said, as neutrally as he could.

She snorted, and produced a cigarette box and a lighter. "Want one?"

"No, thanks. If you want to ruin your vocal cords, be my guest."

"Ah, but—now—I have a *smoky, haughty voice*," she said, stressing the quotation marks with a mocking lilt. "It's part of my delightfully French charm." She lit her smoke with faint distaste. "Bloody journalists."

Nicholas made a sound of wordless agreement and leaned back against the green-painted gates of the Gardens, seeking the warmth of the sun on his face. Further below, under the tall, trimmed trees, Chaudhuri had approached Chris. He took direction with grave acquiescence, then stood at her cue.

Tired and serious was a good look on him. *Oh, damn it.*

Andrée dragged on her cigarette; the movement was fitful and curiously abrupt. She patted at her hair, mussing up her pale curls. "It's a rotten situation for you, I don't deny it."

"How kind of you," Nicholas murmured. "But?"

"He's very—very *very*. And young."

"Robbing the cradle, am I?" Nicholas said dryly.

"I don't doubt that Chris is plenty capable of making his own decisions; *you*, on the other hand, may be construed as someone who fell for his charms, and was taken unaware… don't look at me like that. There's worse being said, and some of it by the right people. It's a potential strategy for you, you know. Playing the victim."

"No," said Nicholas. Disgust came up in his mouth, sour

and nauseating. Sacrificing Chris to the altar of his own reputation had been hard enough. Turning him into the villain of the tale would be unfathomably cruel.

"Then why," she asked, suddenly damnably angry, "are you going along with production? Why not come out in Chris's favor?"

He set his teeth. She made it sound easy: she had that immunity. And yet he knew that she had faced tougher challenges, and spoke from experience. "Standing up for your countryman?"

"I like Chris," Andrée demurred. "He's genuinely kind, which is a hard sell in our business—and in his. Fashion is a harsh mistress; Hollywood is a worse spouse. He deserves better than a hard fuck and a toss-up of his—and your—priorities."

That was harsh, and Nicholas took it as intended. "None of us deserve better. We take what we're offered, and we give thanks for it."

Andrée contemplated her cigarette. "Mn. That sounds, sorry to say, like prime bullshit. You're a good actor, but you're not so good as that. How many times have you raged and stormed on the job? The privilege of work! Of saying *no, thanks* to the barest touch of human decency!" She threw the cigarette butt to the ground and crushed it with her heel. "It's sad for me to admit it, Madden, but you've never been so pleasant as you've been these past weeks. Almost close to human. It was spectacular."

"Thanks very much."

"You damn fool." She curled her hand around his elbow. "You should stay in Paris, you know. We're not so bad when you get down to it."

"No. No, I don't think so." Nicholas tilted his head. A vaguely familiar figure had walked through the arcades opposite the set, striding with unearned confidence towards... "What the fuck is he doing here?"

Andrée, blinking at the sudden harshness in his voice, looked over. "What—oh. Is that Reg's journalist?"

Nicholas started forward, nausea and fury warring in his chest. "Reg's—? That's Damien fucking Jones."

"Jones...?" Andrée trailed off. "Oh, *mince*."

Jones, slick as hell in a grey suit, advanced on Chris with the single-mindedness of a rattlesnake. He held out his hand to Reggie to shake, but his eyes were on his prize. Chris was frowning down at his phone, paying little attention to the vermin in their midst. And in a moment Jones would turn away from Reg, and speak to him.

When Nicholas reached them, Andrée hot after him, Jones had Chris's hand in his own and a glossy smile firmly anchored on his lips, and was saying: "...love an interview. To clear the air."

"That's—I'm afraid I have some commitments," Chris said absently. "Sorry, who are you?"

Jones's smile went a fraction tighter. "Jones. Damien Jones. With *Vogue*. I was contracted to talk to Mr. Jarrett—but I would *appreciate* the opportunity to—"

And then it didn't matter what Nicholas could, or couldn't have said. Chris dropped his hand as though burned.

"Chris." The name came in a voice so foreign Nicholas barely recognized it as his own. Chris gave him a colorless glance and turned away his shoulder.

"Thank you," he told Jones, the accent out in full force. "I am not interested."

"Mr. Lavalle—"

"You," said Chris, his voice pale with anger, "should not be here."

Jones blinked hard and pulled himself up. "Mr. Jarrett has *committed* himself to a full interview."

"But *I* haven't. Nor do I ever wish to speak with you again. You *serpent*."

God, he was magnetic. Had Nicholas ever thought he was not an actor? Chris would have blown them all out of the water if he had only decided to. The fact that he hadn't—that he had held something of himself back until this moment—was staggeringly sweet, and staggeringly sad. Perhaps it was the tragedy itself that had made him capable of acting in this way; perhaps he had always been like this, brilliant and beautiful, and Nicholas had been a fool.

But it was only fair that Chris should defend himself in this way. Chris had made enough sacrifices for *The Throne*.

"It is incomprehensible to me that you should still have a job. How dare you come to my city and do what you have done."

Jones gave a rabbity stare in Nicholas's direction. "Whatever Madden has told you—"

"He hasn't told me anything. I did not require direction to read your filthy article."

"Ooh, *burn*," said Jason, who was apparently there too. As was the rest of the cast. And crew.

Reggie, mouth half-open, stared at the scene in blank horror. He puffed out his chest. "I promise you, dear boy, I had no idea—"

"It does not matter." Chris's gaze on Jones was contemptuous. It was a wonder the man had not deflated yet. "I am done. We will do the final scene, and then—*I am done*."

Jones's countenance changed progressively from hunted to interested. He might as well have started to signal the headline *French Diva Chris Lavalle Walks Out of The Throne, Refuses to Comment* in blaring neon above his head.

And if Nicholas intervened, it would include *Madden Throws Chair at Reporter's Head* as a sub-header.

His reputation was in tatters. His sexuality had been splashed around in the media; his private life had been violated; industry contacts had abandoned him, and doors had slammed in his face. He wavered on the edge of this feeling, throat tight, brain empty.

Then he took a step forward.

Chris shot him a glacial look. It stopped the heart in his chest.

Then, very deliberately, he turned his pale, otherworldly eyes on Jones again.

"You'll leave now."

"Now, listen here—"

"You will indeed!" blustered Reggie. "I shan't have another word to say to you!"

"Nor will I," Andrée said.

"Nor I," said Jason, jumping on the Spartacus train. Murmurs of agreement circulated through the crew. Jones began to look rather alarmed.

"In fact," said Chris, with great sweetness, "here comes security now."

Also came Chaudhuri, looking thunderous, flanked by Mel, half of *The Throne*'s PR team, and two heavy-duty bodyguards in black suits and earpieces.

Chaudhuri's famed contempt for the press carried its weight now. She apprehended Jones at a glance, went straight through to judgement, and instructed the muscle to act accordingly. Jones, with much protest, was led away from the scene.

"Lavalle!" he shouted, struggling in their grasp. "Is it true?"

Chris looked disgusted.

"Is it true?" Jones repeated, avid, his voice lifting dizzyingly above the crowd. "Who else did you sleep with to get onto *The Throne*? Or did you leverage your family relations to get the part? What have you to say about your sexual *tendencies*—"

"Enough," said Chaudhuri. Crushing. "Get him *out of my set*."

The sun shone on, ruthless.

It took some time after Jones's disappearance for the cast's ruffled fur to settle; the crew murmured behind raised hands. And everyone was looking now. There could be no looking away. The scandal and the silence stretched on and on, horribly.

Chris, infernally cool, said to Reggie: "You are consulting with this man?"

"Not anymore, I ain't," Reg said. "He contacted my agent with a request for a short interview. *Vogue*, you know..." He trailed off. "My dear, I am *truly* sorry. Had I known, why—"

"It's alright." Chris tucked a stray lock behind his ear. "No harm done."

The gesture went straight to Nicholas's head. He flinched, and then he could not stand it—the sunlight and the anarchy, and Chris's pride, his unbearable, almost inadvertent bravery, as though he had thought no one would stand up for him. As though there was no one else.

It was humbling. It was powerful, too, in that awe-inspiring way that made Nicholas want to follow in his steps. Chris had blazed his way through this last, final conflict, and Nicholas ached to believe that he could be as unflinching.

They proceeded to shoot the final scene. Nicholas remembered little of it. There was the mandatory explosion of confetti, and the delighted cheer, and the applause; he was kissed on both cheeks by Jason; Chaudhuri, with a half smile, shook his hand; Andrée hugged him hard. Then champagne. Then a full buffet table, laid out with petits-fours and charcuterie trays and platters of fruit, for an early supper, here in the declining sun. Wrap-up party. Goodbyes.

And Chris was gone, when someone thought to look around.

*The Throne*, such as it had been, was over.

# Chapter Twenty

When I was contracted to conduct an interview with Reginald Jarrett on the set of the highly-awaited period piece *The Throne*, I knew that I had a chance to meet the one actor whose name has been on everyone's lips: Christian Lavalle, Priya Chaudhuri's newest protégé and French influencer extraordinaire.

When Lavalle was cast as "Angelo" in what has clearly become an early contender to the awards season, I was one of the first to be interested in his working relationship with the so-called Big Bad Wolf of Hollywood. Nicholas Madden has been a frequent presence in this very column, by virtue of his inconstant fits of temper on various film sets over the years—and his closeted private life.

Since his arrival in Hollywood more than a decade ago, many were they who demanded Madden be truthful to his fans about his dating history and sexuality. On many occasions, I was one of those who tried to confront him. I was always immediately shut down, insulted, demeaned, and thrown out of interviews and hotels. No wonder, then, that his relation to Lavalle, who seemed at first sight to embody everything Madden most detests, should have awakened my...curiosity.

It turns out Madden is as susceptible to a pretty face as everyone else. Let me be the first to say: I called it.

If you haven't seen the pictures by now, where the hell have you been? Witness Madden's hypocrisy and deceit.

When I arrived on set of *The Throne* earlier today, I was not expecting to be made into the scapegoat of Lavalle's own unflattering fit of temper (sounds like he and Madden are made for each other!) or to be insulted, mocked, libeled by what seemed to be most of the cast and crew, and then forcibly escorted out of the set. Bear in mind that I was there under CONTRACT!! (Yes, Reginald Jarrett will hear from my lawyers)...

Autumn came. So did the rain.

As the days darkened, so did Chris's mood; he was unenthusiastic about the projects that were directed to him, yet did the work without protest, without a moment's grace. His agent called in for a part in a recent drama: auditions in October, filming next spring. Chris went through the script. It was a period piece, set in 1942 Paris, during the Occupation. His role was small, but crucial to the plot, and it had its share of pathos. The show had an international release and had stood for a number of awards the previous year. It was a step up, by all accounts, from a soap stand-in to a serious production with an eye for talent. "You're good for it, Chris. They asked for you personally."

Chris accepted the audition, took part in photoshoots for several online fashion magazines, and mostly stayed off social media. His online presence trickled to a stop. Damien Jones had, without knowing it, hit at a particularly vulnerable place when it came to the personas he cultivated: there was a chasm between the Instagram boy-prince, who adored his city and loved talking with fans, and the real, unhappy young man, who was slipping into the latter part of his twenties, whose fashion career would potentially stall to a stop, whose reputation was fragile. There was a wound there. Chris had thought himself long beyond being hurt by disparaging comments, and yet the awareness of them, the physicality of them, now, was stinging.

He had spent most of his teenage and adult years being condescended to. He had begun *The Throne* being condescended to. It was fitting, in an ironic, awful way, that he should end it the same way. Narratively, it made perfect sense.

It still felt like being punched in the solar plexus.

He would have to be self-sufficient in all things. No one would protect him now.

It was a harsh lesson to learn, loneliness. He had dared to imagine, for those eight weeks he had spent with Nicholas, running lines in his trailer, eating noodles with him, kissing him in the rain—he had dared to imagine that loneliness was a thing of the past. Nicholas had, he now realized, sheltered and protected him from much of what made being part of a million-dollar Hollywood production a nerve-racking and strenuous experience. He had given him support, companionship, affection, and that daring sweetness Nicholas had not shown anyone else. Chris had not realized how much he had come to rely on his presence, on his warmth and his temper and his unbearable kindness.

Being away from him now—being on the other side of the world, separated by a rift of their own making—was searingly painful.

"Eat," Antoine advised, nudging a bowl of peanuts in his direction.

Chris reluctantly pulled his cherry-sweet beer towards him.

"You look tired."

"I am." Chris rubbed at his temple, feeling a migraine sink its roots in. He had, the previous night, shot for *Brazen*, a glam-rock boutique of body-positive lingerie. He was still wearing smudged eyeliner and black lace panties. "It was a long...evening. Night."

Antoine, who had been awake for no more than four hours and looked diabolically well rested, took a long pull off his own pint. "That'll teach you to work with Brauer again. He's a monster on a shoot."

"But *so* talented." Antoine and Andreas Brauer had once been on-again off-again enemies-with-benefits for the better part of two years. They had since settled into resentful professionalism; but every now and then a strain of the old dislike crept back into Antoine's voice. Now, though, he was mostly amused.

"Yes, well." A shrug. Antoine leaned back in his chair, resting his chin in his hand. "I'm glad you did the shoot, for what it's worth. Putting on makeup and looking beautiful is good for the soul."

Chris smiled and closed his eyes. The light was too bright. But he felt the weight of Antoine's attention on him.

"You don't sleep very much, do you."

"No," Chris admitted. How could he sleep in the bed he had shared with Nicholas? He kept waking up, reaching out, and finding nothing but cold emptiness.

"*Chris.*" Antoine's voice was softly exasperated. "Darling, you have to speak to me. I invite you out, and you are sad. Sadness won't do. Shall we go out tonight? Would you like that?"

He couldn't stomach it. "Antoine..."

"Dancing. Shots. Questionable anonymous hookups."

"I tried that," Chris said wryly. His past hookups had been cheerful affairs, and though on more than one occasion he had walked the walk of shame at ridiculous hours of the morning, they had never left him with more than passing regret. His affair with Nicholas had left him split in two. "It had an... adverse effect."

Antoine's fingers curled loosely around his pint. "So Madden fucked you over. Take stock, regroup, move on."

It sounded easy enough, laid out in such clear terms. Antoine was known about their circle for never sticking around longer than he needed or wanted to. He was a good lover, to hear others tell it; but he was a truer friend, daring and tireless in time of need. He had no patience for doomed love stories. His longest relationship to date was with his favorite camera lens.

"Get yourself a handsome *beau* and take him to the premiere," was his sage advice. "Some jacked fuckboi with a heart of gold. Think Channing Tatum. Think *muscles.*"

Chris laughed, despite himself, and Antoine's foot knocked his under the table. He seemed pleased by Chris's laughter. "You won't be tabloid-bait much longer."

Paparazzi had tailed him for a time—not, it must be said, with an ounce of discretion or tact—in the vain hope that he would meet indiscreetly with Nicholas. A few of the more daring sort followed him in the metro; the others lobbed questions at him when he went out to the corner store. Photos of him in his most faded jeans and (comfy, but hardly elegant) parka went up on Twitter faster than he could breathe, generally with such sub-headlines as *Depressed or on the Rebound? Chris Lavalle & Mystery Bagger Caught in Private Conversation!* As the light dimmed, however, and Paris descended into wintry climes, they seemed to have lost a bit of their *élan.* It had been almost two weeks since he'd last been inferred to have a secret sexual relationship with his concierge.

"There goes the way of all flesh," said Antoine. "They'll forget about you in a couple of weeks, and then—"

"And then," Chris reminded him, "in January, the premiere."

"And you'll look amazing, well rested, and romantically fulfilled. We'll pull off something grand. Show up and show off. Fuck them," said Antoine, with a sudden flash of anger. "Fuck all of them. Madden too. I can't stand to watch you like this."

Chris took his hand. Antoine had long, large hands, flat-fingered, and strangely comforting to hold. "I'll be alright. I'm auditioning for *The Long Winter* next week. It should give me something new to worry about."

"*The Long Winter*?" Antoine perked up. "Joanne Engels's pet project?"

"Mm-hmm. They have the part of a Resistance spy for me, whose role it is, as far as I can tell, to infiltrate occupied Paris strongholds, poison as many Nazi officers as he can at dinner parties, and then die tragically for the cause. Shush, of course." He paused. "You look surprised."

"I *am* surprised. Engels is a master director. You'll be great, though—you excel at playing the ruthless beauty. The fans will lap it up."

"It should go some way towards boosting my social capita, at least."

"Darling, you should look at the fan blogs. Whoever is daft enough to imagine you might screw Madden for a role doesn't know very much about you at all. You have a loyal fan base."

Chris scrubbed a hand through his hair. "I haven't been online. To put myself out there has…lost a lot of its appeal."

The storm and song of internet fame was no longer as captivating as it had once been. *The Throne* had provided illumination in the disconnect between the lies of the game and the reality of who he wanted to be. Not, as he had thought, to smile, and smile, and take what he was given, but to have decision power over the projects he starred in. *The Long Winter* was one of them. It was a powerful and intriguing historical drama, the first season of which he had watched since getting the audition call, and subsequently adored. If he nailed the part, similar proposals might follow.

His shoot with *Brazen* had shown him fashion that was inclusive and meaningful and...*sexy*. Fashion that didn't exploit models, that paid a living wage and focused on different body types and skin colors. He wanted to focus on that. It meant giving up on the great houses, the contracts with Dior and Armani. But he was twenty-five, and he felt the pressure of looking ever younger, ever thinner, ever blonder. He was aging out of the business.

They took a cab home. Antoine was uncharacteristically silent, though his shoulder was pressed, in a companionable way, against Chris's. The dark streets blurred together in a haze of intermittent lights, the soft roar of cars muffled in the distance. Chris was reminded of the last cab ride he had shared: when Nicholas's head had rested against his, and Nicholas's hot, dry hand was curled in his own. The world had been small then. There had been no need for worry. No need to look beyond that night, that single moment of intimacy.

He had tried, and mostly failed, to keep his thoughts from straying back in time. Those few days they had spent together, weathering the storm, now seemed ten years in the past—detached from him, as though he had aged eerily fast in the meantime.

He had found in his work the professionalism and clarity he needed to keep his head in the game; but when he was home, in bed, lying awake, the loneliness and betrayal he nourished came up in him like an ache.

He had been in love before. He recognized the symptoms of being head over heels for someone; he would have been a fool to miss them now. But this was all of the previous loves combined, compounded, magnified, shooting him up like an electric charge. He *wanted* Nicholas—his physical body, his voice, his dry sarcasm and absurd tenderness, his help, his affection, his intensity and impatience. The sadness in him. The harsh temper that had earned him unflattering nicknames in the gutter press.

And that honest emotion that blazed out of him like a star—loyalty to the film, loyalty to himself, loyalty even to others. It was a built-in function of Nicholas's existence that he could be nothing other than who he was. Wholly, proudly, without a moment of doubt.

Which was no excuse. He was stubborn, overbearing, and often an asshole. He lashed out at a word. He had abandoned Chris as soon as the going had got tough.

And Chris...missed him. He missed him horribly.

"You'll get through it, you know," Antoine murmured as he dropped him off. The cab idled by the curb, but Antoine had insisted on coming to the door. "When January comes, I will take great pleasure in saying *I told you so*. Repeatedly. To everyone I know."

Chris smiled. "Thanks." He pulled Antoine in for a hard hug. Antoine laughed, startled—Chris supposed he must be: he was rarely the one to initiate body contact—and hugged him back, so that they stumbled in the middle of the embrace, and would have fallen, had there not been a convenient doorjamb to lean against.

"Well!" Antoine pulled away, looking a little bashful. "I have to say, love, you're better off, sleep or no sleep. You look damned good when you're heartbroken."

"Same to you."

"Self-congratulation will get us far."

Laughter came then, bubbling and almost happy. "Good night."

★ ★ ★

"…he's very pretty, but *really*…"

"No wonder he was cast. Madden probably isn't the only one he's…"

"…can't act at all."

"…wouldn't *you* go for it? I bet he…"

"He looks like he'd be a proper fuck."

Chris checked in the doorway of the dressing rooms, resting his hand on the wall. The voices were loud and cheerful, and he recognized them. He had been kept on set longer than the other models, for close-up comparisons and a few solo portraits. They had apparently found the bottle of bubbly that had been set aside for the wrap-up party.

"Have you read the article yet? *Lots* of juicy morsels."

"No! Oh, show me!"

Chris's heart was pounding madly. He leaned against the doorjamb. His colleagues, crowded around a dressing-table, were giggling.

He had worked with all of them before. They were pros in the industry. They had greeted him with apparent cheer today. And here they were now: talking shit behind his back. As one did.

"Oh, that's *precious*. So he didn't get the role at all…"

"Can you imagine? Going after Nicholas Madden? You almost have to respect that nerve."

"*I* can't believe it *worked*."

"I'd never go for it. Madden sounds like a right piece of work."

"Yes, isn't he?" Chris said amiably.

Blank silence. A general sense of shock penetrated the room. One of the models had the good sense to turn crimson; another became absorbed in the contents of an eye-shadow palette. The others, caught in various stages of shame or insolence, regarded him with undisguised interest.

"After all," Chris continued, in his blandest voice, "if I wanted to screw my way to the top, I would *absolutely* set my sight on the most hard-ass, most insufferable asshole in Hollywood. Impeccable logic."

"Well, did you?" one of his colleagues said. A fresh burst of giggles erupted.

"No. I didn't." Icy disdain seemed a safe bet.

"But you slept with him. Everyone knows that."

Chris's fingers clenched gently around his elbow. "Do they?"

"Well, *yeah*. We've seen the pictures, you know," his—once, a work friend—continued, undaunted. "I don't blame you, honest. He's *seriously* hot."

"Come on, Lavalle, what's he like?"

"I bet he likes it really rough in bed. He looks the type."

"He's a better man than all of you combined," said Chris, his voice very soft. He registered the looks of surprise around the room with pale contempt, and headed for his dressing-table, turning his back on them. No time to wipe off his makeup; he didn't relish the idea of sticking around more than he needed to. These were people he had worked with—laughed with—he had gone out for drinks with them, had soothed their nerves before a shoot…pain bloomed in his chest, then fizzled out, just as swiftly.

And then he felt nothing.

He changed quickly into jeans and a sweater, and stuffed his equipment back into his bag, ignoring the muffled murmurs behind him. Doubtless his words would make their way to social media before long—*Chris Lavalle, Torch-Bearer*—and he couldn't make himself care. He was long, long past caring.

It was time to leave.

"Hey…" One of the girls, coltish on long legs—barely eighteen—approached him gingerly. Her voice dropped to a whisper. "Look, don't pay attention to him. He's an asshole."

She had large, bambi-ish eyes, very dark. She looked shy. Kind.

"It's alright," Chris said, feeling protectiveness catch in his throat. "I've heard worse." *And so will you.*

The industry was rotten to its core. Girls starved themselves to look the part. Boys didn't fare much better. Anyone who didn't fit in that gender binary might as well not exist at all. And when you dared to step out of line, you were called a gold digger, a fortune hunter, and a whore. Regardless of age, experience, or sexuality.

Lana. That was her name. She was slated to become an ambassador for Louis Vuitton, if the rumors were correct. She was so, so young.

"Lana. You have my number?"

"I—yeah? I think so?" She blinked, very quickly.

"I don't think we're going to run in the same circles much longer," Chris said, as gently as he could. "Sometimes you'll need someone who's done the rounds before. To talk to," he amended, when she looked alarmed. "Call me, if that happens. It won't become any easier. Don't let yourself be alone." He'd done that for years, masquerading behind his online presence. It was an awful, solitary way to live, and he was sick to death of it.

Lana swallowed, but nodded imperceptibly. Chris kissed her cheek, gave the rest of the room a look of grim finality, and went.

Joanne Engels removed her glasses and steepled her fingers together.

"You come from an…unconventional background. I was

not convinced that you were the right fit, given the specifications we usually adhere to. David—" with a nod at the casting director who had welcomed Chris at the door and was, apparently, to thank for his audition "—has had excellent reports of your work with Priya Chaudhuri on set for *The Throne*. Needless to say, I trust his judgement. Previous to this, I believe you have worked on projects that were not, necessarily, up to our—and possibly your—standards of excellence."

"That's a very tactful way of putting it," Chris said wryly.

A brief smile. "Very well. But I *am* impressed. You are not, as I feared, wholly incompetent. That being said."

She set her hand down on the script.

"You speak well, and you know how to pose. That's half the work already done. But you may not be used to the work rhythm we will impose upon you. A series like *The Long Winter* is—well, it is the long haul, Mr. Lavalle. It is not eight weeks of filming in July. It is months of work through the worst days and nights of the year. You will be required to work long hours. Your character is not the most important in the cast, but you must not let that lull you into incompetence. His role is crucial. I do not speak lightly in this matter."

She glanced at David Fontaine. "And then there is the issue of your…latest appearances in the press."

Chris took in a slow breath. "Yes. I have lately been subject to harassment." He met Engels's gaze evenly. "That *is* what you are referring to, is it not?"

"It is indeed," she said, with a flicker of amusement. "You're very bold, Mr. Lavalle."

Chris blinked. It was not the reaction he had expected. Perhaps Joanne Engels, not being part of Hollywood, and therefore not beholden to its rigid code of thought and its strict standards of behavior, could allow herself to look at what had happened to them in a different light. She belonged to a different world.

It recontextualized the treatment they had undergone at the hands of *The Throne*'s production in such a way as left him slightly breathless.

"Chris," he said firmly. "I say harassment because that is what it is. My privacy was violated and exposed to the public in sordid detail. I do not intend to apologize for it. Nor," he added, "for the person I was with."

"I must admit, it brings its fair share of problems. But you are quite a popular man online, scandal or no. *And* you come with a loyal fan base. That is something in your favor, if they should follow you over to *The Long Winter*."

"Of course," Fontaine put in, "our decision will ultimately rely on your performance today."

Chris kept his eyes on Engels. She said: "The spy you will be playing—if we hire you—is a complex figure, by turns Machiavellian and principled. He holds little value for human life, including his own. He will be difficult to grasp. Take the script. Look through it."

"Take as much time as you need," added Fontaine, encouragingly. "We're not looking to pressure you."

That was easily said, but perfectly untrue. Chris felt the pressure like a needle at the back of his neck.

He read the scene straight through, then again, more slowly. It was a verbal duel between Laurent, who he was reading for, and the man he was intent on killing, a corrupt French official working with the Nazi regime. Laurent's task was to convince, seduce, deceive, and entrap his way into an exclusive, secretive dinner party. It was a convoluted, complex scene, full of double entendres and false meanings.

It was thrilling.

"Done?" Engels was watching him intently.

Chris breathed out. "Yes. I think so."

"I'll read opposite," said Fontaine. "I'll follow your lead. Whenever you're ready."

They read through the scene twice. Fontaine was a strangely expressive, reactive partner, which Chris found off-putting until he realized that was the intent: Fontaine was circling through emotions, forcing him to switch directions at a moment's notice. Once he'd grasped that, it became exciting. Laurent's dubious morality, his irresistible charm, his callousness, were utterly unlike Angelo, whose cruelty was based in self-doubt and a deep, quiet melancholy. Laurent worked for a cause, fervent as a priest. He would kill, and kill again, and finally be killed, to free Paris from its chains. Chris fell into the character like a man falling in love.

"Alright," Engels said mildly, after the second read-through. "That's...illuminating."

"Good," Fontaine translated, taking a seat again.

"You were able to grasp the complexity of the script. True, this is a rushed take—the final script will be more elaborate— but it gives us an idea of where we can take him. And what *you* could do with him."

A fizz of expectation coiled tightly in Chris's stomach. "Oh?"

"Of course, we can't commit to anything just yet. I'd like to see you act opposite Philippe, though." Philippe Langlais was *The Long Winter*'s lead actor. Chris had met him at an after-party the year before, and had liked him very much. He was a kind, gentle-spoken, almost shy man, who, in spite of his prestige as one of the new stars of French television, never pulled rank over lesser celebrities. Working with him wouldn't just be rewarding: it would be finding a friend in a friendless place.

Engels gave him a firm, professional handshake, and said

something about looking forward to seeing him again. Fontaine, walking him to the door, said: "Thank you. You've given us something real to think about. This should be very exciting."

Chris walked away with a tense feeling of anticipation. He could not be certain that he had nailed the interview, nor that he would have the part at all. But the act of reaching out into the darkness and meeting a helpful hand had given him courage to see the next weeks through, as Nicholas had done for him in the past. He wished to hell he could tell him so.

The air had cooled drastically over the past few weeks, and he curled his long scarf around his neck as he pushed through to the nearest metro station.

August's storms had long passed; the sky was very white, the wind was picking up. A long, long Parisian winter was about to begin.

# Chapter Twenty-One

weheartmoviespod.com/latest

*[Transcript]...today we're looking at Nicholas Madden's filmography, from his early debut in* Nightingale *to his recent appearances in* One for the Gold *and* Baru. *Madden is an infamous figure in Hollywood—his stellar career and unchallenged talent have received international acclaim, with good reason, we think, but the notorious quarrels he has picked with directors and production managers over the past twelve years have soured the public on him. We have to wonder just how much of it is publicity to drum up ticket sales...*

*...of course, Madden has been in the news recently for reasons completely unrelated to his acting...*

*...Madden, who has been romantically linked with many actresses among Hollywood royalty, has never confirmed any liaison...*

*...scandal broke when racy pictures of Madden and his latest costar, Christian Lavalle, surfaced...*

*...on set for* The Throne, *the period piece adapted from the novel of the same name...*

*...Madden has not given any credence to the rumors and has not commented on either his sexuality nor his relationship with Christian Lavalle.*

★ ★ ★

"All done," said Kay, moving away. "Be careful you don't smudge it."

"I'll be fine," Nicholas said shortly. He gave the makeup artist a tight smile. "Thank you."

"You're a cold-tempered bastard, you know that?" Kay laughed, skillfully rearranging his brushes and paints in his bag. "Well, you're welcome. I'll come back for touch-ups after lunch." He picked up his phone, glancing at the screen. "And *now* I have to attend to Her Majesty." He shuddered. "Wish me luck."

"Is she worse than I am?" Nicholas said, amused. Ariana Hawkins, his costar on *Deep North*, was an extraordinary actress; but she nourished a reputation as a stuck-up princess. Not very much unlike him, then.

"I've worked with you before," Kay said, giving him finger guns. Then he added, ruefully: "No. She's alright. I think she cultivates her image to be…inaccessible. Which I respect, mind. She's had to deal with a *lot* of shit."

"Haven't we all," Nicholas murmured. Kay went silent then, but he squeezed Nicholas's shoulder on his way out of the trailer.

There were ten minutes left before he would be called on set. This was the worst time of Nicholas's day—the in-between moments, the liminal times, when the demands of the work faded away, and all that was left was Nicholas Madden, with the thoughts in his head.

Thoughts of Paris. Night-storms, high fevers, and shared madness.

The cast and crew of *Deep North* were too well versed in the false mystique of Hollywood to ask him to comment. Paparazzi were not so considerate. For a while he had been in the eye of the media circus, followed about and aggrieved by

demands to come clean. His forced outing had had more drastic consequences than even Jim Slater had assumed it would;
Mike Costa, as predicted, had given him up, and doors he had
thought permanently open had slammed in his face. Opportunities lost. Missed connections. *Lie low. Don't make waves.*
Well, he had gone to Alaska, and he would not return until
the promotion tour for *The Throne* began. Then it would be
a *real* party.

His phone pinged. Incoming email. Nicholas opened it.

Hi, it said. This is Antoine Charpentier.

Nicholas paused, the phone frozen in his hand.

Reaching out to you may be one of my worse ideas, considering the circumstances. Rest assured I do not come bearing news from Chris, nor have I been tasked with a message
from him. I doubt you want to know how he fares, considering your disappearing act last August. I care very little for
how you fare, to be entirely honest.

Still, I assume you know how to call someone. On the
phone.

The photos from your session together have come out
well. Contract or no contract, I only intend to use Chris's portraits in my portfolio. You needn't worry about yours doing
the rounds online.

That being said, I thought you might want to have a look
at them. They are…illuminating.

You'll find them attached.

See you in January.

A.C.

It hurt to breathe. Nicholas opened the attachment.

Chris alone. Eyes half-closed, throat bared, a lazy smile

curling at his lips: he was an arrogant young prince, haughty and autocratic, with an audacious twist. His shirt was half-open, and a flash of collarbone showed. That—the hint of bared skin—stung Nicholas deep in the heart.

He swiped past.

Chris, staring at the camera with his hands in his pockets, the light white-gold in his hair. Chris holding out his arms to him. Chris's hand on his waist; Chris's hand in his hand; Chris's fingers twining with his own. Their bodies, encased in light. The dip, the turn. Dancing without music. And Nicholas, looking, as he had never looked, shockingly, stunningly tender.

He had nearly forgotten that moment. The bare, polished parquet, gleaming bronze, and the stream of sunlight through cathedral windows. Chris, real and vital in his arms. The joy rising in him like a flood, at once a threat and a promise.

"Nicholas."

Madalena, framed in the doorway. "What?"

"You're wanted in five."

"Oh."

She glanced at his phone. "Did you…"

"No. I didn't."

"Right." She moved aside so he could pass. They stepped out into the icy Alaskan night, heading towards the glare of spotlights. "Hey, before I forget: you're had four requests for interviews in the last two days alone. Blake Minnow, *Tomorrow Night, EW.com*… PR for *The Throne*. Solo gigs," she added. "Nothing you'd have to share the spotlight for. In another timeline, Chris might have…well, you know."

Nicholas's phone burned in his hand. "I know." He paused. "I really fucked this one up, didn't I?"

Madalena didn't beat around the bush. "You did. But, look—I don't blame you. No one *could* blame you. You were never going to be outed gracefully. There is no decent way to expose someone's sexuality in the celebs press; Damien Jones and his sort were always going to take advantage of you. Whatever wrongs you've committed, staying in the closet wasn't one of them."

Nicholas wasn't so kind to himself as she was. "I wanted to be safe, and I wanted to have him. A self-contradictory paradigm."

"Like I said. Different timelines."

"I wanted to protect him," he admitted.

"And he wanted to protect you." He frowned down at her. "He did, you know. When he saw that you couldn't deal, he went away. He…withdrew himself from the equation. It was the kindest thing he could do, and he did it without protest, without blame."

They walked on towards the set, shivering a little. The landscape, torn up in ice and thorny bush, looked like the dark side of the moon. You could hardly see the sky through the white glare of the spotlights.

The stark, alien-like appearance of this place had made a stranger of Nicholas's past self. He was struggling to recognize himself. Hadn't he once prided himself on his temper, on his talent, on his determination? And when the going had got tough, he had not been brave enough to confront the world at Chris's side. He had begun to run. He had been so concerned about pure survival, he had lost sight of himself.

Now—here—he had no one to face *but* himself. The self he had made for Hollywood, and the self he had been with Chris. Two sides of a man.

He had to choose, and he had to choose soon.

In two weeks, they would be done here. Something else was ending, too. Nicholas was conscious, with a strange, absolute certainty, that a part of his life must now be set aside.

Selfishness and self-loathing—everything he had put in Frederick—everything *The Throne* had forced him to face. He'd had enough of playing the Big Bad Wolf.

Time to see what else he could be.

He slipped his phone in his pocket, but kept his palm pressed against it. "Say yes to *Tomorrow Night*. Who's hosting that now?"

"Leigh Zhao. He's pretty decent. Nothing overly blunt, but he does like a...daring, dazzling style of production."

"That's what he'll get, then."

"You might want to call Slater before committing yourself to making revelations. No?"

"No." A stir of excitement danced inside of him, a spark before the bang. "No, I don't think so. Slater will rant and rave afterwards. I have amends to make."

"*...Welcome to* Tomorrow Night, *where we tackle everything that hasn't happened yet! It's December 14th, nine p.m. Eastern Time, and boy do we have a hefty lineup for you tonight. Congresswoman Natalia Kaufmann will be talking to us about her latest push for youth outreach. The Bridge will perform, live, here onstage—but first, actor, performer, and international pain in the ass Nicholas Madden will be talking to us about his latest role in LGBT period piece* The Throne—*and the controversy that is already attached to the film...*"

"You'll be on in fifteen," a helpful production assistant confided in Nicholas. He nodded, leaning his shoulder against the wall, and watching from the wings.

Leigh Zhao, dressed in a pale grey suit and paisley tie, worked his audience with skillful virtuosity. He was a showman, alright—he knew exactly when to drop the right joke, when to leave a sentence hanging, and when to drum up suspense. His show went from hilarious to somber in the space of a few minutes, veered right back to outrageous by way of cheerful absurdity, and finally settled into comfortable comedy.

Nicholas considered emailing Antoine back.

It was a gamble. He had no guarantee his email would be opened. Antoine, protective as he was, might simply delete it on sight. More significantly still, he might elect to keep their communication to himself. If he wished to shield Chris from further harm...

Tomorrow Night, he typed. He might want to be fore-warned.

What he was planning on doing would shine a spotlight back on Paris, and on Chris. It was a risk he was taking, a new problem he was creating. He did not doubt that Chris, with all his kindness and his generosity, would understand his desire to do this. But Chris had taken hits to his reputation, to his job, and to his life, and he had a right to know before-hand, before the shit hit the fan all over again. He was owed the chance to protect himself.

He hit Send.

"...and now! The Big Bad Wolf of Hollywood, ladies and gen-tlemen, three times Golden Globes winner, sadly overlooked at the Academy Awards—but fear not, this year may be his year—the star of One for the Gold and future headliner of The Throne—Nicholas Madden!"

Bright, enthusiastic cheering. Applause broke out in thun-derous waves as Nicholas walked on set, reaching a crescendo when he leaned in to shake Leigh Zhao's hand.

"Thanks for coming," Zhao said, with an irresistible smile. He was a good-looking man in his late thirties, black hair greying at the temples. His tie was terrible, but he was pull-ing it off.

"Thanks for having me," Nicholas replied, by rote. He

slipped open his jacket as he sat, crossed his legs, and met Zhao's eyes levelly.

"So." Zhao lifted his eyebrows.

"So," Nicholas agreed.

"It's been a busy year for you." Trilling laughter from the crowd. "I know, I know, what a cliché! But it really has been a *long* year. I feel like I've aged a full decade in the last, oh, three months. You ever get that feeling?"

"All the time." This earned him a rush of laughter from the audience. Zhao smiled.

"You've just returned from… Alaska, was it? Working on a secret project?"

"Not that secret," Nicholas said. "It's a high-stakes thriller set in the Alaskan wilderness. A small town gets cut off from the rest of the world after a thunderstorm, a spate of murders disrupts their lives. Very intense, very claustrophobic."

"It's a bit of a change from your usual fare, isn't it? A thriller?"

"Yes—it was an interesting script. And an interesting challenge. I play a classic Noir protagonist, transposed in a non-Noir, yet almost-Noir, setting. Eternal night, ice storms. We've worked very hard on it."

"You're well-known for portraying complicated characters with powerful backstories and moving story lines. You were the favorite for an Oscar for your role in *One for the Gold*, weren't you?"

"I was one of the nominees."

"Well, there's plenty of people who will swear you were robbed that day. Myself included."

A single *Woot!* burst from the audience, to much laughter.

"*And*," Zhao pressed on, "there's some talk you might be nominated again this year? Not for *Deep North*, of course—

when is that coming out?—but for your role in *The Throne*, which is coming out...next month? Correct?"

"Yes. The premiere is in early January."

"In Paris, I hear?"

"That's right."

Zhao nodded, folding his hands together. "Of course, there's been a lot of controversy surrounding the shooting of *The Throne*. Surprise casting choices, the infamous August Storm, and of course—what everyone has seen, what's on everyone's lips is..." He made an eloquent gesture.

"Yes," Nicholas said gently. "My affair with a costar."

Zhao blinked.

The cameras were reeling in, evidently seeking an emotional close-up. Nicholas kept his face neutral.

Zhao took his time choosing his next question. This was not part of their pre-shoot arrangement. Zhao had intended to stick to double entendres and heavy insinuations.

"Sorry," Nicholas said. He was almost enjoying this. "I'm derailing."

"Not at all." Zhao had regrouped superbly. "Are we to understand that you are *confirming* your relationship with Chris Lavalle?"

"The photos have been seen around the world by now." And, if he had his guess, the live-show screens were showing them now in glorious Technicolor. "They speak for themselves, do they not?"

"You," said Zhao, "have been very careful in *not* confirming *nor* denying...anything at all."

"That's true. I'll tell you a secret, Leigh." Nicholas leaned in and lowered his voice, just enough that the mics would pick it up. "Internalized homophobia is a bitch."

A moment of shock in the audience, punctuated by nervous laughter. A flicker of genuine amusement passed over Zhao's face. "Oh?"

"Chris—" Nicholas paused. "Chris Lavalle is a remarkable man. He is also, by accident or chance, a remarkable actor. It has been said that he must have—what was the wording?— *fucked* his way into *The Throne*. That is untrue. It has been said that he has turned me gay. That is also untrue. I have been gay for a very long time."

He took a sip of water.

"Wow," said Zhao.

"Mm-hmm."

"You actors sure choose your moments. Coming out in style, huh?"

"Well." Nicholas smiled. "There's something to be said for extraordinary circumstances."

"Tell me if I've got this straight." Zhao was enjoying himself now. "You and Christian Lavalle met on set of *The Throne*. You hit it off straightaway—"

"Not quite. I called him a phony. I thought he *was* a phony. An Instagram boy-prince with his eye on an Armani campaign, as I recall. And then he…surprised me. He understood Angelo in a charismatic, visceral way. I loved to watch him act. I am not," said Nicholas, wryly, "a method actor. I have never conducted any relationship with one of my costars. A fictional love story remains a fictional love story."

"Then what changed?"

"Chris happened."

"Just like that?"

"No, it was…gradual. Before I knew what had happened, I—we—were already taken in… We worked together. Were constantly together, by necessity. Priya Chaudhuri had us reading lines. I doubt she would have done so had she predicted the result."

"Let's talk about that," Zhao said, with precise direction. "Priya Chaudhuri is famous for her dislike of on-set affairs. You were not daunted by this injunction?"

Nicholas was quiet for a moment. When he spoke again, his voice was soft. "There was a storm. What is now being called the August Storm, across Western Europe. Paris was flooded. Nothing but rain and thunder. No filming. And we were...caught in it." Those days in Chris's small apartment seemed light-years away. They had been safe. Nothing could touch them there. It was only when they had wandered *out*...

"Storms are strange, liminal spaces. We didn't think about Chaudhuri. We barely thought about the rest of the world.

"When the news broke out, I was—concerned. Worried. About my reputation, and the opportunities that might offer themselves to me—or be rescinded. I severed my connection with Chris, and he did not stop me. Of course," Nicholas added, with a touch of asperity, "it was very much *recommended* to me that I no longer pursue a relationship with Chris. He, I know, received the same speech. The PR team of *The Throne* was emphatic. Chris was pushed out of the promotion circuit. We could not overshadow the greater picture, which was, and remains, the success of *The Throne*."

Zhao nodded, his face grave. He was good at this. He could command the crowd's attention with a gesture, with a glance. Now he was self-possessed and sympathetic, and the audience was so quiet you might have heard a coin drop.

"That sounds like a harsh sentence."

Nicholas shrugged. "It's Hollywood. A year ago, I would have agreed with them. I saw love affairs as purely accessory to—and, sometimes, antithetical with—the work that needed to be done. Nothing mattered so much as the job. The movie. And *The Throne* means a great deal to me. I have been planning on being part of its execution for a very long time."

"But?"

"But…" He had prepared this little speech—every accent, every emphasis, every small revelation. Now the words seemed to fall short of the emotion he wanted. "I have always considered the novel to be almost prophetic in its scale. It deals in miracles and epiphanies. It seems only fitting that I should have suffered one of these during the filming."

"What epiphany was that?" Zhao was grinning, caught in the moment. He must be visualizing the audience ratings going steeply upwards.

"For fourteen years I have lived my life purely and absolutely for the job." Nicholas gave the cameras a wry look. "And when the job gave me a man I could fall in love with, I have failed—miserably—to resist it."

The audience took a collective intake of breath, and then burst, almost of its own volition, into stunning applause. It took a sweet time to die down. By the time it did, Zhao had got over his initial amazement, and was laughing.

"I have to say, Nicholas, you know how to stage a confession. Does he know, though?"

"Chris? No, he doesn't. Didn't."

Zhao's eyebrows hiked up. "Taking a risk, are you?"

"Yes and no. I didn't come here for Chris, Leigh." *I came here because I failed him, and I owe him. I owe him my life as I know it now. I have been lying to myself for years, and he showed me who I truly am.*

Zhao looked bewildered. He was loving every minute of it. "Not that I don't enjoy having my show derailed by an egocentric Hollywood actor, but *do* go on."

Nicholas took a moment—both to rally his thoughts and, if he were honest, because the thrill of the moment was quite real.

He felt punch-drunk on relieved happiness. At last it was

said. It was out. He no longer had to be afraid. "We judge the success of a movie to be more important than the safety and well-being of those who forge it. We judge the work—in all its aspects—to be more meaningful and more worthy of our protection than the blood, bone, and brain of its creators. I have been guilty of that sort of thinking. And there is some truth in it: a proper story is in itself a miracle. The story of *The Throne* is one well worthy of being told, and it will be, I think, a great movie, awards or no awards.

"That people should be hurt in the making of it—and hurt in such a way that concerns and affects the rest of their lives—is perhaps unavoidable. But we should *strive* to avoid it. We should not put severe restrictions on those who are giving their all to the creation of the story. We should not shame them for experiencing emotions beyond their control. We should not exile them once they are no longer of use.

"We are beholden to ourselves to try."

Zhao drummed his fingers on the desk. Then, with great deliberation, he took a gulp of water, and wiped his mouth. That was a show too—it all was a show—the surprise, the concerned interest, and now the thoughtful understanding. He was good at it, Nicholas had to admit it. He adapted to the situation as it happened.

"Let me ask you something," he said.

"Sure."

"Have you talked to Chris Lavalle since you left Paris?"

"That's a very private question, Leigh," Nicholas said, with a swift smile.

"Well, you've filibustered my show with a romantic declaration of feelings, so I'd say you owe me an honest answer. As honest as it can get, anyway."

So they were on the same page. "No, I haven't. I have told myself I didn't want to intrude on his privacy, and that I could not—I would not—force my presence upon him. But that was a lie, too," Nicholas admitted. "I was a coward; the worst sort of coward. I couldn't face him, so I stayed away."

Zhao's expression became a touch more honestly concerned. "It takes some courage to admit it."

"No, this isn't courage. It's fear. I was badly frightened by the way the press reacted to our…liaison. Threats and abuse, insulting comments, disgraceful, horrible invectives. I ought to be used to them, and yet—" He broke off, summoning as much pathos as he could. "And yet the worst of it wasn't concerned about me at all. They wanted to find a scapegoat, and Chris was the better target. I only wish I had spoken sooner."

They wrapped up the rest of the interview in record time. Zhao shook his hand with a smile.

"Well played," he murmured, so low that the mics could not catch his words.

# *Chapter Twenty-Two*

**WATCH:** *Nicholas Madden Comes Out Live On* Tomorrow Night

*"We are beholden to ourselves to try and do better": Nicholas Madden makes impassioned plea for compassion and honesty, condemns invasion of privacy, comes clean about affair with costar Chris Lavalle*

"You *asshole*."

Chris lowered the screen of his laptop and started to laugh. After a moment he pulled his knees up, rested his arms on them, and put his hands over his face.

The whole setup was at once unreal and staggeringly clear. It was very much like Nicholas to come out in this manner—in a blaze of fury, with a righteous tirade against the press, *The Throne*'s production team, and the rest of the rotten, twisted world. Condemnation had never sounded so good as it did in his mouth.

*When the job gave me a man to fall in love with.*

God. Chris adored him. Nicholas wasn't an easy man to love—he was too irritable, too ferocious, too prone to quick, outrageous judgement. Too grim, in a hot sort of way.

And yet Chris had seen beyond the fury and the thunder. The storm had seen to that. It had altered them, until they could no longer recognize who they were: their masks had been torn away, and all that was left was tenderness. He remembered, in vivid color and sensation, Nicholas's hand brushing down his naked back; Nicholas's mouth, smiling under his mouth.

There was no coming back from that.

Nicholas had hurt him very badly. Chris recognized that: he prodded at the edges of the wound and felt it slowly scarring over. But Chris had hurt him, too, had abandoned him in the worst moment, hadn't stood by his side when it truly mattered.

Which left the question of what he was going to do about it. Nicholas had set one pawn into motion, and it was left to him to decide if he wanted to play.

He could call. He could wait. He could say nothing at all, and he could come clean on social media. None of these options were tempting. They lacked something...cinematic.

His phone chimed. Philippe Langlais's name—he had been given his number at the end of their double-audition—was showing brightly on the screen.

Welcome to the team 😊, it said, and then: The core cast is meeting for dinner next Saturday. It's been ages since we were all together. You should come!

Chris hesitated. He picked up his phone. Langlais had been smiling and a little shy when they had met. The second he had picked up his script, he had transformed into a different man. His character was by turns cynical, suave, and vulnerable, and Philippe hit every beat without missing a cue. He was a stunning actor. Chris would have accepted the job for nothing but the privilege of working with him; the fact that his own role was captivating, the team friendly and engaging, and the project one he truly thought worthwhile, was turning the next year or so of his life into a genuinely exciting prospect.

He swiped his thumb across the screen. I'd like that.

The reply was instantaneous. Great! We're having Thai. Meet up at Republique at 8?

See you then, Chris sent back, and had barely put the phone down before it pinged again. *Incoming email.* Priya Chaudhuri.

Chris's battered heart gave a little *thump*. He wasn't ready to speak to Chaudhuri. His respect for her had not lessened; he admired her profoundly. But his feelings towards *The Throne* were a tangle of resentment and grief, and he was neither willing to apologize to her nor prepared to accept her own apology. He couldn't unravel his esteem for her work and character from the bitterness of the last few days before *The Throne* had wrapped up—his loneliness, his anger, his self-doubt and his worry.

He hit *open email* timidly.

Her message was short, and to the point. It had, as far as he could tell, been written by Chaudhuri herself, not jotted off by an assistant. She expressed herself in reserved though sincere terms, making direct apology for her thoughtlessness and oversight. She was not interested in making excuses for herself: instead, straightforwardly, she made amends for his loneliness, his exclusion, and his neglect at the hands of *The Throne*'s production team. You deserved better, Chris.

How much of this was due to Nicholas's intervention? Chris did not know, and did not care to know. It was enough that Chaudhuri felt a keen sense of obligation and of loyalty towards her cast: whatever production might say, she had done what she believed was right.

Chris was not such a fool that he thought himself blameless. He *should* have spoken out. He'd had the platform for it. He had an advantage over Nicholas, of being already out; and having long come out of the closet, had comforted himself with thoughts that *he* had nothing to fear. He should have stood by

Nicholas when society had shone its spotlight upon them. He had failed to recognize his fear. He had thought he was being forsaken, and he had taken his anger and he had nourished it, until it was the easiest thing simply to turn away for good.

Privilege and prejudice were tangled up together, a hopeless labyrinth of good intentions and sorry mistakes. Everybody was to blame.

Chris laid aside the laptop with a sigh. He was…tired. Winter was driving him out of himself. He wanted spring, and the warm long sun-drenched days of August. Whether that was the August to come, or the August that was past, had yet to be determined.

Antoine had offered to be his date to the January premiere. Chris had appreciated his concern, but that would send rather the wrong message. As Antoine had appeared in the press as his potential live-in boyfriend before this mess with Nicholas, it was even odds he'd be dubbed a serial cheater before the end of the night.

It was something he thought he wanted to do alone. Face the cameras with his brightest smile and a metaphorically lifted middle finger. Put on a real show.

*Who you present as on the red carpet is just another role.* Nicholas had been gifted with prescience when he'd said that.

Or he'd been trying to warn him. Nicholas, whom the tabloids so loved to portray as a stuck-up jackass on a short fuse, knew the dangers and the pitfalls of failing to publicize oneself in the correct manner.

Chris pressed *Play* on the video again.

*A proper story is in itself a miracle.* Nicholas's face was dark and grave. He'd grown a beard again. He was dressed, impeccably, in a black suit and a white shirt. He looked damn good, and he knew it.

*A proper story.*

Don't cower and hide and wallow in your own doubts and self-condolences. Only show up, and do it with style.

The limo wove slowly through the early-night traffic of the boulevard, gliding past purring cars and curious onlookers. Up ahead, a gigantic crowd had formed around the tall building of the cinema; they swarmed around the red carpet, craning their necks, pushing forward to catch a glimpse of the stars. Cameras flashed. Even through the tempered windows of the limo, the noise from the crowd was a muted roar. Some of them had placards. *Love You!!!* these read, and *WE STAND WITH*—the rest was lost in the chaos.

This was not the first time Chris had walked the red carpet. After two years of doing Paris Fashion Week, the dread of treading on that hallowed ground and posing for photographs had pretty much faded.

"Nearly there," his driver remarked. "You ready?"

Chris hummed, nodding, and pocketed his phone. "All fired up."

"Good for you, man."

And then the limo slowed, then stopped; and Chris pushed open the door, and stepped out.

The noise hit him first, a slamming wall of bruising voices and shouts. Then the flashing, throbbing lights. And then the sheer *scale* of the thing—the immense, glittering facade of the building, and the soft red velvet underfoot, and the realization that this, this moment, this *instant*, was what it had all been building to. This was the peak of the mountain.

He had, briefly, considered going low-key with his outfit. Then he'd thought better of it. No: he had flouted convention and tradition and opted for an electric-blue suit, over a white shirt embroidered in silver fleur-de-lys. A little extravagant, a great deal elegant, a real twist on the expected. Also makeup, because *fuck you*. Antoine's favorite artist was a master with a smoky eye and a magician with the highlighter wand. He looked really goddamn good.

Andrée was a little way away, breathtaking in a backless burgundy pantsuit and Louboutin heels. Perhaps alerted by the shouts of his name—who wouldn't be? they were loud— she turned to look at him; then held out her arms, and Chris went easily, stepping into her embrace and slipping an arm around her waist.

"Hello," he said, kissing her cheek.

"Hello, you." Andrée angled her head against his shoulder, directing a blinding smile at the nearest cluster of cameras and smartphones. "So you decided to come. It was even odds with us if you'd show up at all."

"And miss the opportunity of looking this fabulous? Not a chance."

She laughed, head thrown back. She was fantastic at this, an old pro. She worked the cameras with a wink and a smile. "Come on," she murmured. "They're waiting for us."

Chris tried, and failed, to be casual about it. "Has…Nicholas arrived?"

She cast him a smoldering look. "Yes, as a matter of fact. He's asked me the same thing, and looked very disconcerted when I said you weren't there yet. He's inside, posing for more photos and answering probing inquiries about his recent… social appearances."

"Oh, Lord."

Andrée's grip tightened on his arm. "So are Chaudhuri and the Hendersons. Listen—"

"It's alright."

"It shouldn't be. You were treated like dog shit." She grinned cheerfully at a group of fans, who collectively squealed and held up their phones, flashes popping. "It was rotten of us all. I've heard about *The Long Winter*," she added, with a neat, sharpish swerve. "Good for you."

"It looked like an intriguing prospect," Chris demurred.

Andrée laughed. "You'll be an expert at this yet. Come on—I'm freezing in this godforsaken suit."

"You do look good, though," Chris noted.

"Granted. I always do." She slipped her hand into his, and led the way into the cinema.

It was grandiose inside, all red velvet and gilded staircases. The auditorium, Chris knew, was a grand structure with multiple balconies, plush seats, and a star-studded sky. The air was noticeably warmer now, almost uncomfortably so. At the foot of the stairs stood the cast of *The Throne*, in various arrangements of black tie and silk dresses; likewise Chaudhuri, and the Henderson siblings.

Chris, it seemed, was fashionably late.

The journalist who, holding up a microphone under Chaudhuri's nose, had been asking pressing questions, left off with a theatrical gasp when Andrée and Chris joined the group. Then there was much exclaiming, and air-kisses, and all smiles: the five months they had spent apart had done enough to smooth over the awkwardness of their last few days together, when the entirety of the cast had suffered from Nicholas's bad mood and Chris's airy introspection.

"Chris! My man! It's good to see you!" Jason's broad shoulders tightened the excellent line of his suit.

Reggie was wearing a patterned silk waistcoat threaded through with blue roses. "My *dear*." He bussed Andrée's cheek. "It's been too, too long."

"It's been less than a month, Reg," Andrée said dryly. "I saw you at the after-party of *O, Hero* before the winter holidays."

Nicholas, by the time Chris had done away with the attention pressed upon him long enough to look for him, wore a grim expression. He also looked extraordinarily good-looking. His black suit was impeccably cut, his beard well trimmed, his dark hair cut close. Chris smiled. The months that had elapsed since their last encounter—since those last few bright afternoons in late August, when Nicholas had looked miserable and broken-down and *sad*—felt suddenly inconsequential.

Nicholas *now* seemed…calmer. Kinder to himself. He looked like he'd been eating. Something inside him, which had so tormented him, had gone quiet and dormant.

"Hi," he said.

"Hey."

Nicholas's glance cut down, and Chris was thankful, all of a sudden, that he *had* gone with the blue suit, and foresworn the usual black tie. There was hot admiration in Nicholas's gaze.

"Mr. Lavalle—a few questions?"

"Yes, alright," Chris said, and turned his back deliberately on Nicholas. The interviewer faltered for a moment; she had clearly intended to speak to them both. Still, impervious, she rallied.

"May I say, you look gorgeous. This *blue*! This is your first ever movie premiere. How are you feeling?"

"It's extraordinary. Overwhelming, too; I'm not used to that sort of attention," Chris lied, laughing, and the dialogue devolved into pretty platitudes for a few minutes before the young woman—who stood a little in awe of Nicholas and spoke with a strong French accent—went in for the hard question.

"Your costar—Nicholas Madden," she corrected, breathfully, into the mic, "has given an interview last month with *Tomorrow Night*—well, everyone has heard of it. Any comment you'd like to give?" Her tone was teasing.

"Well," said Chris. And then: "No."

She blinked hard. "No?"

"Nothing that shouldn't be said behind closed doors instead." He smiled, charmingly. He was very, very good at charming smiles. Nicholas could stand there and glower for the rest of the night if he wished to; Chris was off flirting and bantering his sweet tongue away.

Nicholas's hand brushed his shoulder. "We are going in."

"Oh, already?" The young woman pouted. She held on to Chris's wrist. "Surely you can spare us a few minutes."

"You've had more time than you were slated to," Nicholas said flatly. This close—he was standing behind Chris, his arm half-stretched out across his back—his voice was low and somber, with a touch of imminent doom. "Chris?"

"They won't start without us," said Chris. "And I am having *such* fun."

Nicholas's exasperated eyes met his. And that was mindblowingly familiar—that displeasure, that dark flare of anger. He had never looked so good. The first time Chris had felt that slow-burning fury was at the start of all things, on the Place Colette. Nicholas's disapproval could have broken rocks.

Chris gave him a melting look.

Cameras flashed and flamed behind them. Nicholas's hand rested lightly against the small of his back. Each press of his fingers was a small spark of light.

"Chris," he repeated, his voice low. "Come."

Chris's hand made its way, quite by chance, to the breast of Nicholas's suit. His fingers dug in, creasing the smooth blackness of the fabric. "Alright," he said softly. The flare of the cameras was burning hot against his cheek.

They climbed the staircase together. Chris looked back one last time, and nearly stumbled at the sight of the horde of cameras and microphones aimed in their direction. Nicholas steadied him, almost caressingly. His hand slid down to Chris's hand, and then it was the easiest thing in the world, after all that had occurred, after all the grief and the pain, simply to lace their fingers together.

It occurred to him that the story they had started tonight would make its way into tomorrow's tabloids in much re-vamped detail. Celebrity Twitter must be lighting right up. The thought of it made him grin.

"Christ, you're a menace," Nicholas muttered.

"Had you forgotten?"

"Not for one fucking moment." Nicholas gave his hand a squeeze. "Come *on*, danger."

The auditorium, well lit and well crowded with the fans who'd scored a premiere ticket, welcomed them with breath-less applause. They were the last to arrive. Their seats were together—why should they not be?—in the VIP section, and as they sat an usher handed Chaudhuri a mic, pointing to the stage.

She was wearing a floor-length gown of shimmering white-gold, her hair a gorgeous fall of black tresses over one shoul-der. She looked poised, confident, and as wholly at ease in front of a thousand avidly watching people as she was on set, calling for silence. The mic crackled in her hand.

"Hello!"

The auditorium responded with resounding applause. She laughed, motioning for it to die down.

"What a beautiful evening! We're very thankful for the extraordinary welcome you've offered us tonight, in such a gorgeous place as this is. We're *incredibly* thankful that you've all bought tickets." Laughter. "The movie you're about to see has been a long labor of love and effort. Our crew has worked beautifully and wholeheartedly, over the span of months, to offer the best cinematic experience you could wish for—thank you, they deserve applause—stand up, all! Take a bow!"

The cast stood and waved, laughing, and the great auditorium exploded with applause.

"Julian Chamberlain—your script has brought *The Throne* into stunning detail. You have crafted each word, each moment, each scene, so Angelo and Frederick's story could be told *right*. Thank you.

"And our amazing cast. It has been an honor to work with these men and women; they've truly given it their all... This project would not be the same without them. This project would not be *anything* without them. What started as a vanity project with a decent budget has become over the months a true undertaking. I would like to thank them all today.

"Andrée, you are a bright star in the firmament of French cinema. Sir Reginald, you are already a legend and do not need any more compliments. Jason—" She broke off, and on Chris's other side Jason let out a bellow of laughter. "You've stepped out of your comfort zone and given the performance of a lifetime," Chaudhuri said seriously. "Well done.

"Nicholas...ah, Nicholas. You came with a well-earned reputation. You have been present from the very start. You believed in *The Throne* long before any one of us did. I could not imagine any other person in the role of Frederick: you have given him life. For this I thank you.

"And Chris." Chaudhuri's spotlight eyes turned on him. "Chris Lavalle, our wild card, our surprise. Ten years from now, when you've become a star in your own right, it will be our privilege to say that we were with you when you started. You wowed us during your audition, and in the months since you have only ever exceeded our expectations. No one who sees *The Throne* will ever doubt you again. Thank you.

"Thank you all," she added, and if her voice caught fractionally Chris could never tell. "You have worked through the night and the storm, and you have given *The Throne* beauty, dynamism, and flair. We are proud to have worked with you."

She returned to her seat, and Andrée stood to hug her on her way. Her eyes caught Chris's again, and this time he was able to read fondness and sorrow in them, stark yet genuine.

He blew her a kiss. Someone behind him squeaked in delight.

Katherine and Brian Henderson spoke next, thanking investors, shareholders, production managers, and various associates. Then Julian Chamberlain, with a great deal of emotion glittering behind his enormous glasses.

And then it was down to Nicholas and him.

"Ready?" Nicholas murmured as they stood and made their way to the stage. The flashing cameras were so bright, the applause so deafening, it was all they could do to climb up the wide, shallow steps.

Chris took his hand.

"I am."

# *Chapter Twenty-Three*

**aimez-vous** @aimeesays • 25m
Pics!! From the red carpet!! #THETHRONE
instagram.com/p/Pb8zoxHhNX5/
instagram.com/p/Hg7ejkNnNY9/
instagram.com/p/Zg9Pjdfjk9ikd/

**nathalia** @unautrejour • 18m
@aimeesays Ahhh I'm so excited & so proud of them ;;;;

**Bob** @boomboom52 • 11m
#thethrone cast looking g o o d #thethrone #love #red-
carpet #chrislavalle #nicholasmadden

**Hey** @downtou • 5m
#TheThrone Priya Chaudhuri's speech was phenomenal!
The applause is deafening. A once in a lifetime event.

**o, muse** @singinme • 1m
Chris Lavalle and Nicholas Madden presenting #TheTh-
rone together at the official premiere in Paris...be still
my beating heart.

"Keep the change." Nicholas threw a few crumpled euro bills
at the driver, and stepped out of the car before it had even
stopped by the curb.

He walked briskly towards the rue des Saints-Pères. It was cold and he was shivering in his fine suit. He had left the after-party, with its shimmering lights and delicate petits-fours, well on its way to getting blind drunk and waking up in the morning with a glaring headache. But Chris had cut and run before the champagne had even started to flow, had gone before Nicholas had had time to speak with him alone. Chris had *left*, and it felt ghastly—and well deserved.

*Nothing that shouldn't be said behind closed doors*, Chris had said, and he had known—he had to have known—that Nicholas, standing behind him, would hear him. Closed doors. Well, he knew what that meant.

The door of number twenty-seven had been left slightly open. Nicholas pushed it with his shoulder and closed it softly behind him.

Chris, because he was a pain in the ass, lived on the last floor, and there was no elevator. By the time Nicholas got to the final landing, up a flight of red-carpeted stairs, he was breathless and seriously questioning his sanity. A normal human being would have called first. He had staunchly refused to call—despite Madalena's frequent reminders since his stint on *Tomorrow Night*—in favor of…this. This cliché nonsense. A grand gesture: showing up in the dead of night.

Maybe he had gone a little *too* method after all.

A moment of glassy uncertainty stretched out after he had rung the doorbell, and Nicholas leaned his shoulder against the doorjamb as the tinny sound slowly faded.

Perhaps he had failed to recognize Chris's amiable complacency at the premiere for what it truly was: understanding and forgiveness, but not encouragement. Sympathy and help, but not an incentive.

Then soft, padding footsteps; then the door opened, and Chris was there, framed in dim light, wearing pajama pants and a soft-looking t-shirt.

"Hi," Nicholas said.

"Hi." Chris didn't move. He didn't invite him in, either.

"You didn't come to the after-party."

A vague shrug. "It was…a little overwhelming."

"Yeah." Nicholas raked a hand through his hair. "No, I get that." Watching the movie for the first time had felt extraordinary; but, like most extraordinary things, it made it difficult to feel human again once it was over. One felt a strange dissociation: watching oneself onscreen. The person you'd played became more real, more substantial than you really were.

And he was starting to question the wisdom of coming here.

"Are you alright?" Chris asked, softly.

Nicholas gave him a wry smile. "As much as I can be. I've got jet lag coming out of my skull."

"Ah." Chris hesitated. He held out his hand. "Come here?"

Nicholas went. He folded himself up against Chris, slipped both arms around his waist, and sighed when he felt Chris's hands sink into his hair, cupping his neck.

Chris's voice went warm all over. "You were fantastic tonight."

"As were you. As predicted. You will be deluged in audition calls once it comes out."

"About that… Nicholas, I won't be starving anytime soon."

"Yes, I heard." He'd watched *The Long Winter,* and had been impressed by the immense production values and the flawless acting. "You must be proud."

"Right now," Chris admitted against his hair, "I find it very difficult to think about anything at all. We've made a right mess of ourselves, haven't we."

Nicholas swallowed down a slightly-hysterical laugh. "God. I missed you."

"I missed you, too." Chris pulled him up, curling his hands in his hair, so that they could look at each other. His body was warm and giving in Nicholas's arms. "I don't understand it at all," he said. "How we could hurt each other. It feels unreal now."

"I abandoned you," Nicholas admitted. "I was a craven coward."

"You had a right to be scared." Chris's fingers pressed against the base of his skull. "I should have understood that. I should have made it clear I didn't blame you."

"I was a fool."

"So was I."

Nicholas's hands tightened around his waist. "I came here to apologize. To make things right. I wanted to call you—earlier. I ought to have told you directly."

"Ah, but you're good at grand gestures. The temptation of shaming your haters on international television must have been too great to resist."

A short laugh shook through Nicholas's chest. "You might say that. Still. I should have warned you earlier than I did. It was an...impulsive decision, and you were owed better from me."

"I loved it," Chris said frankly. "You were—forceful and persuasive and...scary. And *sexy*." He grinned. He looked so young when he grinned, in the way that some people looked young their entire lives—full of brilliant, dramatic vitality. No wonder he was an actor. Nicholas should have seen it the moment he'd met him.

He had fairly shone off the screen tonight. Angelo and Frederick had come to life in all their desperate, hateful passions.

"I love you," Nicholas said, quietly. He had known it for a long time now, and yet it still felt like nothing short of a damn miracle.

Chris's hands stroked down around his neck. One flattened against his collarbone; the other cupped his jaw; and then Chris kissed him, a brief touch of his lips against Nicholas's.

Nicholas's mouth parted, and he kissed him back, gently, his tongue touching his, until Chris made a very soft sound and deepened the kiss, biting him sweet and sharp. His thumb pressed against Nicholas's cheekbone. On and on the kiss went, seeking and responding in slow waves of mutual pleasure, until pleasure itself was all that mattered, itself was sufficient. Nicholas found himself backed up against the door, which had closed, without his knowing how or when; his fingers tightened on Chris's waist, gathering him up against him. Chris moaned in his mouth. The sounds of their kissing were soft and wet.

"Chris." He buried the name against his throat. "Chris—"

"I know." Chris's hand was resting on his chest, on the left side. "I know, sweetheart."

"I missed you like hell."

Chris's lips touched his cheek. His teeth bit lightly at his ear. "Come to bed—please. I need you with me."

They went, discarding clothes. Nicholas's untied bow tie was the first to go, then his well-tailored jacket; Chris's hands pulled open his dress shirt, finding warm skin below. Nicholas skimmed his fingers across Chris's abdomen, slid beneath the waistline of his pajama pants, copped a feel of his ass, and felt Chris's laughter shuddering deliciously against him. They kissed against the bedroom door, while Chris removed his belt and tugged lightly at the button of his pants. Then they were stumbling in, ridding themselves of the last layers, the last clothes—underwear, off—and they were standing in the middle of the bedroom, in the dim lamplight, stark naked and kissing again, kissing more, never stopping. It was impossible to stop. It was impossible to fathom ceasing to kiss Chris.

"Bed," Nicholas mumbled.

"I know. I know…" Still they did not move, too caught up in relief mingled with pleasure. Chris pulled away far enough to bury his face in Nicholas's neck, one hand wandering down to brush at his aching cock. Nicholas's fingers dug in at the small of his back, where the dip of his spine met his ass. Desire was flaring in every place they touched.

"What do you want?" Chris mumbled.

"I—" Nicholas kissed his jaw. "Want you in me, if possible."

Chris reared back, his eyes wide as moons. "Um. Yes, please."

Nicholas laughed against his mouth. "Tell me you have something."

"I do. Oh—" Chris pulled himself away, lingeringly, smiling when their hands were the last to part. "I have. Condoms, I think. Somewhere. This has been celibacy central."

"I sure hope so," Nicholas growled, and Chris gave him a *look* of unadulterated exasperation that belied the fondness in his voice.

"Come *here*."

Somehow they made do.

"Have you ever—?"

"No."

There was no awkwardness in Chris's eyes; no judgement whatever. "We can—like this. If you—?"

"Yes. Please," Nicholas articulated, breathless with the feeling of Chris's fingers on his back, his hips, his thighs. The bedsheets were cool underneath him, and Chris's touch was gentle. Chris's lips skimmed his shoulder. His hand stroked down Nicholas's arm, down to his fingertips.

"Breathe."

It was very, very strange. Nicholas had never been on the receiving end. Until tonight he'd not thought that he would ever want to be; but Chris had changed him, had turned him from the inside out. This felt merely like the next step in a dance, a new narrative opening. Another role to take to heart.

Where were his ideas of masculinity, of taking and giving, of what submissiveness entailed, or didn't?

He would have done anything Chris asked of him. But Chris *didn't* ask. He sat back on his heels and watched, and he waited until Nicholas could find his voice to demand more.

Then Chris pushed inside him, and Nicholas's hands dug into fists in the pillows. Chris's lips were open against his shoulder blades, pressing down fervent kisses; Chris's moans were muffled against his skin. They moved together, finding rhythm and purchase. Chris's chest pressed stickily against his back. It felt stunningly, ridiculously good. The breath was punched out of Nicholas's lungs with every inward thrust.

"You are so beautiful," Chris murmured, stroking his hands down his spine, fitting them to the dip of his hips. Nicholas blinked back sudden, hot tears. "So so good—oh, Nicholas, I want—"

"Wait," Nicholas said, "hang on—I want," the words rough in his throat, and pushed him away and rolled onto his back. His legs cinched around Chris's hips, gathering him close; his fingers went to Chris's face, tugging him down to kiss.

Chris caught himself on one hand, laughed, bent low to brush his lips to his, and took him slow and sweet and good.

"I think I just had a near-death experience," Nicholas said, afterwards.

Chris propped his chin up on one hand. He looked unbearably, adorably smug. "Oh?"

"I'm still floating somewhere near the ceiling," Nicholas said seriously. "Your ass looks amazing from this vantage."

Chris shook with laughter. "How have I lived a month without you? Four? It must have been a long, long hallucination."

"Lots of sexually frustrated nights on my end."

"Well, that too."

"Antoine sent me the pictures," Nicholas added, lifting one

hand to push messy curls from Chris's eyes. "From the shoot we did together."

Chris's lips parted. He had been a little pale; now, not unbecomingly, he flushed. The tips of his ears went pink. "He would. Shameless interferer. I didn't know."

"We look damn good."

"Of course we do."

Nicholas's thumb pressed down against Chris's lower lip. Chris's blush had not receded, but he opened his mouth and licked gently at the tips of Nicholas's fingers, and then it was Nicholas's turn to get hot and bothered.

"Come here," he murmured.

Chris straddled him in one smooth movement and lowered his head to brush their lips together. His hands caught Nicholas's hands and pushed them back into the bedsheets. "Hey," he said, against Nicholas's mouth. "I love you, too."

Nicholas blinked. "Oh."

"Oh?" Chris's tone was light. "Are you much surprised, Mr. International Star?"

"No one loves me like you do." Nicholas struggled against his grip, mostly for show; he was enjoying being pinned down a hell of a lot more than he'd ever thought he would. This was a night for surprises.

And miracles.

Chris kissed him again, his fingers lacing with Nicholas's. "Well, then. That's the love declarations sorted. I'm glad we know where we stand."

"The best possible outcome."

Chris gave him a wry smile. "And where does it leave us? I am Paris-bound for the next year or so. You…"

"I don't want to give this up," Nicholas said frankly. Chris softened then, and mostly flopped on top of him, tangling their legs together. Nicholas's hand, liberated from his grip, threaded through the fluffy blond hair. "I don't *plan* on giving this up. I only just got you. But long-distance relationships are—well. Not the easiest thing in the world."

"Stay here, then." Chris's tone had gone from light to serious in a second flat. "Stay with me. Here. In Paris."

Nicholas's hand brushed his cheek. Chris folded his hands over his shoulder and propped his chin on top of them, watching him seriously. "Would you be alright with that?" Nicholas asked. "I know that you're jealous of your privacy. It's hard to come by in this world."

"*You* are part of my private life."

Nicholas's foolish, traitor heart gave a painful throb. God, he was going soft.

"It's true, you know." Chris's eyes were dark and full of meaning. "The two days we spent here together were the best I've ever had, and I didn't even know it. I only found out once it was over."

"Lots of sex and baked goods."

"I'm a man of small, easy pleasures. But with you. That's my one condition." Chris pressed a featherlight kiss against his throat, where it met his shoulder, and reached down to pull the duvet over them both. A car roared past in the street below, and something in Nicholas's chest clenched with sudden, diffuse happiness. He'd missed this bed, this city, this man. His man. "Alright: maybe movies, too. And books. We'll make it up as we go. There are no rules."

"I love you," Nicholas said. He cleared his throat. "Again. In case you'd forgotten."

Chris had closed his eyes; Nicholas felt the flutter of his eyelashes against his skin. "I know."

"Don't you Han Solo me."

A soft laugh. "You're forgetting, Nicholas Madden: I'm a movie star now, too."

★ ★ ★

Nicholas's phone buzzed to life some hours later, once they'd thoroughly exhausted each other and had fallen into a light, pleasant doze. Nicholas groaned, and reached out blindly, nearly knocking his elbow into Chris's stomach. The phone, damn it to hell, continued to *whizz whizz* incessantly, somewhere in the near distance. The duvet fell from his shoulder.

Chris muffled a wordless noise into the pillow, and waved a hand at him ineffectually. "Come back."

Nicholas's hand closed around his phone. The screen was lighting up with notifications.

Jim Slater. Unknown numbers. And, at the top, Madalena. She had sent him a link to an article, and a text.

Madalena: whoops. busted 😜 😜 😜.

Nicholas swiped to find a picture of himself, getting into a taxi. *Nicholas Madden and Chris Lavalle flee The Throne after-party*, the caption read. *Is it too much to hope the two star-crossed lovers might be making up?*

"What's wrong?" Chris asked, sleepily.

Nicholas looked down at him. His tousled hair was spread over the pillow, his pale eyes half-open in the darkness. The light from the window touched his collarbone, the dip of his throat. Chris's hand brushed his thigh under the duvet.

"Nothing."

Nicholas set the phone to mute, dropped it on the floor, and sank back down, throwing one arm over Chris's shoulders. Chris made a pleased sound and burrowed a little closer.

"Nothing," he repeated. "Come here, lover. We'll be alright."

# Epilogue

## TEN THINGS YOU NEED TO KNOW BEFORE SEEING *THE THRONE* THIS AWARD SEASON

buzzfeed.com
10:01 est

1. Priya Chaudhuri made her big-picture debut with *American Heroes*, a neo-docu/fiction about second-generation immigrants in New York. *The Throne* is her eighth movie and her first period piece. She has never won an Oscar, despite being nominated for two. She did win a Golden Globe for *The Scarab on the Beach*, her fourth long picture.

2. *The Throne* has received accolades from most major critics, including a 98.9% score on Rotten Tomatoes. It has so far grossed $150M, far outbidding its budget.

3. Julian Chamberlain, the scriptwriter for *The Throne*, said he wished to *"convey a sense of what it might have been to be queer at the turn of the twentieth century. The violence in the text is constantly at odds with the secret tenderness underlying the relationship between the two mains. They are caught between love and hate, a push-and-pull of attraction and contempt—and yet they forge a happy ending in these constrained circumstances. It is a*

*movie about pain and self-loathing, and living in a society that uses you for pleasure then discards you with baseless cruelty. But it's also a movie about finding affection in unlikely places."*

4. Andrée Belfond, reputedly the greatest star of French cinema in a generation, looks frickin badass in period clothing and shorn blond hair. But be warned: her character arc will break your heart.

5. Somehow Jason Kirkhall is in this??? Our #dumbboy has briefly abandoned his beloved action movies for a spin in the big leagues. This marks his first foray in auteur cinema. We're not spoiling you for his role in the plot, but where he ends up is unexpected, to say the least. You've *definitely* never seen him like this before.

6. Sir Reginald Jarrett rocked a different waistcoat every day on the shoot. Click here for a photomontage of all his greatest hits.

7. Though a latecomer in the awards race, *The Throne* is already presumed to be one of the strongest contenders for the Oscars this year. Nominations aren't coming until next Tuesday, but Nicholas Madden might be up for a Best Actor nom.

8. Speaking of which, Madden has surprised us all by making his coming out on *Tomorrow Night* a month before the movie premiered. His scathing critique of Hollywood double standards was perhaps not surprising from a man once dubbed The Big Bad Wolf of Hollywood, but his plea for understanding and compassion were a little out of character. It's almost as if someone changed his mind!

9. Chris Lavalle, a total newcomer on the scene, has wowed audiences with his subtle, complicated, almost disturbing portrayal of Angelo, the movie's most perplexing and enigmatic character. It helps that he's also very, *very* easy on the eyes.

10. No official comment has yet to be made by either actor on the topic of their relationship, but Madden and Lavalle have been spotted together, <u>holding hands</u> and <u>visiting museums</u>, in Paris. They have also been seen <u>kissing passionately</u> in airport Charles de Gaulle and then getting into a taxi together, destination unknown... It would seem that the Big Bad Wolf of Hollywood and the brainless diva have made a happy ending of their very own.

★ ★ ★ ★ ★

# Acknowledgements

I would be remiss if I did not praise the team at Carina Press for their support as the publication and editing process started. My thanks especially to Kerri Buckley, for her approval and welcoming spirit, and to John Jacobson, for their invaluable contributions and enduring kindness.

To my parents and my brother, who've been reading my stories since I was four: look, you brought this on yourselves. Love ya.

To the friends who've supported me during the writing of this book and all the stages that came after: you're the best. Thank you. Special mentions go to the Saturday Crew, for all those coffee meet-ups in the Quartier Latin; to Heemy, for their enduring friendship during the last decade; and to Lydia, for her kind reminders to go and edit my book.

And, last and best, to Tam, who holds my hand and keeps me sane, and whom I love: this last year would not have been possible without you. One day we'll get to the dark on the river.

# About the Author

S.R. Lane lives in Paris, where she alternates between teaching high school English and strolling from bookstore to bookstore, looking for more books to add to her already-towering shelves. After studying Shakespeare, gender, and sexuality at the Sorbonne and King's College, London, she fell in love with romance and romance scholarship. She is especially drawn to queer love stories, messy characters with a sense of agency, a strong setting, and a truly deserved HEA.

She lives online at srlane.com, or on Twitter at twitter. com/foesandfoxes.

*A fiery restaurant owner falls for her enigmatic head chef in this charming, emotional romance.*

*Keep reading for an excerpt from*
The Romance Recipe *by Ruby Barrett.*

# Chapter One

## *Amy*

A restaurant has a certain indefinable quality on a good night. With every seat filled, it's loud. The bartenders sling drinks with panache. The front of house staff moves around each other like dancers, while the bussers are more like ghosts, slipping in and out so fast you never notice there was a table waiting to be flipped. Expo quality controls every single morsel so that the plates are always Instagram-worthy, and nobody has to wait more than twenty minutes.

A good night smells like the signature cocktail and the house special, perfectly paired.

A good night smells like money.

Tonight is not a good night.

"I'm done, Amy."

Chad throws his white chef's coat onto the hostess stand, sending a cup of pens flying and toppling the tablet displaying the seating chart off its stand. Maggie yelps, righting the tools of her hostess trade.

I cover the phone receiver with my palm. "Chad. What the— So sorry. Can you hold another moment?" I say into the phone. "You're done *what*?" I hiss at him.

He slaps his Sox cap onto his head. "Here. I'm done here." He rips open the front door, letting in the smell of cold and rain.

The customer on the other end of the line has hit a rhythm that seems like she did not, in fact, hold for another moment. "I don't see the problem," she says. "Give the table away," the woman says.

As if I would be having this conversation with her if there were anyone I could give the table away to. The door slams shut behind my sous-chef, and the few people who are currently in the dining room stare. Which I'm sure was his intention.

I am putty, slowly pulled apart by a line cook and absentee reservations.

"We have a twenty-four-hour cancellation policy that I reminded you of on our confirmation call," I say, my Customer Service Voice cracking under the strain of wanting to run after Chad. I sound like the Stevia version of myself, artificially sweet—and not as good as the real thing, if I do say so myself. "If you can't keep your reservation we'll have to charge you the twenty-five-dollar cancellation fee."

As if twenty-five dollars will cover the hundreds this table was probably going to spend.

The tabletop set for ten guests sits pride of place at the front of the room. Framed by the floor to ceiling window, the empty table is reflected back at me, so really it looks like twenty empty place settings. The visual equivalent of poking a finger in an open wound.

"Listen." The woman who was supposed to be here with her nine friends forty-five minutes ago drops her *oops I forgot* act. "We're not showing up. And your cancellation policy is nice and all but you never asked for my credit card and I'm not giving it to you so no, you can't charge me for the table anyway. But if you keep *harassing* me…"

I left her one message asking where she was.

"…I might be forced to leave a less than stellar review."

The worst thing restaurant owners ever did was decide that the customer is always right. Customers can be right. Sometimes. So can a broken clock twice a day. Doesn't mean I'm going to give it free food. And it certainly doesn't mean I'm going to let myself and my business, that I've spent years preparing for and countless hours building, be bullied by a no-show.

"You know what?" I turn toward the wall, hunch over the phone to spare Maggie this "do as I say, not as I do" behavior. "Leave your bad review," I hiss. "I don't give a shit. We don't need your business."

A damned lie.

She laughs like a person who wears coats made out of puppies. "Are you sure about that?" The line goes dead.

That went terribly, but the great thing about running your own restaurant is that you never have a second to stop and think about how you could have handled that better.

Or that maybe you should have listened to your head chef when she suggested taking down customer credit cards at the time of booking a reservation, for situations just like this.

Or to pee.

Or breathe through the sick feeling in your gut.

Because there's always another crisis to deal with.

I grab Chad's chef's coat and run out the door after him.

He slouches against the window of the brunch place next door, cigarette glow lighting his face. I knew he wouldn't go far. He'd want a chance to tell me his side. I dodge the crowd of umbrellas on the sidewalk, holding his coat over my head to get to him.

"What the hell." I'm breathless from that ten-foot sprint. "You're quitting in the middle of a service?"

His gaze slips away from mine and he shifts on his feet. Suspicion prickles the back of my neck.

"She's gonna be the end of this place, Ames." He waves his hand around, the ash drifting toward me. I step back. "She's all..." He throws his cigarette on the ground. "She's all show," he says in disgust.

"Why don't you come back inside and we can talk things through with Sophie?" I suggest with more artificial sweetness than I gave the no-show on the phone.

He sighs and shakes his head with a quick jerk.

Chad came with me from our old restaurant and has been with me since I first opened Amy & May's. He's been loyal and hardworking, and that's the *only* reason I gave him a second chance on our zero-tolerance harassment policy. But his second chance is burning up with the cherry at the tip of his cigarette.

I punch his coat into a ball and toss it at his chest. "You did it again, didn't you? I vouched for you, Chad," I hiss.

A passerby snorts their laughter as they walk past. This is just great. An empty dining room, a bad Yelp review, and now the owner of Amy & May's is having a conniption in the middle of the street.

"It was just a joke, Amy," Chad whines.

I step in closer to him as incentive to keep my voice down. "It's not fucking funny. I don't want to hear it," I cut him off, slashing my hand through the air as he opens his mouth, most likely to tell me how Carly, the new dishwasher, actually *likes* it when he makes comments about her body.

I've been working in restaurants since I was sixteen and I've been harassed in every single one of them. Now that I'm in charge, no one working for me is going to experience that.

Sophie "Hollywood" Brunet and I don't agree on much but on this one thing we do.

"You can come by tomorrow to clear out your locker and get your last paycheck. And fuck you for saying that Sophie is going to ruin my restaurant when it's your behavior that caused this." I spin on the heel of my über-unfashionable, ultra-comfortable black canvas slides.

"I'm not the only one who thinks so," he says to my back. I stop at the edge of the awning, the rain already soaking into the toes of my shoes. "She cries in the walk-in."

I absolutely love it when men tell me things I already know.

"She's always worried about her Instaspam."

He knows exactly what social media platform he's talking about, he just thinks he's better than anyone with a profile.

"She can't make a decision to save her life."

"She made the decision to fire your ass," I say, but only so I can hide the sinking feeling in my gut. My staff has lost confidence in their kitchen leader.

And so have I.

He shakes his head. "Whatever, Amy."

"Goodbye, Chad."

The restaurant seems even quieter since I ran out mere minutes ago. My head chef, Sophie, stands at the expo station. A lock of her auburn hair has fallen loose from the black bandanna around her head, and her face glows from the heat of the kitchen. The light makeup she wears to work has run, leaving her wide eyes with a smoky look. I nod to her and tell Maggie I'll be back in a bit. I stomp—because it feels good despite being totally unprofessional—down the hall next to our open concept kitchen and the bathrooms and push through the door with a sign that reads Staff Only. I bypass the staff locker room and throw myself into a chair in my cramped office, kicking the door closed with my foot. I flip through my problems like my mom used to look for dinner inspiration in her Rolodex turned recipe book.

There are three unanswered texts from my brother on my phone but zero returned phone calls from my father.

After a year of success my dream restaurant is inexplicably tanking. We're bleeding staff and customers.

Despite years of experience, I can't find one surefire strategy to get more butts in seats.

There's an unopened email in my inbox from the landlord and I know what it's going to say. That I have three months to make up the rent owed, or we're out.

And yet, like the losing end of a CW Network love triangle, the only thing I can think about is that lock of hair and how it stuck to Sophie's lip, the way her hazel eyes only seem to get bigger and bigger when I walk toward her.

Sophie is my biggest problem of all.

Ever since I first watched her on the final episode of *Pop-Up Kitchen*, I've wanted to kiss Sophie Brunet. The idea of kissing her hooked me but watching her hold her own against the biggest asshole TV chef of our lifetime and a kitchen full of men made me want to take a chance on her. After watching the finale, I fell down a wormhole of past episodes, watching her skill and passion turned into easily consumable reality TV fodder. I scrolled through years' worth of her Instagram grid until, stupidly, I felt like I knew her from the carefully curated snippets she gave followers, starting as a line cook at a five-star hotel in Montreal all the way to her job as a sous-chef at Table Hanover, her last job before she quit to join the cast of *Pop-Up Kitchen*.

When I sent an email to the address listed for her agent, I chalked it up to a mild crush, a strong Negroni, and the frenetic energy that comes with being wide-awake at two in the morning. When Sophie herself responded, excited, *thankful*, for the opportunity to run her own kitchen at my zero stars restaurant, I thought I could set aside the attraction and focus on putting Amy & May's on the Boston scene. It was a relief to finally have someone to do this with, to share the absolute panic that comes with fulfilling your dream before you turn thirty, and watching it light up around you. To have someone to help put out the fire.

But if anything, my attraction has grown, despite that everything Chad said is technically true.

She does spend a lot of time in the walk-in. She's always bent over her phone, worrying at her plump pink lower lip, frowning at the screen. The change was like whiplash. One minute our restaurant was thriving. Reservations months in advance, the atmosphere electric every single night. There were plenty of rubberneckers. People wanting to eat food prepared by someone who was on TV once, like the tangential proximity somehow made the food taste better.

And maybe it did. Until it didn't. Because suddenly it was like Sophie's fame ran out. And everyone just…stopped coming.

The last few months, she's been nothing like the badass woman she was on the show, quietly acquiescing to all my ideas, blindly nodding to everything I say. Even her suggestion to take credit cards at the time of reservation was more of a question. But still, I should have listened.

Now I'm back where I started, doing it all alone. Except this time with a side of an even bigger unrequited crush, on a straight girl, no less. Maybe my biggest mistake of all was thinking I should rely on anyone but myself.

The rest of dinner service goes off without a hitch. If only three tables but no more no-shows counts as not a hitch. "Where's Sophie?" I ask, after the last table has settled.

Carly jumps, dropping a pan into the sink. "Sorry, ma'am."

The restaurant is quiet. Only the closing staff still here.

"Please, no. Don't…" I shake my head. "Don't call me that."

She bends over the pan in the sink, the *shwish shwish* sound of the scouring pad grating at my shot nerves. "She's in the walk-in," Carly says.

Of course she is. I sigh. When we were eight, my twin brother, Wes, and I snuck out of bed and watched *Jurassic Park*. I was so traumatized by the scene with the raptors in the kitchen that to this day, the chill I get when I close a walk-in freezer door behind me is as much from fear as it is from cold.

Sophie doesn't turn around, writing the date on a sauce container, as the door slams shut behind me.

"Next time, can you at least warn me you're going to fire someone?" I wrap my arms around my middle in a fruitless attempt at staying warm.

She doesn't turn but bobs her head in a curt nod.

I take a few steps deeper into the freezer. "I'm not upset. I shouldn't have given him a second chance in the first place. I'm sorry that you had to deal with him."

"You don't have to apologize to me," she says. There's no accusation in her voice. None at all. I hear it nonetheless. Sophie wanted Chad gone the first time Carly came to her asking if she could be scheduled on the days he wasn't working. But we'd lost so many staff already, I panicked and fought to keep him against my better judgment.

She turns to face me, her chef's coat undone, her nipples, hard from the cold, visible through her white tank top. Sophie and I blink at each other and quickly look away. Her cheeks turn a darker shade of red.

So, great. Not only have I failed Carly, I've made Sophie uncomfortable, too.

"Sorry," I say quickly. "It won't happen again." Second chances or checking her out. "And you were right about taking credit card numbers."

I start to rearrange stacks of individually wrapped dough on the shelf beside me for something to do with my hands. I hate it when other people are right. I hate admitting it more. I'd scoffed when she'd suggested it at our last meeting. Actually scoffed. Because taking credit cards wasn't something we'd ever done at the restaurants I'd worked at before.

"I don't want our guests to feel like we don't trust them," I'd said.

Sophie sighs so audibly Carly can probably hear her. It's the only pushback I ever seem to get from her anymore, this sound she makes when she's frustrated but won't say anything. She takes the dough from my hands, putting the frozen disks back where they were. This close, I watch as her chest rises and falls with each breath. Underneath her foundation, dark purple rings her eyes. This close, she's so *warm*, even in this dark freezer. When she's close like this, I get caught up in her and forget my own frustrations with my head chef or that my restaurant is slowly crumbling around me or that I feel lonely at the end of the night and for once I don't like it.

Sophie's jaw is rigid and she is conspicuously not looking at me.

Sometimes I want to grip her shoulders, under her coat, skin to skin, and tell her—*beg her*—to fight with me. Tell me I was an asshole for giving Chad a second chance. Tell me if my ideas are bad. Or good. Anything.

Whenever I get this urge, it's time to eighty-six myself from the conversation.

"Let's talk tomorrow," I say, backing out of the freezer, too warm after being so close to her. "About the new menu. Ten?" I ask.

"Actually," she says. "There's…" She presses her lips together.

"Spit it out, Hollywood."

She narrows her eyes. She hates that nickname, she is so totally done with me.

Same, girl.

"I got an offer. From a guy I know from *Pop-Up Kitchen*?"

Mom gave me breathing exercises when I was kid. A way to manage my anger when it came up on me fast, to keep me from jumping to conclusions, lashing out at her or my brother, but mostly my dad. In the freezer, each breath is so conspicuous, so obvious. But I focus on them anyway because even though she hasn't *said* anything—even though I'm *not*, I'm absolutely not jumping to conclusions—I know exactly what she's going to say.

"He offered me a job," she says.

"Head chef?" Somehow my voice sounds totally normal even though I am screaming internally.

She shrugs, in this effortless, cool way she has. "Sous."

"Why are you telling me this?" I ask. Kitchens are cutthroat. You don't tip your hand, unless you want to get fired. Or maybe I'm about to be leveraged.

"I know things aren't going well." She stares pointedly at me. "You won't let me see the books but... I know that part of it is my fault. I want to stay here and run this kitchen, but I just needed you to know that I'm considering it."

"If you know things aren't going well then you know I probably can't match whatever they're offering you."

She shakes her head, her eyes worried. "No. I'm trying to be...helpful."

"Well, thanks," I say. "For the help." My voice sounds exactly as bitchy as I feel right now. "I got to go."

"Amy."

"It's fine." Everything is fine. My restaurant is tanking and I'm losing my chef and I'm only upset about that for professional reasons and not because I find myself periodically wondering how soft her skin is. My stomach growls. And I've forgotten to eat. Again.

Everything is really fricking great.

"I made you a take-out plate," she calls. I turn in the door-way and sitting on the expo counter is a silver take-out tin, most likely filled with what's left of tonight's under-ordered special. In moments like this, my crush for her absolutely leaps, but I know these moments aren't for me. She's always caretaking our staff in small ways that I'm completely inept at, like making meals for folks who've had a grumpy guest or who were run around all night. Or who have absolutely no idea what they're going to do next.

The plate is still warm. "Good night, Hollywood."

She looks at me only as the door starts to close. "Good night, Amy."

For once I am relieved to not be the last person out of the restaurant if it means I can get some space from the woman who turns the center of my chest into warm goo, while si-multaneously sending me into a panic.

"Carly." I lean against the wall beside her sink. "I'm really sorry about Chad. I broke my own policy when I didn't fire him the first time. It won't happen again."

Carly can't be much older than I was when I started work-ing in a restaurant. She smiles at me, so huge she reminds me of Wes. They both show you what they're feeling with their whole chest.

"That's okay, Ms. Chambers—"

"Amy. Please."

Carly smiles down at her feet. "Most kitchens don't have a policy at all. I really appreciate you standing up for me."

"Yeah, well, it was Sophie, mostly," I mumble. Carly is en-tirely too wholesome. If Wesley were here, they'd be instant best friends. But my brother and I aren't as similar as we seem. "Make sure you descale the espresso machine tonight," I say.

I say good-night and take the back door to my car. By industry standards, eleven is early. I could get a drink at Luxe and meet a nice girl, have another one of those emotionless hookups my brother accuses me of having to avoid "intimacy" and "feelings." Or see if Jeremy wants to take a breather from studying for once to hang out with someone who's not dumbstruck in love, like Wes.

But I drive in the opposite direction of my apartment, away from my favorite gay bar, and Jeremy's new place, and park my old red VW in front of a house with all the lights off except for the one over the front door. I pull the take-out plate and utensils from the paper bag. The weight of this entire day, every one of my problems, is enough to turn me off this beautiful meal but I make myself eat it, even if it's ash in my mouth. I haven't had anything since breakfast.

This is where I feel closest to Mom. Outside her old house that's filled with a new family. Wes hasn't been back since we sold it last year. He says he's ready to move forward, which is hilarious considering I had to convince him to sell in the first place.

It's fitting that I do this alone. Commune with my mother alone. Cry, into pasta with cream sauce, alone.

I do everything else alone. Why not this?

*Don't miss* The Romance Recipe *by Ruby Barrett,*
*available now wherever Carina Adores books are sold.*

*www.CarinaPress.com*

# Discover another romantic love story from Carina Adores

**Amy Chambers: restaurant owner, micromanager, control freak.**

Amy will do anything to revive her ailing restaurant, including hiring a former reality-show finalist with good connections and a lot to prove. But her hopes that Sophie's skills and celebrity status would bring her restaurant back from the brink of failure are beginning to wane...

**Sophie Brunet: grump in the kitchen, sunshine in the streets, took thirty years to figure out she was queer.**

Sophie just wants to cook. She doesn't want to constantly post on social media for her dead-in-the-water reality TV career, she doesn't want to deal with Amy's take-charge personality, and she doesn't want to think about what her attraction to her boss might mean...

**Don't miss *The Romance Recipe* by Ruby Barrett.**
**Available wherever Carina Adores books are sold.**

CarinaAdores.com

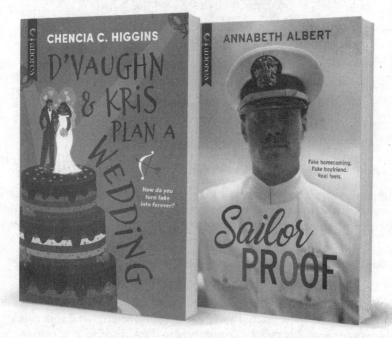